ACCLAIM FOR MARK W. DANIELSON
AND WRITER'S BLOCK

"Brace yourself, this book comes at you like a fire hose. Homicide cop Maxx Watts —that's double-X for excitement—makes for a compelling hero, and his story is written by a man who knows how."
—Shane Gericke, *TORN APART*

"Mark W. Danielson hits a home run out of the publishing ballpark with his first Detective Maxx Watts mystery. *Writers Block* is an intriguing behind the scenes police procedural that keeps the reader guessing. Laced with humor as well as romance, it's definitely a book that's hard to put aside."
—Jean Henry Mead, *Murder on the Interstate*

"You'll like Maxx Watts. He's just like us with a personal life and issues to work on. He's also a dogged, determined cop who'd rather follow his instincts than take orders from higher up."
—Earl Staggs, *Memory of a Murder*

"A philandering publisher/writer gruesomely murdered, smacked on the head with a book memento, tied to a chair and a manuscript stuffed down his throat. Detective Maxx Watts knows someone felt white-hot betrayal. But who? A hot wife, who also served as a literary agent, someone feeding the deceased manuscripts of wannabe writers no one else would publish, or one of the writers who were swindled out of royalties as the deceased promoted his own books? Or someone else? Too many suspects; too many clues.

"Mark Danielson hits his stride with Writer's Block. Wait for a rainy day, then pick up Writer's Block. You won't care if the floors flood. Bravo!"
—Ben Small, *The Olive Horseshoe*

"Mark Danielson's latest, Writer's Block, is a must read for fans of mystery novels. Its attention to characters, smooth dialogue, brisk pace, and cleverly structured plot kept me reading well into the night.
—Shane Cashion
Govern Yourself Accordingly—The Chronicles of a Brainsick Lawyer

Books by Mark W. Danielson

Danger Within

The Innocent Never Knew

Diablo's Shadow

Writer's Block

MarkWDanielson.com

WRITER'S BLOCK

Mark W. Danielson

NIGHT SHADOWS PRESS

Copyright @ 2011 by Mark W. Danielson

This book is fiction. With the exception of my grandmother's name, Daisy Woods, all characters, places, and incidents are products of the author's imagination, or are used fictitiously. In other words, it's all made up. Any resemblance to actual events or locales, or persons living or dead, is coincidental.

First Edition

10 9 8 7 6 5 4 3 2 1

Printed in the United States of America

Library of Congress Registration: TXu1-619-521

ISBN 978-0-9846044-3-2

Night Shadows Press, LLC
8987 E. Tanque Verde #309-135
Tucson, AZ 85749-9399

For Lyne

Lyne, you are my muse, my rock, my best friend, and critic. Thank you for your unconditional love and encouragement. Your relentless pursuit of perfection has significantly contributed to this book. I love you always.

Maxx, you are my constant companion, silent writing partner, and occasional foot warmer. You always know when I should toss your plush squirrel toy. Thank you for your special love that only a dog can give.

Helen Ginger, thank you for your superb editing. You open my eyes, and provide excellent guidance.

Joan Hansen, thank you for your tireless support, not only for me, but for all the Men of Mystery authors. Your Raven award was well deserved.

Michele and Ron Gerbrandt, thank you for another fine cover.

A special thanks to all the law enforcement officers and military personnel who make our way of life possible.

Roger Lopez, thank you for creating the Writer's Block whose engraving graces the book cover.

"DEATH COMES TO THOSE DESERVING."

—Charlie CC Coulter

ONE

Lead Detective Maxx Watts smelled death as he approached the old ranch house nestled among shade trees and scattered homes. Rubbing the raised scar on his left shoulder, he dropped his hand when he noticed his partner Blaine Spartan watching. The home's mortar was cracked, its shrubs nearly gone. All was brown except a thin strip of grass running from a corner like spilt green paint. Cicadas screeched like Banshees. A dog barked incessantly. Trees rattled like vipers in the scorching wind.

Badging his way into the house, the stench led him to a side room where a middle-aged man lay slumped over a desk, hands and feet bound behind him. Patrol Officer Porgy Mulberry briefed him that the vic was a mystery writer and small publisher. Another beat cop waited in the living room with the vic's widow. Watts nodded, but wasn't ready to see her yet.

First impressions are crucial at any crime scene. Being told the vic was slumped over his desk wearing a flowered shirt and Bermuda shorts wasn't much to go on. He could study the photos until he went blind, but nothing compared to seeing things first-hand. How else could he experience the smells, the struggle, the blood, the death? The smell told Watts this guy had been dead for hours, the urine on his shorts already dry.

The setting flashed Watts back two years when that bullet took him down. Partner Blaine Spartan was supposed to be covering him, but Spartan never drew his gun. That event affected both of them, but in different ways. Spartan turned to drinking, and Watts no longer trusted his partner. Reunited a mere week after Spartan completed his rehab, Watts wasn't sure they were ready to work together again.

Although Spartan might be the catalyst to this recurring nightmare, Watts realized that ever since the shooting, he also found himself ending his personal relationships after just a few dates. Since none of his post-trauma counseling had helped, he refused to date anyone new until his head was on straight.

As far as Watts was concerned, Spartan had it easy. Rehab was nothing like taking a bullet. Bullets tear through flesh and then scar the mind. His one father had unknowingly taught him that alcoholism was the result of choice. With Spartan near, he continued walking through the crowded home office, taking in the scene. His scar became even more irritated when he bent over to observe the scene from a different angle. An inch lower and that bullet would have killed him. Knowing that Spartan could have prevented the shooting had the memory lingering like the stink in the room. Not a single night passed without Watts thinking about it.

The screeching cicadas made Watts tense. "Christ! It's like those damned bugs are inside!"

Spartan calmly pointed to the window. "It's open, Maxx."

Overly sensitive to noise and smell, Watts went to the window, shooting an angry gaze as if he could influence the bugs. Suddenly, it got quiet again. While there, he took a moment to scan the grounds.

"The temperature feels the same inside and out, but that strip of green grass suggests the swamp cooler on the roof is operational. So why isn't it on?"

"Good question," Spartan said, loosening his tie.

Watts ambled through the twelve-by-ten room while the Crime Scene Special Unit documented the scene. He flipped his notebook open to jot a few notes: Vic bound to his chair with plastic tie straps. Hands and ankles identically bound. Head face-down on a bloodied document. Nothing else appears disturbed. Trash can upright, framed Manhattan photo level. A woman's voice caught his attention. He barely turned in time to see her leave the room. If she was with CSSU, he had never seen her before. He went back to searching the room.

The constant wind and sweltering heat reminded him why he loathed summer. Now ready to touch things, he pulled some latex gloves from his pocket and slid them on as he walked. To his left, two EMTs stood next to Officer Mulberry. On his right, CSSU photographers clicked like paparazzi, one shooting stills, the other videotaping. Tired of them following him like he was part of a reality show, Watts quickly turned and made a face in their cameras. Not amused, they lowered their lenses and backed away.

Satisfied, he turned to Spartan. "The vic's name is Charlie Coulter," he said, "although with no prior arrests or run-ins with the law he may as well be John Doe. It's an interesting murder, Blaine. He's bound but not gagged, his hair is perfectly groomed, and his Hawaiian shirt is neatly pressed. From the back, you might think he's asleep."

"Yeah," said Spartan, moving around the desk for a better look. "Dead asleep."

Watts ignored him, inhaling the scent of dried urine and blood. "Urine flows with death, but it also streams from fear. I wonder if Mr. Coulter knew his attacker."

"Beats me, but his blood pool on the desk suggests a frontal assault."

"I agree, but the amount seems too minute to be fatal. I wish the ME would get here so we could move the body."

Watts said that out of frustration, but also with intent. He squatted near the vic's chair to examine the body's position, clothes, chair placement, and the floor. Had the floor been carpeted instead of being hardwood, he may have seen footprints. As it was, he saw nothing but dust.

Standing again, everything on the desk looked tidy, the computer, printer, and overhead light still on. The desk drawers were closed, as was the closet door. The only things in the closet were reams of printer paper, old travel magazines, and a dusty pair of black wingtip shoes. The dust layer on the top shelf meant nothing was missing.

He found his partner as he closed the closet door. "Nothing remarkable in there."

Spartan nodded, reading the scene. "I know what you mean. Remove the body and the bloodied papers and there's nothing remarkable anywhere."

Spartan's comment sent Watts crouching behind the chair to peer under the desk again. Everything looked as it should for a drafty room. The wood was polished where Coulter's feet rubbed. The corners had dust where they didn't. Coulter's Huaraches were still on his feet. Still crouched, Watts stepped back a few feet pondering the setting. The modern swivel chair with its chrome spine and leather pads looked out of place in this setting, but its design perfectly accommodated the killer. A single tie strap through Coulter's bound ankles secured him to the base. Another through his bound wrists secured him to the chair's spine. The million dollar question was how did the murderer get Coulter into this position when Coulter should have been able to resist?

Watts reluctantly faced his partner again. "I have to wonder if the killer knew about this chair ahead of time. I mean, how many murderers do you recall using tie straps?"

"Not many," Spartan said, inspecting the chair's design. "Tie straps certainly wouldn't work on an executive-style chair."

"Exactly."

Beads dripped from Watts' brow as he stooped again. He preferred dressing like Coulter and knew some undercover cops that wore bowling shirts and shorts to work, but considering the seedy places they hung out, wearing a suit didn't seem so bad.

One of the EMTs seemed offended when Watts pressed his finger to Coulter's jugular vein. Watts returned the look and said, "You didn't move the body did you?"

"No, sir. I just checked his vitals is all. He's exactly the way we found him— cold and blue. He was long gone before we arrived so we made no attempt to revive him."

"I understand. Hang around until the ME shows up. He might want to talk to you."

"Yes, sir."

Watts eyed Officer Porgy Mulberry who was leaning against the far wall. Their history together dated back to their childhood. Back then, Mulberry was skinny. Now, he resembled the donuts he favored. People like Porgy motivated Watts to work out. No doubt unable to give chase in this condition, Mulberry would have to be lightning-quick with his Taser.

"So, Porgy," Watts said, "when did you arrive on scene?"

Mulberry gazed back with his thumbs tucked under his Sam Brown belt. "Maybe two minutes after the EMTs."

Watts snubbed him as he studied the small marble block on Coulter's desk. Carefully lifting it, he estimated it to be three inches square by one inch thick, every corner sharp, its surfaces polished smooth, weighing perhaps a pound. The engraving on the top had a menacing guillotine within a circle, blade drawn, painted blood dripping from its edge. The front had a brass plaque that read "Writer's Block". He glanced at Spartan, returning it to the desk.

"Interesting paperweight," he said to Spartan.

"Yeah, and also a potential weapon."

Watts nodded as he suspended his right palm over the block. Pretending to hold it in his hand, he swung his arm in an arc toward where Coulter's head would be if he was sitting upright in his chair. He had no way of knowing whether the block was used as a weapon or not, but its desk placement made it likely. He straightened himself and faced his partner.

"Blaine, striking Coulter with the flat side of this block might stun him long enough to get him tied up, but it wouldn't split his skull."

"But an edge strike would sting and spill blood."

"I agree, but the only red on this paperweight is what's painted on the guillotine blade." Sliding the block into an evidence bag, Watts said to CSSU Tech Tim Westin, "So there are no prints on the paperweight?"

"It appears that way. We'll check it at the lab and let you know if we find anything."

Watts nodded his understanding while staring at the desk photo. He presumed it was of Coulter and his wife since both wore million dollar smiles and little else. The sapphire ocean in the background looked like Hawaii, but since he had never been, he didn't mention it. Several unpaid bills jutted from a giant paper clip. Two pens sat idle; one red, one black. A dental appointment reminder from three weeks ago lay near a corner. The half-empty Kleenex box and used tissues in the trash inferred that Coulter had allergies. Westin would study them, too. When his gaze shifted to the floor, Westin pointed to an area near the chair.

"I found traces of blood splatter here, but it's invisible to the naked eye," Westin said.

"So, the murderer cleaned up?"

"No, Maxx, it's microscopic spray like you'd find from a gunshot."

"Except there's no gun wound."

"Not that we can see."

Watts sighed. "I'm still thinking the killer cleaned up. I'd like every piece of trash in this house bagged and taken back to the lab. Make sure you label them by room."

"No problem."

Watts moved on to the plastic tie straps binding Coulter. They looked generic, like the ones sold in nearly every hardware store. It seemed unlikely they would have much value, but sometimes the smallest shreds carried the most weight.

He found it interesting that the blood pool under Coulter's head had been confined to the paper. A closer look revealed the soiled document was actually Coulter's own manuscript titled *Deadly Wrap*. If the killer intended to leave an impression, he or she did a fabulous job. He pointed this out to his partner.

Looking over Watts' shoulder, Spartan lifted a corner with his pen. "The numbers imply four pages are missing, but since they were printed front-to-back, only two sheets are missing."

"I concur," Spartan said. "Did you notice the business letterhead is The Guillotine Press, and the logo matches the engraving on the Writer's Block paperweight?"

"I did. So, did Coulter create this paperweight as a memento or is it something else?"

"Perhaps his widow can answer that one."

Watts mopped his brow. The heat was hard on everyone, especially the vic who was swelling by the minute. Since the ME had yet to show, Watts decided to expedite matters by sitting Coulter up in his chair. Normally, he wouldn't touch a body without the ME's approval, but considering that CSSU had documented the scene and the heat was accelerating Coulter's decay, he believed the breach was justifiable.

"Blaine, get on the other side and give me a hand."

Understanding his partner's intentions, Spartan took a position across from

Watts. Their action set the photographers in motion, clicking and shooting footage of the detectives raising the dead. But rigor mortis wasn't allowing it, and that caused the detectives to back away. Watts started to remove his coat, but thought better of it when it was half-way down his arms. Deciding the coat was a good germ barrier, he would keep it on and drop it off at the cleaner's on the way home. When he moved back into position, so did his partner.

"Okay, Blaine, one hand on his shoulder, the other on his thigh, push on three."

With considerable effort, the body gave way and sat up in the chair like a Ken doll. Watts smiled for the first time. "Seeing Coulter like this gives a whole new perspective, don't you think?"

Hands on hips, Spartan nodded. "I understand why his face is covered in blood and his skin is dingy gray. I can even accept his wide eyes and parted lips, but that gash on his forehead looks pretty deep. I'm willing to bet it came from the marble block's edge."

"X-rays should confirm that, but it's the fear in his face that concerns me. The gash on his forehead doesn't look deep enough to kill him instantly."

"I concur. And he certainly didn't bleed to death."

Watts noted that Coulter's nose and lips were both undamaged. Leaning closer, he noticed something odd and waved the photographers over.

"I need close-ups of Mr. Coulter's face, particularly his mouth," he said.

That drew Porgy Mulberry, who inadvertently bumped into Watts. "Sorry, detective. What's so interesting?"

Watts looked beyond the patrol officer he detested to find the EMT. "Do you have any tongue depressors on you?"

The EMT handed him one, which Watts used to part Coulter's lips. He thought he might find a killer's note inside. When he saw the giant obstruction, his body tensed and face flushed.

"The blow to the head didn't kill him, Blaine. Mr. Coulter suffocated."

After saying that, Watts cast an evil gaze at Mulberry, unable to harbor his years of disdain toward the portly patrol officer. "What do you think, *Porgy*? Can you imagine anyone gasping for air like that?"

"I'd have to take your word on that one, Maxx."

Mulberry's reply sent Watts back to his childhood where he was held under in a neighbor's pool, staring at the sun, his lungs ready to burst. Even underwater, he heard Porgy's distinctive *Ha, ha, ha, hee* laugh. And with all the laughing and splashing, no one noticed Watts struggling for his life. Desperate for air, he kicked Porgy in the groin and swam free. Once on deck, he stormed off, vowing never to speak to Porgy again. Their reunion at the police academy shocked both of them. Today's unexpected rendezvous reminded Watts why he would never be able to exorcise Porgy Mulberry's demon from his mind. Seeing his own drowning eyes in Coulter's face, his heart hammered his chest, his lungs ached, his vision narrowed. Fists bunched, he gulped in a breath to calm himself.

Spartan moved closer. Keeping his voice low, he said, "You don't look so good. You okay, Maxx?"

Watts nodded, staring at the ground. Heavy blinking helped shake off his panic attack. When he looked up, he noticed the smug look on Mulberry's face. Yes, that fat bastard still remembered, and that's why he could never forgive him.

Spartan touched his partner's shoulder, calling his name.

"I'm fine," Watts said, still eyeing his rival.

A squeaking gurney announced the ME's arrival. Dr. Frank Morton slowly came through the door hunched over, wearing thick black-framed glasses. He took a moment to look around before acknowledging Watts.

"Smells like I'm in the right place," Morton said. "The body stinks, too."

"Back atcha, Doc. You look worse every time I see you. Why don't you retire?"

"Careful, detective. As I recall, you're the one that got shot, so the odds favor me outliving you."

"Thanks for the thought, Doc, but I hope to attend your funeral. Anyway, glad you could join us—not that Mr. Coulter has any pressing engagements."

Morton frowned, pulling some Latex gloves from his pocket. "Are you upset because I had another commitment? I assure you I came as quickly as I could."

"No, Doc. My mood stems from a suffocated victim, not your arrival time. There's a large obstruction in the vic's throat. Mr. Coulter must have suffered terribly before he died."

Morton drew his sleeve across his brow, studying the body. He showed little concern other than being physically uncomfortable. He looked up a moment later. "Why is it so hot in here?" he said. "Didn't this guy pay his electric bill?"

Spartan flipped the light switch on and off. "Everything works except the a/c."

"Doesn't matter, we rarely had a/c in the old days. Let's have a look at your vic."

Watts raised his palm. "Before you get too involved," he said, "did you need to speak to these EMTs? They've been here all morning. I asked that they wait for you."

Morton gave them a cursory glance and shook his head. Watts nodded his apology to the EMTs and they took off. Ignoring the videographer who was filming over his shoulder, Morton lifted a tongue depressor from his lab coat and attempted to insert it into Coulter's mouth. When Coulter's rubbery lips barely budged, he calmly set the wooden tool aside and retrieved the liver temperature probe to determine the time of death. The victim's seated position took him longer than normal to find a suitable location to insert the needle, but he was eventually successful.

Morton gave his best smile imitation. "Once I get him to the morgue, I'll open him up to see what's in his throat," he said.

"Time's critical, Doc. Any chance you can remove it here?"

Morton cocked his head, squinting at Watts. "You know that's not how we do things, detective." He paused, scanned the room, and then focused on the probe. "But just this once, I'll see what I can do."

Morton's wink confirmed his procedural break cleared his debt with Watts' private consulting matter. Ignoring the detectives, he set the probe aside and moved around the desk, studying the vic's body from different angles. His gaze traveled from the desk to Coulter's forehead and back to the desk several times.

Frowning, he said, "Since you've already moved the body, I presume it's okay to swivel the chair."

Watts grinned. "The photographers documented everything, the body was getting stiff, and I had no idea when you'd get here. They took additional photos of Coulter sitting up. His chair has never been moved, but there's no problem in moving it now."

Morton nodded, swinging the chair so Coulter faced him. After a brief glimpse, he opened his bag to fetch more tools. It was a struggle, but he eventually pried Coulter's jaw open and inserted a rubber block to keep it that way. Using his penlight to inspect the mouth cavity, he said, "Whatever it is, it's jammed in there tight, and I'm not sure I can extract it without damaging it."

"Do your best, Doc."

Head tilted, he gave Watts an annoyed look. "I assume you want it intact."

"Absolutely," said Watts, feeling a tingle as he fixated on Morton's rubber block. His childhood dentist used one like it to keep him from biting. Sadly, it worked and his mouthful of fillings proved it. Did Coulter's killer use a block like this for the same reason? If so, the killer took it with him because no one found anything like it in the room. Still, the notion suggested that Coulter's murder was premeditated.

Spartan moved in to see. "Man, that thing's huge!"

Watts snapped out of his trance and crowded the ME to see for himself. Morton seemed to be under his own spell, humming while maneuvering his tongs.

"It looks like a giant paper wad," Morton said. "You're absolutely sure you want me to do this here?"

"Yes, Doc, I really need it. Please do your best to keep it intact."

Morton's shrug implied he was re-evaluating his options. His humming became erratic as he fiddled with the object. After several agonizing minutes, he pulled the mucus-filled wad from Coulter's mouth. Smiling now, he dropped it into an evidence bag and then handed it to Watts.

"Is this what you wanted?" he said. "I believe it's all there."

Watts accepted the bag, beaming. "You're amazing, Doc. Simply amazing."

The ME smiled back. "I've never lost a patient yet. No complaints from them either."

"Good one, Doc. Thanks again."

Grabbing the desk for support, Morton slowly rose to his feet without further comment. After stretching his back, he motioned for his assistant to bring the gurney over. Watts stood next to him so he could speak privately.

"By the way, Doc, what did the liver probe tell you?"

"Based on the temperature, I estimate the time of death was eight to ten hours ago."

"So the attack occurred somewhere between 2 and 4 AM."

Morton nodded as he checked his watch. "I can live with that."

Watts turned to his partner and held the evidence bag in the air so they could both see. Though soggy and tinted pink, the ink on the paper was still legible.

"Well, Blaine, you're the paperwork expert. What do you make of this typing?"

Spartan examined the wad closely, comparing it to the manuscript on the desk. "Looks like a perfect match to me."

Tim Westin re-entered the office and immediately zoomed in on the bagged wad. "Jesus, Maxx, that thing's big enough to choke a horse," he said.

"You got that right, and I need you to spread it apart so we can read what it says."

The forensics tech took the evidence bag, cocking his head several times to examine it at eye level. Several facial contortions later, he silently dug into his tool kit and removed some tweezers and a waxed paper roll. After peeling off his old gloves, he slid on a fresh pair and then covered the desk with the waxed paper. When he set the wad on the desk, he stared at it a while, shook his head a few times, and timidly went to work knowing the slightest error could permanently shred clues.

Watts hovered over him, watching him poke and prod the soggy wad. A sudden wind gust nearly blew it off the desk, but Watts stopped it with his gloved hand. A dog's yelp made him look out the window. Curtains blew and trees danced. Everything else looked the same.

Dr. Morton interrupted Watts, tapping him on the shoulder. "Any problem with me cutting the vic free?"

Watts glanced at the tie straps carving into Coulter's wrists and ankles and shook his head. "I think we're good, Doc, but please drop the straps into an evidence bag, okay?"

Spartan's stomach growled. He apologized with a goofy look.

"Ten thirty's too early for lunch," Watts said. "Why don't you and Porgy canvas the neighborhood while we finish in here?"

"Will do."

With Coulter's closest neighbor being forty yards away, Watts knew it would keep them occupied for a while. Seconds after Spartan and Mulberry left, the cicadas screeched again. Oddly, no dogs barked. Another gust made Watts wonder why the window was still open. With no reason to keep it that way, he slid it shut and then felt a cool draft coming from the air vent. So, why were the windows open if they had air conditioning? He double-checked for a break-in, but found the office window frame and screen undamaged. A grunting noise had him looking over his shoulder. He spotted Dr. Morton and his assistant trying to flatten Coulter's torso so it would fit into the body bag. Another grunt preceded a *snap*. Suddenly the cadaver fell flat, groaning as its remaining air expelled. Creepy as it was, Watts kept watching until they zipped the black bag shut.

Westin had made little progress in smoothing the wad since Watts last looked. Finally, the forensics tech heaved a sigh, backed away, and headed for the door.

"I'm not giving up," Westin said. "I just need to grab a few things."

"No sweat, Tim. By the way, I saw a young woman in here earlier, but she's not around anymore. Is she part of your team?"

"Nice looking brunette, petite, maybe five four?"

"That's the one."

"That's our new lab tech. Came here from Houston or Dallas, I don't remember which. Anyway, she's heading back to the lab. Why do you ask? You got a crush on her?"

"No, I just like to know who's in and out of my crime scene. If she's new, that explains why I haven't seen her before." *I would have remembered her.*

Westin's grin implied he didn't believe his lie, but it didn't matter. While waiting, Watts surveyed the office's dingy walls, their pale yellow color even except for a large rectangular area where something once hung. The holes and shape suggested it may have been a framed poster, but that was pure speculation. He was more curious about why the holes were still exposed in this otherwise tidy office. Soon, Westin returned carrying a deep dish pan, a funnel, a spatula, and a bottle of drinking water.

Watts gave him a look. "What are you doing with that stuff? Baking brownies?"

Westin sneered. "Detective Watts, I'm not sure how you managed to convince Dr. Morton to remove the throat obstruction in the field, but before I do anything further, I need you to go on record stating you'll assume all risk for what I'm about to do."

Watts raised his right hand, palm out, middle three fingers extended. "Scout's honor, Tim. I assume all risk, blah, blah, blah. You happy now?"

"Yes I am, but I could have done without the blahs."

Westin then poured some of the bottled water into his pan, dunked the wad, and held it under while the CSSU photographers documented the action. After letting it sit for several minutes, he used the blunt end of the tweezers to slowly unfold the paper. He painstakingly worked for fifteen minutes to separate the two papers and finally they floated like ghosts. Giving no hint of gratification, the tech then slid his spatula under the first paper, scooped it from the pan, set it atop the wax paper, and spread it as much as he dared. He did the same with the second sheet and shot Watts a concerned look.

"I refuse to flip them over, but you can read whatever's visible." He then drained the pan water into the plastic water bottle, capped it, and labeled it as evidence. "When I get back to the lab, I'll analyze this water for toxins."

"Thanks, Westin. You do great work."

"I know."

Once the photographers took their final shots, Watts sent them away. He spotted Spartan and Mulberry in the entry. Spartan's head-shake indicated they had no luck with the neighbors. Watts waved Spartan over, but not Officer Mulberry.

"Westin did a great job separating those papers," Watts said. "The header on them proves they're the missing manuscript pages. Too bad we can't flip them over so we can read both sides."

"I'm sure we'll be able to once they're dry. By the way, the neighbors know nothing."

"No surprise there," Watts said, reading a wrinkled manuscript page. He zeroed in on one line and pointed. "This is kind of odd, don't you think? 'Death comes to those deserving.' What do you suppose that means?"

"Beats me, but it's not the best grammar I've seen."

"I agree, but it is commanding. I wonder if Coulter was using it to make a statement."

"It's a bit premature to make any connections, Maxx. Especially since it's taken out of context."

Watts' eyes roamed the manuscript while his brain contemplated Spartan's comments. Though there was nothing wrong with his statement, it rubbed him the wrong way. Still, Spartan was right. They did need to read Coulter's complete manuscript, but it could wait. His gaze shifted to the so-called Writer's Block. *Award or advertising gimmick?* Could be either. Some authors give away pens, pins, and bookmarks to promote their books. For all he knew, CC Coulter gave away marble paperweights and decided to keep one himself. This made him consider Coulter's financial obligations to his authors, printers, editors, and publicists. Tough economic times and e-readers meant people weren't buying as many bound books. Somehow it all tied together. He turned to his partner.

"Blaine, if Coulter wasn't paying out royalties, I can see how someone might come after him. Money and passion are classic murder motives, and Coulter's gruesome death certainly suggests it was personal."

Spartan placed his hands on his hips to spread his coat. He nodded his accord, staring at the smoothed wad. "You're thinking the killer got fed up and used the Writer's Block to make a statement?"

"That plus the manuscript pages. You can't deny the irony."

"Yes there's irony, but does the manuscript-wad in itself make Coulter's death personal or was it merely a convenient tool? For that matter, we can probably say the same thing about the Writer's Block."

Watts sighed. "Hopefully Coulter's widow can enlighten us. She's in the other room."

"Let's go."

Watts noticed the musty odor as soon as they entered the living room. It could have come from the yellowed lace drapes, the crushed velvet wallpaper, or both. Either way, these features contrasted sharply with the chrome lamps, IKEA furniture, and contemporary wall art. He searched for family photos, but saw none.

When Spartan took a seat across from Mrs. Coulter, it took Watts back to his shooting. Not unlike today, everything seemed fine until the distraught woman they were interviewing pulled a gun. Today, Officer Mulberry stood guard over the widow who slumped in her overstuffed chair like she was boneless. But looks were often deceiving and Watts wasn't going to let Mulberry leave without his permission. Having the officer there served two purposes: protection and reprisal. Revenge didn't come often, but today it was sweet.

Watts changed his focus to Kat Coulter's physical appearance. Her frazzled blonde hair, pale skin, and bloodshot eyes contrasted sharply with her manicured nails and waxed eyebrows. The thin lines at the corners of her eyes hinted she was in her late thirties. The swaying curtains distracted him. The outside noise was less than in CC's office, but with cool air flowing through the vents, why was the window open? Without asking, he closed it and then gestured for Spartan to follow him into the hall. He waited until they were out of ear shot before saying anything.

"So, partner, does the scene bring back any memories?"

"It's been over two years, and she appears to be in shock. Can we move on?"

"Sure," Watts said, looking around. I wish I hadn't sent those EMTs home. If Kat Coulter needs medical assistance, they could have provided it. If she's faking, we'd know." He peeked in the living room to make sure nothing had changed, then looked back at Spartan. "Blaine, we know she spoke to a uniformed officer before we arrived, so why is she suddenly stoic? She admitted to being home when her husband was murdered, but claims she slept through the assault. This is a tiny house. Why do I feel like I'm being played?"

"She's certainly a suspect, but being passive could be a delayed grieving response."

Watts sighed, allowing his brain to take him back to when he and Spartan were interviewing a pretty blonde woman not unlike Kat Coulter. Watts allowed a momentary glance at his partner and then suddenly he was falling backwards, his shoulder on fire. Instinctively, he returned fire as he hit the floor. The persistent twinge in his shoulder reminded him that while he killed his shooter, he never wanted her dead. Hopefully Kat Coulter wasn't hiding a gun under a pillow.

"Here's the plan," he said, certain that Spartan was reliving the same memory. "We walk in together and I'll question her. I realize that Porgy Mulberry is also in the room, but if Mrs. Coulter so much as twitches, I expect you to subdue her. Got it?" Taking Spartan's head bob as a "yes", he said, "All right, then. It's show time."

Watts led the way with his hands behind his back. His peripheral vision confirmed that Officer Mulberry was paying attention so he calmly seated himself next to the widow.

"Mrs. Coulter, I'm Detective Watts. I'm sorry for all that you've been through this morning and I know you've told others your story, but Detective Spartan and I need to hear it first-hand." He bit his lower lip allowing her time to respond, but she never looked up. "Mrs. Coulter, we really need to talk. If you prefer, we can do this downtown."

Their eyes met briefly before hers shifted to Spartan, who was standing behind Watts. As her fingernails clawed at the sofa, her face strained like she was giving birth. Still, she kept silent. Watts tried a different tact.

"Ma'am, from what I understand, after you awoke you went into your husband's office to see how he was doing and found him slumped over his desk, dead. Is that correct?"

Her hands relaxed and her skin color lightened. She laid her head back and her eyes closed like a doll's. Her pouty lips completed the image.

Unimpressed, Watts said, "Mrs. Coulter, may I get you some water?"

Her eyes still closed, she softly said, "Bottled water, in the fridge."

Spartan went into the kitchen and returned with a bottle. He unscrewed the cap and offered it to her. When she failed to reach for it, he set it on her end table.

Watts gave her time to sip but the bottle never moved. Leaning forward, he said, "Mrs. Coulter, it's quite warm in here. Perhaps you'd be more comfortable talking in an air conditioned station."

She gently shook her head, waving her hand. "Please, call me Kat."

Making sure his partner was taking notes, Watts leaned forward. "Well, at least now we know you can speak, so thank you for that." He looked for a reaction, but saw none. "Mrs. Coulter, people grieve in various ways and we're not here to judge you. However, we do need to hear what happened from your perspective."

Nodding, she slowly opened her eyes as if waking from a trance. "Are you married, Detective Watts?"

"No, ma'am. Never been."

Suddenly her expression hardened and she leaned forward in her seat. "Then how can you possibly know what it's like?" she said.

Watts didn't reply to her jab. It's always better sticking to the subject. But if she intended this to defer his questions or play him for a fool, he would soon prove her wrong.

TWO

Watts stared at Kat Coulter, still pondering her marriage comment. Her face burned with anger and her body was stiff. At this point, he wasn't sure what to expect. Mulberry looked bored, but Spartan had his hand inside his coat covering his pistol. Relieved, Watts smiled and eased his back into the chair.

"Mrs. Coulter," he said, "my partner and I are here to discuss your husband's murder, not my love life. Before we get too involved in the details of what happened here, would you mind explaining why your windows were open when your air conditioning seems to be working?"

"First of all, it's a swamp cooler, not central air conditioning."

"Noted. Now, let's get back to the windows."

She rubbed her forehead like she was in an Excedrin commercial. Stretching her neck and heaving a sigh before making eye contact made it appear more convincing.

"CC gave up a successful career as a stock broker to become a fiction writer," she finally said. "He was gifted enough for a New York publisher to offer him a three book contract, but was insulted by their low-ball offer and no money to promote it. Rather than waste time searching for a new publisher, he decided to start his own publishing company to publish his work and help other frustrated authors. I believed in his talent and encouraged him to do it, but we learned that the book business is better at draining resources than replenishing them. We quickly became frugal, and limiting the swamp cooler operation was one way to cut our expenses. We only ran when it became unbearable inside and turned it off whenever we could open the windows."

"But it was running while the windows were open," Spartan said.

Her face blew up like a balloon. "If you hadn't noticed, the wind has been gusting through here all morning, and if the swamp cooler was on, one of your people must have turned it on."

Watts showed his palms to calm her. "Relax, Mrs. Coulter. I'm only trying to understand why the windows were open."

"Detective, we live in the sticks. No one has any problems out here. In fact, we're probably the only ones who locked our doors. So, how could this happen? Why would someone break in here and murder CC?"

Watts bit his tongue hoping she would continue ranting, but she added nothing further. "Moving on—earlier, one of the officers informed me that you have a bent window screen out back. Has it always been bent?"

"Of course not. I may be frugal, but I keep a clean house. I cleaned every window screen two weeks ago and they were all perfect."

"And you didn't hear anything unusual last night?"

She pressed her hands against her head. "I'm not stupid, detective. I know this looks bad, my being in the house and not hearing anything, but the truth is I was out cold. CC often worked late, and last night he was intent on finishing the final read of his manuscript."

"*Deadly Wrap?*"

"Yes, but if you want to hear my story, you won't interrupt again."

Watts and Spartan exchanged curious glances. "Forgive me," Watts said.

She closed her eyes, tilted her head back, and drew in a breath. She let it hang a while before exhaling through her nostrils. Finally, she opened her eyes looking more embarrassed than angry.

"I went to bed around eleven, but couldn't sleep," she said. "After tossing for an hour, I figured CC needed a break so I went to his office to seduce him. He turned me down cold saying as much as he'd like to, he had to finish his manuscript. So I left him to his work, took two Tylenol PM, and went to bed. The next thing I knew, the sun was in my eyes and the clock read six-fifteen. CC never came to bed so I went to his office figuring he was still laboring away. I screamed when I saw him lying on the bloodied desk and immediately dialed 911. An ambulance showed up about ten minutes later, soon followed by the uniformed cop standing behind you. Ever since then, people have been arriving non-stop, coming and going, taking whatever they please. I can't believe he's gone," she said, burying her face in her hands. "I don't know what I'll do now."

Watts glanced at his partner before repeating several questions to verify her story. She answered each one without error. Satisfied, he rose to his feet.

"I think we've heard enough for now," he said. "We'll set a time when it's convenient to discuss things further. Thank you for your time and cooperation, Mrs. Coulter." He took a couple of steps before stopping in the hallway. "Before we leave, would you like us to confirm all your windows are all locked?"

Nodding, she said, "Thank you."

This pleased Watts because it afforded him another tour through her house. When he returned, he held out his business card. She didn't reach for it so he set it by her water bottle. "The number on my card will reach me anytime day or night. I'll need to know if you're staying somewhere other than at your home. Again, I'm sorry for your loss."

Tears trickled down her cheeks as she stared at the card. "Promise me you'll find the bastard who killed my husband."

"We will, ma'am. We always do."

THREE

All Fort Worth Police homicide detectives work out of the Police Headquarters building located at 350 W. Belknap Street. Affectionately known as "350", Headquarters stood adjacent to the imposing Tarrant County Courthouse that overlooked the Trinity River. To the north, 350 overlooked the historic stockyards. Its south view faced downtown. Its central location made it ideal for handling murder cases anywhere within its jurisdiction. It only took twenty minutes to drive back from the Coulter residence.

Watts parked the unmarked Crown Vic and returned to his metal desk to download his brain onto a notepad. Blaine Spartan would do the same one cubicle over, except he would be typing it into a Word document. Believing his written script would hold up better in court, Watts preferred shorthand and only used a computer when he had to. His theory had yet to be tested, but he was ready for the challenge, should it ever arise.

Spartan's fingers were banging his keyboard so fast that it sounded like squirrels shelling peanuts. Unable to concentrate, Watts leaned back in his chair, evaluating his partner's performance this morning. It was hard accusing Spartan of any wrong-doings when he had done so little. His canvassing the neighborhood turned up zilch, and he said only one line during Kat Coulter's interview. In retrospect, Spartan's time would have been better spent interviewing the barking dog.

But Spartan did deserve credit for watching his back during the interview and he was also brilliant at handling paperwork. Skills like that come in handy with warrants and reports, so in this regard, Watts was happy to have him back. Re-thinking the Coulter's scene, he wondered about that female lab tech that slipped out the door and the swamp cooler that was supposed to be off. He was pondering that when his phone rang. His boss, Lieutenant Ryder, was on the line. Ryder didn't sound happy.

"I'm waiting to be briefed," Ryder said.

Watts checked his watch. Fifteen minutes hardly seemed enough time to be concerned.

"We'll be right down, sir." Watts hung up and tapped on his partner's cubicle. "Let's go, Blaine. We've been summoned."

Spartan grabbed his coat and joined him.

The *squish* from Watts' mismatched shoes echoed down 350's dreary hallway. He didn't know his left leg was slightly shorter than his right until he started running high school track. His podiatrist solved that problem by recommending custom shoes that leveled his hips. Doing so made the physical pain go away, but the resulting stares took some getting used to. In high school, he countered with jokes about being a one-man band. Nowadays he didn't care what people thought.

The vintage police station looked much as it did when it was first constructed. Like most community buildings, 350 received minimal upgrades over the years. In some areas, Watts swore the original air lingered. Ryder said it was nonsense because the ventilation system had been overhauled more than once. But Watts' nose never lied. With Spartan tailing him, he peered into Ryder's glass office, scrutinizing the lieutenant's worn Indian rug. Ryder waved them in. Watts had already agreed to let Spartan speak first.

"Mrs. Coulter found her husband dead in his office and called 911. When we spoke to her, she appeared to be in shock and wasn't saying much. We found a possible break-in point at the utility room window, but so far there is no evidence confirming that."

Ryder nodded, looking at Watts for more.

"Apparently Mr. Coulter had a habit of staying up late," Watts said. "Particularly when facing a deadline as he did last night."

Ryder raised his hands. "How so?"

"CC Coulter was an author and small press publisher. According to Mrs. Coulter, he needed to spend the evening reviewing the final draft of his manuscript. She tried to seduce him and he turned her down. Then she took some Tylenol PM, went to sleep, and never heard a thing. CSSU didn't find any footprints out back, but the bent window screen Blaine mentioned suggests a possible forced entry."

"Forensics told us about the bent screen, not Mrs. Coulter," Spartan said.

Ryder nodded and signaled for Watts to continue.

"Doctor Morton pulled the giant spit wad from Coulter's throat and Tim Westin managed to spread it out. Turns out they are pages from Coulter's *Deadly Wrap* manuscript."

Scratching his head, Ryder said, "Coulter's manuscript is titled *Deadly Wrap*?"

Spartan grinned. "Ironic, isn't it?"

"I guess." Ryder looked at Watts again. "You were saying?"

"That's about it for now," said Watts. "Forensics is still analyzing evidence, the ME has Coulter on ice, we're writing notes, and as soon as you're finished with us, we'll try to identify some suspects."

The lieutenant pressed his palms together, raising his fingertips to his lips. Following a long pause, his sunken eyes gazed at them. "So we have open windows, locked doors, nothing appears missing or disturbed, and a small publisher dies from his *Deadly Wrap* manuscript."

"Yes, sir."

"Something doesn't add up. Go back there and see what you missed."

Watts eyed at his partner, pivoted on his right heel, and walked out.

Spartan rushed to catch up. "Gee, Maxx, that went well. What are we supposed to find?"

Watts didn't comment. Instead, he thought about what his dead father always preached. *No matter what, never let your guard down.* Dad was a lousy drunk, but sometimes he offered good advice. That pearl was his favorite. As soon as he sat down at his desk, Spartan was hovering over him.

"What now, Blaine?"

"Just wondering when you want to leave."

"After I finish my coffee."

Spartan stared at the vapor rising from the black brew in Watts' mug. "How can you drink that stuff when it's blazing hot outside?"

Watts held it to his lips until it was empty. "Ah, that's good," he said with a grin. Predictably, Spartan headed back to his cubicle to sulk.

Alone again, Kris Kristofferson's *Sunday Morning Coming Down* settled into Watts' brain like coastal fog. Dad spent a lot of Sunday mornings complaining about headaches, and frequently had beer for breakfast like in the song. That got Watts thinking about Spartan's bout with alcoholism. Perhaps ridded with guilt over the shooting, his partner abused the bottle like Dad did. Thinking he should ease up on Spartan a bit, he rose from his chair and leaned over the thin wall that divided their desks.

"Okay, partner—ready to roll?"

Glued to his computer screen, Spartan said, "Give me a second to finish this thought."

"Take your time. I need to hit the head anyway."

Spartan was ready when Watts returned. Side-by-side, they descended the stairs to the basement garage where their Crown Vic awaited them, its engine still warm. Watts slid behind the wheel and keyed the ignition while his partner strapped in. A quick twist sent a burst of black smoke out the tailpipe and the car started to vibrate. While steering the wheeled beast out of the parking garage, Watts busied himself re-running the case in his head.

Spartan spoke first. "Are we going to discuss this case or go for a joy ride?"

"Joy ride," said Watts, gripping the wheel at ten and two.

Delighted with his response, Watts couldn't do this job without humor. It kept him sane when fragments were all that remained of a person. Sometimes the stench got so bad he had to leave his clothes outside when he got home. And when he lay down at night, it wasn't unusual to sleep in fear of what might haunt him. Compared to many cases, this one seemed easy. Feeling Spartan's gaze, he knew his play time was over.

Glancing his way, Watts said, "How about this? CC Coulter was a writer and a publisher, so we should find out who didn't like his work or might have been upset with him. If the Writer's Block split his head open, then maybe it was a spur of the moment crime."

"As in the result of an argument?"

"Maybe."

"Except arguments usually involve yelling and Mrs. Coulter claims she slept through it."

"And according to her, that's correct."

As Watts drove, he realized there was a lot more to her story than her sleeping through the murder. "You know, Blaine, I still can't get over that odd 'Death comes to those deserving' phrase from the manuscript. I don't know what it means or why it sticks with me, but it does."

Spartan nodded, admiring the sun-struck Fort Worth skyline. "I know what you mean," he said. "The marble block, the odd phrase, and suffocation all seem to imply CC's death is the result of a personal vendetta."

Unwilling to restate the obvious, Watts handed the briefing folder to his partner. "We have twenty minutes before we get there. See what we've missed and come up with some questions for Mrs. Coulter."

Spartan took the folder. "Shouldn't we call her to tell her we're coming? I mean, when we left, you said you'd be in touch. I'm not sure arriving unannounced is what she expected."

"It's not what I expected either, but Ryder sent us so that's what we're doing. Don't call."

Spartan shrugged, opened the folder, and scanned the murder file. He went ten minutes before saying, "You do realize that if the media picks up on Coulter's murder, *Deadly Wrap* could become a best seller because of how he died."

Suddenly Watts' eyes lit up. "*That's* what was missing this morning. No reporters! Why do you suppose that is?"

"I have no idea."

"Neither do I, but it sure seems odd since this is the city's first murder in seven months. Usually, reporters swarm over us like flies on poop. So, where were they this morning?"

Spartan gave a puzzled look. "Maybe there's more to this case than we realize. Maybe the media was shut out."

"Maybe, but regardless of why it happened, our job is to nail the killer."

"I concur. And for the record, I was prepared to shoot Mrs. Coulter if she drew a gun."

Watts' face softened. "I noticed, Blaine. And I appreciate it."

When they arrived, the Coulter's house looked different than it had earlier. The sky was brighter, and yet the farm house seemed darker, more desolate. The yellow police tape was still in place but now only one patrol car remained on scene. The oak trees also seemed taller, the distance between neighbors longer. In spite of the sweltering heat, Watts slid on his sport coat.

Kat stood in her doorway in a white robe, a towel covering her hair. Even without makeup she looked beautiful, her blue eyes captivating. But Watts also knew that beyond her splendor lay a potential killer.

Kat tightened her waist strap and crossed her arms. "I wasn't expecting you. Did you forget something?"

Watts shook his head. "Sorry, but our boss sent us back for a few more questions."

"Can you wait in the living room while I get dressed?"

"Absolutely. Take your time."

They took the same seats as before. The room felt cooler but the musty smell lingered. Watts assumed it was from mold in the swamp cooler pan, not that it mattered. He found the lack of any family photos in their living room more disturbing. He sat there rubbing his face, wondering what to say when Kat entered the room. She would probably ask for an explanation as to why his boss sent them back, but the fact is he didn't have a good answer. He could say that he planned to meet Dr. Morton later today. Then again, she didn't need to know that. Right then, Kat Coulter appeared in jeans, sneakers, and a white Tee. Watts and Spartan stood, as gentlemen do, when a lady enters the room. They sat once she sat.

Watts cleared his throat. "Mrs. Coulter, it's easier tracking down killers when we have the facts, so feel free to interrupt whenever something comes to mind. First off, has anyone from the media contacted you?"

"No."

"Don't you find that odd?"

"Frankly, I hadn't thought of it until now. No one's called, but I wouldn't take it if they did. And if they showed up unannounced like you did, I wouldn't open the door."

Watts bowed his head, getting her drift. "I'll try to be brief," he said. "First of all, our initial impressions seem to favor this murder being a personal assault, and since you were asleep at the time, we're thinking it may have been one of your husband's friends or colleagues. That means we need to know your husband's routine and who he contacted in the past few weeks."

Squinting, she leaned forward. "Are you suggesting one of our *authors* killed CC?"

"No, ma'am. I'm just saying we need to know all we can about your husband."

"I already told you, CC's writing success led to his establishing The Guillotine Press. We met in New York when he was seeking a literary agent. I took him on as a client, and continued that role seeking new talent for The Guillotine Press. CC wanted to publish unknown authors who might otherwise not be in print. The publishing world is very perplexing, detective. CC was always very honest with his authors. I assure you that every aspect of our press is legitimate, and that certainly includes our authors."

Watts nodded, jotting that down. He hoped she would continue, but she didn't.

"What kind of novels did CC publish?" Spartan said.

"Murder mysteries."

Watts gaze immediately went to the bookshelf near the window. On the top left were four hardbacks bearing CC Coulter's name. Next to them were ten trade paperbacks bearing The Guillotine Press logo. Moving closer, he jotted down their titles and authors. When he finished, he looked back at Kat.

"Are any of these books published under pen names?" he said.

Her face wrinkled sharply. "No, but what difference would that make?"

"Probably none, but I need to know."

She frowned as she stared at the book shelf. It took a while before she faced the detectives again. "CC always said that if you can't sign your own name to something, it's not worth publishing. That's why he never published anything using a pseudo name."

Watts paused to re-read his notes. Out the corner of his eye, he watched her dab her eyes, then wad the tissue in her palm. He held his silence a moment longer before lowering his notebook.

"So Courtney Dridelle, Hank Azar, Lance Ballard, Jolene Lundgren, Ben Striker, Pao Lee, Luke Harper, Toby Roberts, Mick Taggart, and Arlene Buck are all real names?" he said.

"Absolutely. Personally, I've only met Pao Lee and Courtney Dridelle, but I believe CC met them all at one time or another. Their contracts and royalty checks use the same names."

Watts nodded, intrigued by The Guillotine Press' logo. "Whose idea was the bloodied guillotine emblem?"

Kat stared at the books. "It was CC's idea. He said it parodied Poe's *Pit and the Pendulum* like Chubby Checker did Fats Domino."

"You lost me."

She fired a stern look. "You've never heard of Edgar Allan Poe?"

"I read Poe's *The Pit and the Pendulum* in high school, but the only checkers I know of is a board game and an auto parts store."

Her sigh implied he was the most ignorant person she had met. After a long pause, she explained that Fats Domino was a popular singer in the 1950's, and an upcoming performer decided to change his name to Chubby Checker to parody Fats. "Get it?" she said. "Fat is to Chubby as Domino is to Checker. Chubby gained a lot of notoriety from it. Pretty clever of him."

"Yeah, clever," Watts said, wondering what ancient pop singers had to do with The Guillotine Press. "Moving on. As its literary agent, what can you tell us about your authors' writing styles?"

"Well, Courtney Dridelle and Arlene Buck write romantic murders. Attorney Hank Azar writes legal thrillers. Lance Ballard's book involves a dude ranch murder. Jolene Lundgren and Ben Striker both write gory murders. Pao Lee writes Hong Kong murders. Luke Harper's story concerns a Texas cult mass murder. Toby Master's victim dies on a golf course, and Mick Taggart's is about death at forty thousand feet."

As an avid admirer of westerns, Lance Ballard's book caught Watts' eye. "Murder on a dude ranch sounds kind of like that movie, *City Slickers*."

She quietly watched the floor. "I wouldn't know about that, detective. Perhaps the description on the book jacket will provide some insight."

Watts nodded and pulled Ballard's *Hard Ride to Cimarron* from the shelf. "A dude ranch cattle drive turns deadly when campfire secrets are revealed," he said, reading the description out loud. It was printed directly below a painting of four mounted greenhorns swinging their ropes at full gallop. Billy Crystal meets Louis L'amour, he mused. Murder theme or not, Ballard's book seemed an unlikely match for The Guillotine Press. He slid it back on the shelf.

Kat locked her knees together and swung her legs in Watts' direction. "I sense your disapproval, detective, but whatever opinion you have of this book is irrelevant. What you should take from this is that Lance Ballard and all of our authors are real people with real faces, and none of them use pen names."

Watts nodded, studying her body language. *Is she confident, angry, or hurt?* To break the tension, he stared at the bookshelf to avoid her eyes.

Kat hugged her ample chest looking increasingly frustrated. "Look, I've been answering your questions. Now how about telling me what happened to my husband. It doesn't make any sense. CC wouldn't hurt a fly."

Watts settled into his seat allowing his unbuttoned coat to expose his holstered 9mm. He wanted her to see it so she knew he was in charge, and that he would use it if he had to. Unfortunately, it failed to make an impression.

"As of now, all we know is your husband died a brutal death in his own home and we have no suspects," he said. "However, it's interesting that all of your authors write about murder. And since that seems to be your genre, do any of these books describe a death like your husband's?"

She glanced at the GP books and then back at him. "Now what are you suggesting? That this was a copy-cat murder?" Seeing Watts and Spartan nodding, tears trickled down her cheeks. "All I know is CC didn't deserve this."

Watts tilted his head remembering the line, *Death comes to those deserving*. While she recovered, he realized that physically seeing the GP books made their second trip worthwhile. It took a while before he asked his next question.

"Can you think of anything that might help us identify the killer?" he said. "Perhaps you heard a voice or maybe a car's engine disturbed your sleep?"

She adamantly shook her head. "Like I said, I was out cold and didn't hear a thing." In seconds, her face transformed from sad to accusing. "Detective Watts, I may not know much about our authors' personal lives, but I do know that CC was good to all of them. He did everything possible to promote their work. He even took their books to the Frankfurt Book Fair, so if their sales aren't what they expect, it's their own fault. Even the big houses demand that their authors promote their work."

Her sudden aggression surprised Watts. He silently glanced at Spartan and back at Kat. Her face softened when their eyes met.

"I'm sorry," she said. "It's just that he spent so much time promoting these authors—" She didn't finish her sentence.

Watts scratched his head, wondering if she even considered the possible author/suspect connection before he mentioned it. Leading a witness is not allowed in court, and yet that's what he seemed to be doing here. He didn't like it, and liked it less that Spartan was standing around like a stuffed bear instead of participating. Watts blew out a breath and looked at her.

"Mrs. Coulter, we honestly have no idea what we're looking at, but I assure you we will do everything possible to find your husband's assailant. Of course, I must also remind you that everyone is a suspect until we have a resolution."

She half-rolled her eyes and looked away. "I wondered when you'd get around to that."

FOUR

Watts wasn't ready to leave Kat Coulter's house. Not when his interview with her was getting interesting. Wanting to get a better sense of things, he suggested they step out back so he could show her the bent window screen. Instead, Kat led the way, touched the screen, and then looked around the yard. In the distance, the Jack Russell bounded at leaves, its owner nowhere in sight. Watts noticed four shaded seats on her porch and edged toward them.

"Let's sit out here for a moment and take in the scene," he said.

Without waiting for a response, he and Spartan took the outward seats to place Kat in the middle. That way she had to choose who to speak to. Sometimes a seating arrangement like this made people say more than they planned. As it turned out, the sweltering heat toiled on all of them. The neighbor's kid came out to play fetch with his pup. Nothing else was remarkable.

Smiling, Watts pointed at the kid. "Looks like he's doing more fetching than the dog."

Kat watched the boy and nodded politely. "We're not here to discuss the boy, detective. What do you make of the window?"

Watts delayed his answer because the scene stirred summertime memories. *Funny how heat never bothers kids.* Back then, he went outside and played because that's what kids did. He never had a dog, but the neighbor's dog loved him more than its owners and that suited him fine. Those days, people sat on their porch swings sipping lemonade telling tales, none of which involved homicide. The thought of murder brought him back. He glanced at the bent window screen and then at Kat.

"The window is certainly a possible entry point," he said, "but forensics hasn't found any evidence that can confirm or deny your husband's assailant entered through it. No fingerprints, footprints, clothing threads, nothing."

She stared at the window clasping her hands. "Detective, we've been cursed ever since we moved here. First, the book sales weren't what we expected and now CC's dead. Call it New York paranoia, but I kept telling him we shouldn't leave the windows open. I should have put my foot down and insisted they stay closed and locked. Had I done so, CC might still be alive."

"Unfortunately, we'll never know." Watts waited a moment and then said, "On a different subject, you said you were CC's literary agent. Can you expand on that?"

"Of course. As the sole proprietor of the Kat Bleuette Literary Agency, my New York City address attracted countless hopefuls. I read a lot of queries and summaries over the years, but I was immediately drawn to a stock broker named CC Coulter who wrote murder mysteries. I wrote him back and after exchanging a few e-mails and phone calls we agreed to meet for dinner, my treat. I didn't expect he would be so handsome and charming, but I assure you I signed him as a client for his writing ability. Tossing my ethics aside, we began dating and soon fell in love. Over the next few months I received several offers for CC's manuscript, but the numbers were so disappointing that CC decided to establish his own publishing business. Even when we first met he said he was tired of the New York rat race, so going into business for himself seemed like a good idea. I supported it and he invested nearly all of his assets in The Guillotine Press. For a while things looked promising, but soon The Press consumed our lives." She grabbed her hands to stop the trembling. A deep breath seemed to help. "I'm sorry. It's just that I miss him so much."

Watts glimpsed at his partner. He sensed Spartan got his drift. They weren't back to their pre-shooting/pre-alcoholism days yet, but they were getting in sync again. Watts got up and went to the window where gray fingerprint dust gave up nothing. The baked ground beneath it kept its secrets, too. How anyone could sleep in this heat was beyond him. No wonder Kat took two Tylenol PM capsules. Too bad they didn't take her blood to confirm that.

He studied the oak trees expecting the cicadas to screech. Could they have masked a break-in? Seconds later, the monstrous bugs shrieked as if to answer his question. In unison, they suddenly fell silent for a moment and then chimed in again. Their random behavior ruled them out as accomplices. He quickly moved on.

Keeping his back to the wind, Watts jotted a note to look into The Guillotine Press' financial affairs. Clearly, CC wasn't a robbery victim because nothing was taken, and even if a burglar walked in on him, why torture him like that? Considering this, Watts kept reaching the same conclusion. This murder was an emotional act performed by someone with a grudge. He couldn't share that with Kat, though. Not yet anyway.

Kat grew impatient. "I'm roasting out here," she said. "Can we go back inside?"

"Of course."

Watts scanned the area one more time before following them inside. Assuming Kat was knocked out from the sleep aid like she said, with no surrounding fence and an oak forest filled with deafening bugs and barking dogs, it was plausible the attacker could have come and gone undetected. So far, their only evidence was a small marble block, a spit wad, and plastic tie straps that bound CC to his chair. Gloved hands hide fingerprints, but the lack of footprints still gnawed at him. Staring at the dead lawn, he hoped CSSU snapped photos before trampling the area. With luck, their pictures might reveal something.

After stepping inside, he gave a look of urgency. "Mrs. Coulter, I'm afraid I had too much coffee this morning," he said. "Mind if I use your rest room?"

"Help yourself. It's right down the hall."

Watts excused himself and locked the bathroom door behind him. After raising the toilet seat, he let the sink faucet dribble, slid on a Latex glove, and opened the medicine cabinet. True to her word, an unsealed bottle of Tylenol PM sat on the upper shelf. He eased the cabinet shut, lowered the seat, turned off the water, and waited a few seconds before flushing. It was a trick he used to spit out vegetables when he was a kid and he hoped she was as gullible as his parents. He tucked his glove in his pocket, washed his hands, and casually returned to the utility room to inspect the bent window screen. Obstacle free and a four foot drop, he figured that any average sized man could enter through it. Adding credence to the break-in theory, the room was close to CC's office. After jotting more notes, he joined Kat and Spartan in the living room.

"Thank you," he said. "I'm better now."

"Good." Her eyes narrowed. "Find anything while you were back there?"

"Nothing of interest."

Watts answered while searching for the killer's mark. Murderers always leave something behind, but in this case, the bloodied manuscript and Writer's Block may have sufficed. Clearly, those items were meant to be found, but why rest CC's head on the manuscript instead of the guillotine-inscribed paperweight? Had the media reported the story, the Writer's Block would have created a more powerful impression. Thinking about that, he was still baffled by the lack of reporters. The news should have reported his death on at least one broadcast.

"Mrs. Coulter, can you enlighten me on the story behind the Writer's Block?"

"There's not much to say. One of our authors gave it to CC as a joke. A play on words."

"Yeah, I figured that. Which author gave it to him?"

"Pao Lee."

"And how long ago did this happen?"

"Two days before CC died, Pao came by because he was starting his US book tour. CC loved it. He and Pao shared a good laugh over it."

Watts nodded at Spartan. *Finally, a break.* "Mrs. Coulter, would you mind if we borrow your Guillotine Press books?"

"No, but be careful with them because they are signed first editions. One day they might be worth something."

"We'll be careful."

Admittedly, Watts knew little about the book business, but from what he'd seen in book stores, the odds were against any small press author making it big. Regardless, he looked forward to reading these stories because any one of them might reveal something pertinent to the case. He took half of the books and headed for the door. Spartan could get the rest.

"I'm truly sorry for your loss," he said. "We appreciate your time, and if anything else comes to mind, please call me."

She gave a sad nod as they carried her books away.

FIVE

Watts brooded over the GP books during the drive back to 350. He kept thinking that something inside one might lead them to the killer. The wildfires out west had thickened the brown haze. The smoky smell was coming through the vents even though the a/c was set on recycle. He didn't recall a summer when a drought had caused so much devastation.

Spartan seemed to be lost in his own thoughts so Watts tuned the radio to classic hits 97.1. An old Kris Kristofferson song transported Watts to his childhood, riding in the car with Dad behind the wheel. Though not a polished singer, Kris' voice gave a genuine quality to his tunes, and he wrote some good ones. *Sunday Morning Sidewalk* was one of Dad's favorites. When Watts joined in for the chorus, Spartan turned the volume down and angrily stared outside. Watts beckoned for an explanation.

"What's the matter, Blaine? You don't like my singing?"

"Your singing's fine. It's the tune I don't like."

"But it's a classic. How could you not—"

Suddenly it dawned on him that Kristofferson's song wasn't one a recovering alcoholic wanted to hear. He was quiet for a moment, trying to backtrack. Rather than apologize, he said, "I like most music. Why don't you pick another station?"

Spartan nodded and punched in 99.5. Ironically, Alan Jackson's hit drinking song, *It's Five O'clock Somewhere* was playing. This time Watts reached over and turned the radio off since there was no way to predict what the next song would be.

After that, Spartan relaxed a bit. He stared out the window for a long while before looking back at Watts. "Any preference on which Guillotine Press book you want me to read first?" he said.

Watts swerved to avoid a large tumbleweed. The move flung Spartan against the side of the car and then back toward the center. After watching the giant weed roll across the road in his mirror, Watts grinned at his partner.

"Sorry, Blaine. Years ago one of those things punctured two of my tires and left me stranded in the middle of nowhere. Since then I've made a point of avoiding them at all cost."

Spartan waved his hand at him. "Not a problem."

"Anyway," Watts continued, "to answer your question, pick any book except Courtney Dridelle's *Deadly Voyeur*. I want that one because the title is similar to Coulter's *Deadly Wrap*."

"That's fine. I'll start with Arlene Buck's *Administrative Affair*. I'm also going to Google these authors when we get back. I won't do a deep search unless it's warranted."

"Sounds good. Let me know what you find. I'll be at my desk, reading."

Spartan gave an odd look. "You think that's wise? I mean, Lieutenant Ryder's bound to give us grief if he sees us sitting around reading novels when we're supposed to be working this case."

Watts gave it some thought. Even though the GP books could be linked to the case, Ryder probably wouldn't like them reading in a semi-public setting. Even so, considering that CC's assailant might be a Guillotine Press author, reading these books was essential.

"Tell you what, Blaine. Instead of going back to 350, why don't we go to the library? I'll tell Ryder we're in the field tracking down leads. You with me?"

"Sure, so long as the librarian knows they're our books. After all, they are signed first editions."

Watts grinned again.

SIX

After spending two hours in the library skimming through the GP books, the only known facts were CC Coulter was dead, and either his wife killed him or she didn't. Earlier, Watts reminded his partner that they would treat Kat Coulter the same as anyone else who was home when their spouse died. She would remain a person of interest along with all of the Guillotine Press authors until her name was cleared. When they got back to the station, they both felt they had wasted the afternoon.

Back at their desks, both started writing reports. Watts' only reference to Kat Coulter was she agreed to e-mail him the final draft of her husband's *Deadly Wrap* manuscript. So far, it had not appeared in his inbox, but he expected it before the day ended. Satisfied, he slid his chair back so he could peer into Spartan's cubicle.

"Hey, Blaine, I'm going to visit the lab to see what they've found. Care to join me?"

Spartan nodded while typing. He saved his document, closed the program, and climbed out of his chair. When they arrived at the lab, the attractive young woman that Watts had seen at Coulter's office came forward to meet them.

"May I help you, detectives?" she said, as if she didn't recognize them.

"Yes," said Watts, leaning over to read her name. Spartan was watching so he immediately backed off, but he thought it said Woods. "We were hoping you could brief us on the evidence collected at the Coulter crime scene."

"Let me get Tim Westin. He's handling that case."

She vanished before Watts could say anything else. Now feeling self-conscious, he and Spartan stood behind the counter, taking in the surroundings. Other than some desks, chairs, computers, back rooms, and a conference room, there wasn't much to this place. Finally, Tim Westin emerged from a back room, clipboard in hand.

"Hi, guys," Westin said. "I understand you're here for an update on the Coulter case?"

Watts nodded. "What have you got, Tim?"

"First, the water I used to separate the wad showed no toxins so the vic wasn't poisoned. We double-checked the tie straps for any distinguishing marks or prints, but found none. I believe the killer was wearing gloves, and the tie straps like the ones used can be purchased in any hardware store so we struck out there. The tissues in the trash were free of toxins, and when we went through the house trash there were no discarded gloves, tie strap packs, medicines. However, there was a tiny super ball like the kind you get out of a toy machine at Fuddruckers's or Six Flags that had chew marks from a dog. I set it aside figuring you'd want to look at it. Also, the marble paperweight has traces of CC Coulter's blood so it was definitely wiped down and intentionally left on his desk. The blood splatter on the floor came from Coulter, and no one else's blood has been found. Right now we're investigating a single black hair that was sucked up in our vacuum." He paused to review his notes, then looked up. "Unfortunately, that's all we have right now."

Watts took it in, shifting his gaze from Westin's clipboard to his partner, hoping to catch another glimpse of that attractive lab tech. He couldn't understand why she was so elusive unless she was intentionally hiding from him. He thought about that for a moment and realized it was not only ludicrous, but arrogant of him to think she would even notice.

The black hair and toy ball intrigued him, though. He was interested in what Kat Coulter had to say about them, but decided to wait on that. If Kat's e-mail didn't come though soon, he would have reason to pay her another visit. Westin coughed as if waiting to be excused.

Watts smiled at him. "Thanks, Tim. Blaine, do you have any questions for him?"

"No, I'm good," Spartan said.

"Okay," Watts said, patting the counter. "Let me know if anything else comes up."

"Will do." Westin promptly turned and left.

Watts left thinking more about Spartan than the evidence Westin presented. Something in his partner's voice suggested he had something else on his mind, too. When they were halfway up the stairs, Watts stopped and looked at him.

"I can always tell when something's on your mind," he said. "Spit it out."

A smile spread across Spartan's face. "So, what do you think of her?"

"If you're referring to the Kat Coulter, I expect we'll need to talk to her again."

"Don't play dumb, Maxx. You know I'm referring to the cute lab tech that greeted us. I could tell you're sweet on her. You practically drooled on her while trying to read her name."

Watts stared back at his partner. "First, you're not my matchmaker.

Second, I haven't been 'sweet' on anyone since I was an infatuated kid. Third, I've never had a conversation with her. Fourth, while she is attractive, she's also cold as a fish. Finally, the only thing we have in common is we both work for the police department, and that alone is reason not to get involved."

Spartan hiked his shoulders and continued up the stairs.

Watts stayed quiet after that. When he got back to his desk, he immediately checked his e-mail and was disappointed the one from Kat Coulter hadn't shown up. He slid his chair back to relay that to Spartan. As he spoke, a plan came to mind.

"I'm going back to Kat's with a flash drive so I can copy the file," he said. "While there, I'm going to ask her about the black hair and toy ball. I'm taking my pocket tape player so I can record our conversation. Want to tag along?"

"Of course. I go where you go. That's what partners do."

"I was hoping you'd say that."

Watts grabbed the flash drive from his desk and soon they were heading up the familiar drive to Kat Coulter's. Since he expected her to complain about police harassment, he let Ryder in on it before they left. Ryder said he would handle whatever came up and made it clear their job was to solve a murder.

"If it takes you a dozen trips to find the truth, that's fine with me," he said.

Watts and Spartan were both relieved to hear that.

When they approached her driveway, Watts had to brake for that same Jack Russell puppy he saw playing and chewing on a newspaper earlier today. The dog ran toward the neighbor's house and came prancing back as if to torment them. After stopping momentarily to look at their car, it made a beeline toward the neighbor's house. Watts stepped from the car smiling. "I think that dog's had too much caffeine," he said.

Spartan glanced at it and nodded. "I wish I had that kind of energy."

They headed for the door without giving the dog a second thought. This time Kat Coulter wasn't waiting for them. Her curtains were drawn and no sounds came from inside. Watts rang the doorbell and waited. When no one came, he peeked around the side of the house.

"Check out back," he said.

Spartan nodded and took off in the opposite direction. He came back a few minutes later shaking his head. "Maybe we should have called first," he said.

Watts turned and silently headed back to the car. He climbed in, started it, and turned the a/c on full blast. Spartan climbed in and started to fasten his seat belt, but Watts shook his head at him. "We're not going anywhere, Blaine. Sooner or later she'll be back, and when she arrives, we'll question her. What did you learn from the GP book you were reading?"

"That I'm not a fan of romantic mysteries. Granted, I only had time to skim through Buck's book, but it seems like I've seen the same TV plot several times before."

"I know what you mean. Can't say that I'm looking forward to skimming through those books either, but it has to be done. I didn't get much out of *Deadly Voyeur*, either. I'll take a hard core action book over this crap any day."

Watts no sooner agreed that a dust cloud appeared in his mirror. He recognized Kat's BMW before seeing her behind the wheel. "Must be our lucky day," he said. She's back."

The detectives stepped from the Crown Vic as soon as Kat pulled into her garage. She gave an annoyed look as she stepped out.

"You know, your constantly showing up unannounced is getting old," she said. "What do want this time?"

Watts could have told her about the lab results, but that would be tipping his hat. In situations like this, it was better tossing out snippets to trigger reactions.

"Mrs. Coulter, do you like those tiny super balls that bounce sky high?"

Shielding her eyes from the sun, she squinted at them. "If you're referring to the one in the trash, CC tossed it because that stupid Jack Russell grabbed it when he was bouncing it out back. I could have cared less about it, but that ball was CC's grand prize from a Fuddruckers toy machine and he loved it. Imagine trading your coins for a toy in a plastic bubble. How stupid is that?"

The detectives exchanged glances without commenting.

"Anyway," she continued, "CC was in his chair bouncing it and didn't catch it one time and out of nowhere this obnoxious little dog flies over, grabs it in his mouth, and takes off running. CC spent ten minutes running that little dog down to get it back. Personally, I think he should have let him keep it. Maybe the dog would have choked on it so it wouldn't bark any more. Anyway, after that, the ball never bounced right so CC got rid of it."

"It is a fast little dog," Watts said, recalling the bite marks on the ball. "By the way, I never got your e-mail so I brought a flash drive so you could transfer CC's manuscript onto it." He took it from his pocket and handed it to her.

She accepted it, slipped off the protector cap, inspected it like she was checking for a hidden device, and replaced the cap. "The house is a mess," she said. "Would you mind waiting here?"

Watts shook his head side-to-side. "I'll go with you to make sure it transfers properly."

She made a face, looked at her car, the house, and then back at the detectives. "Give me a minute to change and I'll meet you at the front door."

Watts found that peculiar, but didn't challenge her. Instead, he watched her go into the house and then squinted to see his partner. "What do you suppose she's hiding, Blaine?"

"Beats me, but I'm willing to bet she's doing more than changing her clothes."

"I know what you mean. Sure wish I had a warrant so I could force the issue, but that's not gonna happen. Whenever we go in, feel free to let your eyes roam while I sit with her at the computer."

"Will do."

Finally the front door opened. Kat stood there in denim shorts, a faded red Tee, and sandals, appearing more worn out than stressed over having to face them again. They followed her into the living room where she had set her laptop up. Watts gave a surprised look.

"You don't use CC's desktop?" he said.

"No, detective, we've always had our own computers, and after what happened, I don't want to touch his. He sent me copies of his manuscripts as another means of backing them up."

She inserted Watts' flash drive, copied the *Deadly Wrap* document, and opened the flash drive to confirm it copied okay. She then closed the program and gave a snooty look when she handed the flash drive back.

"Anything else?" she said.

"Yes," said Watts. "You're blonde and your husband had sandy brown hair. Who do you know that has jet black hair?"

Without hesitation, she said, "Beats me. Why?"

"No reason. This should do it for now. Thanks again. We'll be in touch."

Watts was pleased to have the complete manuscript. Having witnessed her every move, he had no reason to doubt this was CC's final version of the manuscript. He and Spartan held their silence until they were driving back to 350.

Finally, Watts looked at his partner. "See anything interesting in the house, Blaine?"

"It's not so much what I saw, but what I didn't see that concerns me. Clearly she didn't want us going through her house. Unlike before, all of her doors were closed. As I said before, changing her clothes had nothing to do with keeping us outside."

"I'm sure you're right. It doesn't take long to change into shorts and a Tee shirt. Even so, she calmly sat at her computer and gave me what I requested. Her hands weren't shaking, her body looked relaxed, and without a warrant, we're shut out."

Spartan pursed his lips. "What do you expect to find in that manuscript she gave you?"

"I have no idea, but I'll probably end up reading it on my own time." Watts took a moment to reflect on that before looking at his partner. "Anyway, we can't waste any more time on her. When we get back to the station, we need to line up those author interviews."

Spartan silently voiced his disapproval by checking his watch and staring through the windshield. He didn't speak for five minutes. Finally he said, "It's getting late. Shall we schedule the interviews for tomorrow?"

"Well, since we don't have any suspects, tomorrow should be fine. Hopefully, they'll allow us to rule some people out. I'll look at their profiles while you book the interviews."

"Fine with me."

SEVEN

By the end of their shift, Watts had a handle on who these authors were and Spartan had lined up interviews with each of the local ones. None had any remarkable histories. They would interview the out-of-state authors on a recorded phone line, but Watts didn't want to do that until he heard what the locals had to say. Seeing no value in depleting his personal cartridges on official police business, he printed out a copy of *Deadly Wrap* and stuck it in a folder to take home. Once that was done, he headed out the door.

Seeing his green 2010 Dodge Ram pickup always brought a smile. Watts named him Leroy after the man in Jim Croce's *Bad, Bad Leroy Brown* song, and bad he was. Lifted struts, overhead light rack, and custom wheels distinguished Leroy from every other truck on the road, but his custom exhaust really turned heads. Even idling, Leroy growled like a cougar ready to pounce. Leroy rivaled nearly anything on the quarter mile track, too. But Watts wasn't compensating for anything when he bought his truck. Leroy was the fulfillment of his dream. He saved for ten years before he could afford him and never regretted his decision. Especially since Leroy was his most faithful companion. He listened to him, and never protested or questioned where Watts wanted to go. He never cared if he got dirty, and never dripped oil to mark his territory. Too bad the gas prices soared after Watts bought him.

Watts climbed in and lowered the windows to let the heat out. The silver windshield screen did a good job of reflecting the sun, but its dark green exterior still made it an oven inside. Leroy stopped for a pedestrian who admired him more than he should as he crossed in front.

"Nice truck," the man said.

From behind the wheel, Watts nodded, studying the bald twenty-something man whose black combat boots gleamed with each step. His ragged beltless blue jeans hung low on his hips. A sleeveless white Tee exposed well-toned biceps covered in tattoos. He had the bald head of a Marine, but his menacing Snake-Eyes made it clear he had never been to boot camp. He was the kind of guy you didn't want to meet in a dark alley.

Watts acknowledged him with a chin-lift. "Nice tats," he said.

Snake-Eyes grinned back and quietly moved on.

Anxious over the guy's appearance and gaze, Watts didn't move until Snake-Eyes was halfway down the street. To the best of his knowledge, he had never seen him before, but for some reason felt they would meet again. Watts raised the windows, cranked up the a/c, and stepped on the gas. Leroy thundered down the road without a care.

In spite of reading *Deadly Wrap* well into the night, Watts couldn't shake Snake-Eyes from his thoughts. Some people look evil, but this guy exuded it. He also reminded him of Dad's drinking buddy, Bubba. Not only did Bubba have a shaved head, but his arms were bigger than Watts' thighs. That bastard delighted in slapping Watts around at least once per visit, and yet Mom was the only one who stepped in to protect her twelve year old son. She'd haul him away saying drunks have no logic, and from what he saw, he couldn't argue with her. The one good thing about Dad passing was he never saw Bubba again, but people with bald heads still made him anxious.

Going back to his reading, he found *Deadly Wrap* more entertaining than expected, but like the other GP books he had skimmed through, he didn't believe this was a future blockbuster.

The phone rang and Watts promptly answered. He didn't expect it to be Spartan, particularly since Spartan's kids were talking in the background. "Hi, Blaine. Did you miss me?"

"Not really, but I meant to tell you I'm still checking into The Guillotine Press' financial status and CC Coulter's insurance policies."

Watts smiled. *The old Spartan is back, emptying his thoughts before turning in for the night.* "Thanks, Blaine. Anything else?"

"Nope, that's it. See you in the morning."

"Have a good one."

Watts hung up and glanced at his stack of GP books. Iron-Fist attorney Hank Azar's fictional courtroom drama, *Forsaken Alibi*, and Spartan's earlier comments about Kat Coulter delaying entry into her home gave him doubts about the authenticity of the *Deadly Wrap* version she gave him. He regretted not making a copy of CC's death-wad papers so he could compare them. He still needed to determine if the killer chose specific pages for the wad or if they were conveniently lifted from the open manuscript. Holding that thought, he set everything aside and headed for bed.

Sleep found him quickly, but he kept waking to Snake-Eye nightmares. After the third time, he went to the bathroom to splash water on his face. When he looked in the mirror, he half-expected to see Dad's friend Bubba. Thankfully, he never appeared. As he lay in bed now wide-awake, he considered thumbing through mug shots when he got to the office, but soon realized there were plenty of evil people lurking the streets, and he couldn't justify wasting his time doing this when the only words he and Snake-Eyes exchanged were compliments. Somewhere during the night he fell asleep again.

Breakfast consisted of peanut butter toast and chocolate milk because it could be downed in a couple of minutes. He hoped his work would relieve his nightmares. It only took twenty minutes for him to get ready, lock his apartment, and head out to his truck. It wasn't a record, but it was close.

Leroy looked ready for battle in his covered stall. Once Watts backed him out, the red sun reflected in his hood. As soon as he turned the radio on, the news reported that as of yesterday, Fort Worth had exceeded three consecutive months with temperatures over ninety degrees, and eighty of those topped one hundred. The last measurable rain fell nearly four months ago. Every living creature congregated near whatever water they could find. That was especially true for kids. The lucky ones frolicked in water parks and pools. The rest settled for fountains, fire hydrants, and murky ponds. On days like this, beat cops found it easy to spot wrong-doers because the sane people tended to stay inside. As Watts steered Leroy toward 350, he contemplated his uniformed days. He recalled how full moons stirred odd behavior, and wondered if the high temperatures may have incited CC's attacker. He changed lanes thinking that anything was possible, especially for screwballs strung out on drugs.

His thoughts then turned to his partner's alcoholism. Watts respected Spartan for admitting his problem and seeking help before he lost his job or his organs succumbed to the poison. Dad's organs failed one at a time until he died a shell of the man he once was, and because of this, Watts swore on his mother's death bed that he would never drink like Dad. She passed a year later, but she was always in Watts' thoughts. He turned the volume up to ease his pain. Thankfully, he arrived at the station soon after.

Attempting to sneak past Ryder's office was pointless when wearing noisy support shoes. Instead, he flashed a smile when Ryder looked up. Watts peeked into Ryder's office and said, "Morning, sir. I was going for some coffee. You want some?"

Ryder shook his head, chewing on his reading glasses. "I'm warm enough, thanks. I haven't seen you around much, Maxx. Got any news for me?"

"Yes, sir."

Watts spent the next ten minutes briefing his boss on the lab report, and the ME listing the official cause of death as suffocation. "For the record," he said, "I still believe the writing on the paper wad pages holds some clues. And before you say anything, I'm reading the *Deadly Wrap* manuscript on my own time. Today, Blaine and I are conducting author interviews."

"That's fine, but since you've seen the widow three times now, what's your take on her?"

"All indications are she's clean and dirt poor."

Ryder rubbed his chin like a scholar contemplating a Pulitzer Prize. "How much life insurance did Mr. Coulter have?"

"Two million."

Ryder's eyes lit up. "That's substantial," he said.

"I agree, and it reminds me of the *Deadly Voyeur* plot."

"Pardon me?"

"*Deadly Voyeur* is another Guillotine Press novel." Watts waited for his boss' brain to catch up, but when it became clear that wasn't going to happen, he explained further. "Sir, In *Deadly Voyeur*, a voyeur's wife and her two lovers conspire to kill her husband for his life insurance payout. That's the association I was referring to. Anyway, while we know the insurance amount, we lack the details. I'm hoping to know more today."

"How long can it possibly take to get insurance information?"

Watts gave a silent shrug.

Ryder's fingers popped as he spread his palms on his desk. "Go do your interviews, Maxx, and keep me posted."

"Yes, sir."

Watts left Ryder's office realizing he could save time, or at least gain confidence in the authenticity of *Deadly Wrap*, if he compared the death-wad pages to his newly printed manuscript. At the time of Coulter's death, the manuscript was open to page 252 and the next page was 257. Pages 253 through 256 were double-sided so he took two blank sheets of printer paper and wadded them tight. The dry wad seemed too large and stiff to force into someone's mouth so he went to the break room and ran it under the faucet. The wet wad was much smaller and more pliable and compact, and also explained the lack of cuts in the roof of Coulter's mouth. He went to the lab hoping the cute lab tech would make him copies of the salvaged pages, but in the time it took Westin to copy the four pages, he never caught a glimpse of her. It seemed the less he saw of her, the more intriguing she became. He thanked Westin for the papers and headed upstairs, trying to rid her from his thoughts.

Watts returned to his desk expecting Blaine Spartan to be at his, but it was still early. Matching the four pages that Westin recovered to the manuscript copy Kat provided restored his confidence in her. He read CC's back-cover description of his Hollywood betrayal story out loud to himself.

"Actor Pico Rivera meets a horrific demise on stage while filming *Deadly Wrap*."

Coulter's novel and fictitious movie of the same title seemed to pun the film industry with "wrap" being a term for completing a scene, but meaning death in the novel. In Hollywood, there was no better drama than a lead actor dying in front of the camera, regardless of how many times it had been done.

That disturbing line in Chapter Four still caught Watts' eye. The one where Actress Simone Paramount says to leading man Pico Rivera, "Death comes to those deserving." Perhaps it was his English classes that made it so bothersome to him, but no matter how many times he re-read the phrase, it never sounded right. He wrote it several different ways trying to improve its grammar. "Death comes to those who are deserving." *Nope.* "Death comes to those who deserve it." *Strike two.* "Death shall come to those deserving." He gave up at strike three realizing he would never be a writer.

Afterwards, he wondered how a detective with a criminology degree could become so preoccupied with a goofy phrase from a novel. Perhaps he was searching for a subtle message, or wondering if CC wrote it this way to confuse his readers. If the latter was his goal, then he certainly succeeded, but if it contained a subdued message, it still eluded him. Too bad he couldn't ask the author for clarification. Like Snake-Eyes, that pesky line continued to haunt him.

Normally, Watts considered himself an accomplished reader, but whenever Coulter's manuscript started to drag, Watts' brain followed suit. The many grammatical errors and typos had him comparing *Deadly Wrap* to Disney's *Ratatouille* movie, except instead of *Ratatouille's* "Anyone Can Cook" theme, Coulter's seemed to be "Anyone Can Write". It's no wonder he didn't find any bookstores that carried The Guillotine Press books. But CC's amateurish writing also had Watts questioning Kat's literary talent. Then again, he had read some pretty horrible books that were published by New York houses. Unable to stomach *Deadly Wrap* any longer, he re-examined only the four re-printed paper wad pages to see what he might have missed:

Coulter / Deadly Wrap   253

"Tempers had been heating up between Anna and Gabriella for some time," Simone said to Detective Sam Juacinto.

"You're referring to Anna Hyme and Gabriella Alhambra?"

Stone-faced, the actress took a drag from her cigarette and blew smoke from her nose. She rubbed her eye and then checked her nails to exaggerate her boredom. Her ploy must have been working because the detective cleared his throat in annoyance. "Of course I'm talking about Anna and Gabriella," she said to him, still admiring her nails. "Who else would I be referring to?"

Juacinto ignored her question. "You said Anna and Gabriella weren't getting along? Why?"

Simone Paramount hesitated, her eyes barely visible under her fashionable hat. Love triangles were never good, and whenever they started falling apart, things got ugly. But how much could she tell Juacinto without incriminating herself? After all, she, too, had spent time with Pico Rivera—but not this week, this month; no, make that this year. She still couldn't believe Pico was dead. He was a superb actor, and to watch him die on the set was doubly upsetting. The police were more concerned with finding whoever traded Anna's prop gun for a real one rather than why Rivera was murdered. Why didn't the prop manager notice it?

Simone had tuned out, so Detective Juacinto readdressed his question. "Ms. Paramount—the trouble between Anna and Gabriella? You never answered."

The actress dropped her cigarette, grinning. A quick twist of her shoe snuffed it. "Sorry, detective. Would you mind repeating your question?"

Juacinto sighed. "We were discussing the tart relationship between Anna Hyme and Gabriella Alhambra."

"Well, they weren't very close, if that's what you mean. In fact, off screen, they didn't get along at all."

The detective raised a brow. "And why is that?"

Simone leaned against the studio wall staring at the props that crowded the studio's back lot. The airplane, spaceship, and boat mockups that looked so real on the big screen were now rusted relics. It seemed cruel to let them waste away like that, but that's Hollywood for you. Use, abuse, and move on.

She turned away when a tour bus approached. In spite of this, she half-expected, or at least hoped, that someone would recognize her and call out her name. It hurt when no one did.

After the tour bus passed, she quietly faced Juacinto. "Detective, there are a lot of personalities in this business and not everyone gets along, but none of that matters because actors can be best friends on screen, then pull each other's hair as soon as it's a wrap. But that shows how talented they are. Not everyone can put their differences aside to make everything look believable on screen. It's truly a gift, which is why we all can't be actors. Personally, I can't see Anna and Gabriella ever getting along. It's just not in the stars—no pun intended."

"I see," Juacinto said, recalling that you don't necessarily have to be friends to conspire to commit murder. "Now here's how I see it, Simone. Anna and Gabriella were both on the set when the gun fired, and they both had affairs with Mr. Rivera. Even more interesting is that your director, Glen Dale, stated that neither actress seemed particularly shocked when Rivera was shot in the head."

Simone lit another cigarette, drawing in its poison. After teasing her lungs with it, she cracked her lips so the smoke could float out. "Well, detective, since you have all the answers, what do you make of my relationship with Pico?"

Juacinto deliberated over her question. It was rare when suspects asked an investigator anything, and when they did, it was usually to distract them. He wasn't biting. At least not yet. Instead, he said, "If you don't mind, let's stick to Ms. Hyme and Ms. Alhambra."

Coulter / Deadly Wrap   255

Simone's eyes rolled as she exhaled the last of her smoke. She seductively pressed her back against the wall, hiking one leg for affect. A smile unfolded as her skirt rode up, exposing her milky thigh. She set her foot down and innocently straightened her skirt as only an actress can, then allowed a smile as she lifted her face to the sky. "The sun feels great, doesn't it?"

The detective squinted into the red ball dangling above the horizon. The nearby Santa Monica Mountains lay buried under a smog blanket. In an hour or so, the heat would have the asphalt repairs sticking to his shoes, but thanks to Hollywood magic, non-residents still saw Los Angeles as a sinful playpen with clear skies and beaches filled with beautiful people lying on the sand. Hollywood worked hard to keep that illusion, which is why the police were being pressured to keep Rivera's death quiet. In trade, Juacinto was granted full run of the movie set, and was promised he would receive full cooperation by the cast and crew of Deadly Wrap. But while all of the cast members willingly spoke to him, he could never tell how much of what they were speaking was the truth. After all, as Simone so aptly pointed out, actors are deceivers, second only to politicians.

"Getting back to Ms. Hyme and Ms. Alhambra— "

Simone snuffed her second cigarette and calmly hugged her Gucci bag. "I'm not sure what you expect me to say. I already told you they didn't get along, they both knew Pico on and off the set, and they were both fine actresses. I don't know what I could possibly add to that."

Juacinto stared at her handbag, certain it was a Shanghai knock-off. His eyes traveled from the handbag to hers. "How long have you known Anna and Gabriella?"

She thought for a moment. "I guess I've known Gabriella for three years, now. Anna and I go back at least ten. We met at an audition."

"Was that for television?"

Simone's face contorted. "I've never done TV."

"So, it was for a movie?"

"Actually, it was for the stage production of Little Shop of Horrors. Unfortunately, neither of us got a role, but we stayed in touch because we were both struggling actresses." The detective nodded, waiting, but she added nothing.

Juacinto sighed. "Did either of them ever use firearms before?"

"Are we talking on screen or off?"

"Either one."

"Well, Anna and I went to a shooting range as part of a self-defense class. After a few hours of classroom instruction, we were taught how to shoot a nine millimeter pistol. We both did surprisingly well," she said with a smirk. "Did you know that women are better shooters than men?" Juacinto didn't answer. "Anyway, I can't speak for Anna, but I've never shot a gun since."

"I see," he said, jotting some notes before looking up. "What about Gabriella?"

"Hell, I don't know. My only real contact with her was when we had bit parts in the stage production of Chicago three years ago.

Thankfully, we both got noticed, which is why we're on this set. It's not like I really know her, though. You know what I'm saying?"

"I believe I do," Juacinto said, tucking his notebook into his coat pocket. "Thank you for your time, Ms. Paramount."

She gasped. "That's it? That's all you need from me?"

He smiled, pleased with himself. "That's it for now. I'll be in touch. Good day."

*   *   *   *   *

Watts scratched his head thinking how whacked Hollywood actors must be to make such unbelievable dialogue sound believable. Coulter seemed to be poking fun at this element in his story. But *Deadly Wrap* also stirred thoughts of how the most believable actors are the ones who completely immerse themselves in their roles. In this regard, he wondered whether these cameleon actors even recognized their own identities. He smiled, thinking of how Charlie Sheen messed with the industry. Great actors play crazy extremely well whenever money is involved. Unfortunately for Sheen, his gamble backfired, but he still deserved an Emmy for his YouTube rants. A passage in *Deadly Wrap* from actress character Simone Paramount convinced Watts there must be a connection between the author's grizzly death and his murder mystery: "Love triangles were never good, and whenever they started falling apart, things got ugly. But how much could she tell Juacinto without incriminating herself?"

Watts saw little value in CC's love triangle plot, but, "how much could she tell Juacinto without incriminating herself?" raised a flag. Authors write what they know, so did *Deadly Wrap's* characters evolve from CC Coulter's lady friends? Was CC having a fling with one of his female authors? Lacking any better leads and convinced he was on the right track, Watts was eager to interview the female GP authors. If there was any connection between CC's novel and his personal love life, one of these ladies would know.

EIGHT

Spartan came to work looking glum. He seated himself across from Watts like he wanted to talk but said nothing. Judging from his expression, Watts thought his wife Sandy may have kicked him out. She had done it before.

Watts turned on the charm, hoping it might help. "Morning, Blaine. You ready to hit the road? Lots of interviews today."

"I take it no one's told you that Pao Lee is dead. He and his Chinese friend were killed in Forest Park."

Watts' blood ran cold. "Pao Lee, as in our The Guillotine Press author, is dead?"

"It appears that way. A jogger found them this morning. Their bodies were tentatively identified by their passports. Skip Parsons has the lead on this one and is currently in the field. Lieutenant Ryder says to stay focused on our own case and leave Parsons alone. By the way, he directed that comment at you, not me."

"But I've been at my desk for an hour and saw him when I first came in. Why would he tell you and not me?"

"Don't take it personally, Maxx. Lieutenant Ryder just found out about it, and since I was coming down the hall, he cornered me and said to pass it on."

Watts shook his head, dismayed. "I can't believe one of our persons of interest is dead."

"I know, but what's really strange is Ryder said it's a coincidence that Lee's a murder victim as if it's no big deal. According to him, two Chinese tourists were taking an evening stroll when some thugs took them out. It wasn't a robbery because nothing seems to be missing. Personally, I think it's a hate crime."

"How so?"

Spartan grimaced as though picturing it in his mind. "Maxx, their chests were stripped bare and they had swastikas carved into their chests. Also, a witness reported seeing a couple of Skinheads speed out of the park in a pickup."

Watts' brain snapped him back to Snake-Eyes. "Any tattoos on these Skinheads?"

"Be serious. How many guys with shaved heads don't have tattoos? It was dark, we don't have a vehicle description other than it was a pickup, and it's not our case. We need to leave it alone. Skip can handle it."

Watts stared down the hall, collecting his thoughts. He wasn't buying it. Coulter's and Lee's murders had to be connected, and it was disturbing that his boss was holding his leash. "CC Coulter died a gruesome death and nothing was taken," he finally said. "I think we should swing by the crime scene on the way to our interviews—as observers, of course."

"Maxx, the boss specifically directed us, meaning you, to stay away. The last time Parsons had the lead, he complained that you interfered in his investigation. Ryder won't tolerate it again."

Watts leaned his head to one side, hearing his partner's concerns. But Parsons liked to whine, and since there was no basis for his complaint, it never went anywhere. "You were in rehab when that happened," he said, "and yes I poked around a little, but I never disturbed any evidence. At the time, murders had been on a steady decline so when that prostitute's throat was slashed, every Fort Worth detective wanted in on that case. I will say this—Parsons did a good job on it. He wrapped it up in three or four days, and the killer is now serving thirty to life in San Quentin. But this case is different. Three people have been murdered in two days and two of them are directly associated with The Guillotine Press, so to me, that hardly seems a coincidence."

"I'm not arguing with you, Maxx. Only relaying what Lieutenant Ryder said. Go talk to him if you want to go against his orders. All I did was deliver his message."

"Then consider it delivered."

Watts leaned over his desk skimming his notes summarizing the GP authors and their novels:

Courtney Dridelle: *Deadly Voyeur* -- "A voyeur spying on his married neighbors is shocked to see his wife in bed with them having a threesome. But taking matters into his own hand was only the beginning."

Arlene Buck: *Administrative Affair* – "Working late becomes a fatal mistake for Dick Robertson."

Hank Azar: *Forsaken Alibi* – "Courtroom drama at its finest. A must read."

Jolene Lundgren: *Butcher's Cut* -- "This book makes Slaughterhouse 5 look tame. Freddie, beware!"

Ben Striker: *The Blade Within* – "A clever tale of deception and death. This one goes straight to the heart."

Lance Ballard: *Hard Ride to Cimarron* – "A dude ranch cattle drive turns deadly after campfire secrets are revealed."

Pao Lee: *The Mariner's Club* – "Kowloon's infamous seafarer's club is haunted, but can its ghostly reputation cover up a sailor's murder?"

Luke Harper: *In God's Will* – "Reverend Lucifer McAdams is leading his followers to their maker, but will the cult's mole foil his plan?"

Toby Roberts: *Gentlemen Only, Ladies Forbidden* – "It's the final hole of the Crowne Plaza Invitational and crowds line the fairway. All eyes are on Keith Calloway as he kisses his ball for luck. The shock of his sudden collapse is nothing compared to his autopsy."

Mick Taggart: *Terminal Approach* – "ValueSkies Lieutenant Debbie Griffin is making her final flight before retiring. Though enduring many oddities over her career, nothing could prepare her for what happens behind closed doors."

Watts moved his mouth around before looking at his partner. "Did you double-check the police computer on these GP people?"

Spartan leaned his chair back and nodded. "I verified your results, and as we both know, other than Luke Harper being cited for illegal dumping at a Salvation Army store and a few others cited for random speeding and parking tickets, that's it for the criminals of The Guillotine Press. Not that this comes as any surprise. Criminals don't normally write novels about the murders they commit."

Watts exhaled through his nose while studying Courtney Dridelle's book jacket photo. He hoped it would take his mind off Pao Lee's murder, but it didn't. Parsons would spend all day working the case while he'd be out interviewing authors and there wasn't a damned thing he could do about it. But nothing said he couldn't run through the park when he got off work and if he happened to stumble onto the crime scene, well, no one could accuse him of interfering.

He tapped on Dridelle's' photo to get his partner's attention. "This stunning green-eyed brunette certainly has the aura of a romance mystery writer. Though her male protagonist murders his cheating wife, any other similarities to CC Coulter's murder are minimal."

"I agree. And Arlene Buck appears equally attractive, and her tale of a jealous secretary killing her cheating executive boyfriend might be pertinent because when her protagonist Dick Robertson fails to leave his wife as promised, his secretary takes revenge by killing him with a bullet bearing his name. I find the personal nature of Buck's fictitious murder to CC Coulter's death intriguing."

Watts crossed his arms and looked up. "So you're thinking that Arlene Buck became so infatuated with her publisher that she killed him because she couldn't have him as her lover?"

Spartan nodded. "It could happen."

"Okay, then what do you make of the mindless gore in Jolene Lundgren's *Butcher's Cut*? When I looked through it, it took me back to *Prime Cut*."

"Say what?"

Watts smirked. "*Prime Cut* is an old Lee Marvin movie from the early seventies. My folks rented it when I was a kid and it scared the hell out of me because the mob was killing people and then grinding up their bodies in a slaughterhouse. It took me years before I could stomach a hot dog again, and I barely touched Lundgren's book because of the memory. Besides, Lundgren's gruff appearance makes any love connection between her and CC as far-fetched as me winning the lottery."

"I think I'll pass on *Prime Cut*, but thanks for the insight. Any thoughts on the male GP authors? Any that might bear a grudge?"

"None that I know of."

Watts nodded again. "In Toby Roberts' *Gentlemen Only, Ladies Forbidden*, the protagonist is poisoned in front of thousands of spectators when he kisses his golf ball. What do you think about that? I mean that seems pretty personal."

"Let me guess. It takes place at Pebble Beach and Tiger Woods is his partner."

"Actually, it happens right here in Fort Worth at the Crowne Plaza Invitational and Tiger didn't even qualify for the match."

"Poor Tiger. He gets no respect anymore. But the fact is Coulter wasn't poisoned so I don't see any link. By the way, Toby Roberts is our first interview so we should go. It'll take us about 40 minutes to get to Mansfield."

Watts got to his feet and slid his chair under his desk. After flipping through his notepad to make sure he had plenty of blank pages, he tucked it and his recorder into one pocket and stuffed some spare batteries and cassettes in the other. He made sure everything fit and then said, "Let's roll."

NINE

Watts and Spartan headed to the Crown Vic, eager to get moving. The GP authors were so spread out, it would take a miracle to see them all in one day. Even though the morning rush should be over, getting to Mansfield, Waco, and Plano without getting stuck in gridlock would require minimal time with each of them. Since that notion contradicted the reason for their visit, they would have to evaluate their progress as they went.

The morning sun was high enough not to be blinding, but low enough to still create glare. The miserable heat was already generating dust devils. In another hour, kids would be wrenching fire hydrants open to cool off. A while later, an emergency vehicle would respond, shut the water off, and the beat goes on. Watts was glad he wasn't playing the bad cop anymore. At least not in uniform.

Glancing at Spartan, Watts said, "While we're driving, let's bounce some ideas off each other about the possibility the Forest Park and CC Coulter murders are linked."

Spartan fiddled with the a/c vents to aim them at his face. The air dried his eyes, but it was worth it. "I'm willing, so long as you don't discuss it with Skip Parsons or Lieutenant Ryder."

"No problem. So, let's go out on a limb and say that these murders were the result of gang initiations. Three dead men means three new members were allowed into the club."

Spartan's head rolled like a puppet's that lost its string. "First of all, I think we can rule out the Aryan Nation. I've never heard of a White Supremacist cult conducting initiations like this, especially against someone like CC Coulter who fits Hitler's ideal description of a male."

"Okay, how about a meth addict? He sees an open window, slips inside to steal supplies, and stumbles onto Coulter. Remember that Coulter's office light is probably the only one on in the neighborhood at the time. There's no reason why this can't be random."

Spartan gazed out the window. A while later he casually checked his watch, and then stared at the scenery. It took him a while to glance at his partner.

"While random hits are possible and all of these murders involved gruesome suffering," he said, "I don't believe that Coulter's suffocation fits into the same category as chest carving. Then consider the Caucasian versus Asian aspect. To me, the Forest Park murders fit the hate crime scenario, but Coulter's death seems personal."

"I agree. Now on to a different subject, how are things at home?"

Spartan's gaze hardened. "You can drop me off here if you plan on blabbing all the way to Mansfield."

Watts immediately lifted his foot off on the gas and coasted to a stop on the shoulder of the road. Looking at his partner, he gestured that he was free to leave. A semi passed close by and rocked the car with its wind blast. Watts held his pose and his silence.

Spartan frowned back. "Very funny," he said. "Keep driving."

"Fine. Back to the case, did you know that Kat Coulter is friends with Mayor Jordon?"

"Yup. She worked on his campaign. Ryder mentioned it while I was talking to him this morning."

Watts eyed him. "Did Ryder also mention that Olyn Jordan is quite the lady's man?"

"Maxx, everyone knows that about OJ, but what the hell—he's single."

"Actually, he's a widower. Lost his wife about seven years ago. Really nice lady, too. Everyone said he wouldn't have gotten elected without her. I drove a radio car in her funeral procession. Lots of tears that day."

"Yeah, I saw the highlights on TV and OJ looked pretty broken up. Can't blame him, though. If something happened to Sandy, my life would never be the same."

Watts silently bobbed his head thinking about Mom's funeral. It was a small gathering, but far more people paid their respects to her than to Dad. He thought about Mrs. Jordan's service and suspected that many of those in attendance were fulfilling political or social obligations rather than mourning her passing. That had Watts wondering who would have attended his funeral had he died from his gunshot wound. With no parents, girlfriend, or wife, and only a few close friends, he figured Porgy Mulberry would be leading the way looking like the Michelin Tire Man with a badge. It wasn't a happy thought.

He glanced at Spartan. "Did you know Porgy Mulberry has an elephant's memory? For that matter, he wears elephant pants."

"Really, Maxx? I didn't realize elephants wore pants. That's pretty random. Where'd it come from?"

"Beats me. Anyway, after we talk to Roberts we're driving to Dallas to see Arlene Buck and Courtney Dridelle, right?"

That's the plan. They all know we're coming. Too bad we can't fly there."

Watts gave a nod. He had never ridden in the police helicopter, but it would be really fun to land on someone's lawn, interview them, and then take off again. Realistically, he knew that would never happen.

Spartan pulled out his iPhone and punched in Toby Roberts' number. "Mr. Roberts, this is detective Spartan. We're about twenty minutes away and I wanted to make sure you were home."

"I'm on the fourteenth fairway and there's no one ahead of me. Call me when you're five minutes out."

The line went dead so Spartan tucked his phone away. Deep in thought, he blew out a breath, scratched his head, and stretched his back as though a demon was aching to get out. Watts stared at him, confused. "Something bugging you, Blaine?"

Spartan tapped his lips for a moment before speaking. "It occurred to me that in spite of my extended leave, we still have the best arrest record in the department. Pretty amazing isn't it?"

"That's because we make a good team. But we also know it only takes a second of inattention for situations to go bad, so keep your head on a swivel. By the way, I tucked some water bottles under the seat. Grab one if you want."

Spartan found one, removed the cap, and raised his bottle in salute. "Cheers."

* * * * *

Spartan picked up his phone as they approached the Mansfield city limits. Once distanced from Arlington, the two towns now shared common borders amid tall oak trees, high tension wires, and signs. Auto traffic, once sparse, was now steady. He noted that Watts also seemed to be reminiscing how things were before the great Dallas/Fort Worth expansion. He pressed Talk on his phone and the call went through.

"Mr. Roberts, Detective Spartan, we're about five minutes away. Are you home?"

"I will be by the time you get here. You need directions?"

"We're turning onto Country Club Drive now. According to my GPS, it looks like we turn right onto Muirfield Drive."

"That's correct. See you soon."

Watts parked the Crown Vic in front of Roberts' house. In his mirror, he saw a golf cart pull up behind him. He eased his door open in case the cart continued forward but it stopped. He climbed out and offered his hand. "You must be Mr. Roberts," he said.

"I am, and it's too hot to chat outside. Let go in where it's cooler."

They followed Roberts into the living room where golf trophies filled an entire wall. Opposite from them were paintings of Pebble Beach, Augusta, and an island golf course he didn't recognize. There were no personal photos of a wife or kids, but if Roberts was married, his wife had no say in the décor.

Roberts paused in the kitchen entry.

"Make yourselves comfortable. Can I get you some lemonade or iced tea?"

Watts nodded over his shoulder. "Lemonade would be great."

"Same for me, please," Spartan said. He then looked over the assortment of golf magazines spread out on the coffee table.

Watts searched for confirmation that Roberts had a family, but it appeared he had no one else in his life. Not a single photo of a beloved one or a pet anywhere. From what he gathered, Roberts' sole existence involved clubbing dimpled balls. He heard footsteps and accepted his beverage from Roberts. The golfer then seated himself in the easy chair that faced the detectives on the sofa.

Roberts took a sip and set his drink aside. "So, what can I do for you gentlemen?"

Watts drank some lemonade and held onto the glass. "Did you hear about CC Coulter?"

Roberts' head tilted like a curious-dog. "As in what?"

"He was murdered in his home the other day."

The mystery author's tanned skin suddenly lost its color. Roberts raised his glass to his lips, but didn't drink. He set it down a moment later, shaking his head. "How did he die?"

Watts stared back, skeptical. News like that travels lightning fast on social network sites. Licking his lips left a lingering tang on his tongue. "It appears that someone didn't like him. Mr. Coulter died from a giant paper wad stuffed down his throat."

What? How big was it?"

Spartan glanced at his partner and then said to the author, "Does size matter when your publisher is dead?"

"A paper wad," Roberts said, looking remorseful as he stared at the floor. "What a way to go. How could anyone do that? For that matter, why?"

Watts followed the author's eyes to the novel on the fireplace mantle.

Gentlemen Only, Ladies Forbidden by Toby Roberts. No surprise there. "Mr. Roberts," he said, "Where were you two nights ago?"

Roberts grabbed his head, scanning the room with crazy eyes.

"I was here, alone, same as every night. And before you ask if anyone can verify that, the answer is no because I have always lived alone." He paused, his expression pale, confused. "I can't believe CC was murdered. Why would anyone kill a small-time publisher?"

"We don't know," said Spartan, "but it appears to be an act of vengeance."

Watts cleared his throat signaling he would ask the next question. "Mr. Roberts, how well did you know CC Coulter?"

Roberts hiked his shoulders and tossed his hands in the air. "I barely knew him," he said. "We once had lunch together to discuss The Guillotine Press, and later shared a table at a book signing, but we basically handled everything by phone, text, and e-mail."

Spartan made a show of flipping his notebook open and clicking his pen. "So you were here, alone, two nights ago?" he said

Roberts took in his surroundings as if this was a self-revelation. "I already said I was here alone, but I play two rounds of golf every day with various people in the morning and evening, and the club house maintains the schedule. When I get back from my evening round, I watch some TV and go to bed. Some might say it's not much of a life, but it works for me. My experience is you can either have a relationship with golf or a woman, but you can't do both at the same time."

That made Watts smile. "We're not here to judge you," he said, "but we do appreciate your candor. What can you tell us about your book contract?"

Roberts scoffed as he reclined his chair. "What's there to tell? I wasted two years looking for a publisher, so when CC made me an offer, I took it. It wasn't the contract I had hoped for, but at least I got my book published."

Watts signaled for his partner to take the next question.

"No one faults you for signing with The Guillotine Press," Spartan said. "However, we are very interested in the terms of your contract."

Roberts' face flushed and body tensed. He crossed his right leg, held it a few seconds before reversing it with his left. "I was never CC's partner, if that's what you mean."

Watts observed Roberts' body language. His mannerisms suggested he knew more than he was saying, but there was no way to prove it. He allowed plenty of time for Roberts to expand his answer, but the golfer added nothing. "Mind showing us your book contract?"

Roberts leaned forward clutching his hands so hard his veins bulged.

"Detective Watts, my contract is between my publisher and me. It is privileged information and I fail to see how it has any bearing on this investigation."

Spartan tapped his fingers together, staring at the author. "Sir, this is a murder investigation," he said. "No one is accusing you of any wrongdoing. We're here to gather facts, and your contract may provide some valuable insight into this case."

Roberts grabbed his drink and gulped. He set it down, eyeing them. "You seem to be implying that my contract with CC Coulter is a murder motive."

"We're not making any implications," Watts said. "We simply need to consider everything, and that includes your contract. Texans pride themselves in being law abiding citizens. Can we count on your help to solve this crime?"

Roberts quietly rose from his chair and headed to the front door. He gave the doorknob a firm twist, opened it, and faced his guests. "Gentlemen, thank you for stopping by to tell me about my publisher's demise. I'm not sure how this affects my relationship with The Guillotine Press, but that's an issue I intend to pursue. It's a furnace out there. I suggest you finish your drinks before you leave."

The detectives glanced at each other, downed their beverages, and walked to the door. Watts offered his business card on his way out. Courtesy was key in this job, even when things got nasty.

"Thank you for your time, Mr. Roberts. We'll be in touch."

TEN

The heat out-paced the sun's climb as Watts slid behind the Crown Vic's wheel. A furtive glance confirmed that Toby Roberts was at his window watching them. Watts' back immediately stuck to the car seat so he started the engine and turned on the a/c. He waited until he heard Spartan's seat belt click, then spun the wheel to point the car toward Crowley where Arlene Buck lived. Twelve miles west on 1187 would get them there. If their interview with Ms. Buck went as quickly as Roberts', they could interview all the local authors by mid-afternoon. A mile down the road, the Mansfield golfer still consumed Watts' thoughts.

"So, Blaine, what do you think about Mr. Roberts?" he said.

"I'm not sure. I mean, it's plausible he was home polishing his golf trophies the night CC Coulter died, but he sure got defensive when we mentioned his book contract. He was in the kitchen window when we drove off. He ducked when I turned around to look. Don't you find that a bit suspicious?"

Watts checked his mirror as he completed his turn. "I saw him, too, but he seems more like an oddball than a killer. Didn't you ever hide behind a curtain thinking you were invisible? I bet every kid does that one time or another."

"Which is probably why they used the invisible blanket in the Harry Potter movies, but Roberts isn't a kid and he's knowingly withholding information."

"That's true, but for now we'll note that he's being uncooperative and move on."

"Hopefully, the remaining authors will oblige."

"Yeah, hopefully."

Spartan looked unhappy. "Why do you think Roberts got so defensive about his contract?"

"Maybe it contains a clause he doesn't want us to see. Let's see how the others react before we get upset over it. Now, if everyone refuses to discuss their GP contracts, we may have legal grounds to obtain copies. For now let's concern ourselves with Arlene Buck. We'll approach her tag-team style like we did Toby Roberts."

"Sounds good."

Along their route, a small plane banked toward Spinks Airport. Bouncing like a toy, it flew so low they could see both pilots. When it crossed in front of them, the detectives spun their heads to keep it in sight. In seconds, the wing dipped left, then right, then left again. Inches above the runway, the nose pitched up, the left wheel puffed smoke, and then the right wheel touched down. As the nose wheel bounced, the engine roared and the plane took off again.

Spartan smiled as he watched the plane. "Now, *that* looks like fun," he said. "One day I'm gonna try it."

As the plane disappeared behind them, Watts said, "It does look like fun, but I bet it's as hot up there as it is on the ground. I'd wait until winter if I were you."

"Not a bad idea. You know the Army Air Corps had a lot of training bases here in World War II. Not many of them left anymore."

Watts' smiled, enjoying a memory. "Yeah, I used to race down a deserted runway on my bike when I was a kid. I'd park myself at the end of it and then pedal as fast as I could pretending I was taking off. Texas was probably ideal for training pilots in the forties, but as you said, most of those airports have been plowed under. In fact, this might be one of the few surviving airports. I wish we had more time. I love visiting places where time stands still."

"Well, I hate to disappoint you, but Crowley has changed with the times."

Watts stared at his partner. "Don't tell me suburbia invaded Crowley."

"I'm afraid so, Maxx."

"Well, that's a damn shame."

"Tell me about it."

Spartan's GPS said Arlene Buck's Ash Street residence was west of South Texas Street, but it didn't look right to Watts. He parked in front of the weathered wood-sided house, but wasn't ready to get out. Buck's place may be a step up from a barn, but not by much. Her trashy residence sent Watts back in time again. He was having way too many flashbacks and didn't like it much.

He sighed as he opened his door. "You know, Blaine, Crowley may have new construction on its outskirts, but its core still has the same crappy homes with rusty cars in their lots that I remember as a kid." Watts' voice trailed off as he pictured his drunken father chasing his mother around the yard. *Yeah, Dad, you were a real gem.* He shook off the memory and climbed out. "Let's go, Blaine."

With drill team precision, the detectives stepped out together, straightened their coats, and headed toward the front door. When they got within fifteen feet, a woman appeared behind the screen door casting a firm gaze. Watts wondered if they had the wrong house because she looked nothing like the book jacket photo, and unless lip balm qualified as makeup, she wore none. Her figure seemed nice enough for a forty-something lady, but her brown eyes looked as empty as a cow's. He showed his badge and tucked it away.

"Ms. Buck, I'm Detective Watts and this is my partner, Detective Spartan. Thank you for seeing us. I hope we're not intruding."

From behind the screen door, Arlene Buck casually looked up and down the street. "How can you be intruding when there's no one else around?" she said.

Watts smiled at her humor, expecting to be invited inside. When that didn't happen, he said, "Ma'am, may we have a moment of your time?"

Buck crossed her arms and stood her ground like a grizzly protecting her cubs. She stared long and hard at Watts and then at Spartan as if she wanted to remember their faces. Finally, she opened the door. "You can come in, but you won't be staying long."

Watts moved through the door feeling the dark paneling made the house as gloomy inside as it was out. Its décor as absent as light, he moved uncomfortably close to Buck so Spartan could squeeze in. The woman made no attempt to invite them into her living room. Instead, she kept everyone in the hall.

Breaking the awkward silence, Watts said, "Ms. Buck, we're here to gather information about your publisher's death, but frankly, I'm rather puzzled by your reception. Have we done something to offend you?"

"Yes," she said, scowling like she caught them stealing her fresh-baked pie. "You interrupted my writing and made me lose my thought in the middle of a sex scene. I may as well have gone to the market."

Watts glanced at his partner wondering if he was equally confused. Spartan's smirk validated their wonderment of this jaded woman writing about sex. He was wrong about Buck's eyes resembling a cow's. Cow eyes were empty, but also content. But Buck's intimidating gaze was one you wanted to avoid. Doing his best to stay neutral, he said, "You were standing at the door when we drove up. How could we have disturbed you?"

"You think I don't know what you're up to?" she said, waving her finger at them. "Toby Roberts warned me you'd be calling, saying you think one of us authors killed him. Just because I live in a dump doesn't mean I'm stupid. Mystery authors are very perceptive and also know how to get away with murder. On paper, that is."

Spartan's face tightened. His stance followed suit. "Did Mr. Roberts mention anything about your book contract?" he said.

"He did, and since that's the first thing you brought up you can leave now. Good day."

Watts stood his ground. "Where were you two nights ago?" he said.

"I said, good day."

Watts stared back at the woman and slid out the door. "We'll talk another time."

"Don't count on it. Drive safe, detectives." As soon as they were out, she pulled her screen door shut and blocked the entry.

With Spartan beside him, Watts shook his head walking back to the car. "That was bizarre," he said. "I'm glad you're here to back me up because Ryder wouldn't believe me."

"I know what you mean. A lot of words could describe that woman, but bitch is the first one that comes to mind."

Still fuming when he reached the car, Watts threw his door open and looked back at the house where Buck still stared. He quickly snapped his head back and turned the key. "Don't look at her, Blaine. Her gaze might turn you to stone."

"I said she was a bitch, not a witch."

"Bitch, witch, who cares? Let's head over to Dallas. No doubt Courtney Dridelle already knows we want to see her contract so she'll either talk to us or throw us out."

"You want me to call her so we can save some time?"

"No. We're still building our case, and if the authors refuse to talk to us, we'll go back to Mrs. Coulter to discuss their contracts. Recording these interviews is my insurance policy."

"Considering how our boss operates, that's very wise, Maxx."

ELEVEN

Watts had Spartan call Lieutenant Ryder during their drive to Dallas to give him an update. While on speaker phone, the detectives filled their boss in on the book contract situation and why they would probably need to speak to Kat Coulter again. Ryder wasn't pleased and didn't say why. So far, they had spent two hours on the road for less than ten minutes of interviewing their persons of interest. To make matters worse, it would take at least five more to visit Courtney Dridelle in Plano, Hank Azar in Garland, Mick Taggart in Irving, and Luke Harper in Waco. It seemed unlikely they would return before Ryder was gone for the day.

During their conversation, Ryder played Devil's Advocate asking what they would do if Kat Coulter refused to cooperate further. His question had Watts thinking about the marble paperweight that Ryder kept on his desk. It was similar in size and shape to the Writer's Block, but Ryder's adorned a replica police shield instead of a guillotine. Ryder's was a gift from the Police Officer's Association when he made lieutenant. Watts and Spartan attended the ceremony. Later that night, cheers and beers flowed freely at the local tavern frequented by off-duty police officers. The occasion had been memorable until someone found a dead hooker in the dumpster out back. Although the investigation proved that no one at the party was responsible, the media made such a fuss over it, the department never organized another affair like that. Watts remembered that evening every time he saw Ryder's award, and now CC's Writer's Block was equally tainted.

Still on Spartan's speaker phone, Watts said, "Lieutenant, paperweights always tell interesting stories. Do you have any idea who fabricated yours?"

"None whatsoever, Maxx. As you recall, it was presented to me. Why?"

"Just wondering if the Writer's Block came from the same trophy shop. Can you get someone to track it down?"

"I'll see what I can do. Anything else?"

"Yes. Do you have an update on the Forest Park murders?"

"Nothing new, and nothing that concerns you. What else?"

Watts raised a finger at the phone, thinking before answering. "I guess that's it for now," he said. We'll keep you posted."

Watts gestured for Spartan to end the call, but apparently Ryder beat him to it. After tucking his phone away, Spartan stared through the windshield at nothing in particular. Moments later, he glanced at his partner and said, "So, when are you gonna ask that pretty lab tech out?"

Watts eased his head to the right, his face devoid of expression. "You sure bring her up a lot. Why?"

"She came to mind when you mentioned the Forest Park murders. You have to admit it, Maxx. She's cute."

"We've been over this, Blaine, and I'm not interested. She's like an elusive cat that comes around for food but never lets you pet it. Either she's uncomfortable because she's new, or she's uncomfortable around people. If it's the latter, it might explain why she's no longer at her previous job."

"I'm sure you're right, Maxx. Don't ask her out."

"Nice try, Blaine, but remember, I took the same psych courses you did."

* * * * *

Compared to Fort Worth, Dallas resembled the Emerald City. Its cultural differences were as distant as the Moon was to Earth. One would never know the two cities were only separated by forty miles. But when it came to murder investigations, there were no boundaries. If Watts required assistance, all he had to do was call the local PD. That was one thing the two cities had in common.

Watts had hoped to visit self-proclaimed Iron-Fist attorney Hank Azar first, but his paralegal informed Spartan that her boss was in court. Considering his annoying ambulance-chasing TV commercials, it seemed likely that Azar was suing some insurance company on behalf of his client, but mostly to benefit himself. Mulling that over, Watts recalled how Azar's protagonist in *Forsaken Alibi* deceived the court in his murderous drama. From what he read, it seemed likely that Azar's protagonist was also his alter ego. Perhaps the defense attorney wrote about the judicial system to vent his frustrations using the old, "If you can't beat 'em, write about 'em" tact. Regardless, attorneys were usually well paid, so Azar should have no reason to hide the details of his low-budget book contract. A thought came to mind.

"Blaine, would you mind calling Azar's office and remind his receptionist that I need to hear from her boss as soon as possible. Make sure she understands that I mean today."

"No problem."

After making the call, Spartan punched in Mick Taggart's number. Taggart's wife answered and informed him that the airline pilot was called out early this morning for an overseas trip and wouldn't return for four days. Spartan passed on that information to his partner.

Watts wasn't happy. "Okay, so scratch Taggart," he said. "How about calling Courtney Dridelle and Luke Harper to see if they're home?"

"No problem," said Spartan, rubbing his fists into his eyes. He put it on speaker when it started to ring.

Watts looked at his partner with concern. "You okay, Blaine?"

Spartan kept rubbing. "It's just the smog. I'll live."

Watts held his gaze, thinking there might be problems in the Spartan household. Courtney Dridelle answered before they could discuss it.

Following Spartan's introduction, she said, "What can I do for you, detective?"

Spartan nearly choked when he heard her sultry voice. He turned off the speaker, covered his mike, and told Watts, "If her looks are anything like her voice, she probably does well selling her books at signings." He turned the speaker back on after Watts nodded back.

"Ma'am, we'd like to meet with you to discuss The Guillotine Press. We're heading your way now. Is this still a convenient time?"

"Sure, Hon. I'm not going anywhere."

"Great. We'll be there within the hour."

Spartan ended the call, grinning like a fool. "Did you hear that? She called me Hon and she has no problem seeing us."

"And I bet she'll have some fresh squeezed lemonade, too."

"I don't remember her saying anything about lemonade," Spartan said. "You're getting way too cynical for your age."

Watts grinned at him. "Aren't you two years older than me?"

"Yeah, which makes me two years wiser, so chill out."

Watts mulled that over for a moment, then said, "If you're so wise, why'd you turn to drinking?"

Spartan looked away and stared out the window. It took him a while before he looked back, but when he did his face was still flushed. "Several years ago, I started taking life too seriously," he said. "I'd go to a neighborhood party with my wife and then leave alone because I didn't fit in. Then you took a bullet and guilt rode me. I couldn't sleep or eat, and no matter what I did, I couldn't get the shooting out of my head. I discovered that drinking made me more genial because it hid the pain. Before long, I found myself drinking after work because it put me in a better mood when I got home. But a bottle is lousy company, Maxx. I soon found myself drinking alone and couldn't stop. Pressures from the job and marriage began taking their toll and it seemed I couldn't please anyone. The stress gave me an ulcer, so I started chasing my beers with medicine. Sandy forced me into counseling, but I was an unwilling patient so it didn't do much good. Whenever Sandy got fed up, I'd head back to the bars so I could have fun with people I'd never met. I know you can't relate because you rarely tip a glass, but alcoholics drink to escape their troubles. It wasn't until Sandy threatened to leave me that I sought help from the department. Granted, it's nothing like the physical therapy you had to go through, but detox was pretty damned rough. Thankfully, everyone stood by me." He paused to draw in a breath and slowly ease it out. "Anyway, that's my story. I'm not proud of it, but I relate better to people now because of that experience. I find good in people I've never seen before, and also know my wife and kids are far better than anything I ever got from drinking. That's why I'll never down another beer."

Watts reached over and patted his partner's shoulder. "That's great, Blaine. And thanks for spilling your guts. All our years together and this is the first time you've let your guard down. I've never mentioned it to you, but my dad was also an alcoholic. I never understood why he chose booze over me, but I suspect he was having problems at work and I was probably a pain in the ass when he came home. That's no excuse for choosing the bottle over Mom and me, but your explanation helps me understand him better."

Watts stopped talking as childhood memories filled his head. He was surprised at how bitter he was even though two decades had passed since he last saw his father. Like his partner, his past would always haunt him.

Since Spartan wasn't talking, Watts said, "Getting back to the case, you might think I'm taking this murder case personally, but I always trust my instincts, and from everything I've seen, Kat Coulter had both the opportunity and motive to kill her husband. The problem is I haven't uncovered any evidence that supports that so I'm counting on you to keep things in check. Hopefully Courtney Dridelle will provide some insight. Regardless, I promise I'll keep an open mind with all of our persons of interest."

"That's all anyone can ask, Maxx."

TWELVE

Maxx Watts cruised the north-Dallas community of Plano searching for Courtney Dridelle's address. His unmarked sedan gave two Hispanic gardeners a stir as they blew grass clippings into the street. Three posh homes all had pool cleaning trucks in front of them, each from a different company. Empty backyard swings rocked in the breeze between the custom houses. He didn't see a single kid outside.

Out of nowhere, a teen zoomed by in her late model Beemer. Two blocks later, a Porsche nearly side-swiped them as it sped around a corner, another teen behind the wheel. It was one of those rare times when Watts wished he was in uniform so he could ticket them, but he had no time for such matters anymore. Today was those kids' lucky day. He had to let him go.

Spartan shook his head at the mansions and cars. "Talk about spoiled," he said. "How will these kids make it without daddy's money?"

"Beats me. Does Courtney Dridelle have any kids?"

"Don't know," Spartan said, gawking at the steep-pitched roofs. "You know, I'd rather face some badass with a gun than re-roof one of these homes."

"I hear ya."

Watts slowed the car and confirmed the address. White pillars supported the two-story covered second-floor balcony. Six equally spaced oaks led toward the front door like runway lights. Japanese boxwoods lined the walkway that dissected her perfectly manicured lawn. Identical rose gardens set against the home's red brick walls completed its symmetry. It was indeed a grand house.

"It appears Courtney Dridelle is quite successful. Let's go talk to her."

The home's oak door was even larger than it appeared from the street. Black iron hinges gave it a medieval look. All that was missing were ornamental lions guarding the entry. A dog barked as soon as Watts rang the doorbell. Soon, a furry white pup appeared at ankle level in the side window. A woman said, "Speedo, No!", and her footsteps grew louder. Soon, the door cracked open, closed, and then opened again with Dridelle holding her miniature Westie terrier in her arms.

Watts showed his badge to the alluring woman whose physical grandeur equaled her home's. Her high cheek bones, flawless tanned skin, and radiant eyes were framed by highlighted auburn hair that spilled over her shoulders and down her well-proportioned figure. Plastic surgery or not, stunning was the only word that came to mind. Watts would have been shocked if she wasn't Miss Texas, nineteen years ago.

Her little dog growled at him. "Don't mind Speedo," Dridelle said with a soft Texas drawl. Petting her dog made him stop. "Like so many little dogs, Speedo's rather full of himself. Anyway, please, come in."

"Thank you," said Watts, cautiously petting the dog's head. "It's okay, little guy. We won't be staying long."

Retracting his hand when her dog growled again made Dridelle giggle. "Why don't we go out back?" she said. "I just made a pitcher of ice cold lemonade."

Watts grinned. *What's with these people and their lemonade?* He wasn't sure he could stomach another glass, but didn't dare mention it. Stepping inside, he saw his image in the marble floors. The Great Room looked more like an art gallery than a family setting. Among several landscape paintings were two featuring Longhorn bulls.

"I take it you're in the cattle business," he said.

"Actually, that was Daddy's thing," she said, blinking her eyes at Watts. "I inherited the ranch, but sold it a few years ago to build this house. I'll take passion over cow pies any day."

"So these were his bulls?"

"That's right. *Prize* bulls. Daddy loved them so much that he commissioned a local artist to do these paintings. The one in the field is Maurice, but if I'd named him, he would've been Sir Humpalot. The other one is Bruno, and he's quite a humper, too. I own them now, and their stud fees exceed my living expenses. Because of that, there was no way I could let these paintings go. Too bad men don't have their stamina."

Now Watts understood why this woman wrote romance mysteries. Every word she uttered oozed sex. Oddly, as with Toby Roberts, Courtney Dridelle didn't have any family photos or portraits on display. Not even one of her late father. Perhaps it was an author's thing.

Above the white marble that framed her gas fireplace was a hefty oak mantle. To its right were oak bookshelves that held ten of her books. Left of the fireplace, more shelves displayed Native American pottery. Watts noted this was her first break in symmetry.

Dridelle led them to the screened porch where a ceiling fan blew a draft over the silver pitcher and ice bucket that was centered on the round glass table. Stainless-steel chairs surrounded the table, all perfectly spaced.

"Please have a seat," she said, lifting the pitcher. She teased them with cleavage views as she leaned over to fill their glasses. After setting the pitcher down, she took a seat across from them. "So, what can I do for you, detectives?"

Watts took a sip to cleanse his mind as well as his throat. "As I'm sure you're aware, your publisher was murdered two days ago."

"I am," she said, her Botox expression unchanging.

He sipped more lemonade for effect before setting his glass down. "That's very good," he said, imagining its acid dissolving his stomach lining. "Anyway, due to the nature of his murder, we are interviewing all of the Guillotine Press authors to get a sense of who might want Mr. Coulter dead. What was your relationship with him?"

She leaned forward to grab her glass, eyeing him as she took a playful drink.

"Are you speaking professionally or personally?"

"Either," Spartan chimed in.

Watts disagreed, shaking his head. "Both," he said.

Dridelle leaned back in her seat and seductively crossed her legs. "Let's just say I knew CC personally long before I did professionally. We met at the *Los Angeles Times* Festival of Books several years ago. It's probably the largest book event in the US, but it's also a carnival."

Watts nodded, locked on her face. "How so?'

"Well, first off, it's held at the UCLA campus, so it has a vibrant college feel. Then, live bands and street performers are sandwiched between hundreds of book-filled tents. It's the craziest book affair anywhere in the world, and the place stays packed all weekend. Nothing compares with it."

"Sounds like fun," Spartan said.

"Oh, it is," she said, sliding her finger along the top of her glass. "Anyway, I was signing at the Sisters-in-Crime booth and CC was sitting at the table next to ours. It's rare when I see authors as cute as him, and when we spoke, his silver tongue drove me wild. We flirted in between signings, and ended up having dinner afterwards. CC was a true gentleman, always helping with my chair, opening doors, and he never took his eyes off me. Afterwards, we went to my room and—well, you can fill in the blanks.

"When morning came, we had breakfast and then he went back to his place. I never expected to see him again, but one day out of the blue he contacted me to see if I was interested in having him publish my work. I was flattered not only because of his offer, but because we'd become so close in such a short time. At the time, my book sales were down and I was looking for a new publisher, so his timing was perfect. When we got together a few weeks later, it was like we'd never been apart. In fact, if he hadn't been married, I might have considered proposing to him—and that says a lot because I've turned down so many men."

"You knew CC was married?" Spartan said.

"Oh, pah-leeze. We're all adults and he was a player. Actually, he exceeded my expectations," she said, her grin widening now. "I truly miss him."

Watts stared at the woman, feeling sorry for Kat, who was equally attractive in her own right, and seemingly in love with her husband. Then again, if Kat knew about their affair, jealousy could be a motive. One glance confirmed that Spartan was equally enchanted with the writer. In fact, Spartan appeared so mesmerized that Watts cleared his throat before returning his attention to Dridelle.

"I'm surprised you're so candid about your affair. Was CC as open about his relationship with you?"

"By that, do you mean did Kat know about us?"

Watts nodded.

"Well, she certainly knew I was one of CC's authors. His *favorite* author, I might add. So much so that he became a muse for one of my novels. But don't get me wrong, detective. Kat is neither stupid nor blind. I'm sure she could read between the lines."

"So, you're saying she knew the two of you were having an affair?"

Dridelle's grin flattened. "I have no idea how CC handled his wife," she said. "I only know how he handled me, and he did that very well."

Watts' head bowed. Squeezing his palms together, he took a moment to collect his thoughts. "Okay," he said, "Let's move on to your professional life with him. How many books did you publish with CC versus your previous publisher?"

Glancing at the shelf, she read them off. "Five with Bantam, four with Penguin, and one with The Guillotine Press."

"That's impressive. Admittedly, I'm also no expert in the publishing field, but isn't The Guillotine Press a step down from Bantam and Penguin?"

Dridelle shrugged and took another sip of lemonade. "These days, you take what you can get."

"I see. And how has your success been with them?"

In an elegant move, she re-crossed her legs, winking when Spartan noticed. "Define success," she said, looking back at Watts.

Watts tapped his fingertips together, her answers reminding him of

President Clinton's response to defining "sex" at his Congressional hearing. Looking into her eyes, he calmly said, "In a writer's world, I imagine writing a *New York Times* best seller would define success."

Her eyes teasing him, she said, "You don't have to sell that many books to make 'the list'. For me, success is when you become a household name. Granted, I'm no Jackie Collins or Heather Graham, but I do have a loyal fan base. Even so, my book sales barely cover my taxes. I mean, without those stud fees, I'd be living in a double-wide."

Watts nodded even though he wasn't buying it. "I can't imagine Bantam and Penguin keeping you on without good sales figures."

She shook her head at him, smiling as though he was dumbest person on the planet. "Detective, I earn twenty-five cents for each mass-market paperback sold, and I get nothing from used book sales. Think of how many books sales it takes to buy a McDonald's burger and you'll know what I'm talking about. There are definite advantages in working with small publishers."

"Such as?"

"For starters, how about flexible deadlines and more input in the jacket design? CC had a great touch."

"Yeah, we got that impression," Watts said, glancing at his partner before looking back at her.

She reached over and playfully slapped Watts' arm. "Not that way, silly, although I liked that, too. But I was referring to my ability to talk business over the phone. You can't do that with large publishers. Most of the time CC and I handled things over the phone, but sometimes when we talked over dinner. In that regard, The Guillotine Press suited me well."

"Especially after Bantam and Penguin dropped you."

"Well, that, too."

This time, her expression seemed genuine. Watts couldn't remember a woman speaking so candidly about sex. But if Dridelle handled her business over the phone, chances were good that Kat Coulter could have overheard their conversations and felt threatened by her. Watts was curious why Bantam and Penguin both dropped her, too, but didn't ask because it wasn't pertinent to the case. But why sign with CC Coulter? What could he possibly offer her besides a roll in the hay?

A wind gust whistled through the screened porch. Spartan looked up as the dust devil traversed the yard. As dirt and debris attacked the screen, Watts calmly covered his drink, waiting for things to quiet down before asking his next question.

"Ms. Dridelle, was Kat Coulter jealous of your affair?"

Batting her eyelashes, she said, "I suspect she was, but who wouldn't be?

I mean, think about it—a striking woman who writes steamy romance novels is having dinners with her husband? The only difference between me and my female characters is they get sucked in by passion instead of using it to their advantage. Most of them are also average looking and get hit on by studs that are clearly out of their league. Of course, in real life men are the weaker sex. Show 'em your tits and they go brain dead. CC was no exception, and did whatever I asked. Sadly, I got bored with him like I do with everyone else, and soon our relationship was strictly business. I'm sure Kat knew exactly when our mattress dancing days ended—if you know what I mean."

Spartan coughed, hoping to gain her attention before things got any more graphic. "Ms. Dridelle, can you show us your Guillotine Press contract?" he said.

Dridelle's posture stiffened. "Now, why on earth would you need to see that?"

"We're comparing all of The Guillotine Press contracts. It's no big deal"

"Well, it is to me. I'm happy to discuss anything except my contract."

Spartan frowned at his partner. Watts took that to mean it was his turn again. Leaning forward, palms together, he raised his fingertips to form a steeple. "Ms. Dridelle," he said, "You mentioned that you and CC hadn't shared a bed in some time. What changed your physical relationship?"

After a long drink, she delicately pressed her napkin to her lips. "I've been with a lot of men, detective. Tall ones, short ones, good ones, bad ones—even a few cops—but after a while the thrill is gone. I assure you it's no reflection on any of them. In fact, CC was one of the best. But being a writer lets me create the most seductive studs in the universe—far better than any here on Earth. So in that regard, I view my affairs as research. After all, without experiencing a variety of men, my characters wouldn't be as believable. My readers crave these guys, and the stronger their desire for them, the more books I sell. And before you ask—yes, women do fantasize. Especially these days."

"Why is that?" Spartan said.

She gave him a grin. "Because the pendulum has swung in favor of women, especially sexy ones. Sarah Palin is proof of that. Her sex appeal nearly won a national election and she's still in the picture in spite of quitting her elected position and moving from Alaska Nowadays, women can ask men out without feeling like sluts, but that was unheard of twenty years ago. Social networking sites have made it a breeze to hook up. And look at how TV has changed. Back in the sixties, husbands and wives slept in separate beds, but nowadays, women are swept off their feet—if only in their dreams.

Women crave stories about sex and revenge. That's why Carrie Underwood's payback song, *Before He Cheats*, did so well. Now, more than ever, women are empowered to do as they wish."

"We'll take your word on that," Watts said.

"Of course you will because you're men."

Her comeback had Watts thinking about his failed relationships. But he wasn't shallow like Dridelle, and never once used a partner as a sex toy. Even so, none of his relationships lasted more than a few months and he was beginning to wonder why. Did he have trust issues with women, or was it something else? The more he considered his track record, the less he liked it. Shaken, he returned his attention to her.

"So, CC Coulter became your muse and yet he only published one of your books?"

"Isn't that what I told you?"

Watts sighed and Spartan jumped in again. "Ms. Dridelle, where were you two nights ago?"

"Why, I was here, of course, and no, I didn't have any stud muffins hanging around. I figure I've done enough research for a while. Besides, the sheets stay cleaner when I'm alone."

"Can anyone verify your whereabouts?" Watts said.

With a raised brow, she shook her head, innocently twisting her hair.

Her relationship with her publisher still bothered Watts. He wondered if trading sex for a publishing deal made her feel used. Perhaps she became upset when her deal with CC softened.

Dridelle gazed at them like an angry teacher. "I read faces pretty well, detectives. I'm not a whore and I didn't kill CC. Every lover I've ever had was all over me first. Sparks had to fly before they ever got to second base, and plenty of times they never got to third. CC hit home runs whenever he was at bat, but I can't be with just one man. I know it's wrong, but that's also why I'll never marry."

Watts quietly rose from his chair. He had heard enough, and like her, needed to move on. After smoothing his coat, he reached for her hand.

"We have other appointments, so if you're not willing to show us your contract, we need to be going. Thank you for your time, Ms. Dridelle. We can find our way out."

"Sorry to disappoint you, Hon, but my book contract is a private matter between me and my publisher. Let me know if there's anything else I can do for you, okay? Feel free to drop by anytime you're in the neighborhood."

Watts refused to bite. Instead, he and his partner walked out of her house.

THIRTEEN

Watts wasn't willing to leave Dridelle's neighborhood. Rather than head for their next appointment, he moved the Crown Vic two blocks down the street and turned it so he faced her driveway. It wasn't that he expected her to go anywhere. He simply needed a moment to think. Spartan knew not to speak when he got into this mood. It was best for both of them to give him his space. The dashboard air and police band radio chatter provided welcome distractions.

Spartan's belly growled. He chuckled when Watts gave a disapproving look. "You ready for lunch?" he said.

Watts put the car in gear and pulled away from the curb. "Let's grab something on the way to Waco."

"Sounds good. You want me to call Mr. Harper to make sure he's in?"

"Sure," Watts mumbled, still deep in thought.

After placing his call, Spartan punched one of his favorite Dallas area restaurants into his iPhone. He then checked the GPS to make sure it was doable. His mouth already salivating, he looked at Watts and said, "Luke Harper won't be home for 90 minutes so we have some time to kill. Ever eaten at Kenny's Burger Joint? They have the best gourmet burgers in the metroplex."

"Never been, but if you say it's good, I'm game. Where is it?"

"It at the northwest corner of Legacy and SH 121, ten minutes away, tops. Sandy and I discovered it one day and it's great. Trust me, you won't regret it."

Watts found a parking spot directly in front of the restaurant, which was located in a high-end Stonebriar Commons Shopping Center. Not your normal strip mall or burger joint, Kenny's was upscale, and suited Dallas well. Modern styling, a well-dressed wait staff, and a full-service bar serving wine and "adult shakes" made it totally unique. Watts also liked that he and Spartan blended in with the other guests in coats and ties. He wouldn't be surprised if the two men seated at a nearby table were Dallas detectives.

Watts looked over the menu and ordered a bacon cheeseburger and Coke Zero. Once the waitress took Spartan's order and left, he said, "This place looks great, Blaine. Check out those burgers the waitress is delivering to that couple."

Spartan beamed. "I know," he said. It's a good thing Kenny's is in Frisco and not Fort Worth or I'd weigh a ton. Unfortunately, Sandy will have a beautiful dinner waiting when I get home and I'll have to eat it."

"What's wrong with that?"

"Nothing, other than I'll get fat."

"Oh, right."

Their waitress returned and politely set their drinks on the table. "Your meals should be right up," she said.

Watts smiled his thanks and took a sip of his Coke. "Sure beats lemonade, doesn't it?"

Instead of acknowledging him, Spartan was busy ogling their waitress as she walked away. Watts wasn't going to mention it until he saw him do it again when she delivered their meals. Popping a sweet potato fry in his mouth, Watts thought while munching. Finally, he decided he had to say something.

"You're scaring me, Blaine."

Spartan prepared to take a bite out of his burger, but instead wrinkled his forehead and stared back. "What are you talking about?

"Your eyes are all over her, man. I've never seen you do that before. What's going on?"

Spartan hiked his shoulders and bit into his sandwich. He slowly chewed, swallowed, and took a sip of Coke, ignoring his partner. But Watts held his gaze, demanding an answer. Finally, Spartan heaved a sigh and set his burger down.

"You're single, Maxx. You have no idea what it's like to be married."

"You're right, but since we're partners and it's changed your behavior, I want to know why because whatever's affecting you could affect me."

Spartan kept his elbows on the table as he fed fries to his mouth. When they were gone, he said, "Sandy was very supportive all through my rehab, but now I get the feeling she resents me. Sometimes I think I'm losing her, and it can be a real struggle. You're lucky you're single, Maxx. You have a lot less stress."

Watts scanned the room to make sure no one was listening in. The couple next to them was paying their bill and the ones behind just got up to leave. He downed more of his drink, waiting until they were gone so he could speak freely.

"Blaine, being single gets old. Believe it or not, I'm envious of you. You always look so happy when you're bragging on your kids, and I know how much you love your wife. So here's a tip—stop checking out the ladies before it ruins your marriage. You may not even realize you're doing it, but Sandy sure as hell does. Imagine how you'd feel if the tables were turned and she was checking out the guys while you ate? Roaming eyes can be dangerous."

Spartan resumed his eating without further comment. He quietly stuffed the last of his burger in his mouth and then wiped his face. After polishing off his drink, he set his napkin aside and patted his belly. "Now that was a great meal," he said, as if Watts never mentioned women. "I don't know how Kenny does it, but this place rocks."

"Yes, my meal was great, too, but did you hear what I said? You and Sandy used to be so tight. What happened?"

"Beats me. Like Courtney Dridelle said, people are better off being single."

"No, she said she was better off being single," said Watts. His partner's eyes looked away as if to hide their hurt. "Look, Blaine, I really care about you and Sandy. I've never been married, but I do know that it takes two to make a marriage, and if your roaming eyes don't stop cheating on your wife, you'll lose her forever."

"Thanks, Maxx, but just so you know, I've never touched another woman. *Ever.*"

"You don't have to physically touch someone to cheat. I'm telling you this as a friend, stop checking out the ladies."

Spartan clutched his napkin and squeezed. After balling it with both hands, he set it down again. "I appreciate what you're trying to do," he softly said. "I could tell you to butt out, but I won't. The truth is I love my wife and had no idea I was doing that, so thanks for telling me."

"You're welcome." Watts signed his bill and checked the time. "Mr. Harper's expecting us. You ready to go?"

"Sure am. I hope it's worth the trip.

* * * * *

Even in drought years like this one, Indian paintbrush, blue bonnets, and yellow mustard pop up along Interstate 35 every spring. After waiting all year, they couldn't help but rise from the earth to show their brilliant colors. But the wildflower season ended months ago and now the landscape was as indiscernible as the sky. They had been traveling for an hour and Watts estimated they had another 45 minutes to go. When they finally exited the freeway, Watts pulled into a gas station for a pit stop. While relieving himself of his two glasses of Coke, he thought about Luke Harper's cult murder, *In*

God's Will. When reading it, he got the impression that Harper was inspired by Waco's Branch Davidian cult disaster and Reverend Jim Jones' mass suicide in Jonestown, Guyana. Watts never finished the book because it didn't correlate to Coulter's murder, and compared to the other Guillotine Press novels, wasn't particularly well written. If CC published Harper's book because he thought controversy would sell, he totally missed the mark. Watts finished in the rest room and headed back to the car. When he got in, Spartan decided he needed a pee break after all. Watts reviewed their taped interviews while waiting. Spartan returned moments later.

Driving through Waco sent Watts back to the televised broadcast of authorities storming the Branch Davidian compound. The 1993 standoff between the cult and law enforcement agencies had lasted for fifty-one days before someone decided to end it. Live video from all angles recorded lawmen shooting and getting shot. When the tanks rolled in, flames engulfed the buildings, quickly gutting them with men, women, and children inside. To this day, the event is remembered as one of the darkest in law enforcement history. Even now, no one is sure what provoked the disastrous end to the standoff, but Watts felt certain that Luke Harper would offer his ideas. The Branch Davidian wasn't the first clan to suffer a massive death toll, though. In 1978, Reverend Jim Jones saw his People's Temple falling apart, so he gave his followers the choice of drinking cyanide-laced Kool-Aid or being shot. Jones cared nothing about age, sex, or racial discrimination during his going-out-of-business sale. Everyone had to die, including the US Congressman Leo Ryan who was there examining claims made against Jones and his agricultural Jonestown project.

Watts was still caught up in these disturbing images when they found Harper's single-wide home. The trailer park seemed orderly enough. Some of the wheeled homes adorned fake flowers. Fake windmills and butterflies graced others. Laundry floated from clotheslines. Kids' bikes leaning against trailer walls stood ready for use. Watts recalled Courtney Dridelle's remark that she would be living in a trailer park if it weren't for her daddy's money. Looking around the park, he sincerely doubted that.

Like Arlene Buck, Luke Harper defiantly stood in his entry as they approached. Watts estimated Harper to be in his seventies. Had *In God's Will* included an author's photo, it would have scared potential readers away. His Roman nose drooped to his upper lip and scraggly hairs sprouted from the mole on his right cheek. Atop his ears, hairs rose noticeably because they stood above his hairline. It mattered not that Harper's neck jiggled like a turkey's. What concerned Watts was the old man's body language. He didn't smile or move when they showed their badges. They weren't off to a good start.

"Sir, may we come in?" Watts said. Harper grunted and backed away from his door. Stepping inside, Watts saw the 12 gauge shotgun leaning against the wall. "Is that thing loaded?"

"Isn't yours?" Harper said.

Watts' stomach knotted. Without asking, he opened the shotgun, removed the shells, tucked them in his pocket, and returned the gun where he found it. "I'll give these back after we talk," he said.

"That's fine. And once you empty your guns, we'll get down to business."

"Sorry, Mr. Harper, but we can't do that. We're required to keep our guns loaded while we're on duty. It's for everyone's protection."

Harper grimaced and angrily shook his head. "You're just like all the other government clones! Hypocrites, all of you!"

Spartan and Watts exchanged glances. Driven by paranoia, nut cases like Harper often kept weapons stashed at arm's length. Closely monitoring Harper's movements, Watts said, "Mr. Harper, I'm confused. We set up an appointment, you agreed to see us, and yet you're treating us like intruders. We are investigating your publisher's murder. What's your problem?"

"Apparently you didn't hear me the first time. You two are political pawns who do the government's dirty deeds. You either entrap people and toss them in jail or burn them alive. This used to be a free country. My brothers and sisters earned that freedom in the Revolutionary War and kept it through two World Wars, and yet you torch Mount Carmel's Branch Davidian camp, murdering eighty-three innocent men, women, and children in the worst travesty in US history. The Branch Davidians date back to 1955 as a Protestant sect of the Seventh Day Adventists. The ones in Waco were nothing like that crazy-ass Jim Jones in Guyana. I pray you didn't come here to defend the government's right to invade a sanctuary with tanks, because if you did, you should leave immediately."

"Sir, we're not here to discuss the Branch Davidian compound or debate historical events. We're simply here to discuss your publisher's murder."

Harper sneered keeping his suspicious eyes in constant motion. "Well, I sure as hell didn't kill him. Then again, I wouldn't be surprised if you did and you're framing me for it."

Watts leaned against the cheap paneled wall, searching for signs of a family. Not seeing any seemed to be the common element among the Guillotine Press authors. Well, that plus they loved their lemonade. Then again, Harper was so angry and untrustworthy, Watts wouldn't accept anything he might offer, not that Harper would. He didn't need to be a shrink to know Luke Harper was hurting inside. That came through in his writing. And since anger stems from passion, Harper had his reasons. Watts' goal was to determine if CC Coulter was responsible for his resentment.

"Sir, with all due respect," he said, "You don't appear old enough to have served in World War II, but I agree that war is a horrible thing, and something no one should experience. Losing an uncle and second cousin in Vietnam reminded me of the cost of freedom. Vietnam happened before my time, but I've seen plenty of footage on how it tore this country apart. Did you spend any time over there?"

Harper bowed his head and shook it. "I would have fled to Canada had they drafted me. Vietnam was nothing but a government travesty designed to sell arms and show our military might. The same thing happened at Mount Carmel when President Clinton and Janet Reno authorized that raid. Goddamn bastards!"

"Sir, Detective Spartan and I were both in high school when Mount Carmel was raided, but since you have such animosity toward our politicians and the law, were you somehow involved?"

Harper's eyes narrowed and fists bunched. "What are you implying?"

"Nothing, sir. I'm only trying to understand your pain."

Harper deflated and folded his arms. He sat that way for several minutes, staring at a small wooden box on the bookshelf. He allowed the detectives to follow his eyes without offering an explanation. A hardbound version of *In God's Will* rested atop this box.

Watts waited patiently. Five minutes passed without a word. He couldn't tell if the old man shut down, or whether Harper expected him to ask about the box. The kitchen clock ticked. The woman next door screamed at her child. When a small dog barked, Watts gave in. "Sir, what is in the box?"

"My daughter, or so they tell me."

Suddenly, everything was clear. "Mr. Harper, was your daughter inside Mount Carmel during the attack?"

His eyes welled as he nodded.

"I'm very sorry."

Spartan had barely uttered a word since they arrived, but Watts figured this was a good time to leave. As they started toward the door, Harper fired a gaze.

"Don't you at least want to know what happened?" he said.

The detectives were leery, but the old man looked desperate for an audience. It was probably a waste of time, but Watts figured they owed it to him to listen.

"Please, have a seat," Harper said, softening his tone.

Once they sat, Harper gave his version of the ATF raid. Harper's account matched the official version with stunning accuracy. Believing that Luke Harper lived this tragedy every day of his life, Watts saw no value in adding anything. Branch Davidian leader David Koresh and Reverend Jim Jones of the People's Temple were nothing alike except for the indelible marks they left behind. Clearly, Harper's book may have been his way of dealing with his daughter's death, but publishing it never eased his pain. In fact, Harper became so distraught as he told his tale that Watts never asked about his Guillotine Press contract, or discussed his whereabouts on the night Coulter was murdered. Instead, he felt sorry for the man whose life ended with his daughter's. It must be hell staring at her ashes every morning. No doubt Harper would die a lonely man.

That notion had Watts reflecting on his own life. At least the part about dying alone. He searched for whatever it was that kept him from settling down. Was it fear of things souring like his partner described or fear of commitment? How ironic would it be if that cute lab tech had the same issues? As Watts pondered that, he realized that more than anything, he was afraid he might endanger the life of someone he loved by being a cop. At least that part made sense.

Spartan nudged his partner. "It's getting late," he said. "We should go."

Watts nodded and then warmly shook Harper's hand. On his way out, he removed the shotgun shells from his pocket and set them on the counter. "Mr. Harper, I'm truly sorry for your loss," he said. "We've heard enough. Thank you for your time."

Harper nodded without bothering to get up. Watts gladly watched the trailer park disappear in his mirror.

Spartan glimpsed at his partner. "We have a long drive back. Mind if I give Sandy a call?"

"Have at it. Tell her I said hi."

* * * * *

After acknowledging his partner, Spartan pulled out his cell phone. Their shift would be over by the time they arrived at 350 and he couldn't wait to get home. Their conversation at lunch helped him realize the hell he had put his wife through and he was determined to win her back. Sometimes it took the observations of others to see the obvious. Guilt rode him as he recalled the days when he hit the bars on his way home. His drinking had taken a heavy toll on their marriage and they were still coming to terms with it. Counseling had helped both of them realize that alcoholism was a disease, and Sandy seemed proud that he was overcoming it. His giving up the bottle gave them three more hours together each day, but it wasn't always easy. She knew that alcohol was a mistress that could seduce him at any time. They both worried about that, but he had vowed to stay clean. He was glad she answered the phone.

"Hey there, sexy. Do you have any plans for tonight?"

"That depends," she said. "What did you have in mind?"

Sweating from her cool tone, Spartan said, "I thought we'd all go out to dinner and rent a movie."

"Sure. It's not like we had any plans. It sounds like there's an echo. Where are you?"

"Maxx and I are driving back from Waco, so it will take at least a couple of hours. Nothing special happened today so I don't see any reason to hang around the office. Why don't you and the kids figure out where you'd like to eat. I'll call you when I'm heading home."

"Sounds good. Drive safe."

Spartan heard his eight-year-old daughter in the background. "Sandy, can I speak to Ramsey before you go?"

"Hang on."

There was a short pause and then his daughter came on the line. "Hi, Daddy!"

"Hi, Sweetheart. How are you?"

"Fine. Are you coming home now?"

"Not yet, but I'll be home in a few hours. We're going out to dinner, so help your mom pick out a place, okay? I'm still at work, so I'll let you go. I just wanted to say I love you."

"Thanks, Dad. I love you, too. See you soon."

Spartan ended the call, grateful he still had a family. He would have loved hearing "I love you" from his wife, but those words didn't come easily these days. He didn't blame Sandy though. Fear of losing her is what kept him sober. There were days when he would sit on a bar stool, mindlessly downing beers like Norm on Cheers. What a waste of time and money, not to mention a blow to his health. Thank God Sandy supported him through his detox. But there were times when he wondered if she didn't prefer him drinking. Back then she laughed at his jokes. He wasn't as funny now that he was sober, and that killed him. He knew that she loved him on some level, but it might never be like it once was. He couldn't reverse the clock, but he was determined to balance his career with his family. However things turned out, it would have to do.

FOURTEEN

By the time Watts got back to his apartment, he had tunnel vision, and his body vibrated from the driving. It wasn't a productive day. They had spent the majority of their day on the road for thirty minutes of conversation. His brain was so foggy that he missed the bikini-clad babe by the pool's greeting. Instead, he quietly stepped inside, set his keys and pistol on the kitchen table, stripped down to his boxers, and sank into his easy chair, grateful that no one was complaining about his dirty clothes on the floor. The problem was "no one" provided little companionship. Within minutes, he grew anxious and grabbed a water bottle from the fridge. When he returned to his chair, his dirty laundry bothered him, so he picked it up and tossed it in the hamper. On his third attempt to relax, he plopped in his chair and turned on the TV.

With his frequently interrupted work schedule, he gained solace from his twenty-four hour sports channels. Today, the Texas Rangers were leading 4 to 1 in the seventh inning at The Ballpark in Arlington. He had attended their very first game there, and like everyone else, wondered who came up with the stadium's name. But The Ballpark's classic red brick, green trim, and immaculate playing field made up for its funky name. They even built a similar-style Little League ballpark next to it. The *Texas Rangers* made it to the World Series in 2010, and from all indications would get there again—someday. As much as he wanted to attend another game, it probably wouldn't happen until he solved this case.

When a commercial came on, he scanned the room for something to read. The Guillotine Press books were nearby, but he needed a break from the job so he ignored them. After the game ended, he slid on his shorts, cross-trainers, and a Hawaiian shirt, and headed outside. Upon reaching the sidewalk, he spotted a *Fort Worth Star Telegram* newspaper box and bought a copy. He had no interest in the business, entertainment, or classified sections, so he neatly tucked them under the newspaper stack, and found a shady spot to read. Page Two of Section A described the double murder in Forest Park as a hate crime possibly committed by White Supremacists. No suspects were in custody, but two males with shaved heads and swastika tattoos were seen speeding from the park in a pickup truck shortly before the bodies were discovered. The fact that the victims had swastikas carved into their chests seemed to support the Skinhead account. Everything in the article matched what Watts had been told, including the victims' names. The unanswered question was why Pao Lee and Shing Chow were in the park at night.

Since Forest Park was only two miles from his apartment, Watts decided to walk there, still perturbed over Lieutenant Ryder telling him to butt out. Trinity Park was significantly further and lay across the river of the same name. Both parks encompassed more acreage than a football stadium, and were heavily forested, interspersed with picnic tables, playgrounds, and playfields. Trinity Park boasted the Botanic and Japanese Gardens while Forest Park had the zoo and kiddy train. Each park drew hundreds of visitors each day, but at night they became daunting and dangerous.

The heat burned through Watts' shoes before he reached the park. It seemed unlikely that anyone would still be at the crime scene, but he needed the exercise anyway. Oblivious to the sweat running down his back, he kept his pace, concerned about why his boss avoided the possible Pao Lee connection. Ryder knew the names of all the GP authors and had been briefed on them more than once. So, why not let him work with Skip Parsons? Was Ryder concealing information or was this in response to the last time he interfered? One thing was for sure. Watts wanted the run-down on this double murder before going to work in the morning.

Locating the crime scene proved more difficult than Watts anticipated. The newspaper account said the bodies were found in the grass near the Trinity River, but with the park bordering the river, several areas fit that description. The yellow police tape told him he was in the right place. To his delight, the cute lab tech, Daisy Woods, was working inside the cordoned area.

"Hello again," he said, showing his badge. "Remember me? Detective Maxx Watts, Homicide. I saw you briefly at the Coulter's house and in the lab. Coulter's the vic who had the paper wad crammed down his throat. I'm working that case, and have a hunch mine might also be related to this case. Mind if I ask you a few questions?"

Her eyes gave him the once-over from head to toe. "I don't know any detectives that wear Hawaiian shirts," she said. "How do I know you're not a Thomas Magnum impersonator?"

Watts' smile widened. It was the first sign she had a sense of humor. To appease her, he struck Tom Selleck's lead-in pose from the 1970s Hawaiian detective TV show and danced his eyebrows.

Unimpressed, she said, "Nice try, but Magnum's legs were longer and he wore a mustache."

"Okay, you got me there, I'm no Tom Selleck. But how do you know about *Magnum PI*? It's been years since it was on. You're not old enough to know about it."

"First of all, a girl never reveals her age. Secondly, *Magnum* is on Retro TV. Finally, you're not old enough to have seen the originals, either."

Watts laughed out loud. "Okay, you win. Pretending he didn't know, he said, "Do you at least have a name?"

"Of course," she said, removing her glove to shake his hand. "Daisy Woods, CSSU."

Her firm grip didn't match her supple skin. Watts let go and stuffed his hands in his pockets. "Nice to meet you, Ms. Woods. So, have you found anything interesting?"

"Call me Daisy, and there's nothing that I can share since it's not your case."

Watts respected the perimeter tape and wouldn't step inside unless invited. He would gain nothing by upsetting a lab technician. Especially a cute one. He leaned against a tree, giddy as a teen at a Sadie Hawkins dance.

"I was hoping to speak to Pao Lee as part of my murder investigation, but I'm obviously too late. It's a tough break because he might have given me some insight. Today was a real waste. My partner and I spent all day on the road interviewing people and got nothing in return."

Shielding her eyes from the sun, she looked at him. "I'm sorry, but as I said, I can't share any information."

"I understand. Pao Lee's death sure mucks up my investigation, though. Lee created the Writer's Block, and I'm convinced someone used it to make a statement."

"And then someone made a statement out of Lee," she said. "Can you imagine someone stripping off your shirt and carving your chest?"

"I prefer not to think about it. Any signs of a struggle?"

She stopped what she was doing and frowned at him. "I seem to recall saying I can't discuss the case. You should direct your question to Detective Parsons. He's probably still at 350."

"That's okay. Do you happen to know where the Writer's Block paperweight is?"

"It's in the evidence room where it belongs. We found minute traces of Coulter's blood on it, but no one else's. What about it?"

"Pao Lee gave it to his publisher a couple of days before Coulter died. Since his widow mentioned the marble block's pun, I'm guessing that Lee meant it as a joke, but there's no way to confirm it now that he's dead. By the way, did anyone ever match the black hair found in Coulter's office? I'm thinking it might be Lee's."

"I'm not sure, but as I told you, I can't share anything with you even if your person of interest happens to be Detective Parsons' vic. I'm only a lab tech, detective. Please don't put me in the middle. I'm sure your lieutenant can get you whatever you need."

"Well, thanks for your time, Daisy. Sorry if I made you uncomfortable. Nice seeing you again."

He anticipated a good-bye from her, but that didn't happen. She didn't walk away either. Instead, she stared at him like a dog awaiting a treat. Breaking the silence, he said, "Daisy, is there any way you can walk me through the scene without compromising yourself so I can get a sense of what happened?"

With pursed lips, her eyes roamed from his face to his torso and traveled south. It took a while before her eyes met his again, and when they did, they seemed kinder.

"In a nutshell," she said, "the victims were probably killed behind those trees over there and then dumped in the grass. Whoever did this wanted us to find the bodies."

"Bodies dumped on Forest Lawn, eh? That's as caustic as the Writer's Block."

Frowning again, Daisy said, "I fail to see the humor in comparing two men's deaths to a celebrity cemetery. Can you imagine their fear as the knives carved into them?"

"You're right, and I apologize for sounding insensitive. I meant no disrespect. Like the Writer's Block, it was a bad joke. That's why it came to me. Still, the two puns could be tied."

"Maybe they are, but more likely you're reaching."

After saying that, she did a flirty half-twist and stepped away to get back to what she was doing. Watts followed like a fly would a horse. Not only did her body language signal she was interested in him, she was also discussing the double murder case in a round-about way. That alone gave reason to pursue her. Watts caught up to her and leaned against the boundary tape.

"Okay, so they were killed over there, presumably at night, but the sun doesn't set until late, so why would Mr. Lee and Mr. Chow come here when it's dark? Did their assassins drive them here or were they ambushed as they walked the trail?"

"I don't know, but I'm sure Detective Parsons is looking into it."

She tucked the loose strand of hair behind her ear as she kneeled to pick something up. Twisting her head so she could see Watts, she said, "I've already told you more than I should. It was nice meeting you, detective."

Realizing he had reached her limit, Watts smiled and gave her his card. "Please call me Maxx."

Stuffing the card in her pocket without looking at it, she quickly said, "Have a nice day, *detective*."

Her comment might have deterred Watts, had she not smiled so coyly. As he headed home along the riverbank, he found himself thinking more about her than the case. Woods still seemed to fall into the "look, but don't touch" category, but she was more complex than that. Perhaps she had dated cops and been burned. Maybe that's why she transferred to Fort Worth. In any event, he was probably better off leaving her alone. As much as he loved women, relationships on any romantic level quickly got complicated.

He paused at the riverbank, skipping stones while pondering the thought. When he finished, he wiped his hands on his pants, but couldn't leave without first doing a mental survey of the area. In the distance, downtown Fort Worth choked in the tinted sunlight. Tires whined from the nearby interstate. The kiddy train had made its last run. Cars streamed from the parking lot. Thankfully, most park visitors were unaware anything had happened the night before. For them, today had been great. But the Chinese victims hung on Watts' mind more than CC Coulter. Had Lee and Chow feared darkness like everyone else, they might still be alive.

The cold steel of Watts' snub-nosed revolver pressed into his back as he started to jog. Hawaiian shirts work well for concealing weapons, but carrying a gun reminded him he was never off duty. The world was full of crazy people, and he was no match for a group of them intent on slicing someone in a flowered shirt. Besides, Daisy reminded him more than once that he had no business being there. She was the second person to tell him that Forest Park wasn't his concern. But he was a detective, and detectives tend to be hard headed. Tomorrow, he would go in early to review all pertinent case information. Hopefully his partner was enjoying his evening out with his family. In a very small way, Watts still envied him for that.

FIFTEEN

When Watts' alarm went off at six AM, it was a balmy eighty-two degrees outside, and the air smelled different. Looking outside, he saw the black crickets were back. He never heard a good scientific explanation for this invasion, but they were everywhere; in sewers, sidewalks, trees, and walls. In a few days they would die, leaving a gagging stench powerful enough to mask the wildfire smoke. On his way to his truck, he crunched some of them, the sound as chilling as a winter breeze. With luck, a thunderstorm would come and wash them away, but he would probably solve this case before he ever saw rain.

He arrived at 350 an hour early to see what he could learn. Last night he had called Skip Parsons, pleading to let him see his files. Parsons finally agreed to meet with him and looked over Watts' shoulder as he went through the material.

"The photos speak for themselves," Parsons said. "You'd think those Skinheads would have branded them, not cut them up."

"Why is that?"

"Because they'd carry their brand for life, and the Skinheads gain notoriety every time someone asks about them."

"Makes sense," Watts said, "but it's a moot point since they're dead."

Parsons' face soured. "Anyway, Lieutenant Ryder is hoping to sequester this so the media doesn't reward the assassins with television coverage. That's why he doesn't want you nosing around."

Watts nodded, intent on studying the photos. He flipped through the stack until he found one of Pao Lee.

Parsons seemed to be reading Watts' expression. "Well?" he said. "Is it the same guy?"

"Looks that way to me. Grab a chair, Skip. You might find this interesting."

Watts spent the next twenty minutes briefing Parsons on everything he knew about the Coulter case and his meeting at Forest Park with Daisy Woods. He also mentioned how Woods didn't like being in the middle and wouldn't tell him anything. Parsons gave no reaction, but did confirm that the black hair found in Coulter's office belonged to Pao Lee. He dismissed it, though, because Lee was an invited guest. Watts didn't like it that Parsons knew about the hair before he did. Then again, he was in the field all day.

"You need to scratch Pao Lee off your list," Parsons said. "I kept my word, and now you know as much as I do. Call me if you find any connections and I'll do the same for you."

"Thanks, Skip. I appreciate your coming in early, and please keep this to yourself. I don't want Ms. Woods thinking we've been discussing her."

"I understand."

* * * * *

Watts and Spartan met at the motor pool as they had previously agreed. Doing this avoided Lieutenant Ryder, and also gave them an earlier start. Noticing Spartan's neatly pressed suit and tie in a perfect Winsor, Watts said, "You're looking mighty spry this morning. What's the occasion? Did you get lucky last night?"

"Let's just say we had a good night and leave it at that. You ready to hit the road?"

"Sure," said Watts, sliding into the driver's seat. "You'd be proud of me, Blaine. Yesterday afternoon I went to Forest Park and ran into Daisy Woods, that cute lab tech you keep nudging me about. She's nice, but rather standoffish. I asked about the double murder and she wouldn't say much, so I called Skip Parsons and we met this morning. They confirmed Pao Lee was one of the Forest Park victims, and his hair matches the one found in CC's office."

"Well, that's an interesting twist, isn't it? Does Ryder know?"

"I assume so. Parsons said Ryder was trying to block the media to deny the White Supremacists any media coverage. The problem is all we have is a couple of witnesses claiming they saw two men with shaved heads speed from the park. Frankly, I'm as bothered about why these two Chinese men were walking in Forest Park after dark as I am about who did it."

"Offhand, I can think of two reasons," Spartan said. "Jetlag and ignorance. The last time I went overseas it took a week before my body adapted to the new schedule. And why shouldn't they be able to walk at night? They probably did it all the time in Hong Kong."

"Okay, so that tends to support the theory they were murdered because they're Chinese. I mean, Aryan White Supremacists don't like anyone outside their so-called Master Race."

After giving a skeptical nod, Spartan said, "So you're thinking that we have neo-Nazi Skinheads hanging out in the park who see two Chinese dudes walking along and decide to take them out because they're not white? I mean, stranger things have happened." He paused, waiting for a response. When Watts failed to say anything, he added, "Here's another take, Maxx. Lee and his buddy went to the park to sell something and the deal went bad."

Watts bit his lower lip when he drove over a pot hole. It stung, but he didn't taste blood. "That sounds plausible, but drug deaths don't usually result in swastikas carved into chests. In that regard, the neo-Nazi scenario fits pretty well. By the way, Skip and I aren't mentioning our meeting to Ryder since he told me to stay out of it, which means you also need to keep it quiet."

"That's fine with me," Spartan said. "So, how do you want to proceed? Are we still going to visit Mrs. Coulter this morning?"

"Absolutely, and if we can ever get in touch with Hank Azar, we'll see him, too."

"Then let's go. Whoever we don't see, we'll call. I want to wrap these interviews up."

"Me, too, Blaine."

Watts took the back roads to Kat Coulter's house. It was the fastest route this time of day, and this early in the morning, he couldn't imagine why she would be gone. It was often best to visit persons of interest unannounced because it caught them off guard. Of course, she would still have to agree to see them.

"Maxx? You okay?"

Watts blinked, surprised his partner was staring at him. "I'm fine," he said. "Why?"

"It's not like you to go this long without talking. Something eating you?"

"Yeah. I keep thinking about this crazy world we're passing on to our kids. Somewhere in this country, there'll be another homicide within the next thirty seconds. Even though Pao Lee is dead, we still need more information on him and his friend, and before you remind me that Shing Chow isn't part of our case, Lee's association with The Guillotine Press overrides that. I want to know how long those two had been in this country, and what their personal relationship was with each other. They both came from Hong Kong, and for all I know they're cousins. Anyway, that's what's going through my head."

"Are you sure you want me tagging along instead of doing research at the office?"

"Did you forget about yesterday's interviews? What a bunch of nuts. Harper and Buck were particularly scary. And what the hell was Harper doing with a loaded shotgun? There's no way I'm visiting any murder suspects by myself."

Spartan grinned, seemingly pleased. "Okay, you convinced me. "Now, fill me in on the details of this forensics technician. You say her name is Woods?"

Watts nodded. "As in Daisy Woods," he said, "But you already knew that, didn't you? Your face gave you away."

"Touché. But your face wouldn't be red if you weren't flirting with her. By the way, she doesn't date cops."

"You don't say."

"Yeah, I do. No ring, no fancy jewelry, no mention of anyone else. She's as lonely as the number one."

Watts smiled, recalling Woods' wavy auburn hair, sensual blue eyes, teasing poses, and occasional grin, and yes, he had noticed she wasn't wearing any rings. She was intriguing, but also annoying. And if she didn't date cops, then why ask her out? Then again, he had nothing to lose. "Who knows, Blaine? Maybe our paths will cross again."

Spartan tossed his hands in the air. "You know what? I'm really glad I'm married. Dating is way too complicated for me."

"Then keep your eyes on your wife."

SIXTEEN

Kat Coulter split her kitchen blinds the moment Watts parked in front of her house. Rather than get out, he and Spartan stared at the front door expecting her to open it. When that didn't happen, Watts stayed where he was. Not that Kat was the type to ambush them, but the woman who nailed him in the shoulder didn't seem a shooter either. Unlike uniformed officers, detectives don't normally wear body armor. The fact that everything seemed in order meant nothing because most ambushes happen when everything looks normal. While Watts yarned worst case scenarios, the front door opened. Kat Coulter stood in the entry in a pink robe.

The detectives quickly climbed out and approached her. Watts got within an arm's length, nodded politely, and avoided looking at her attire. "I apologize for not calling ahead," he said, "but we have a few more questions. We can wait in the car while you get dressed."

Kat tightened her robe and combed her fingers through her tousled hair. "Give me ten minutes," she said, and then closed the door.

Spartan scanned the area and then glanced at Watts. "You want me to watch the back?"

Watts shook his head. "She knew we were here, and if she wanted to run, she never would have opened the door. I told her we would wait in the car, so that's what we'll do. Remember, she has friends in high places. If we ruffle her feathers, she'll complain to Mayor Jordan and then we'll take it in the shorts from Ryder."

"I'm willing to bet her knowing the mayor has a lot to do with why Ryder's so anxious," Spartan said.

"Maybe, but so far we're still able to approach her and I don't want to mess that up." He paused to rub his neck, wishing he had applied sunscreen before going to the park yesterday afternoon. "Anyway, I'm glad you're here to back me up. Like I said, I don't like interviewing people alone—especially attractive women like Kat Coulter. Frankly, I'm more concerned about her accusing me of something than I am being shot. That's why I need you to watch my back."

"I'm here to help, Maxx." After saying that, Spartan watched the minutes click by. Five, then ten. At fifteen minutes, he voiced his concern. "Not to second guess you, but how much longer are you gonna give her?"

Watts rolled his head toward his partner. "Have you ever heard Brad Paisley's song, *Waitin' on a Woman*?"

"Of course I have, but it's been over fifteen minutes, and she said to give her ten. For all we know, she's slipped out the back door and is hiding at a neighbor's. What makes you so sure she's still in there?"

"Because running would make her an even bigger suspect."

"Maybe so, but her backyard is wide open and heavily forested. I'm telling you, Maxx, she could be long gone. What could possibly take her this long?"

"Blaine, Kat Coulter is the kind of woman who wants to look good, and from what I've seen, her looks are all she has left. She lives in a humble house, is newly widowed, and we showed up uninvited. We'll give her another—never mind, she's at the door."

Watts took a moment to straighten his tie and preen his hair. Even from thirty feet away, Kat looked spectacular. Her fifteen minute transformation included curls, makeup, and a slip-on form-fitting dress. He found himself attracted to her the same way he was to Daisy Woods. Of course, each had completely different styles, but they were both beautiful in their own way. He supposed this meant he needed a woman.

Kat held the front door open for them. "Sorry for the wait," she said. "I would have been ready if you had called ahead."

Watts considered her comment as he stepped inside. Her polite greeting was unexpected. "Again, I apologize for that," he said. "We appreciate your seeing us."

Spartan nodded as he entered her house. "Mrs. Coulter, I offer my sincere condolences during this most difficult time. I'm sorry to keep bothering you."

"It's okay," she said, closing the door. "And thank you for your concern. I'm sorry it's so dark in here. I'm still trying to adjust to life without CC. The only benefit is I can shut the blinds to cool the house. CC liked them open so he could watch the squirrels, birds, and deer in the yard. He was always aware of movement, even when he was writing. That's why this doesn't make sense. I've seen him deep in thought, and suddenly a squirrel would dart across the lawn. Almost instinctively, he would look up and watch it until it was gone. I can't understand how someone could sneak into his office without him yelling or fighting back."

Watts cleared his throat, thinking the same thing. The only way it would make sense is if CC Coulter knew his assassin. "Mrs. Coulter, is there anything you can tell us that might identify your husband's killer?"

She coughed, waving her hand like she was blowing smoke from her eyes. "I'm parched," she said. "Would either of you care for some iced tea or lemonade?"

More lemonade! Watts declined, but Spartan gladly accepted. Elbowing his partner after she disappeared in the kitchen, he said, "What's with you? We came to see book contracts, not drink lemonade."

Spartan shrugged as he looked around the living room. Her modern paintings were now dull shades of gray, and her chrome Ikea furniture barely shined. It was so dark, he checked to make sure he removed his sunglasses. No mistake. It was dreary inside. Watts looked disgusted so he said, "What's with you? She's thirsty, I'm thirsty, there's no reason to be rude."

Before Watts could counter, Kat was back carrying a tray that held three glasses and a pitcher. Smiling at Watts, she said, "Are you sure you don't want any, detective? I made it last night. My friend has a lemon tree and she dropped off a ton of them. CC loved lemonade, so I always kept it on hand."

Watts smiled back, thinking about what Spartan said. "In that case, I'll have a glass."

Kat's hair fell forward as she poured. Holding it back with her free hand, she finished the task and handed them each a glass. She took the last one, seated herself, and modestly tucked her dress under her thighs.

Spartan tasted his drink and held the glass up, admiring its clarity. "This is wonderful," he said. "Thank you."

Watts nodded his agreement. "Yes, it is, and thank you. Now getting back to business, we just learned that the black hair we found in your house matches Pao Lee's. I'm not sure if you're aware, but he and his friend were murdered shortly after your husband was killed. I'm trying to determine if these murders are linked."

She gave a horrified look and set her glass down. "Pao Lee is dead?"

"Yes. They were murdered in Forest Park."

"That's horrible! How?"

"We think it's a hate crime," Spartan said. "It's very unfortunate."

"That's an understatement," she said, staring blankly toward CC's office. It took a while before she focused on them again. "I'm sorry. What were you saying about hair?"

"The black hair we retrieved from your husband's office belongs to Pao Lee," Watts said. "I'd like to know if Pao ever went in there."

"Absolutely not. He never left the living room while he was here. He gave CC the paperweight, we sat and talked a while, and then he left. I'm sure I told you that."

"You probably did. But getting back to how we might identify your husband's killer, you said your husband noticed everything and should have fought back. How do you think he would have reacted if he saw Pao Lee enter his office?"

"I have no idea," she said, setting her glass aside. "But your eyes are telling me that's not what you wanted to hear, so rather than beat around the bush, are you here because you think I killed my husband?"

Watts hesitated. He wasn't ready to approach that one yet, especially with her political connections. "Mrs. Coulter, I assure you there is a significant difference between interviewing persons of interest and murder suspects." He paused to take a swig of juice, and then lowered his glass. "The truth is we don't have any suspects right now. Identifying Pao Lee's hair certainly raises eyebrows — particularly since he gave CC the Writer's Block. But we really came here to learn about The Guillotine Press contracts because your authors refuse to disclose theirs. We need your assistance to resolve this matter. We need to see those contracts."

Kat settled into her chair and took a long drink. She jiggled her glass until the ice moved and then finished what was left. "I'd gladly show you the contracts if I knew where they were, but since I've never had anything to do with them, I'm afraid I can't help you."

The detectives exchanged confused looks before gazing back at her. "I thought you managed the business," Spartan said. "Aren't you their agent?"

Raising her shoulders, she innocently said, "My primary job was to manage CC's career, screen queries and manuscripts, maintain CC's and The Guillotine Press' web sites, and sort his mail and messages. I never once sent any correspondence, helped build, or got involved in any of their book contracts. CC handled all of that. As far as promoting our authors, they have always been on their own. So if you insist on giving me a business title, it would have to be CC's personal secretary. He was very strict in keeping his contracts between him and his authors."

The detectives were unconvinced. Spartan leaned forward in his seat, looking for an explanation. "Forgive me, but I'm having a hard time believing you never saw a book contract. As I recall, you once said you found new authors for The Guillotine Press. If this is the case, how can you say you weren't involved in this aspect of the business?"

"I just said CC handled all the contracts. He called the prospective authors, discussed the details with them over the phone, mailed them their contracts, and once they were signed, sent their manuscripts to our editor.

The Guillotine Press was a labor of love, but not very profitable. Even so, CC and I never had any regrets."

Watts rubbed his hands together, thinking about that. The house felt cool when he came in, but now sweat was sliding down his back. Everything she said sounded so scripted, but he had to admit it was believable. He looked at his partner to see if he had a question for her. Spartan waved him off.

"I remember seeing a file cabinet in CC's office," Watts said. "Would you mind looking through it for the book contracts? Even a blank one would be helpful."

Suddenly her expression grew cold. Without saying anything, she rose from her chair casting an angry scowl as she gathered their empty glasses.

"As I said, I had nothing to do with the book contracts, and I refuse to disturb CC's files when memories are all I have left of him. We haven't had his memorial service yet, and I haven't set foot in his office since he died." She stopped herself and covered her eyes. "I'm sorry if I sound bitchy. I thought I could do this, but I was wrong." Her eyes were red when she grabbed the tray. She promptly ran into the kitchen to get away from them.

Her weeping made Watts feel small. It didn't help that his partner kept staring at him like he had kicked a puppy. On the rare occasions where he wasn't sure what to say, he studied the body language. The tray trembled in Kat's hands, and her sobbing stabbed his heart. But he was a detective, and he and Spartan came to gather facts. If she refused to produce the contracts, then he would turn this over to the District Attorney and demand she open CC's files. That's how he would handle it for the average citizen, but since Mayor Jordan could make life difficult for him and his boss if he did it that way, he decided on a softer approach. He leaned into his partner so she couldn't hear them.

"Since you seem to have a better rapport with her," Watts said, "see if she will check his computer. I haven't seen a typewriter anywhere, so the contracts are probably in there, too."

Spartan nodded. "I'll do my best. Maybe we'll get lucky."

SEVENTEEN

While Watts watched from the living room, Spartan approached Kat in the kitchen. He moved close enough for her to notice, but stayed far enough away not to intimidate her. Kat was busy rinsing their glasses and didn't seem to notice him so he coughed to announce himself. She heard him and looked his way.

"I'm sorry we upset you," he said to her. "We're only trying to solve this case."

She slowly turned around, pressed her back into the counter, and crossed her arms. "I want you to solve this case more than anything. It's so hard carrying on without CC. No kids, no pets, I feel so alone."

"Have you ever thought about adopting a dog? The shelters are full of pets looking for homes, and a dog might offer some protection."

Kat smiled faintly, staring at the refrigerator. "Thanks for the tip, but I'm allergic."

Spartan glanced toward the living room and then back at her. The faucet dripped when the swamp cooler kicked in. Watts sensed Spartan was struggling so he joined them in the kitchen. "Mrs. Coulter—" Watts said.

"Kat," she fired back. "Please call me Kat."

"Okay, sure. Here's the deal. We need to see a Guillotine Press contract so we can determine whether your husband's murder was a premeditated act. As we said, a blank contract would suffice without compromising anyone's integrity. We understand that you didn't run the business, but no business can survive without records, so if you don't wish to open the file cabinet, will you please access his computer so we can check his electronic files?"

She defiantly shook her head. "CC and I used separate computers, and we never exchanged passwords. He liked it this way because he was secretive about his writing. I only got to see things when he wanted a critique. It had nothing to do with author contracts."

Watts sighed. "Maybe it's not password protected. Can you at least give it a try?"

Her face lost its color, and her body tensed. "Detective, do you have any idea how distressing it would be for me to sit at the same desk where my husband's blood pooled?"

"If you prefer, we can talk in the living room while Detective Spartan gives it a shot."

She hesitated, but finally gave a nod. Spartan went into the office while she and Watts sat in the living room. She shuddered when his computer booted up.

"This is so hard," she said, staring toward the office. "Did I tell you I tried to seduce him that night?"

"You did, and I'm sorry it didn't work out."

"Me, too. I keep thinking he might be alive if I'd been successful."

"That's the glass half full. Half empty is whoever broke into your house may have killed both of you." Her look of horror made Watts instantly regret his words. "I'm very sorry," he said. "I should have been more sensitive. Are you okay?"

She buried her face in her hands, shaking her head, sniffling.

"Maxx," Spartan said from the office. "Would you come in here?"

When Watts got up, Kat followed suit. Spartan was staring at the computer screen as if something magical was about to happen. Watts found himself staring, too, wondering what secrets it held. The password key box was visible, but empty.

Watts leaned over his partner's shoulder. "Did you try 'Guillotine Press'?" he said.

Spartan typed it in, but the computer rejected it. He then varied the case settings and different versions of "Guillotine", but the results were the same. When he ran out of ideas, he glanced over his shoulder at Watts. "Got any more ideas?"

"Try typing Kat," Watts said, scratching his neck. When that failed, he vigorously scratched his head. "Well, I guess our only option is to take the computer downtown and let the geeks break in."

Kat's gaze hardened. "Nothing leaves this house without a warrant," she said. "CC's computer is as precious to me as my jewelry. His fingers polished those keys, and I'm not letting it out of my sight."

"But what if it holds the key to his murder?" said Spartan.

"I'm sure there are other clues," she said to him. "You need to look harder."

Watts stared at the locked file cabinet. "Let me guess. Your husband had the only key and you don't know where it is."

"Actually that's true, and I'm not mentally prepared to rummage through his desk to look for it. Call me superstitious, but until CC's murder is solved,

I don't believe his soul can move on. That's why I want to keep everything as it is. I hope you understand."

Watts stared at her for what seemed an eternity, during which time neither he nor Kat blinked. When he tilted his head toward the door, Spartan rose from the chair.

"Thank you for seeing us, Mrs. Coulter," Watts said. "Again, I apologize for not calling ahead. We'll be in touch."

Watts headed for the door, confident his partner would whisper his own apology. Spartan joined him in the car a few minutes later. Once the car was moving, Spartan struck up a conversation.

"You think she's lying about the password, don't you?" he said.

Watts nodded. "I also think she believes we won't be getting a warrant anytime soon. My concern is if their authors get wind of this, they might shred or delete their contracts figuring they're worthless now that Coulter is dead."

"Coulter may be dead, but the authors' books are still in print, and without their contracts, they won't have a day in court if they stop receiving their royalty checks." Spartan paused to adjust his coat that was riding up his back. "Maxx, she's a grieving widow who wants to protect what's left of her home. Somehow, we should be able to get whatever we need from one of the authors."

"Perhaps, but don't be swayed by her looks, Blaine. We learned that the hard way two years ago. Also remember that she is as suspect as anyone."

"I realize that, but she also never batted an eye when I said I was going to turn on CC's computer. That should count for something."

Watts shook his head. "It didn't bother her because it was password protected. And how convenient to say she didn't know where the file cabinet key was. You don't really buy this thing about CC's ghost not crossing over do you?"

Spartan pressed his head into the headrest, visibly frustrated. "I don't know about ghosts," he said, sounding rather agitated, "but I do consider myself a good judge of character, so rather than agree to disagree, let's press on with our interviews and see what we come up with."

"Fine with me."

Spartan rubbed his eyes again. His sneezing began the moment they passed a field of fresh-cut hay. He quickly switched the air conditioner vent to recycle and held a tissue to his nose. "Crap!"

Watts glanced over at him. "Still fighting those allergies, I take it?"

"Yeah, and I forgot to take my medicine. I'll be fine so long as you keep it on recycle."

"No sweat. Call Azar whenever you feel up to it. Sooner or later, we'll get through."

EIGHTEEN

Watts was eager to talk to Hank Azar, not so much as a suspect, but because lawyers are known for clinging to their documents. They can't help themselves. It's ingrained into their psyche from day one in law school. Unfortunately, Spartan got the same message when he called. "Mr. Azar is unavailable." How convenient. Since Azar was the only local author they hadn't spoken to, he steered the Crown Vic back to 350.

During the drive, Watts reflected on the persons of interest they had interviewed. So far, the Courtney Dridelle/Kat Coulter/CC Coulter love triangle still had the most merit. Watts always suspected CC was having an affair, but didn't know who it was with until Dridelle mentioned it. Then again, that made perfect sense since they both had something to gain from it. Considering the amount of planning that went into CC's murder, it couldn't have been random. It also seemed unimaginable that a small time publisher like CC Coulter could sign an accomplished author like Dridelle. If Dridelle used CC for "research", as she coined it, then she and CC had taken equal advantage of each other. But where did that leave Kat? Watts had considered raising this issue with her today, but instead decided to include it in his request to confiscate CC's files and computer. Having a warrant would nullify the password.

He considered her testimony about how her husband preferred leaving the shades open and never missed anything that moved, but that story didn't jibe with the break-in. She also admitted that her husband should have fought back against his attacker, so the only logical explanation for him not doing so was it was someone he knew. That took him back to Kat because she knew about his affair, may have wanted vengeance, and she was the only person CC wouldn't strike. To him, that theory made more sense than Pao Lee coming back to the house.

When they arrived at 350, Watts and Spartan went directly to Lieutenant Ryder's office to brief him on their progress. Ryder listened, seemingly welcoming their thoughts. He was unusually accommodating when Watts asked him to forward his warrant request to the DA. In fact, the entire meeting seemed canned, as though Ryder knew their every move. Regardless,

Watts felt confident they would soon return to Kat's to pick up the files and computer. But after giving their best pitch, Ryder floored them by denying their request.

Watts' jaw dropped. "What do you mean denied?" he said. "Kat Coulter had motive, was home at the time, and she's withholding evidence. What more do you want?"

Ryder calmly leaned back in his chair and propped his foot on an open drawer. Smiling, he said, "I'm not sure you understand how well Mrs. Coulter and Mayor Jordan know each other."

"What are you saying? That they're sleeping together?"

The lieutenant's foot thumped when it hit the floor, and his smile was long gone. Suddenly, he was leaning over the desk like he was ready to kill something. "Maxx, I warned you not to go down that path, but you did it anyway. Not long ago, I got a phone call from the mayor. An inquiry as he put it. He wanted to know how the case was proceeding. Imagine that, the mayor asking about an unknown publisher's death. Of course, he never specifically mentioned Kat Coulter's name, but from the way he spoke I got the impression she called him soon after you left her place."

Spartan, who usually remained silent in situations like this, made an exception today. "So, what are we supposed to do, lieutenant? Ignore the fact that her late husband's computer may hold damning evidence? Should we wait until she's deleted everything or worse, destroy the hard drive? I'm sorry, sir, but I'm with Maxx on this one."

Ryder snorted as he tore off his glasses. He stared at them for a long moment before sliding a receipt over for them to look at. "You guys might find this interesting," he said.

Spartan picked it up, holding it so Watts could also read it. Ryder was smiling as Watts read the trophy shop receipt twice.

"Okay," Watts said, "So we have proof that Pao Lee commissioned the Writer's Block. So what? Mrs. Coulter already stated that Lee gave it to her husband at her house."

"That's right, and now Lee's dead," Ryder said, gritting his teeth. "By the way, I need that receipt back so I can return it to its proper place."

"And what place is that?" Spartan said.

"Never mind. In fact, forget I even showed it to you."

Watts raised a brow, glaring at his boss. "That receipt links Lee's murder to our case. Shouldn't we share it with Skip Parsons?"

Leaning back in his chair again, Ryder said, "Skip already knows."

Watts bowed his head, trying to make sense of it. To him, since these murders appeared linked, they should form a task force to see if they had a serial killer on the loose. Instead, the mayor was keeping Ryder under his thumb. *What could the mayor possibly have on Ryder?*

"How about this scenario?" Watts finally said, knowingly pushing his luck. "Suppose Mayor Jordan ordered the hit on Pao Lee after Lee killed CC? That way the mayor's lover gets the insurance money and the murder trail ends."

Ryder burst into an insulting laugh. When he finished, he gazed back with wicked eyes. "Maxx, you and your partner need to stop reading those murder mysteries and start digging up some facts. All that fiction is corrupting your investigative abilities."

"Actually, sir, I believe Maxx has a valid point," Spartan said. "I'm not prepared to accuse anyone of anything, but what if the mayor is involved in these murders? It's not hard for a man in his position to drop a hint and suddenly someone ends up dead. We all know this has happened at the highest levels of government, and what better way to cover it up than blaming a hate group? Of course, if this was an intentional hit on Lee, then Shing Chow was simply in the wrong place when it happened."

Ryder's grin widened as he reorganized his desk. "You guys sound so desperate, I actually feel sorry for you."

"Fine," Watts said. "Don't believe us. I admit it's a long shot, but remember, we're paid to think outside the box. So, what if Lee and Chow's murders were intended to cover up CC Coulter's? All that receipt you showed us proves is that Lee created the Writer's Block. So far, we cannot link him to the murder scene because whoever struck CC with the paperweight wiped it clean before placing it back on the desk. Those are the facts, lieutenant. You can't ignore them."

This time Ryder laughed so hard he nearly tipped his chair over. With a red face, he straightened himself, still wearing a grin. "Did you two come from Hollywood?" he said. "That has to be the most preposterous theory I've ever heard. Are you really accusing two of the most highly respected members of our community of conspiring to commit murder? Olyn Jordan has been our mayor for over seven years, and he's known the Coulters ever since they moved here. Kat has worked his social affairs for much of that time, and helps raise his campaign funds."

"Yeah, and maybe her social affairs are raising other things, too," said Spartan.

"Knock it off," Ryder said, his grin lost again. "Had I known that showing you this receipt would cause such lunacy, I never would have passed it on. I only presented it because it gave your case an interesting twist. Whatever connection Pao Lee had with his Writer's Block died with him. I suggest you let it go so you can find the real killer."

Watts leaned on his boss' desk, staring him in the face. "Get us those book contracts and we'll find the killer."

"Forget it, Maxx. It's not gonna happen." Ryder flicked his wrist to check his watch, then glanced at them. "The day is flying by, gentlemen. I suggest you get moving."

Watts tucked his hands into his pocket to prevent sending gestures on his way out. Spartan quickly followed. Once they were a safe distance away, Spartan nudged his partner.

"Maxx, you do realize that one day Ryder's gonna bust you for being so belligerent."

"Screw him," Watts said. "But thanks for backing me up in there. We presented a theory and he didn't buy it. Frankly, after hearing it out loud, I'm not sure I'd buy it either. What bothers me is how quickly he dismissed it."

Spartan frowned. "Don't tell me you think Ryder's involved?"

"Not involved, Blaine. Just blind."

That helped Spartan relax. "Then let's find a reason for him to get new glasses."

Smiling, rested his arm on his partner's shoulder, Watts said, "Now you're talking."

After refilling their coffee mugs, they returned to the murder board. At the bottom left corner of the whiteboard were all The Guillotine Press authors names. Check marks were placed beside those they had already spoken to. The rest they hoped to reach today, Mick Taggart being the exception. Because Hank Azar was the most elusive, they made him their top priority.

Spartan took a sip from his mug and set it aside. His coffee was cold, but it didn't matter. He didn't want it anyway. "Earlier we had talked about doing a conference call with Azar," he said. "Is this a good time to call him?"

"May as well. I don't have any messages that indicate the bastard ever called us back. I hate it when people blow us off. Especially defense attorneys. Go ahead and call, but don't use the speaker. I'll pick up if you're successful."

Watts sorted through his desk drawer while his partner dialed. He found the staple remover he had been looking for, but not his favorite pen. There was the pack of gum he slid in there five months ago. He even found a photo of an old girlfriend from three years ago. Nice looking lady, but overbearing. He promptly ripped it up and tossed it in the trash. Overhearing his partner, it seemed Spartan's conversation ended as quickly as that relationship.

Calmly looking at his partner, he said, "Let me guess. Hank Azar is unavailable."

"Man, you must be psychic."

"How did you know? Let's move on to the out-of-state authors."

Spartan went down the list. "Shall we start with Lance Ballard?" he said.

Watts shrugged. "Ballard's as good as anyone, and ranchers can usually be found."

Spartan nodded at Watts when the call went through. Mrs. Ballard answered, sounding sweet and confident, in a fifty-something way. She had no problem talking to them, and even volunteered how, after breaking bones riding bulls and raising cattle, her husband was quite content letting tourists work their ranch for them.

"Nowadays, urban cowboys and cowgirls from all over the world flock to our ranch so they can act like Billy Crystal in *City Slickers*," she said. "Keeping these cattle moving makes them too lean for meat, but we still get a nice price for their calves. Turning this place into a dude ranch was the best decision we ever made."

"Sounds nice," Spartan said. "Maybe when my kids get older we'll give it a try."

Watts' raised thumb signaled his approval. It was a nice touch, keeping the wife appeased before interrogating her husband. Then again, Spartan might actually mean it.

"Oh, here's Lance now," Mrs. Ballard said.

Without introducing himself, Lance Ballard came on sounding a lot like Sam Elliott. Gruff, deep voice, and irritated as though he stepped in manure and tracked it through the house. "I take it this concerns CC's murder," he said.

"That's correct," Spartan said, seeing where Ballard would take them.

"Well, I should've kicked CC's butt a long time ago for being an ass, but he didn't deserve to die. Hell, no one deserves to die that way."

Spartan hesitated, and then said, "What way is that?"

"Don't play me for a fool, detective. All of us Guillotine Press authors stay in touch. I know all about the paper wad and the Writer's Block. To put it bluntly, CC was a lying, two-faced sonuvabitch. Out here, a man's word is everything, but Mr. New York City was nothin' like that. He made promises he couldn't keep. I figured it must have caught up with him. You know—what goes around comes around."

Spartan wasn't going to debate that. He never knew the vic, but from all he'd heard, CC Coulter sounded like a rat. "Mr. Ballard, can you provide some specifics to fill in some blanks? For starters, I'm not sure I understand why you're so upset with a dead man."

"Ah, hell, I guess CC wasn't all that bad," he said, his voice calmer now. "He just struck me the wrong way. It was probably stupid of me to think that a city slicker like him would share my honor code. Anyway, what exactly do you want from me? Surely there's nothin' in my novel that interests you, and since I haven't been to Texas in over five years, I couldn't have killed him. By the way, plenty of folks on the ranch can back me up on that. Say the word and I'll give you their names."

Watts nodded his approval to Spartan. Ballard sounded agitated, but since he was talking, Watts saw no value in joining the conversation. Sometimes two detectives asking questions adds confusion more than help.

"Names would be great," Spartan politely said. "Sir, you mentioned you should have kicked Mr. Coulter's ass a long time ago. Why is that? Did he take something from you? Withhold royalties?"

"Detective, my daddy always said not to speak until my brain caught up with my mouth, and that's always proven to be good advice. Right now I've got a sick cow that needs tending and that's where my brain's at so if you got more questions, you'll have to ask my wife or call back later."

"Sir, before you go, can you or your wife fax us a copy of your Guillotine Press contract?"

"Not a chance. I burned that sonuvabitch two years ago along with everything else that had Coulter's name on it. He got me nowhere, and burning 'em was a way to close that chapter. I might regret it one day, but it was sure great watching 'em go up in smoke."

"I see. Well, thanks for your time, and good luck with your cow."

"Thank you kindly. Good day."

Spartan hung up staring at Watts who was smugly leaning back in his chair. "Well, you heard the man," he said. "What do you think?"

Hands locked behind his head, Watts rocked his chair. "I think it's bull. Lance Ballard's no simpleton, and he knows we're looking at him. I'm sure he's right about not being anywhere near Texas, but he's still hiding his contract. If we can somehow get him to testify, his word would be as good as any contract, but for now, we'll let him stew over this. It's clear that he wants to discuss Coulter because he's fuming inside, but he's not our killer. Keep the faith, pal—sooner or later we'll find the guilty bastard."

"Or bitch."

Watts smiled. "Okay, so we don't discriminate, let's say we'll get whoever's responsible and leave it at that."

"Fair enough," Spartan said.

Watts rechecked their interview list. "Jolene Lundgren's next. You need her number?"

"No, I'm just wondering how to start the conversation so we get better results. Maybe I should say something about her book, or maybe mention the weather."

Watts dropped his feet and leaned on the desk. "This is police business, Blaine. Not a dating service. Are you treating her different than Ballard because she's a woman?"

Spartan reached over his shoulder and scratched his back. As soon as he did that, he felt another itch on his ribs. Watts was waiting so he put his arms down. It took him a second to remember what Watts said, and then it came to him. "It has nothing to do with Lundgren being a woman. It's because she writes slasher books. I mean, what woman writes crap like *Butcher's Cut*?"

"One who wants to make money?" said Watts. He grinned as an image came to mind.

Spartan gave a quizzical look. "What's so funny?"

"I was just thinking that if Jolene Lundgren and Lance Ballard got together, she could butcher the beef and he'd grill 'em." Watts paused and said, "It seemed funnier before I said it out loud."

"I can't speak for Ballard, but I sure as hell wouldn't trust Jolene Lundgren with my rump."

"Very funny. Now make the call."

NINETEEN

Spartan punched in Jolene Lundgren's number, but wasn't looking forward to talking to her. It had nothing to do with her being a woman, but rather her gory descriptions in *Butcher's Cut*. In fact, he barely finished her first chapter because it was so gross. Page after page of a murderous woman slashing her victims wasn't his idea of entertainment, especially since his job was to investigate bloody crime scenes. Troubled by this, he hung up before his call went through.

"It's busy," he lied. "I'll try again later."

Watts glowered. "I'm not deaf, Blaine. Her phone never rang."

"Look at her photo, Maxx. Deep-set lifeless eyes, long gray-streaked hair, wrinkled skin, wearing a scowl. She's one scary woman. Why would Coulter use this photo on her book? For that matter, why would any respectable publisher print such rubbish?

One look at the book jacket and Watts had to agree with his partner. Jolene Lundgren was ugly enough to make a grizzly bear run. But looks were irrelevant when it came to murder. Besides, Lundgren wasn't even in the same state. Smiling at his partner, he said, "Are you afraid that she'll cast a spell through the phone?"

Spartan stalled. Finally, he said, "This time let's use the speaker phone so she knows we're both on the line."

Watts raised his hands. "If that's what it takes to get you to call her, so be it. Now dial."

After four rings, a gravely-voiced woman answered and Spartan cringed. He couldn't imagine anyone waking up to that voice. Watts motioned for him to say something before she hung up. Rolling his eyes, Spartan said, "Is this Ms. Lundgren?"

"It is, and you'd better talk fast or I'll be hanging up. I don't accept phone solicitations."

"Ma'am, this is Detective Spartan, and my partner Detective Watts. We're with the Fort Worth Police, and—"

"Congratulations," she said, cutting him off. "That gives you two minutes."

"Ms. Lundgren, we're investigating CC Coulter's death, and—"

She sucked in a breath. "Say what? CC's dead? How? When?"

Watts looked at his partner, sensing real hurt in her voice. After Ballard's remark, he assumed that everyone knew. But Lundgren sounded genuine because there was no hesitation in her reaction. Even the best actors can't fake that.

"This is Detective Watts, and I'm sorry to say that Mr. Coulter died in his office a few days ago. He took a violent blow to the head, and then suffocated on an object in his throat."

"I can't believe he's dead," she said, her voice trailing off. "At least he died in his office instead of some skank's bed."

Watts' brows shot up. "Can you expand on that?" he said.

"Oh, please. Everyone knew CC slept around. He flaunted it at book fairs, but other than being unfaithful, he was a true gentleman, and writing was his passion. I'm glad he died doing what he loved."

Watts' face sank. Her comment reaffirmed what he already suspected about CC Coulter. She was the second woman to share this insight.

"Ms. Lundgren, did Mr. Coulter flirt with you?" Spartan said.

Her smoker's laugh ended with a lengthy hack. "Sweetheart, you obviously haven't seen my picture," she said. "I raise pigs in Eaton, Colorado because pigs and the people here don't give a damn about how I look. I treat my pigs well, and when I send them off to slaughter, I never fret about eating their chops. Come to think of it, the only difference between how I treat pigs and how CC treated women is I'm more honest about their temporary arrangement."

"So, you're saying that CC Coulter was a pig?" Watts said.

"Oh, you're so witty. Give yourself a pat on the back. I bet you've been waiting to use that line ever since I mentioned pigs. Do you do stand-up in your spare time?"

Spartan interrupted. "Ms. Lundgren, what my partner's trying to ask is if everyone knew CC Coulter slept around, wouldn't that be a good murder motive?"

"Beats me," she said. "I wasn't his wife or his keeper, but if I was, I would have castrated the sonofabitch like I do my pigs."

Watts wrinkled his face, imagining that. When the thought passed, he placed his hands on the desk and leaned into the phone. "Ms. Lundgren, since you mentioned CC's wife, do you happen to know if she slept around, too?"

"How should I know?" she said, sounding insulted. "I never met the woman."

"I see. From the way you were talking, I assumed that—"

"Never assume, detective. I'd have thought you knew that by now. I knew CC was married and that he cheated on his wife, but that's all. End of story, as we say."

"Let's move on," Spartan said. "You sounded hurt when we told you CC died. What, exactly, was your affiliation with him?"

"He was my publisher, for Christ's sake. He gave me a break when no one else would. I considered him a friend, and I'd like to think the feeling was mutual."

Watts stared at his partner, still trying to get a sense of her. Lundgren's voice turned bitter with Spartan's question. CC Coulter may have been her friend, but there was no way they were ever intimate. But that didn't mean she didn't fantasize about him. Did she resent his wandering off with other woman while she stayed behind at their signing table? Did slaughtering pigs inspire her bloodthirsty protagonist? Watts had Spartan take over so he could contemplate these thoughts.

"Ms. Lundgren, you mentioned that Mr. Coulter gave you a break when no one else would. What kind of break are you referring to?"

"As I said, he published my book when no one else would. I sent queries to everyone and got a ton of rejections. Of course, a lot of them never replied at all. But CC not only replied, he did so with a personal phone call saying my book showed promise. He told me that my genre is dominated by a couple of authors, but there is always room for more. Then he made me an offer, which I accepted, and the rest is history."

"That's great," Spartan said. "How have your sales been?"

"Hell, I don't know. I haven't seen any royalties, if that's what you mean."

Another laugh led to her choking. Her throat seemed to clear after a few hacks. Then it sounded like she spit into a nearby spittoon. It wasn't a pretty picture.

"Sorry about that," she said. "Anyway, I write to vent. Of course, it also feels great seeing my book in print."

"I'm sure," Spartan said, looking to Watts for help.

"So your book sales don't concern you?" Watts said.

"Didn't you hear that I'm a pig farmer? Am I going too fast for you, sonny boy?"

Watts grinned. *No wonder she's single.* "Ma'am, my point is that publishers expect their clients to be motivated and generate book sales. In other words, while The Guillotine Press may have published your book, they still expected you to push it. Am I right?"

"Maybe, but CC never pressured me into anything. I always figured that if my books sell, they sell. If they don't, I'd feed 'em to the pigs."

Since Lundgren was relating better to Spartan, Watts pointed so he asked the next question. "Ms. Lundgren," Spartan said, "What can you tell us about your book's first run? In other words, how many books were published?"

"Don't insult me, detective. I know what a run is, and it was fifteen hundred."

"Fifteen hundred books?" Watts said, stepping in. "That's a lot of books. How many have been sold?"

"Oh, it's you again," she said, harshly. "Didn't I just say I had no idea? You know, re-phrasing or repeating your questions won't change my answers. Not that it matters because your time's up. I have work to do, and you ran way over your two minutes."

"A final question?" Spartan said. "Will you fax us a copy of your book contract?"

"Nope."

"Is it because you don't have a fax machine?"

"What's with you guys? Not only do I have a fax machine, I also have a computer, electricity, running water, even indoor plumbing. Yessir, us pig farmers have come a long way since the Dust Bowl."

"Yes, ma'am. But why can't you send us a copy? Is there a problem locating it?"

"You know, I'm having a real hard time figuring out which one of you is the good cop and which one's bad. Then again, I'm just a—"

"Pig farmer," Spartan said, "and we still need a copy of your contract. We don't care whether you fax it, mail it, or FedEx it, so long as we get it."

"Once again, you're not hearing what I'm saying. Detectives, I'm not sending you shit. I hope that's clear enough for you. Good luck with it. I've got to go."

When the line went dead, the office seemed unusually quiet, but like cicada bugs, the background noise quickly resumed. Spartan stood and angrily clapped his hands in the air. "The show's over, folks. If anyone wants to know the particulars of that conversation, see me now. Otherwise, shut your traps."

Watts grinned when the office staff responded with giggles and snickers. "It's no big deal," he said to Spartan. "Lundgren's annoying. That's all there is to it."

Spartan tilted his head back. "Agreed, but what about the contract?"

"Lundgren's right, you don't get it. I keep telling you we're building this case one piece at a time. By the same token, we're desperately trying to keep it from falling apart. So, intentional or not, Ballard and Lundgren have both given us more insight into CC Coulter's life than we ever had before, and since I recorded their conversations, it's not hearsay. Right now, we probably have enough to ask for a warrant for the contract, but the timing's not right. Don't worry, though. We're fine so long as we keep making progress." He smiled and playfully slapped Spartan's shoulder. "Hang in there, partner. We're doing okay."

"Yeah, right."

Watts showed his disappointment. "Okay, what's bugging you?"

Spartan crossly looked around. "Let's take a walk. Outside. Now."

"You got it."

Spartan didn't say a word at first. The streets were alive with diesel trucks idling, high-pitched lawn blowers, hissing bus doors, and horns. Tires screeched, someone yelled, and then it was silent, not unlike the cicadas in the trees. A cotton cloud dotted a skyscraper while the red sun reminded them fall was still two months away.

"It's a bit toasty and hazy, but an otherwise beautiful day," Watts said, making small talk. Spartan said nothing. Two blocks later, Watts was getting antsy. "Okay, Blaine, now you're wasting my time, so either talk or I'm going back inside."

"Fine," he said, stopping to face him. "Have you heard from Lieutenant Ryder?"

His question confused Watts. "You're forgetting I avoid him like the plague. Why?"

"Don't you find it odd he's not bugging us?" Spartan said, looking paranoid.

"Not really, because he knows we're working the case and he's busy with other things."

Watts noticed an attractive woman approaching from the opposite direction. To re-train Spartan's roaming eyes, he quickly moved to block his partner's view. If Spartan objected, he didn't show it. "Anyway," he continued, "Don't worry about the boss. As far as I'm concerned, the less I see of him, the happier I am."

"But do you trust him?"

"Of course I trust him. What's with you?"

Spartan stared at the sidewalk as he walked. "I don't get it, Maxx. One moment, Ryder is all over us about making progress, and then all of a sudden he drops out of sight. He also acts weird whenever we mention the mayor. It's like he's been muzzled."

Upon hearing that, Watts pivoted on his heel and pointed his body toward

350. A patrol car pulling out of the lot waited for them to pass in front of him. Watts waved his thanks, and the officer merged onto the street.

Spartan hurried to catch up. "Aren't you going to respond?"

"Blaine, I don't have time to waste worrying about Mayor OJ or Lieutenant Ryder. I assure you Ryder will let us know if he has a problem with us. He always does. Right now, we need to focus on our case."

"I agree, but how do you propose we get a publishing contract when no one's cooperating? It has to be the missing link. Why else would everyone be so protective?"

"Beats me, but let's go inside where it's cooler. We still need to call Ben Striker in LA."

"Hank Azar, too. That SOB still hasn't called us back."

"Thanks for reminding me."

TWENTY

With Spartan sitting across from him, Watts called Attorney Hank Azar's office as soon as he returned to his desk. Oddly, he got a busy signal when it should have gone to voice mail. Not that he expected anything spectacular from the lawyer, but Watts needed to speak to him to clear his name. After redialing two more times, he finally reached Azar's secretary, Midge McFarland.

"Ms. McFarland, I need to speak to your boss," he said. "Tell him if he can't take my calls, we can meet in person wherever he chooses."

McFarland sighed an apology. "Detective Watts, at the risk of sounding like a broken record, may I have Mr. Azar call you back? He honestly isn't available right now."

"Very well, but please pass this on. Either Mr. Azar returns my call within the next two hours, or I'll get a subpoena. He, of all people, should know that it's easier cooperating with the law than bucking it."

"Yes, sir. May I place you on hold?"

"Certainly." Watts winked at his partner and covered the phone. "I bet she's in there talking to him right now," he said. He raised his hand when she came back on the line.

"Detective Watts, if you can hold for a moment, I see Mr. Azar coming down the hall."

"Sure, I'll hold." Grinning at his partner, Watts said, "What a crock."

"Maybe, but at least he's going to talk to us."

Watts nodded, shushing him again.

"This is Hank Azar."

The author/attorney sounded exactly how Watts expected he would. Since Azar introduced himself with an aura of self-importance, the detective decided to do the same. "Sir, this is Detective Watts, Fort Worth Police Homicide Division. I must say that you're an exceptionally difficult man to reach."

"Time is money, detective. What's on your mind?"

Watts leaned back in his chair, stretching his legs to get a foot up on the lawyer. Reviewing his notes with pen in hand, he said, "Mr. Azar, you are one of the last Guillotine Press authors we needed to speak to. We're both busy, so we can either do this over the phone or meet somewhere, your choice."

"Aren't we talking now?"

Rule number one, never debate a lawyer. Rule number two, if you debate a lawyer, you will lose. Watts couldn't remember who told him that when he got promoted, but it was true. Funny that it never applied until now. "I'll make this short," he said. "I need a copy of your author contract so I can compare it with the others."

"I see. And what do you expect to find, detective? In my contract, that is."

"I'm not sure. I was hoping you could enlighten me."

Azar gave a hearty laugh. "I'm sorry, detective, but you're only allowed one bluff per phone call. If you're truly interested in solving Mr. Coulter's murder, then I suggest you find the murderer. I'm quite sure that any judge will rule that whatever's in my contract is of no consequence to your case."

"Don't be so sure. You know as well as I do that any and all evidence is scrutinized to either convict or free the accused, and in this case, The Guillotine Press contracts are part of that evidence. Unfortunately, yours is still outstanding."

"As are the rest of them," Azar quickly said. "Come on, detective, you know I'm right. Courtney Dridelle and Arlene Buck called me two days ago. Then Luke Harper called. By the way, he says you're an ass. His words, not mine. Lance Ballard also called. Get the picture? So, what's this all about? You're wasting my time, and as you know—"

"Time is money," Watts said along with him. To quicken the pace, he said the first thing that came to mind. "Mr. Azar, when we first began talking, I never mentioned anything about Mr. Coulter's murder and yet you brought it up, claiming your contract has no bearing. Why would you say that before I ask?"

"I think you've been watching too many cop shows, detective. I assure you I have nothing to hide, but if I did, do you really think I'd admit to it during a recorded conversation? And yes, I'm sure you're recording this." He paused, waiting for a response. "Come on, detective. If you deny it, then it's not admissible in court."

"Yes, Mr. Azar, you are on a recorded line."

"I knew it! I'm having so much fun, I almost wish we could have lunch together."

Picturing Azar's sarcastic glee, Watts squeezed the phone wishing it was the lawyer's neck. "There's still time."

"Not really. After all—well, you know the line."

Watts propped his head in his hand and read over his notes. "Before you sign off, I have a few questions. Did you see or have any communication with your publisher, CC Coulter, at any time within two months of his murder?"

"No."

"Do you know of anyone, particularly your fellow Guillotine Press authors, who wanted to see Mr. Coulter dead?"

"Again, no, although Lance Ballard can't stand him."

"I got that impression," said Watts. "Did The Guillotine Press owe you any royalties?"

"I think you mean, does."

Watts squeezed the phone harder. "Forgive my ignorance. Do they owe you royalties?"

"I can't say."

"You can't say, or you won't?"

"I mean I don't know. You see, I have no idea how many of my books have sold. I received a partial check after the first run and none for my second. They did the second run two years ago, but I only get a royalty check when the amount exceeds three hundred dollars. Considering the profit margin, that means I have to sell about three hundred books to see another payment. So how close am I? Beats me, and I have no way of finding out. It's like Catch-22. I call the distributor and the distributor says they can't tell me because I'm not the publisher. So I call CC and he says he can't get the information from the distributor. All of us Guillotine Press authors are in the dark with no way to get information. We get no answers, no checks, and no accountability. Only speculation. And I'd be willing to bet that Kat Coulter claims ignorance. I had no idea the publishing business was so shady. The business aspect of book writing takes all the fun away."

"Now, let me get this straight. To get paid, you need to sell three hundred books?"

"That's correct, sir."

"That's a lot of books for an unknown author."

"Tell me about it. Thankfully I don't write books for a living because trade paperbacks like mine pay about a buck apiece. Mass market paperbacks pay between twenty-five and fifty cents. This means that nearly everyone makes money on book sales except the authors. Seems criminal, doesn't it?"

"I imagine the same holds true for artists."

Azar sighed. "I suppose, but what amazes me most about this business is the harder I work at it, the harder other authors work to keep me down. I mean, how can my book possibly threaten anyone? What are they afraid of?" He paused and then said, "Honestly, detective, I don't know how anyone can afford to write full time, but my hat's off to those that do. From where I stand, it's clear that unless you get a break like Dan Brown did from pissing off the Catholic Church, you're screwed."

Watts nodded, doodling. "It doesn't sound like The Guillotine Press was well managed."

Azar laughed. "Now, there's an understatement."

The detective unexpectedly found himself empathizing with the lawyer. Was Hank Azar duped by Coulter, or did his ego drive him to The Guillotine Press to get his name in print? While pondering that, Jolene Lundgren's comments came to mind. Clearly, she had a different perspective about her book. She could care less whether she sold one copy, or ten thousand.

"Mr. Azar, what kind of expenses did you incur from publishing your book? In other words, how much did it personally cost you?"

"I know what incur means, but I don't know the amount. It seems my expenses are endless. I've never seen a business where everyone benefits except the creator. I'll spend thousands on a book tour and feel lucky if I bring in a few hundred. And when you factor in the cost of advertising and publicists, I don't even come close to breaking even."

"What about your advance? Didn't that cover your expenses?"

Azar laughed again. "Once more, you've been deluded. The days of large advances are gone. Nowadays with e-books and self-publishing, anyone can get published, and that's completely changed the business. For authors who don't want to invest their own money, there are on-line venues that will e-publish their work for free. Of course, they don't earn much in royalties that way, but for people who want to stroke their egos, posting on line is great because their names are all over the Internet."

"I see."

"But the biggest problem as a small press author is you get very little respect from book stores, reviewers, and even your fellow authors. Part of that is because some small presses aren't as discriminating as they should be. I'd have to say CC fell into that category. Of course, celebrities will always get published by the big houses because of their name recognition, and most of it's pure crap." He paused to clear his throat. "My point is that no matter how serious you are or how good your writing is, the book business stinks unless you're one of the top ten authors, and since fiction only makes up about fifteen percent of all the books published, big publishers aren't taking risks on unknown authors. That's why I signed with The Guillotine Press, detective. It was a gamble that has yet to pay off, but it was worth a shot. Of course now that CC's gone, I doubt it will stay in business."

Watts gave his pencil a rest. "You don't think Kat Coulter will continue running it?"

"Well, I haven't seen any correspondence saying that's her intention."

Thinking how much time Azar could save by saying "no", Watts said, "So, you think Mrs. Coulter will close up shop and sell off her business assets?"

"Assets?" he said with a laugh. "What assets? Unsold books are liabilities, not assets, and since the distributor's warehouse is stocked full of 'em, she probably owes for storage. I suspect she also owes money to their Kansas graphic designer, their San Francisco editor, and their Canadian printer. Of course, I don't know this for certain because I'm not privy to that information, but my guess is The Guillotine Press has run its well dry, screwing all of its authors."

"So, The Guillotine Press only exists on paper?"

"Like I said, I don't know that for sure, but I do know that CC operated from his house and used a rented downtown mailbox to make his business appear larger than it is. Among other things, he was an illusionist. To someone like him, image is everything."

"Like a courtroom lawyer?"

"Precisely," Azar said, laughing again.

Figuring Azar had given his all, Watts thanked him for his time. He sounded like a jolly fellow. Too bad they couldn't talk over lunch. In closing, he said, "You do know that I'd still like to see your contract."

"I'm sure of that, detective. Good day."

TWENTY ONE

Watts cradled the phone, exchanging confused glances with his partner who had monitored Azar's conversation. On the one hand, the lawyer's take on the book business matched everyone else's. On the other hand, the detectives were no closer to seeing an author's contract than before. The one positive was they avoided another drive to Dallas by handling this over the phone.

The consistent theme among the authors was that none of the GP authors counted on their royalties for a living, and that lessened money as a murder motive. Watts and Spartan spent the next several minutes trading thoughts on why authors put themselves through this when there was so little profit. It still didn't make sense to them.

Doing the math, Spartan gasped. "Do you realize I'd have to sell four thousand books a month to pay my bills and taxes? I can't imagine doing that year after year."

"First, you have to write a book before it becomes an issue," said Watts.

"I think I'll stick with my reports. At least I get paid for them."

Watts smiled, knowing how much pride his partner took in his reports. Returning his thoughts to Azar's conversation, Watts accepted the attorney's words as gospel, which is something he rarely did. Azar backed his claims with facts. Everything he said sounded surprisingly genuine. Before wasting more time contacting The Guillotine Press' distributor, graphic artist, and printer, Watts wanted to first contact Ben Striker, author of *The Blade Within*. If Striker was anything like Jolene Lundgren or Lance Ballard, talking to him would be meaningless, but it had to be done.

Watts reached into his pocket and pulled out a quarter. "Want to flip to see who makes the next call?" he said to Spartan.

"That's okay. You spoke with Azar so I'll call Striker. He'll probably want to drive his point home."

"Good one, Blaine. This job's a lot easier when we can laugh. The only people that grow old are the ones that take themselves too seriously."

Spartan nodded his indifference and reviewed his notes before making the call. Something caught his eye. "Hey, Maxx, listen to this review from Striker's book jacket. 'A clever tale of deception and death, *The Blade Within* goes straight to the heart.' Cozy, isn't it? You gotta wonder how CC ended up with all these creepy authors."

"Creeps are everywhere, Blaine. They're not limited to authors. What's sad is how many people buy this crap."

"Yeah, I know, but it's no different than TV. If people didn't watch the crap they air, the sponsors would bail and they couldn't afford to keep it on."

Spartan nodded as he dialed Striker's number. A woman with a sing-song voice said, "Striker Detective Agency." The title was so unexpected that it threw him off for a second. Spartan didn't see anything in Striker's bio about him being a private eye. He wondered what other surprises lay in store. He formally introduced himself and requested to speak to her boss.

The unnamed receptionist hesitated. "What does this concern, sir?"

"The Guillotine Press."

"Hold, please."

Spartan looked at Watts. "You know, whenever people place me on hold like this, it makes me want to run my hand through the phone line and squeeze their throats."

"Relax, Blaine. Remember what I said about growing old? Take a deep breath. Little outbursts like that can cost you days of your life. It's a well-known fact that stress kills."

Spartan closed his eyes, forcing himself to unwind. It wasn't easy because the receptionist's delay lasted longer than it should have. If Striker was there, he should be taking his call. If he wasn't, then there was no reason for the delay. The woman finally came back on the line.

"Mr. Striker's with a client right now," she said. "May I have him return your call?"

"Absolutely," said Spartan, giving her the number. "Tell him it's urgent."

"I will, and have a nice day."

Spartan hung up repeating, "Have a nice day? Didn't that line go away decades ago?"

"Beats me," said Watts, checking the time. "Too bad it's so early. Tex-Mex sounds pretty good right now."

Spartan's head bobbed. "It sure does, but let's wait a while. The day is young."

They returned their focus to the murder board where they had prioritized their suspects from top to bottom. They voted Kat Coulter most likely to succeed while the Pao Lee came in as runner-up, even though he was dead. They both agreed that Mayor Jordan should be included, but it seemed too dangerous to list him.

Considering the mayor's role in this, Watts said, "If OJ's having an affair with Kat Coulter, then it's possible he helped murder her husband. Kat could have easily let him in, or left the door unlocked for him. He could have parked his car a block away and walked there. The neighbor reported their dog barking on two separate occasions on the night of the murder. The first came shortly after midnight, and the second about an hour later. An hour is plenty of time to kill someone, clean up, and leave."

"But this is our mayor we're talking about, Maxx, and so far our wild speculation is his only link to the murder."

"I concur. I'd love to tail him, but I can't with Ryder protecting him like Jordan's watching over Kat. I've never heard of a public official becoming so personally involved in a murder case."

"I know what you mean, but why would the mayor risk a scandal to protect Kat Coulter unless they're lovers?" Spartan stopped suddenly and a grin found his face. "If the mayor and Kat were to elope, would that be considered a political run-off?"

Watts rolled his eyes. "Okay, Blaine, it's official. Your jokes are definitely digressing. Get on the computer and see what you can dig up on Striker before he calls back. I'm going to work some other angles."

"You got it."

Two hours passed without any word from private eye author Striker. Watts heard his partner's stomach growl, so he bounced a paper wad off his partner's head and said, "It's lunchtime, Blaine. You still in the mood for a taco?"

Spartan tossed the wad back and it bounced off Watts' chin. "Make it El Regio's and you're on," he said, disappointed Watts tossed the paper in the trash.

"El Regio's it is," Watts said. "You drive, I buy."

"Considering the price of gas, you're probably getting the better deal."

"Fine. I'll drive and you buy."

"No, that's okay. Leroy burns twice the gas as my car, and it's nice of you to buy. But be forewarned, I'm not ordering off their kiddie menu."

Watts laughed. "Order whatever you like. It'll give us time to talk."

On the way over, Watts shared his latest Mayor Jordan theories. His logic sound, they both agreed not to discuss Jordan outside of the car. On their return trip, they discussed nothing of significance between Pepsi belches. Once inside 350, Watts pulled his chair across from Spartan's desk and stared at the murder board.

"Okay," he said. "Time to get back to business. Other than calling Striker again, what else do we have?"

"I keep looking at Kat Coulter and Pao Lee and think we should reverse 'em. Pao may be dead, but two of his victims in *The Mariner's Club* died from suffocation."

"Good point," Watts said. "I'd forgotten that. It was pillows, right?"

"Yeah. Definitely not the best way to die in bed."

Watts leaned back in his chair. "You do realize it'll be tough convicting a dead man."

"I do," Spartan said, "but it'll be worth it if it clears this case."

"Okay, so we swap Pao and Kat, where does that leave Striker?"

"Nowhere until we talk to him. The same goes for Mick Taggart."

"No idea why Striker hasn't called, but Taggart should be coming home soon."

Watts found the airline pilot's number and dialed. He recognized Mrs. Taggart's voice, and after introducing himself, asked for her husband.

"Oh, dear," she said. "Mick calls me every day on Skype and I told him you needed to speak to him. I'm a little surprised he hasn't called you back. Anyway, he should be landing in Anchorage soon. I'll remind him to call when I talk to him."

Watts considered that and figured Taggart knew Skype calls weren't secure because they were transmitted through personal computers. Mick Taggart could wait.

"Mrs. Taggart, can you do me a favor and look at his schedule for the last two months?"

"Sure. They're right here on the fridge. He always posts them so I know when to clear the Harleys from the driveway and get rid of the pool boy." Sounding disappointed when he didn't laugh, she said, "That's Mick's joke, not mine."

Watts faked a laugh for her benefit. Taggart's schedule revealed he was halfway around the world when CC died. Watts needed to verify that with his airline, but that wouldn't take long. He then thought that with all of his travels, Taggart might not stay up on Guillotine Press affairs. Of course, the odds were equally good that Hank Azar had e-mailed Taggart regarding them wanting his book contract.

Seeing no benefit in prolonging the call, Watts said, "I appreciate the information, Mrs. Taggart. Please have him call me when he lands."

"I'll give him the message, but he might be a Zombie when you talk to him. His jetlag seems to get worse with age."

"I'll keep that in mind. Good day."

Having overheard the conversation, Spartan wrote Taggart's name on the bottom of the list showing he was accounted for, and not a suspect. Watts agreed with the placement while pondering Snake-Eyes and the Skinheads seen fleeing Forest Park. He wondered if Snake-Eyes was in a gang and somehow involved in the Lee and Chow murders.

Spartan gave him a strange look. "What's up with you?" he said.

Watts shrugged. "I've been thinking about Skinheads for lack of any better suspects."

"Sounds like you're drifting into Skip Parsons' territory."

"Maybe, but only because of how Lee and Chow died. I keep wondering if these murders were random. But then the Skinheads I've dealt with never had any remorse for their actions, so if they broke into Coulter's house, they probably would have raped and killed Kat after murdering her husband. I also can't see them stuffing a wad down his throat if they sliced up the other two."

"Then we agree the murders aren't related," Spartan said.

"I'm afraid so, which brings us back to Lee's hair in Coulter's office. Even in the breeze, I don't see how it could travel from the living room to his office."

"I agree, which is why Pao Lee tops our list. I think the key still revolves around the personal nature of this crime. In my opinion, the killer was fed up with CC and took action."

Watts nodded. "To date, not a single shred of evidence suggests anyone outside of CC's inner circle was responsible for his murder, and the method seems too premeditated for gang violence."

"So the question remains, who did it?"

TWENTY TWO

The detectives spent most of the afternoon bouncing ideas off each other, but neither was ready to present anything to Lieutenant Ryder. While Spartan performed more computer searches, Watts visited the evidence room to see what he might be missing. The over-analyzed black hair found in Coulter's office now rested in a sealed petri dish while the chewed up toy ball and marble Writer's Block paperweight remained in separate sealed evidence bags. He carefully studied all of them, but drew no new conclusions. When he returned to his desk, Spartan was still busy on his computer, so Watts tried to reach Ben Striker again.

Living in LA made Striker an unlikely suspect, but Watts still had to speak to him to rule him out. Of course, as a private detective, Striker would know how to make a scene appear like someone broke in even if they didn't. Sliding his chair back got Spartan's attention. "What if Kat hired Striker to follow her husband?" he said. "For that matter, what if CC hired him to follow Kat?"

Spartan rubbed his chin, thinking. "Kat already knew about CC's affair," he said. "But what if CC hired him, learned that his wife and OJ were having an affair, and threatened to go public? In response, OJ either killed CC, or had him killed to keep him quiet."

"That could work. We certainly know there have been people willing commit murder to protect their bosses, and the prospect of this love triangle certainly floats OJ to the surface. All things considered, it's probably not a good idea to list his name. Besides, I'm not sure I buy it."

Watts' phone rang. The caller ID showed it was Ben Striker. Watts held the phone so Spartan could hear. "Detective Watts."

"I understand you're looking for me," Striker said, flatly.

"That's correct," Watts said. "What took you so long to call me back?"

"I get paid by the job, and the job took longer than expected. I'm sure you've had similar experiences in your line of work."

"What kind of job were you doing? Divorce surveillance?"

"Man, you're good," Striker said, mockingly. "As I'm sure you're aware, stakeouts take time, which is why I didn't call you back until now."

"Well, better late than never. As lead detective for CC Coulter's homicide," Watts said, "I've been interviewing his authors. My partner and I have also read The Guillotine Press books. Oddly, I don't recall seeing your photo, or any mention that you're a private detective. Why is that?"

"You, of all people, should know that stakeouts get blown when people recognize you."

Watts had to agree. "Has that ever happened to you?" he said.

"Not yet, and I intend on keeping it that way."

"But what about your name? Don't people recognize it from your book?"

"I doubt it. One book hardly makes you a household name."

"Maybe not, but if you're worried about recognition, why not use a pseudo name?"

"Maybe I'll do that next time. Thanks for the suggestion. Anything else?"

"Yes. How long have you been in the detective business, Mr. Striker?"

"Ever since I got out of the service. I spent twenty years in Army Intelligence."

"My hat's off to you, sir, and thank you for your service."

"We all make choices, detective. Mine worked out well for me."

Watts paused, considering that. "How far up the Army ladder did you climb?" he said.

"Not that it's pertinent, but I'm a retired Lieutenant Colonel."

"O-5, eh? Impressive," Watts said, doing his best to sound sincere. "My dad was drafted into the Army and served in Vietnam, but got out as soon as he could. I think he made E-4."

"That's probably right, assuming he kept his nose clean. Any idea what unit he was in?"

Watts was pleased to have finally made a connection. The Army thing seemed to have softened Striker's tone. It allowed him to lighten up, too, which he preferred.

"Unfortunately, he never volunteered that information and I never asked," Watts said, regretting it. "Vietnam was way before my time and we didn't have the best relationship, so it wasn't that important to me. I do know that he received an Honorable Discharge and earned some medals, though. I'm not sure which ones."

"Our Vietnam offensive couldn't have existed without soldiers like your dad. We may have lost the war, but at least it ended the draft. In that regard, we came out ahead. Had we learned anything from our war experience over there, we might not be muddled in the Middle East." He stopped abruptly, like he wanted to take that back. "I'm sorry," he said. "I got a bit sidetracked. Let's move on."

Though interested in what the colonel had to say about war, Watts didn't ask because it wasn't relevant to his case. Switching to Striker's trade, he said, "Sir, I'm pretty ignorant about the private detective business. Is there any money in it?"

"I'm for hire 24/7, anywhere, anytime. All people have to do is pay me."

"I understand, but that didn't answer my question."

"Then let me rephrase it. I'm still in business. Let's leave it at that."

Watts had been scribbling notes while talking. When he looked down, he was shocked to see he had scribbled his father's Army emblem. "Mr. Striker, which Army unit had an arrowhead shaped patch with a horse and slash?"

"That's the First Cavalry Division. Is that where your dad served?"

"I think so. Anyway, tell me how you came up with the storyline for *The Blade Within*."

"Well, a long time ago, I considered writing a non-fiction story about my Army experiences, but then I figured I'd probably be thrown in jail. You see, the government seems to overlook the fact that our politicians nearly destroyed the CIA because of what was revealed to the press, so I figure I'd be in the same boat. It's quite the double standard. Anyway, I figured I could tell a lot of it through fiction with a disclaimer, so that's what *The Blade Within* is all about."

Watts nodded at his partner who was giving him a thumbs-up. "Makes sense," Watts said. "How has your experience been with The Guillotine Press? I mean, knowing what you know now, would you recommend that a friend publish with them?"

"Detective, I wouldn't wish The Guillotine Press on my worst enemy. CC Coulter may have been a smooth talker, but he was a louse when it came to delivering the goods. On those rare occasions when I actually reached him on the phone, I may as well have been talking to a rock. As for e-mail responses, forget it. He was truly the invisible man."

"Sorry to hear that. Did you have a literary agent before you signed with Mr. Coulter?"

"Actually, I went through a couple of agents before that, and fired them both because there was never any accounting for what they did. All they did was bill me for mailing costs, reproduction costs, administrative costs, whatever, and for that I never saw any results or got feedback. After that, I sent queries to every suitable publisher listed in the *Writer's Digest* book, and heard back from maybe ten percent. Then one day I got a call from CC, and as

I mentioned earlier, he was a smooth talker. I signed with him without doing any research because it was a sure thing. You'd think that a retired Army Intelligence officer would know better, but my actions proved otherwise."

Watts laughed before realizing Striker wasn't joking. He scribbled a note to Spartan saying it was past quitting time, and he could take off if he wanted. Spartan shook him off, mouthing he would wait to see how this played out. After nodding his understanding, Watts said, "Mr. Striker, did you have a multi-book contract?"

"It took me forever to write this one. Maybe someday when I'm retired I'll try writing another one, but for now, I'm done."

Watts paused, re-reading the book jacket's description. "*The Blade Within* is a clever tale of political deception and death that goes straight to the heart. *Midwest Review*." He handed the book over to Spartan. "Mr. Striker, I have to ask, is *The Blade Within* a vindictive story?"

"Let's say it's therapy from my time in Vietnam and leave it at that. On the surface, it has nothing to do with the Army, but if you read between the lines . . ." His voice trailed off.

"That's interesting because I've heard a lot of authors describe their work as therapy. Did writing this book bring any closure?"

"It's hard to say. I probably function better than a lot of Vietnam vets. Frankly, I'm not sure any of us will get closure, but things are better now that we're recognized as patriots. And even though we honor our members of the armed forces now, I think things are worse because our Middle East vets aren't fighting a defined enemy, and they can't fire unless fired upon. Talk about messing with your head every time you enter a building. Everyone inside could have a gun pointing at you. I don't envy them."

Sensing Striker's anguish, Watts silently vowed to re-read Striker's book when he had the chance. The US suffered too many losses in Southeast Asia, and for what? Was Vietnam responsible for his father's alcoholism? He had yet to meet anyone who understood this war.

"Changing the subject, did you visit Texas in the past two months?"

"Yes, I have clients there."

"By chance, was Kat Coulter, CC Coulter, or Olyn Jordan one of your clients?"

"You know I can't divulge my clients. They pay me to be invisible, and that's how I treat them. By the way, that's my standard court response and it always holds up."

"I understand. Can you send me a copy of your book contract so I can compare it to the others? You can fax it, mail it, or e-mail it if you like."

"Sorry, but I can't do that. CC made it clear that we're not to discuss it, and out of respect for him, I shall honor his request. Please offer my condolence to his wife."

Watts' pencil lead snapped, its graphite smearing his paper as he brushed it away. "I'll pass it on should I see her again," he said. "Thank you for your time, sir. It's been a pleasure."

"Any time, detective. Good day."

Watts ended the call and then turned to his partner. "Damn, Blaine. I really thought I would get a contract from him."

"Me, too, but it always ends the same way—Sorry, no can do."

Watts sighed, adjusting his chair. "Blaine, would you mind dropping this audiotape off at the lab to get it transcribed?"

"Consider it done." Spartan removed the tape and started to walk away.

"Oh," Watts said, "Have them make an extra copy. We'll lock one in the safe, and work from the other."

"I'll see what I can do. It's late. Mind if I take off after?"

"Not at all. Go home, take the family out to dinner, and maybe you'll get lucky again."

Spartan grinned. "Sounds like a plan. See you in the morning."

TWENTY THREE

Watts left the office soon after his partner. Spartan would go home to another hot meal while he would run back to Forest Park. That was the difference between being married and single. When he got home, he changed into a clean *Magnum PI* uniform and arrived at the double murder scene at 6:15. Joggers jogged, fishermen cast lines from the riverbanks, and the yellow police was tape gone. Watts wondered how they erased the blood. With clean water in such short supply, the clean-up crew may have tilled the soil. Then again, there was probably an ordinance against that, even though road kills spilled more blood. Staring at the scene stirred memories of Daisy Woods. She seemed like a loner, too. He wondered what she was doing now. Maybe jogging through the same park or having dinner at Subway. Once again, he found himself more interested in her than crime solving. But that didn't keep his conspiracy theories from surfacing like the cricket invasion. Food must be the reason they favored condos over parks.

He sat in the shade contemplating the sad lives of the authors they interviewed. Luke Harper died along with his daughter. Courtney Dridelle got by on a shallow life, probably wondering how she would get by once her looks faded. Arlene Buck and Jolene Lundgren were bitter old women who had let themselves go. Lance Ballard seemed like the only one who was happy with his life.

Watts' phone rang, and saw it was Mick Taggart calling from Anchorage. He didn't feel like taking it right then, but felt obligated to since he had made such a stink about him calling.

"I'm sorry it's taken so long to get back to you," the pilot said, sounding drained. "I had to get some sleep after I landed. These long trips are killing me. Anyway, what can I do for you?"

"Sir, I'll keep this short," he said. "Since you were overseas when CC Coulter died, you are not a suspect in his murder. However, I would like to know why you signed with The Guillotine Press. And don't worry about violating your contract. I've already read it." He was bluffing, but what the hell.

"Well, I had been writing for years, and got published in a lot of newspapers and magazines. I even had a few short stories published that paid pretty well, so writing a novel seemed like the next logical step. I sent my manuscript to twenty or so publishers, but the only responses I received were form letters. Then CC called me out of the blue and said he liked my work and wanted to publish it. Needless to say, I was ecstatic. Then when he told me about the financial commitment, I checked into it and realized that's about what it would cost if I were to self-publish, except this way I was with a reputable company that had an editor who would ensure my book was worthy of print. I looked at CC's offer as an investment in myself, so I signed his contract. I can't say that I've seen a return on my investment, but I am proud of my book. Life is too short not to take chances, detective. I had no expectations, and CC delivered everything he promised. I have no complaints with him, and I am sorry he was murdered. The news came as quite a shock."

"Mr. Taggart, would you mind telling me how old you are?"

"I'm proud to say I'm sixty two, and thanks to a recent change in the law, I can fly for three more years. Pilots joke about flying until they die, but I plan to retire in the next year or two so I can enjoy life and concentrate on my writing."

"Well, good luck with it, and thanks for calling me back. I believe I have everything I need, so have a safe flight home."

"Thanks, detective. Take care."

Glad that he accepted Taggart's call, Watts tucked his phone away and looked around the park. With the crime scene erased, there was no reason for him to stick around. As he began a slow jog through the park, his gun dug into his back. He probably wouldn't notice it if he ran faster, but then his hips would start hurting. Going too slow would kill his exercise, so he tolerated the pain with the jog. He smelled marijuana coming from a picnic area and spotted five large tattooed Hispanics firing angry gazes at him. He had never made an off-duty arrest before, and today wasn't a good day to start. Sometimes it's best to turn a blind eye and let the narcs handle the druggies.

Ryder's reasons for keeping Mayor Jordan out of this seemed clear enough. Everyone had skeletons in their closets, so Jordan must have some, too. But truth be known, Ryder seemed more interested in keeping his job than protecting OJ's political career. Maybe that was why the mayor called Ryder on the carpet. Bad things happened when you crossed OJ. But Watts always had a difficult time butting out when someone ordered him to. If anything, it made him more determined to find the truth. If it took concrete evidence to prove the mayor was involved, then by god, he would get it.

He jogged four miles before calling it quits. It was a shorter run than usual, but long enough to break a sweat. He wished he could see Daisy again.

He should have asked for her number instead of giving her his card, but at the time that seemed too forward. Why couldn't he get her out of his head?

After showering at home, Watts turned on his computer and called up his Facebook page. Typing in Daisy Woods produced numerous profiles showing photos of cats, dogs, and even a penguin, none of which remotely resembled his favorite CSSU tech. He gave up and turned on the evening news, then went to the fridge to find a yogurt. While spooning it in his mouth, he watched an update on the wildfires west of Fort Worth, the worst of it being near Possum Kingdom Lake. A report on freeway gridlock followed that, along with some local interest stories, the unchanging weather report, and sports. The news addressed everything except the Forest Park murders, and he still found that odd. For Mayor Jordan and the park visitors, the deletion was a blessing. To Watts, it was still suspicious.

After a quick shower, he donned the last of his clean Hawaiian shirts and took Leroy out for a drive. Though unplanned, he soon found himself in Kat Coulter's neighborhood. During his last visit there, her clean kitchen suggested she didn't spend much time at home and he wanted to see if his hunch was right.

Even pickups like Leroy blend into rural neighborhoods, but his Hawaiian shirt was another story. Wearing a ball cap and shades for camouflage probably didn't help, but since Kat Coulter would never believe a Fort Worth native would be seen in a flowery shirt, he wasn't worried. Within minutes of arriving, he spotted Kat Coulter climbing into her car wearing a flashy black cocktail dress, high heels, and matching purse. He ducked down in his seat until she had backed her Beemer out of her driveway, and then slowly raised himself up. She showed no concern as she sped off.

Watts gave her a head start because Leroy towered over most everything on the road. When she pulled into the Convention Center parking garage, Watts parked on the street. After contemplating the possible repercussions for his non-scheduled stakeout, he decided it was worth seeing where she was going, so he removed his digital camera from Leroy's glove box, stepped from the cab, and hurried up the parking lot stairs before she could get there. When he heard her spike heels stabbing the concrete, he began snapping tourist photos of the Convention Center until she had started her descent. He didn't follow until she was two levels beneath him.

He soon spotted her pacing alone in front of the convention center while couples in black-tie attire wandered inside. Across the street, train passengers leaving Union Station scattered like ants, eager to get home. Sweeping his gaze back to the Convention Center, Kat Coulter was gone. Thinking she may have spotted him, he watched for her to come back to the lot. When that didn't happen, he snapped a few photos for effect and went back to his truck.

His gut cramping all the way home, he remembered Spartan talking about ulcers. But you don't get ulcers from one lousy stakeout. More likely, it was his nervous stomach rebelling. As soon as he went in the door, he darted to the medicine cabinet for a Zantac. Once that was done, he settled into his easy chair to mull over his solitary life.

Spartan was right about the complexities of being single. There was something to be said for sharing a bed, even if all you did was sleep. An idea popped into his head, and he flew to his computer to do an Internet search on Fort Worth Convention Center events. It only took a few key strokes to learn that tonight's affair was a fund raiser for Mayor Olyn Jordan's re-election campaign. Feeling better now, he searched for images of OJ with Kat Coulter. Since she had worked with him for years, he expected numerous photos of them together. Finding none was very strange.

Now obsessed with the Coulter/Jordan connection, Watts learned that the mayor attended a conference in New York shortly after his wife died. Within two months of that conference, the Coulters had relocated to Fort Worth. Whether Kat's Texas move was coincidence or planned, it certainly raised flags about OJ's personal affairs. But what really infuriated Watts was someone with the mayor's clout could possibly get away with murder.

Watts called FWPD operator to request Daisy Woods call him. He knew they couldn't give out her home phone number, and handling it this way put the onus on Woods. If she hadn't called him within fifteen minutes, it would wait until morning. Five minutes later, his phone rang and his mouth went dry. *It's her.* He greeted her using his best spur of the moment excuse, "Sorry to bother you after hours, but I wanted to share a few thoughts of you. I mean, of the case." He wished he had put more thought into it.

Her giggle was a relief, but his hands were shaking, awaiting her response.

"Which case are you referring to, Maxx. By the way, I assume it's okay to call you Maxx since it's on your card."

"Absolutely. As I said before, I'd much prefer you call me that."

"Well, since it's after hours, you can call me Daisy. What can I do for you?"

The way she spoke turned it into a loaded question, her playful tone teasing him, daring him to say something stupid. She was an entirely different person on the phone.

"Well, I had some serious doubts on this case and needed someone to share them with," he said. "We touched on a few of them when I met you in the park. My partner knows about some of these things, my boss doesn't want me to touch some of them, and I found some interesting things on the Internet. If you don't want to talk or get involved, I understand."

"So, do you want me to listen, or get involved?"

Another loaded question. She sure knew how to put him on the spot. But two can play that game. "Either." A second later, he added, "Both, if you're willing."

"I'm listening."

Watts proceeded to brief her on all that had transpired since they last spoke. She wasn't saying much, but she was an excellent listener. One he felt comfortable confiding in. They talked for thirty minutes, and soon Watts found himself even more attracted to her. He loved feeling giddy over a new crush. It was the first step in any new relationship. Unfortunately, without being able to see her face, he had no way of telling whether she shared similar feelings. He saved her number in his phone, just in case.

His stomach kept rumbling even after he ended the call. Thinking it might need food, he checked his freezer, but found nothing enticing. He didn't crave sweets often, but today he needed a Dairy Queen Banana Boat. Calling it health food because it contained Vitamin D in the ice milk, and potassium in the bananas, he figured it was as good a rationalization as any. Besides, he jogged today. Satisfied, he headed out the door.

He pulled into a corner spot at the DQ and pressed his key fob. Leroy beeped, and he proceeded into the restaurant. Inside, two beefy men with shaved heads and tattoos leaned against the far wall looking mean. Watts nodded at them as he approached the counter, preferring a high-calorie dessert to low-life trouble. To be safe, he stood so he could keep them in sight, calmly placed his order, and backed away trying not to think about the Forest Park murders. The taller one had barbed wire tattoos that completely wrapped around his biceps. His arms had other designs, too, but Watts couldn't make them out. Barbed Wire had cigarettes tucked into his Tee's sleeve, Brando style. The shorter one looked equally scary. A Minnie-Me version of the first, but bearing skull tattoos instead of barbed wire.

Staring at Watts, Barbed Wire said, "Nice shirt, Pops. I could use one like that."

"Try the Goodwill," Watts said as calmly as he could. "That's where I found this one."

Watts hoped his lie would buy him some time. He had planned to eat his dessert here, but decided to take it home instead. He had hoped that Wire was finished talking, but that wasn't the case.

"What about your truck?" Wire said. "Did it come from the Goodwill, too?"

Minnie-Me snickered, drawing his index finger across his crooked nose. The moment Watts saw that, he knew Minnie was the follower. The teen behind the counter looked worried, his hand shaking as he scooped ice milk for Watts' order. Watts hoped he would finish before splitting.

Barbed Wire moved closer, his boots clanging like they had spurs. "I asked you a question, Pops. Where'd you get the truck? I've been looking all over for one just like it. Who knew you'd deliver it to me?"

Nothing raised Watts' blood pressure like an assault on his truck. Feeling the cold steel of his service revolver against his back, he slid away from the counter so he could draw it if he needed to. He slid the DQ kid a five-spot as he grabbed his dessert, and told him to keep the change. The kid quickly snatched the bill and disappeared into the back leaving the place deserted. Then the Skinheads split up like raptors, each taking a side. When Barbed Wire stuck his hand in his pocket, Watts reached for his gun and showed his badge.

"Police," he said. "Don't move!"

Suddenly, Barbed Wire was all smiles, raising his hands as he backed away. "Hey, man, I was just messin' with ya. No need to get all fired up."

Watts held his gaze, motioning Minnie-Me to join his buddy. He wanted to bust them, but on what charge? Neither showed a weapon and intimidation was hardly a basis to bust them. Keeping both hands on his pistol, Watts aimed it directly at Wire's chest. "Since you two aren't eating, why not get out of here before someone gets hurt."

Wire smirked and dropped his arms. "Sure thing, Pops." On his way out, he glanced at Watts over his shoulder, sneering. "I still like your truck."

Watts nodded and watched them leave in a red/white/and rust 1980s vintage F-150. It would be easy to track with no front license plate and exhaust so loud it deserved a ticket, but without backup, he didn't dare follow. Dad had his problems, but he was right that there was no point in dying a hero because as he put it, dead is dead. *More sound advice from the departed.*

Seating himself with his back to the wall, Watts drew in a deep breath and spooned his dessert. The whipped cream had gone flat, the ice milk was melting, but he figured it would taste the same. After taking a bite, he looked around for the DQ kid. "All's clear," he said, loud enough for anyone within a block to hear. "You can come out now."

But no one answered. After repeating himself with no response, Watts leaned over the counter to take a look. Seeing no one, he figured the kid was either hiding in the bathroom, had left, or something bad happened. Praying it wasn't the latter, he drew his gun, leaped over the counter, and found the place empty, the back door swinging in the breeze. Fearing the worst, he pulled the door shut and called the police before searching for the kid. When Watts returned to the dining area, two officers with drawn guns drawn were ordering him to freeze.

Watts released his grip and let his gun dangle from his finger as he raised his hands. "Detective Watts, homicide. I'm the one who called you. The kid's missing."

"Ah ha," the black cop said, his burly hands steady on the trigger. "And I'm Robert E. Lee. Now ease the gun down and we'll talk."

Watts complied, sliding his gun across the floor and then raising his hands again. "My badge is in my breast pocket if either of you would check."

The black cop nodded for his Hispanic partner to approach Watts while he kept him covered. A quick search turned up Watts' badge and cell phone that still showed his 9-11 call. Satisfied, the black cop picked up the gun and handed it back to Watts. "Sorry, detective. You can imagine how it looked."

"Hey, I have no problem with how you handled it," Watts said, "but I can't believe you got here so fast. You must have been right around the corner."

"Actually, we were. Right before we got the call, I was asking Tomas here whether he wanted DQ or Whataburger and he picked DQ. The rest is history. Sometimes it's meant to be, you know? By the way, I'm Jimmy D."

After exchanging handshakes, Watts said, "Nice to meet you, Jimmy D. And you, too, Tomas. Like I said, the kid who works here is gone. I don't suppose you saw a frightened teen dart out the back door, did you?"

Both cops shook their heads. Jimmy D then asked what happened.

Bewildered, Watts hiked his shoulders. "When I came in, two Skinheads started giving me a hard time. When they wanted to play rough, the kid disappeared in the back room, not that I could blame him. The Skinheads took off after I showed my gun, but what concerns me is the kid might have taken off about the same time. I pray they didn't grab him."

"We'll put out an APB if you can give us a description of the Skinheads and the kid."

Watts pointed to the security camera. "Assuming this thing works, they should be on the surveillance video, but they are white males with shaved heads, early twenties, tattoos, reeked of smoke, white tee shirts, blue jeans, black motorcycle boots, driving a late 80s Ford F-150 rust-bucket pickup with no front plate and very loud exhaust. I'd say the tall one is six-two, the shorter maybe five-nine. Both have muscular builds. The missing DQ kid is maybe seventeen, bad skin, wearing a red DQ shirt and blue jeans. He's a bit pudgy around the waist, but otherwise an average man-boy. Now that you're here, I'll call the store manager to see if we can get the surveillance tapes."

"Sounds good."

DQ Manager Jeff Stockman answered Watts' call. After explaining the situation and some disagreeing, Watts convinced Stockman that he shouldn't blame the kid for running away in a situation like this. Stockman also agreed to call the kid's cell phone to check on him and be right down to lock up. The manager's attitude suggested something like this had happened before. Whether his restaurant had experienced prior problems or not, no kid should be working alone in a place like this, especially at night. Watts tucked his phone away, flipped the "Open" sign, and dimmed the lights. A young Hispanic couple approached the door, but quickly turned away when they saw cops inside. Watts watched them leave and then looked back at the officers.

"So, what do you think, guys? Is this a safe area for kids to hang out in after dark?"

Jimmy D removed his hat and wiped the sheen from his forehead. "I'm not sure that anyplace is safe these days, Maxx. When I started this job, I never wore Kevlar, but now I don't leave home without it."

"That's probably a good idea. I'm re-thinking that myself. But isn't Kevlar hot?"

"Better fry than die from some trigger happy turd."

Watts chuckled. "Good point," he said, feeling his bullet scar, scanning the restaurant's interior. Even in dim light, its colorful walls were still vibrant. Then his thoughts turned to the DQ kid. His concern grew because Stockman never called back. If he ran outside when the Skinheads were leaving, they could have grabbed him without anyone knowing. *Why hasn't Stockman called?*

The two cops sat at a table, drooling over the menu. The enduring smell of burgers and fries wasn't helping matters. Jimmy D said they were coming here for dinner, and now both cops were checking their watches. Then a stomach growled. Watts wasn't sure whose it was, but they needed to eat, and could certainly be more productive elsewhere.

"If you guys want to take off, I'll wait here for the manager," he said. "He's on his way."

Jimmy D looked relieved. "Thanks, Maxx. My man Tomas is starving. Here's my card," he said, handing it to Watts. "Call if you need us."

Watts glanced at it and put it in his wallet. "Thanks, man. You guys be safe."

"You, too, Maxx." Jimmy D said, hurrying out the door.

No sooner had they left when Watts' phone rang. It was Daisy.

"Sorry to bother you," she said, "but I wanted to remind you to call whenever you feel like talking."

No sooner had she said that, Watts' had an incoming call. Caller ID showed it was Stockman. *Damn!* "Daisy, can you please hold for second? I have another call I have to take. It'll only take me a second."

"Sure, go ahead."

Stockman sounded tense, speaking before Watts spoke a word. "I haven't been able to reach Tony Fazelli," the manager said. "His parents haven't seen him, and he's not answering his cell phone."

"I'm waiting for you at the DQ," Watts said. "How long before you get here?"

"Five minutes."

"Make it three."

Watts punched a button and Daisy was still there. "Daisy, I'd really love to talk," he said, sounding anxious, "but it appears I'm caught up in a kidnapping." After thinking about what he said, he added, "Just to clarify, I haven't been kidnapped, but a DQ kid might have been. Can I call you later?"

"Of course," she said, her tone soft, comforting. "I'll be up late, so call whenever you want. I hope you find the kid."

"Me, too, and thanks for understanding. I'll talk to you later."

Watts quickly hung up and called Jimmy D back. "The kid's definitely missing," he said, "and I'm worried those two Skinheads may have been involved in the Forest Park murders. Can you head over to the park and see if they're doing round two on the kid?"

Jimmy D hesitated. "Sure," he said, "but you really think the kid's in jeopardy?"

Watts' voice grew tense. "Jimmy D, all I know is the kid's boss is nervous, and his parents don't know where he is. I have no clue whether he's in Forest Park or not, and the punks I saw at DQ may not have done anything wrong, but I'd appreciate you checking it out."

"No sweat, Maxx. We're on our way."

Watts ended his call figuring he probably interrupted their second attempt at a meal. But that's how it was. Always on call ruined his night, too. He glanced at his dessert, which now resembled a floating log in a polluted lake, and dumped it in the trash. *C'est la vie.* He didn't need the calories anyway.

Two minutes later, a portly man in polo shirt, sweat pants, and flip-flops leaped from his car and rushed toward the door swinging a key ring. "I'm Stockman," he said, sounding more desperate than before. "I was hoping Tony's car would be gone, but it's still in the parking lot."

Watts nodded, feeling responsible for ruining his evening, too. "Okay, here's what I need you to do," he said, trying to calm the manager. "Lock your place up, then take your surveillance tapes to the police station so we can ID the suspects and put an APB out for them and Tony. That way, every police car in the city will know who they're looking for." Stockman's head bobbled, but nothing else moved. "Hurry," Watts said. "I have to go." As he pushed on the door, he added, "Don't get mad at Tony, okay? He's a good kid, and we'll do all we can to find him."

"Thanks, detective. I'll deliver the tapes right away."

Watts ran to Leroy and fired him up, images of chest carvings racking his brain. He raced toward Forest Park, praying he was wrong. Flashing red lights bounced off his mirror, so he pulled over, prepared to explain why he was speeding. To his surprise, the radio car flew by. Seizing the opportunity, Watts followed, lagging slightly so as not to draw attention. When he arrived, Forest Park was blinking red while white spotlights speared the woods. Jimmy D had done a great job getting units on scene. Watts was amazed no one even glanced at Leroy.

After looping through the park, Watts stopped next to a radio car and identified himself to the burly cop inside. "I'm searching for a noisy rust-bucket F-150," he said. "Seen one?"

"Not tonight," he said, sounding bored. "Are you the guy who started this free-for-all?"

Already on edge, Watts showed his badge and lit into the baby cop. He didn't stop until the guy's chin was trembling. "Now call Dispatch and tell them that Tony Fazelli's car is at the Dairy Queen and he's nowhere to be found. It doesn't matter whether the kid's in the park or not. He's missing and we need to find him."

"Yes sir."

Watts didn't move until Baby Cop had delivered his message. Once he heard Dispatch acknowledge the call and instruct the patrol cars to resume their beats, he drove off, unsure where to go next. Leaving the park, he reflected on how he dressed down the rookie cop. He guessed the cocky kid was in his second year, and still believed he was bullet proof. Having also been belittled by a detective while a beat cop, Watts regretted duplicating the incident, but Baby Cop needed to know there were reasons why detectives did certain things. As he floored the accelerator, Leroy's turbo kicked in. He probably blew out four bucks worth of gas right then, but hearing the throaty exhaust was worth it. Unlike Rust-Bucket's pipes, Leroy's sounded glorious. He quickly backed off on the accelerator since he just insisted that Baby Cop watch for noisy pickups. Thankfully, he didn't see any red lights coming his way.

Heading to Trinity Park was a whim, and like before, didn't produce Tony, any Skinheads, or a rusty red pickup. At the park's exit, he killed Leroy's engine, then rolled down the windows. Cicadas shrieked, an upset man was scolding his dog, a distant train warbled, but nothing resembled Rust-Bucket's pipes. Now nine-thirty, forty-five minutes had passed since he left the Dairy Queen. Tony could be anywhere, assuming the bastards hadn't killed him. Considering Dairy Queen's proximity to the Trinity River, they could have tossed Tony in, and no one would know until his body turned up on the bank. Clearly, these bullies had no scruples. Anyone willing to pick a fight with an adult in reasonable shape would have no problem pounding on a soft teenager.

He returned to the Dairy Queen, circling the dark building where Tony's '02 Escort sat in the otherwise empty lot. Nothing looked out of place. Heading to the river, he realized that its gradual slope made it unlikely a body could reach the water if tossed from the bank, and using a bridge would likely produce witnesses. His head throbbing and acid burning his stomach, he drove to the nearest police station and squished his way toward the front desk.

A patrol officer who was booking a cuffed prostitute smiled. "Maxx Watts!" he said. I'd recognize that sound anywhere. You working undercover now?"

Watts walked with him, shaking his head. "Just doing a little after-hours research."

Ignoring the crying teen, the officer stopped and opened a door. "Gotta go, Maxx, but good luck with it."

"Thanks, man."

Watts approached the front desk trying to put a name to the officer he had just spoken to. Normally, he was pretty good at names. Desk Sergeant Bernie Verani, who was busy talking on the phone, was a perfect example. He rarely forgot a face, and yet he drew a complete blank with the guy who sounded like they had a history. Verani hung up, so Watts stuck out his hand.

"Howya dooin', Bernie?"

Verani smiled back, shaking it. "I'm dooin' good, Maxx. How you dooin'?"

"I'm dooin' good, too."

After sharing the laugh, Verani said, "Ya know, Maxx, I always love it when you Texans try to imitate a New Yawwker."

Arms together, palms open, Watts faked a frown. "Hey, it's what we do. I mean, ya gotta wonder about Long Islanders that move to the Trinity shore—if ya know what I mean."

"Yeah, Maxx, I do. But you didn't come here to bad mouth me, so what's up?"

Dropping his accent, Watts said, "Here's the deal, Bernie. I've searched the parks and river and Tony Fazelli's still missing. I asked the DQ manager to drop his tapes off. Did he deliver them here?"

"He did, and the stills went out right away. Everyone has the faces, but no one's seen a thing. Imagine that."

"Yeah," Watts said, tapping his nails on Verani's desk. "Well, I'd better take off. Do me a favor and call if you hear anything on the kid."

"Will do, Maxx. Now get outta here and get some rest. You look like shit."

"That's how I feel, too."

Walking away, Watts wished he could have told Verani that rust-bucket's license plate. Unfortunately, red and white was the favorite color combination for that vintage. In the Dallas/Fort Worth Metroplex, hundreds of F-150 pickups probably fit that description, but only one had those custom pipes. He would recognize them anywhere.

TWENTY FOUR

Tired as he was, Watts wasn't ready to go home. That's when it dawned on him that Daisy had called. He immediately punched in her number and she picked up. After spending the next ten minutes filling her in, he said he was heading back to Forest Park on a premonition.

"How about picking me up first?" she said. "I know the park well, and two flashlights work better than one."

He liked her logic and agreed. Guilt rode him on his way to her place. Would any of this have happened if he had stayed home instead of going out for that banana split? Did his Hawaiian shirt somehow provoke the Skinheads? With the exception of wearing an Oakland Raiders jersey to a Dallas Cowboy's game, the notion of fighting over clothing choices seemed absurd. But when considering Barbed Wire and Minnie-Me's scarred bodies and junkyard dog dispositions, anything seemed possible. Pondering that, he steered Leroy into Daisy's apartment complex. Recalling Wire's admiration for Leroy, Watts wondered if stealing him was their real objective. Two drivers would make that easy. They might have hurt him and Tony to make it happen had Watts not been armed. Wire was certainly bold enough to try.

Daisy was already halfway down the stairs before he climbed out, and had no interest in sweet talk. Watts helped her into the truck and then sped off. On the way, he continued his rant on the Skinheads' audacity.

"They had to have known about the surveillance cameras," he said, "and yet neither made any attempt to conceal their faces."

She glanced at him. "Did they look strung out on drugs, or are they just plain stupid?"

Watts shook his head. "We'll never know unless they sing like canaries when they're arrested."

She nodded and stared out the windshield. Neither were talking, so Watts considered Leroy's features. If the Skinheads were searching for his truck, the custom features he loved so much made him easy to spot. They also knew he was a local cop, and assuming they could read, saw *detective* on his badge. That made him even easier to find. All they had to do was wait outside the station until he left, and then follow him home. Of course, he didn't mention any of this to Daisy, but she had probably already figured that out. Secretly, he hoped these guys ran for the border.

They were spotlighted not far into Forest Park. Flashing lights immediately followed. Watts rolled down his window expecting Baby Cop, but the approaching silhouette he knew. Smiling, he said, "Hello, *Porgy*."

"Well, well. If it isn't the infamous Maxx Watts. Funny how we keep bumping into each other." He paused to shine his light into Daisy's face and then aimed it at Watts. "I take it you two came out to see the submarine races?"

"Don't be an ass, Porgy, she's with CSSU. I'm sure you know about Tony Fazelli and we're here to look for him. I have a premonition he's somewhere in the park."

"A premonition," Mulberry said, tucking his thumbs under his Sam Brown belt. "That's a big word, Maxx. "But then I'm just a beat cop, so I guess I don't rate premonitions."

"Except for when donuts are fresh," Watts sarcastically said.

"Touché. So, what about this premonition? It's a big park. Is she psychic?"

Daisy leaned over to see Mulberry. "I'm currently working the double murder case," she said, putting an end to their macho nonsense. "I'm also very familiar with this park."

Mulberry crossed his arms, contemplating that. "Well, in case you didn't hear," he said, "We've already searched this place and came up empty."

Then everyone was silent. Up close, Mulberry's red lights bounced off the trees, but in the distance, it was an abyss. The freeway noise now minimal, they heard frogs croaking. The serene beauty of the lights reflecting in the Trinity River probably drew tourists like Pao Lee and Shing Chow to the park. Watts and Daisy opened their doors at the same time and climbed out. Watts glanced at Mulberry.

"Care to walk with us, Porgy? We could reminisce over old times and swimming pools."

"Go to Hell, Maxx. Some of us have to work for a living."

"Suit yourself, but Tony Fazelli's out here somewhere. I can smell him."

"Yeah, right. You and your lady friend enjoy your stroll. Call me if the Boogeyman shows up, and I'll come to your rescue."

Porgy blocked the spotlight as he lumbered back to his car. Soon after climbing in, the night turned black again. He didn't bother waving as he drove away. Watts was glad to see him leave.

Daisy stood with her hands on her hips demanding an explanation. "I sense some animosity here. What's going on?"

Watts raised a shoulder, then let it hang. "Porgy and I have known each other since we were kids. He tried to drown me once and I'll never forgive him. Simple as that."

"My, what a cozy story," she said. "Moving on, take a sniff, Mr. Bloodhound, and tell me which way to go."

Watts was still grinning when he took the triple-cell flashlight from his glove box. Daisy already had hers in her hand. The Boogeyman never scared Watts, nor was he concerned about being mugged. However, saying the wrong thing to Daisy terrified him. She was smart, witty, and even more attractive than he thought. Her perfume was nice. Having never smelled any on her before, he hoped it was for his benefit.

Looking from the Colonial Country Club west, the only light was from a few sparsely placed lamps, seemingly placed to have minimal value. Zoo animals squawked, leaves hissed, crickets joined in the cicada's sing-along, and yet the park felt eerily quiet. Watts scanned the area knowing that to catch criminals, you have to think like them. Porgy's response implied that the police had given the park a reasonable scan, but after finding nothing of significance, probably gave up quickly. Watts was immediately drawn to the water. Even at this time of year, the Trinity had a current, so anything tossed into it would turn up downstream.

Aiming his light into the distance, he said, "Isn't there a hidden creek that flows into the river up this way?"

"There is," she said, using her beam as a pointer. "Remote and surrounded by trees, it would be a perfect place to dump a body."

"I agree. Let's go there first."

There were few trees along the jogging trail that parallels Colonial Parkway and the river. Watts chose this route so they could check the riverbank along the way. So far, all they had spotted was blowing trash, a raccoon, and a few squirrels. Turning up the creek got Watts' heart pumping, though. Territorial water moccasins loved places like this, and they didn't have rattles like diamondbacks.

Trying to hide his fear, he said, "Stay close," and inched his way forward. Thinking he heard something, he abruptly stopped. A peacock from the zoo blared, dogs howled, a donkey hee-hawed, and then the cicadas chimed, but nothing resembled the moan he thought he heard.

Daisy tapped him on the shoulder. "Are you okay?" she said. "You seem rather edgy."

"I'm fine, thanks. Stay alert. I swear there's something out here."

Moving closer to the water, Watts aimed his light up and down the inlet but saw nothing. Right after a tree limb snapped under his feet, he heard another moan.

"I heard it that time," Woods said.

"Yeah." Watts grabbed his phone and dialed 911. When the operator came on, he identified himself and asked that she send a radio car to his location. After tucking his phone away, he called out into the darkness. "Hello! Police! If anyone's there, please yell!"

The only noise came from his foot plunging into the creek.

Son of a bitch! It took all his willpower not to scream that. He probably would have had Daisy not been with him. Every step reminded him that his only defense against cottonmouths was his long-handled flashlight and pistol. That meant the odds heavily favored the snake, should one decide to attack. He was about to mention that to Woods when another moan came. Immediately, both of their lights shined upstream. Ten yards up, lying half submerged and motionless, lay Tony Fazelli's bloodied body.

They tried to run, but the mud tugged at their shoes. Climbing higher on the bank improved their traction, but the shrubs and branches were a problem. Forgetting about the snakes and undergrowth, Watts darted ahead. Surprisingly, Daisy kept pace. The approaching sirens assured them his message got through, but now they needed an ambulance. Watts made his second request while running toward Fazelli. He scooped up the teen and followed Daisy's beam to the road. Seconds later, Mulberry was on scene in his radio car.

Denying Porgy any opening remarks, Watts said, "Bring me your First Aid kit—and also some water, if you have it."

Daisy sat down and slid her thighs under Fazelli's head trying to make him comfortable while Watts checked the boy over. The air may have been warm, but his core temperature was low. His jeans were on, but his torso was stripped bare. Blood ran down Fazelli's chest, and he had a lump on his head. Although the wounds didn't look deep enough to be life threatening, their intended message came through loud and clear. *Damn Skinheads!*

Watts grabbed a smelling salt and waved it in front of Fazelli's nose. "Tony, wake up, it's the police. Everything's okay. You're gonna be okay."

Porgy Mulberry resembled the Goodyear blimp with its landing light on as he hovered over them. They all watched Fazelli when suddenly the kid's face twitched. Almost immediately, his frightened eyes opened, and Daisy held him down. As the sirens grew closer, her gentle touch kept him from struggling.

"Tony, it's okay," she softly said to him. "Help is here. You'll be fine."

Fazelli squeezed his eyes shut and tears streamed down his cheeks, but he still wasn't talking. Knowing the ambulance was on its way, Watts didn't attempt to clean the wounds. Instead, he removed his own shirt and covered the boy to protect him from the scratchy wool blanket Mulberry was holding in his hand.

"So it's really him," Mulberry said, sounding more agitated than relieved.

"We'll discuss it later," Watts said, shutting Porgy up. When the ambulance whisked Fazelli away, he added, "We'll meet you at the hospital. I need to talk to the kid."

Mulberry climbed in his car and rolled his window down. "You need a ride back to your truck?"

"Thanks, Porgy. We'd appreciate that."

When they arrived at Texas Health Harris Methodist Hospital, Mulberry was at the front desk gathering information, and Tony Fazelli was in the ER. Seeing Watts topless, someone tossed him a scrubs shirt. After pulling it on, Watts badged his way into the patient's room. He wondered why no one seemed to care that Daisy was tagging along.

Fazelli stared at the ceiling while the doctor cleaned his chest wounds. His lower body was wrapped in a blanket not long enough to cover his feet. Watts whispered to Daisy that the kid was either sedated, in shock, or both. She quietly nodded back watching the boy's pulse on the electronic monitors. When the doctor finally looked at them, Watts flashed his badge.

"I'm Detective Watts. How's he doing, Doc?"

"He needs an MRI to check for concussion and brain swelling. His wounds aren't deep, but they're ugly and could get infected." Shaking his head, he angrily said, "What kind of animal carves swastikas into a kid's chest?"

"Probably the same kind of animals that slice up Chinese men, except in that case, they went deeper. Will Tony's cuts scar?"

"Every wound scars, detective, but because of his age, I've requested assistance from a plastic surgeon. They can stitch him up with a lot less scarring than me."

"That's very kind of you," Daisy said. "Has he said anything to you? Is he cognizant?"

"I can't tell. So far, he hasn't spoken a word or even flinched. His parents are on the way. Hopefully, he'll talk to them."

Down the hall someone frantically yelled, "Where's my baby?" From the tone, Watts suspected it was Fazelli's mother. Overhearing Mulberry talking to her confirmed that. She would arrive any second.

"Thanks again, Doc. We'll be in the waiting room. Please come and get us if Tony starts talking."

Tony Fazelli's eyes widened when Watts turned to leave.

"Detective, wait!"

Watts and Woods stopped in their tracks and turned around. Approaching the bed, Watts said, do you remember us?"

"Not her, but you're the guy that ordered the banana split and took on those Skinheads."

"That's right, and this is Ms. Woods. She and I found you in the park. I'm glad you—"

"Tony!" a middle-aged woman shrieked, rushing in with Mulberry at her heels. "Are you okay?"

Fazelli pulled the covers over his chest like he had a girlfriend hiding in his bed. "I'm fine, Mom. Can you give us a few minutes? I need to talk to this detective."

The woman gave Watts the once-over as though wondering why someone in a blue scrubs shirt would have a gun strapped to his back. She seemed less curious about Porgy Mulberry, and completely ignored Daisy Woods.

"Tony, the nurse and I will be back shortly," the doctor said. "Mrs. Fazelli, may I have a word with you in the hall?"

Mrs. Fazelli glared at her son, and then at the others. From her expression, Watts sensed she was hurting. He couldn't blame her, though. She must be terrified. He waited until the doctor had escorted the woman out before saying anything further.

"Tony, I'm Detective Watts, and this is Crime Scene Special Unit Forensics Technician Woods and Patrol Officer Mulberry. Can you tell us what happened at the Dairy Queen after I confronted the Skinheads?"

Fazelli's eyes narrowed and anger filled his face. "One of them grabbed me when I ran out the back door," he said. "They tossed me in their truck like I was a piece of trash. I tried to yell, but the big guy covered my mouth and forced me face-down in the other guy's lap. After we got a few blocks away, they ripped off my shirt and started slicing my chest. When I struggled, one of them hit me. The next thing I knew, I was in the creek with my chest on fire. I knew I was bleeding so I didn't touch anything so I wouldn't infect it. I had no idea what was going on, so when I got to the hospital I kept quiet and listened. People were poking and prodding and stripping off my clothes, but I didn't care. Then I recognized your face, and suddenly everything was coming back like I turned on a switch. The Skinheads told me you'd know where to find me, and they were right. They said I was an example—a warning for you to butt out next time. They also said they can find you anytime, but good luck finding them. Those were their exact words. I'm sure of it."

Daisy gave Watts a confused look. "What does he mean by that, Maxx?"

Watts shrugged her off and focused on Fazelli. "Tony, I never saw those punks until I walked into your DQ today, and I have no idea what their quarrel is. Did they say anything else, like why they mean that you're a warning?"

Fazelli grabbed his pillow and pulled it around his head. "No! They just cut me, and I don't have a clue why! God, my head hurts!"

Watts took his business card from his wallet, set it on the table, and gently rested his hand on the teen's shoulder. "I'm truly sorry, Tony. I wish I could give you a reason why this happened. If anything else comes to mind, please call me. A couple of years ago I spent some time in this very room. They'll take good care of you."

Daisy smiled, kissed her index finger, and touched it to Fazelli's forehead. "Take care of yourself, Tony. I'm glad you're okay."

To make sure Mulberry left, Watts grabbed his arm and dragged him away. After telling the hospital staff they were finished, he asked Mulberry to retrieve the DQ tapes from the police station, and to list the Skinheads as murder suspects. Mulberry didn't look happy, but had no say in the matter. When they climbed inside Leroy, Watts looked at Daisy.

"I know it's late, but are you up for some coffee or dessert?"

"Sure. I must say that I prefer your *Magnum* costume to scrubs, though."

Watts grinned and started driving.

TWENTY FIVE

The evening ended on a good note. Watts spent an hour with Daisy, drinking coffee and sharing a chocolate volcano. It helped that Ryder had assigned Fazelli's case to another detective. While exchanging small talk with her, Watts explained his Police Academy history with Porgy Mulberry. In exchange, she told him that she transferred to Fort Worth from Dallas because she liked the town better. When he took her home, he walked her to her door and promptly left before things got awkward.

He slept surprisingly well, but when he awoke, the first thing that came to mind was Fazelli's warning about the Skinheads. On his way to work, he took several detours to see if he was being followed. He would have recognized the F-150's exhaust had it been within earshot, but they could have been keeping their distance. When he parked, he checked to make sure no one was watching before stepping from the cab. Once inside 350, he made a beeline for Ryder's office.

Ryder had already heard about what transpired last night, and assured Watts that he did the right thing by getting involved. He went on to say that the DQ Skinheads had yet to be identified. Suddenly, Tony Fazelli popped into Watts' head. The fear and humiliation Fazelli faced would last a lifetime. Watts felt certain the kid would never set foot inside another Dairy Queen, so long as he lived. Watts also suspected that after this incident, Fazelli's former boss would either double his evening shift or close his restaurant early. After all, how many banana splits does it take to justify late hours?

Spartan walked by as Watts was leaving Ryder's office. Having heard the rumors, Spartan asked to hear about it first-hand. At first Watts was hesitant, but then he realized that Ryder probably spread it around the office. It wasn't easy re-telling the story, but he managed. He left out the part about having dessert with Daisy.

"Anyway, how was your night, Blaine?"

"Great," Spartan said, wearing an impish grin. "Sandy and I slept very well together, if ya know what I mean."

"Well, congratulations, partner. Glad things are looking up. Have a good meal?"

146

"Did I ever. Poached salmon, brown rice, green salad, and for dessert, Angel food cake topped with strawberries and whipped cream. It was fantastic."

Watts gave a bewildered grin. "How could you eat all that after a huge lunch?"

"Like I said, it was fantastic."

"You know, you keep telling stories like that and I may have to find a wife. Now for the big question—what did you do to deserve it?"

"Well, before I went home, I called Sandy to tell her I had tickets to the opera."

Squinting in disbelief, Watts said, "I thought you hated opera."

"I do, but I love my wife, she loves opera, and sometimes it's best to put her first."

"I understand. You're a good man, Blaine."

"Thanks, Maxx. I appreciate that. And now that your kidnapping/chest-slicing/ DQ Skinheads are murder suspects in the Lee/Chow case, why don't we re-look our murder board?"

"Sounds good."

They ducked into Spartan's cubicle and stared at the whiteboard that was full of names, dates, places, and photos. Their post-author interview comments suggested that most of them had personal issues.

"Maybe these people write fiction to rid their demons," Spartan said. "You know—kill them with words."

"Possibly, Watts said, holding his chin. "What I find interesting is the more I study our evidence, the more convinced I am that Coulter's *Deadly Wrap* manuscript holds clues about his murder."

"Well, good luck finding them. We've both looked through it countless times, and never found any link to that *Death comes to those deserving* line you're so fond of."

"I know. On a different note, last night one of the cops at the DQ said nowadays he always wears his Kevlar vest. I'm thinking I might start wearing mine until those Skinheads are behind bars."

Spartan nodded, sticking out his lower lip. "That's probably not a bad idea," he said. "After all, they know your vehicle, and that you can identify them."

"Don't remind me. By the way, have you seen the DQ surveillance video?"

"Nope. Keep in mind I only heard about this an hour ago."

"No sweat. Let's go check it out. I seriously doubt those Skinheads had anything to do with CC's murder, but they might provide some insight into Lee and Chow's killers. "

When they reached the lab, Daisy Woods met them at the counter. She was smiling brighter than she had been, and only had eyes for Watts. And since she wasn't wearing any perfume, Watts took it as a sign that she had indeed worn it for his benefit. Her clothes were her standard polo and pants uniform, but she wore a glow he hadn't noticed before.

"What can I do for you, detectives?" she said.

"We'd like to see the Dairy Queen surveillance video," Watts said, as professionally as he could.

"Sure. Tim Westin already scanned it so he could do some computer enhancements, so it's no problem."

As soon as she left, Spartan elbowed his partner in the ribs, grinning like a fool. "I knew it!" he whispered. "I knew you two would hit it off."

Watts casually looked over at him, playing dumb. "Come on, Maxx. Mulberry spilled the beans about the two of you last night. Personally, I think it's great."

"She helped me search the park, Blaine. That's it. She's a professional in every sense of the word. Don't blow this out of proportion."

"Oh, I'm not, but her eyes say she likes you. You should spend more time with her."

"Let me worry about that. Now be good, she's coming back."

Daisy looked at them as if she knew they were talking about her. "Here you go," she said. "Sign on the dotted line and it's yours. The player and monitor are set up in the room next door."

Watts smiled at her. "Thank you very much. We'll have it back shortly."

The surveillance tape showed nearly everything that happened in the DQ. The Skinheads standing there, Watts coming in, Barbed Wire's challenge, and then Watts pulling his gun and showing his badge. Tony Fazelli ran into the back room right after that, and then the Skinheads left. Spartan was impressed at how Barbed Wire and Minnie-Me stared into the camera. It was hard to believe no one could identify these cooperative thugs. Few people like this had clean records. Then again, now there might be enough people with shaved heads and tattoos where they blended in. Watts didn't buy that, but it was the best excuse anyone had come up with. The fact that Skip Parsons' Forest Park witnesses couldn't identify the guys in the getaway pickup seemed to validate that possibility.

But Watts didn't need printouts of these guys to know what they looked like. Their images were burned into his brain like the sound of their rust-bucket pickup. He hoped—no, prayed—that one day they would tail him. Following a few deviations and with some backup, he could nail the SOBs. He would really love to do that. His partner's gaze made him look.

"What? Please don't tell me you're gonna say something about that lab tech."

"Not at all," Spartan said. "This tape got me thinking about Ben Striker. Here's an author that's involved in surveillance, and openly admits to being in Texas before the murder. To me, that gives credence to the possibility that he was spying for CC Coulter."

Watts' forehead sunk. "So your saying CC hired Striker to spy on his wife?"

"It's a possibility, especially if CC promised him a book deal. I mean, why would Kat hire him when she already knew her husband was a player? But CC may not have known about OJ boinking his wife until Striker came along."

"Okay, so what's your theory? That Kat and OJ put two and two together, had Pao Lee kill CC to keep their affair a secret, and then took out Pao and his buddy to cover their tracks? That seems like a longshot to me, pal."

Spartan mournfully bowed his head. "If you say so."

"It was sarcasm, Blaine, but who knows? That would explain why they found Lee's hair in the office. Still, it doesn't explain why Lee would murder his publisher, or why OJ would import a hit man from Hong Kong when there are hundreds of willing mercenaries in Texas. As for Striker, even if we can place him in Fort Worth at the time of CC's murder, we don't have a shred of evidence on him. The irony is I practically solved Skip Parsons' case by stumbling into a Dairy Queen, and we're still left hanging. This case stinks worse than the outside air."

"I certainly hope we'll solve this case before the wildfires are extinguished."

Watts nodded, still thinking about Striker. Yes, he is a private detective, but he's also a man of honor. A retired Vietnam Veteran Army lieutenant colonel, no less. Watts thought about his surveillance experience, losing Kat Coulter at the Convention Center. Striker would be out of business if he ever allowed that to happen. Striker also wouldn't leave until he found out why Kat was there.

Watts looked at his partner. "You ready to go for a ride?"

"Don't tell me, we're going back to Kat Coulter's again."

"Nope. We're gonna pay a visit to the *Fort Worth Star Telegram* to check out their stories on the mayor's social events."

Suddenly Spartan's light came on. "And we're doing this to make a connection between Kat Coulter and the mayor, right?"

Watts nodded.

"I like it," Spartan said. "Let's go."

They turned in the surveillance tape and left in their Crown Vic without informing Ryder. The newspaper building was only nine blocks away, so it didn't take long to get there. Flashing their badges, the security guard let them inside. Watts asked who handled the social affairs page and they were directed to Reporter Leslie Malone. Amongst the chatter of desperate reporters and ringing phones, they headed toward her desk. Malone barely acknowledged them when they arrived. Her short-cropped hair, masculine attire, and thick-framed glasses couldn't hide her beautiful blue eyes. She didn't look impressed by their suits or badges.

"May I help you?" she said, twirling her pen between her fingers.

"Yes," Watts said. He introduced him and his partner and then seated himself across from her so they could see eye-to-eye. The only problem was her computer screen blocked his view, so he moved his chair to one side. Spartan chose to stand. "I've seen your name on some of Mayor Jordan's stories," Watts continued, bluffing. "They're quite good."

Malone folded her hands together, alternating stares between Watts and Spartan. "You should know that sucking up has never worked for me," she said. "What do you want, detectives?"

Other than interrupting her day, Watts wondered what they had done to piss her off. Before sitting down, he noticed a framed photo of her with the mayor, both wearing tuxedoes. It appeared to be quite recent. "That's a nice shot of you with the mayor," he said. "What was the occasion?"

"He presented me with a journalism award, but somehow I doubt you care anything about that. In case you didn't know, newspapers run on deadlines, so again, what do you want?"

Watts gazed at her wondering who assigned her to the social detail. Maybe she acted nicer around women. Then again, maybe not. Pointing at the photo, he said, "When was it taken?"

"A few days ago, why? Are you gay? I mean, you're handsome enough. I could introduce you to some friends."

Watts smiled sheepishly at his partner, and then at her. "No, I'm not gay, but thanks anyway. Tell me about this black tie affair with the mayor. It wasn't from last night was it?"

"Had it been last night, I would have given that reply instead of saying a few days ago. And last night's affair was another fund raiser. It seems the mayor has them constantly. Maybe he plans to run for President one day.

Anyway, the awards ceremony was a much bigger deal, and was also held at the Convention Center. When I say a bigger deal, I'm referring to the opportunity for the really big wigs to wear tuxedoes and rub elbows with the mayor while the people receiving the awards stay in the background except for their photo op. Personally, I don't understand that kind of schmoozing, but it was nice of the mayor to present the award to me. It's my first one with this newspaper."

"Congratulations on your award," Spartan said. "May we see a copy of the program?"

She opened her desk drawer like she was going to look for it, but then hesitated. "Why do you want it? What does this concern?"

"We're not at liberty to discuss that," Watts said, "but we'd like a copy of the program."

After exchanging glances, she reached into the drawer and pulled out the pamphlet. "You can find it on line, but I'll make you a copy anyway," she said. "I'll be right back."

Watts watched the pear-shaped woman waddle toward the copy machine. Clearly, her sharp mind made up for whatever her physique lacked. When she reached the copier, he sensed she was eyeing him in her peripheral vision, and could practically see the cogs spinning in her brain. Her return trip seemed faster.

"Here you go," she said, handing Watts the program. "Anything else?"

Watts picked up the program, amazed at how many people he had faced with similar attitudes since CC Coulter died. "I think we're good," he said. "We appreciate your assistance. I wish you continued success with your newspaper career."

They wasted no time heading for the door. When they first came in, Watts had no idea what they would find, but they left with a bounty.

TWENTY SIX

If there is a god, Watts believed He was watching over them today. Once they returned to the station, he made two more copies of the awards program so he and Spartan each had one, and he could put one in the evidence folder. Without explaining himself, he began circling certain attendees. Hank Azar was there. So were Courtney Dridelle, Kat Coulter, and Ben Striker. Reading through the program helped piece things together.

"Can you believe they gave CC Coulter a posthumous award for an environmental piece he wrote for the *Fort Worth Star Telegram*?" he said to Spartan.

"I know. Who would have thought a fiction writer would publish an article about corruption within the oil industry, and how it relates to our current energy and financial crisis. I bet he didn't score any points with the oil barons."

Watts set his pen down, thinking about that. "Let's forget about the oil guys for now and concentrate on the murder. I can see why Kat Coulter would attend the affair, but why would any GP authors show up for CC's environmental award? Something's not right."

"I agree," Spartan said, "but my point was that maybe the oil barons he offended decided to take him out. We know they've ordered hits before. I admit it's a long shot, but nothing can be ruled out."

Watts nodded as he set his program aside. Going back to his computer, he surfed the *Star Telegram's* web site for CC's prize-winning article. When he found it, he printed two copies. He expected to see a photo of Kat Coulter all dolled up and teary-eyed as she accepted the award on her husband's behalf, but her photo was missing. He mentioned this to Spartan and picked up the phone. "I'm calling Ben Striker," he said. "Feel free to listen in."

This time the private detective answered promptly. After exchanging greetings, Watts said, "I noticed that your name was among the attendees at a *Fort Worth Star Telegram* awards banquet and wondered why you were there. Were you working, or—"

"Detective, before you go any further, I was already working in Fort Worth when Hank Azar told me CC was getting this award. My planner showed I was free that night, so I made plans to attend. While I would have preferred seeing the mayor hand the award to CC rather than his wife, it was good that they recognized him. By the way, Kat looked stunning."

Watts delayed commenting, wondering how a private investigator who claimed to work 24/7 could know his schedule that far enough in advance. "Do you recall where you sat at the banquet?" he said.

"Of course. I was with Courtney Dridelle and Hank Azar."

Watts nodded, chewing on his lower lip. Striker sounded so casual, he wondered if he wasn't wasting everyone's time.

"Mr. Striker, did Mayor Jordan pose for photos with the recipients?"

"How would I know?"

"Because you were there, and you would notice details like that."

Striker paused, so Watts looked at his partner. Spartan's hiked shoulders confirmed he was equally clueless. Finally, Watts said, "Mr. Striker, are you there?"

"I am, and I was trying to recall the event. I suppose the mayor posed with each award recipient, but honestly, I wasn't paying attention. Why do you ask?"

"Because it's odd that Kat Coulter's acceptance photo is the only one missing."

"Oh, my god!" Striker sarcastically said. "Kat's photo's missing? I promise I won't sleep until this mystery is solved!"

Watts covered the phone to hide his partner's chuckle. Thankfully, Spartan quickly recovered so he could uncover the phone. "Okay," Watts said. "I probably deserved that, but why would her photo be the only one missing?"

"Beats me. Maybe it was overexposed."

"Nice try, but they used digital cameras."

"Then how about she didn't like it, and requested they not use it?"

"Okay, but a second ago you said she looked stunning."

"She did, but that doesn't mean she couldn't take a bad photo. My god, you can snap an entire set of *Cosmo*-worthy shots, and women find something they hate about every one of them. Even when I'm testifying in court, my female clients seem more concerned about their looks than they are about their defense. It's truly amazing."

"I'm sure," Watts said, now changing the subject. "So, why were you in Fort Worth?"

"We've been through this before. I can't divulge that."

"I know, but it never hurts to ask. Have a good day, Mr. Striker."

"I will, detective. Bye now."

Watts cradled the phone and propped his feet on his desk. He found it a lot more fun dueling with a PI than a lawyer. He and Striker each had their jabs, but it ended in a stalemate. Their conversation reminded him of the *Magnum PI* episodes where Magnum toyed with the police. *Castle* and *Hawaii Five-0* had their share of cops versus PIs, too. Watts loved these shows because he could relate to them. He pictured an episode where Kat Coulter and Mayor Jordan were kissing next to CC's dead body. The image vanished when Spartan called his name.

"Dude, you're daydreaming again," Spartan said.

"Not daydreaming, Blaine. It's called thinking about the case. I thought I was getting somewhere with Striker, but the conversation fizzled before it ever started. Striker answered all of my questions without hesitation, or fear of repercussion."

"I think you're overrating him," Spartan said. "I mean, how hard is it to admit that you attended a banquet when your name's printed in the program? Remember, he refused to answer why he was in Fort Worth."

"Which means it's still possible he was working for one of the Coulters."

"Or someone in high places."

Watts sighed, wishing Spartan would stop playing the Devil's Advocate. His constantly second-guessing everything he did was getting real old. Then again, he provided a good balance, which was probably why detectives worked in teams. Watts got up and slid his chair under his desk. "I'll be back in a few," he said. "Keep looking into Striker. I want to know his plane tickets, hotel reservations, rental car, and whatever else you can dig up on him while he was here. He probably isn't our killer, but he might inadvertently lead us to him."

"We can only hope."

Watts headed to the lab while Spartan did some research. Tim Westin had started toward the counter, but turned around when Daisy said she would handle it. She seemed happy to see him, and that put Watts in a better mood.

"You're back," she said. "What can I do for you now?"

Watts leaned over the counter and whispered, "I need your opinion on something. Would you mind joining me in the screening room?"

She casually glanced at her co-worker and said, "Westin, Detective Watts needs some help with something. We'll be in the screening room. Come get me if you need me."

Watts followed her into the room amazed at how quickly she could turn her charm on and off. Though intrigued, it made him wonder who the real Daisy Woods was. On the one hand, it made perfect sense since she was so new to the job, but it sure made things confusing on a personal level. He intentionally left the door open to preclude any rumors or innuendos, and recounting all that had happened, introduced his theory that either of the Coulters could have hired Striker for surveillance. Daisy listened intently, but offered no ideas. Still, it was good talking to her, and Watts no longer felt anxious like he had when they first met in Forest Park. He also felt that their experience in finding Tony Fazelli gave them a connection. Her professional demeanor made it difficult to determine if she had any feelings for him, but this wasn't the time or place to be worrying about such things. Watts checked his watch and rose from his chair.

Reaching across the table to shake her hand, he said, "Thanks for meeting with me, Ms. Woods. You're a great listener."

"I'm always happy to help," she said, returning a firm grip. "Call me anytime."

Taking that as a positive sign, Watts floated up the stairs to meet with his partner. Spartan stopped what he was doing and leaned back in his chair. Since Spartan didn't ask about the lab tech. Watts said, "I can't imagine Kat Coulter taking a bad photo, so why is hers the only one missing from the web site?"

"I don't know, but I have a feeling you're going to tell me."

"I think it's because Mayor Jordan was in the picture."

Spartan swiveled his head, stretching his neck. Too much time at the computer had kinked his neck. Swiveling it to ease the tension, he stared at the ceiling for a long moment before looking at his partner.

"Sorry about that," he said. "I wish I had some Motrin. Anyway, Mayor Jordan would have been in all the photos because he was the one handing out awards."

"I realize that, but maybe OJ's expression wasn't what either of them wanted. You know—like maybe his arm was too snug around her waist, or maybe he was gazing into her eyes instead of the camera. Scandals arising from less have toppled politicians."

Spartan pinched his lips shut until he was ready to respond. Following a long pause, he said, "Kat Coulter is newly widowed and OJ's been single for years. No one's going to care if OJ's grab-assing."

"Well, I care," Watts said. "Especially if they co-conspired to kill CC. For all we know, OJ and Striker both crossed over to the Dark Side when Jordan hired him to take CC out. Striker could have planted Lee's hair and made it look like a break-in. To me, that seems more plausible than Lee coming back to kill him."

Spartan's face went blank. "Wow," he said. "You're getting quite a straw collection."

"Very funny, but you heard Striker's response when I asked why he attended the banquet."

Spartan nodded. "He said he was already in town, but since his plane didn't arrive in Fort Worth until the day after CC died, I'd say he has a pretty solid alibi."

Watts snapped his head around. "Why didn't you tell me that sooner?"

"You never gave me the chance. You kept running your mouth like you always do."

Watts wasn't sure how Spartan intended that, but his jab reminded him of Striker, Dridelle, and Azar trashing their publisher during their interviews, and then afterwards attending the awards banquet. So, why would anyone attend an event honoring someone they couldn't stand? Striker may have had an alibi, but the others didn't. In fact, Dridelle could have easily distracted CC while his wife was knocked out on sleeping pills, tied him to the chair in a kinky sort of way, killed him, and then staged the break-in. It was another long shot, but at least it explained why CC didn't fight back.

Spartan clasped his hands and bowed his head. "Sorry, Maxx. I didn't mean to take my frustration out on you. Maybe we should explore the disgruntled oil baron theory again."

Watts started laughing. "I can just see some fat-cat oil baron standing inches from CC Coulter's face saying, 'This is a giant spit wad, the most powerful spit wad in the world. It will stop your breathing so fast you'll wish I would blow your head clean off. So, you've got to ask yourself one question: Do you feel lucky? Well, do ya, punk?'"

Spartan cocked his head, casting a frown. "I fail to see how Dirty Harry's celebrated line has anything to do with this case."

Watts sighed. "It was a joke, Blaine. I said it to lighten the mood, but now you're pissing me off. I'm gonna hit the head. I'll be back."

In the rest room, Watts went right for the sink to splash water on his face. The man in the mirror said he hadn't been sleeping enough lately, and he was right. He toweled himself dry, combed his hair, straightened his tie, and went back to feeling more normal. Spartan's look implied it wasn't.

Standing next to his partner, Watts said, "I've been thinking about it, and in light of CC's award, we can't rule out the possibility the oil industry is involved in CC's murder. How do you want to proceed?"

"For starters, we should add OJ's name to our suspect list. His initials can suffice."

"Sure, and if anyone asks, we'll say OJ means Overly Jealous, referring to Kat Coulter."

Spartan cracked a smile. "I like that. We should probably bump Dridelle up, too."

Thinking about it, Watts began pacing, squishing his left shoe with each step. He made four trips back and forth, ending up at his partner's desk again. Staring at Spartan's computer jogged his memory. "I think it's time we approached Lieutenant Ryder about impounding CC Coulter's computer and files," he said. "If he balks, then we'll know Jordan's pulling his strings."

Moving his mouth from side-to-side, Spartan agreed, and followed Watts down the hall with their murder board. They stopped in front of Ryder's office like two prisoners waiting to see the warden. Watts tapped on the door and Ryder waved them.

Smiling, rubbing his hands together, Ryder said, "So, are you ready to make an arrest?"

"Hardly," Watts said. "We're still lacking evidence, and the GP authors are still withholding information that's key to our investigation. Sir, we're here because we need your help acquiring The Guillotine Press contracts. I know we've been over this, but we have to get our hands on at least one of them, and the most likely source is CC Coulter's computer and files. The problem is we'll need to subpoena them."

The smile slid off Ryder's face like mud in a carwash, his new expression more angry than disappointed. "You're right, we did talk about this, and as I recall, I told you to let it go. Nothing upsets me more than constantly having to repeat myself."

"Then give us the tools to finish our investigation," Spartan said.

Suddenly the room fell silent. Watts and Spartan stood their ground like matadors in the ring, sabers ready, prepared to strike. But Ryder wasn't backing down. The standoff continued for another minute before Watts said, "Let's forget about Coulter's computer for a moment. What happened to the media coverage on these murder cases? Did Mayor Jordan somehow manage to suppress them?"

Ryder got up, locked the door, and returned to his chair. "I wondered how long it would take you to bring up his name. You think I don't know who OJ is on your whiteboard? Any moron in the office would know who it was."

Lines plowed Watts' forehead. "No one's above the law, lieutenant, and withholding information can't protect the mayor."

Ryder scowled like a captured beast. "Listen carefully because what I'm about to say doesn't leave this room." He waited for their nods before continuing. "So, here's the deal. Mayor Jordan is not a suspect, so scratch him from your list. I know this for a fact because he and some nameless individuals were playing poker when Coulter was murdered."

A grin spread from Watts' mouth like an earthquake. "And were you one of these nameless players?" he said. "I mean, how else would you know this?"

Beet red, Ryder said, "Yes, I was there, and it's perfectly legal since we don't play for money. But since the voters might not see it that way, the mayor has gone to great lengths to keep the poker playing and Coulter's murder quiet."

The two detectives broke out in simultaneous laughter. The longer it went on, the worse it got, and their boss' look didn't deter them in the least. Still snickering, Watts said, "So, if you're not playing for money, what are you playing for? Pink slips? Spa treatments? *Votes*?"

"Now you're pushing it, Maxx. How about none of the above?"

Watts' smile faded. He had spent his career exchanging barbs with Ryder, and this was the first time Ryder kept his mean face. Watts knew he should leave it alone, but that wasn't his style when it came to murder investigations. Rather than provoke his boss, he chose a different tact.

"Okay, we'll forget about the mayor," he said. "But why won't you get us those book contracts?"

Ryder slammed his fist on his desk and hunched over them like a vulture. His angry eyes piercing them like lasers, it became clear that Mr. Hyde had taken over. Baring his teeth, he said, "I'll talk to the DA, but you'd better come up with something or I'll have you both in uniforms faster than you can say 'where's my patrol car?' Got it?"

"Got it," they said with one voice.

Watts was about to leave, but had another thought. "Any update on Tony Fazelli?"

"Yes. He's home and doing well. I'll pass it on that you asked about him."

"I'd like to send him a note. Can you get me his address?"

"I'll e-mail it to you. Now get out of here and get back to work."

Once clear of Ryder's office, Watts reached into his pocket and turned off his tape recorder. Another thing that Dad always preached was having good insurance, and today Sony provided it. When things get strange, you get sneaky. He didn't tell Spartan about it, either. Sometimes it's best that way. On their way back to their desks, Watts squished his shoe extra loud so everyone would know they survived Ryder's ranting just fine. He even remarked to his partner how well things went. The office now quiet, the only sound came from Watts' shoe.

TWENTY SEVEN

Today's lunch came from the vending machine, and Watts' stomach had been rebelling all day. When he got home after work, he searched his pantry for something to eat. He tossed the macaroni and cheese that expired five years ago. Three dusty tuna cans soon followed. The jar of spaghetti sauce looked okay, but he didn't have any spaghetti. He had peanut butter, but no bread. The two unopened mustard bottles were leftovers from a party two years ago, so he tossed them, too. Sadly, his freezer's contents were as dismal as the pantry's. Staring at a box of pizza rolls, he thought about the fabulous dinner Spartan described. Slamming the freezer door, his melted DQ banana split then came to mind. Whether he ended up there for a burger and a replacement sundae or went somewhere else, he knew he had to get out. Still concerned about the Skinheads, he decided to don his Kevlar vest.

He slipped a Hawaiian shirt over his vest and pistol and took a drive, contemplating Ryder's relationship with Mayor Jordan. He rarely doubted his ability to solve cases, but CC's might be the exception. Whether his subconscious planned it or not, he ended up at the same DQ where he had the problem. As he was parking, he noticed that Tony Fazelli's car was gone. He also noticed a new door sign that showed the business hours were from six AM until eight PM Sunday through Thursday, and six AM to ten PM on Friday and Saturday. He appreciated Stockman keeping his word.

This time, two teens in blue DQ visors and polos were standing behind the counter, eager to take his order. The ponytailed blond girl wore too much makeup, but nicely filled out her shirt. The boy standing next to her was probably a basketball player, not because he was black, but rather because of his height. His muscles would develop later, but his lean body showed he worked out. Standing at least six-five, the kid seemed to relish in towering over Watts.

"Nice shirt," the kid said with a toothy grin. "Where'd you get it?"

"Goodwill," said Watts, looking over the menu. A reflection made him glance over his shoulder. He smiled at the father and daughter that came through the entry and they smiled back. He moved so he could read the menu and still see Leroy. Maybe his Kevlar vest increased his paranoia, but the three teens seated near the window seemed to be admiring Leroy a lot more than they should. They seemed harmless enough, sending text messages between cheap talk and grins. Minutes later, they left without tossing their trash and headed straight for Watts' truck. Tracking them with his eyes, he reached into his pocket, and when they got too close, pressed Leroy's panic button. At Leroy's sudden honking and flashing, the kids jumped back looking horrified. Soon, they were glaring at Watts, so he waved at them. He thought they would leave, but were soon back at their seats, talking again. Pretending to ignore their glances, he ordered a burger, fries, and water. Barely three minutes elapsed before the future NBA star with the DQ visor said his order was ready. Watts thanked him, grabbed some napkins, and took a seat where he could eye the kids and his truck. A few minutes later, the teens left, allowing him to enjoy his meal. When he finished, he ordered a banana split, and ate it before it melted.

Watts regretting ordering the dessert, though. By itself, a banana split was fine, but after a burger, it felt like a five pound weight in his stomach. He had planned to wash Leroy when he got home to burn off some calories, but then an old red and white Ford pickup appeared in his mirror, two car lengths behind. Pulling into a gas station to let it pass, he soon realized it was too quiet to be the Skinheads' F-150. The old cowboy behind the wheel confirmed that, his hands at ten and two. Watts' realized that his obsession with the Skinheads and their rust-bucket pickup was affecting his judgment and stealing his pleasure. Ridding them from his mind made the drive home less stressful.

After stripping off his Kevlar and bathing Leroy, he went inside and skimmed through the newspaper's entertainment section. *Dirty Harry was playing at the Movie Tavern at West 7th Street?* He couldn't believe it. When he was a kid, Clint Eastwood's tough-guy Inspector Harry Callahan was his hero. A modern day Wyatt Earp, Callahan was respected and feared at the same time. Of course, it helped that Eastwood's character always had more action than dialogue. Watts raced to the theater and found his seat right before show time. Something brushed against his head and he smoothed his hair. Seconds later, he felt it again. On the third time, he angrily swung his head around.

Spartan waved back, grinning. "I wondered how much popcorn I'd waste before you turned around," he said.

Watts smiled at his partner and waved to his wife and kids. "We'll talk after the show."

Calm again, he turned around, eager to watch the sniper take out the girl in the pool in the opening scene. By today's standards, *Dirty Harry* seemed cartoonish, but in its day, it was quite intense. After the show, he met the Spartans in the lobby. Cute as ever, Sandy's perfect skin, perfectly groomed hair, and perfectly groomed kids truly made her a Stepford Wife. Sandy was the first to speak.

"Isn't this place great?" she said. "We haven't been here in years. It was a spur of the moment thing."

"Same for me," said Watts. "I dare you to name a detective who would pass up *Dirty Harry* on the big screen."

"I know," she said, looking at her husband. "Maxx, I promised the kids a Dairy Queen sundae on the way home if they were good, so we'd better get going. You want to join us?"

Watts looked Spartan, wondering if he had mentioned the DQ incident to Sandy. Blaine's eyes implied that she was making the decisions, and he didn't dare interfere. With that in mind, he said, "I appreciate the offer, but I just came from there. I don't know about the other DQs, but the one near here now closes at eight, Sunday through Thursday. I'm afraid you're too late for tonight."

Looking relieved, Spartan smiled at his kids. "How about Baskin Robbins?" he said.

"That sounds great," said Sandy. "Thanks for telling us, Maxx. See you later."

"Good night, Sandy. Blaine, I'll see you bright and early."

"I'll be there."

Watts headed for his truck and pressed the fob button. Shining under a street lamp, Leroy welcomed him back by unlocking his doors turning on his interior light. Watts climbed in, wishing he possessed Callahan's ability to skirt the law. Like him or hate him, Dirty Harry could sure clean up a town. So, what would Harry do in a situation like this? Since he couldn't discuss it with Harry or Clint, he decided to call Daisy.

"Sorry to call so late," he said, "but I just got out of a movie."

"Not a problem. You want to come over? I have something we should discuss."

Watts' heart stopped. Nothing in her tone sounded personal. He said he would be right over and pointed Leroy in her direction. Twelve minutes later he was knocking on her door.

Greeting him in a white halter and cut-off jeans, she said, "Come on in. Would you like something to drink?"

"Water would be great," he said, admiring her outfit. Once she left, he let his eyes roam though her apartment. Her UT diploma was the first thing he noticed. A Bachelor of Science in chemistry. *Nice.*

She came out of the kitchen giving an odd look. "What's that noise?" she said.

"It's my shoe," he said, apologetically. "Sorry. It's a long story."

"No need to explain. I've heard that noise before. Just wasn't sure where it came from."

Suddenly, he felt naked. Clearly, she didn't invite him over for small talk. He didn't smell her perfume, either. It made him wonder if he had imagined it before. Since she wasn't talking, he said, "On the phone, you mentioned you had something to discuss. Is everything okay? Does it concern the case?"

She handed him a water bottle, and then plopped down on the love seat. Watching Watts dither, she gently patted the seat. "It's okay," she said, smiling . "I showered, and I don't bite."

Watts sheepishly sat next to her, angling his body so he faced her. She wore no makeup, and didn't need it. It was the kind of setting men dream about, sitting next to a beautiful woman alone in her apartment, the night getting late. The only problem was nothing in her eyes even remotely hinted that she was interested, and that crushed him. "Okay, now that I'm settled—".

"Lee and Chow's bodies are gone," she said.

Suddenly all business, Watts' eyes opened wide. "How can they be gone when they've only been dead two days?"

"I found it suspicious, too, which is why I thought you should know. When the bodies were brought in, the ME contacted the Chinese Consulate in Houston who then contacted his counterparts in Hong Kong. After an extensive search, no one came forward to claim either Lee's or Chow's body. The Chinese claim that neither one has any relatives in Hong Kong or Kowloon, but you have to wonder how hard they tried in a city of over seven million residents."

"Good point, particularly since Lee and Chow are such common surnames."

"Right," she said, cutting him off. "Anyway, late this afternoon, the Chinese Consulate called back and instructed the ME to have their remains cremated, so now all that's left of Pao Lee and Shing Chow are crime scene photos, DNA samples, and their passports."

Watts folded his hands, conspiracy on his mind. How convenient that one of his primary persons of interest had been reduced to ashes. Frowning at her, he said, "Call me stupid, but why wouldn't someone claim their bodies? Why would the ME so willingly dispose of them during an ongoing homicide investigation? Why would a Hong Kong author like Lee seek out a Texas publishing company when his backyard practically promoted copyright infringement? Hong Kong had tons of publishers, and Lee wouldn't have to translate a thing. So, why go with CC Coulter? Why Texas?"

"I can't explain that, but since Britain ruled Hong Kong until 1997, both men probably spoke fluent English."

Watts gave a jumbled look. "Why would you know that?"

"My parents took me there shortly before the British returned rule to the Chinese."

"That must have been fun. Is Hong Kong really as crowded as they say?"

"Absolutely. The streets are so crowded there that Jackie Chan could disappear without a trace."

"Wow. Unfortunately, I'm still in the dark over Pao Lee's cremation."

She moved her mouth to one side. "Sorry I'm not more help."

He desperately wanted to prolong their conversation so he could stay longer. His hands sweaty and mouth dry, he gulped his water, and clung to the bottle. Her looks had melted his brain, just like Dridelle said. *Men truly are the weaker sex.* When he managed a thought, he said, "Is it odd watching Chinese people speak with a British accent?"

Smiling, she gently patted his thigh. A sisterly touch. He didn't pull away.

"Sometimes I'll see one on CNN, and it catches me off guard because I was expecting a Chinese accent," she said. "A Japanese friend once told me that when she visited Japan, everyone assumed she could speak the language, but she could barely manage to say, *moshimoshi*, their telephone greeting. Both show how biased we are."

"That's true. Imagine how you'd react to a Chinese guy speaking with a Texas twang."

Giggling, she said, "Actually, that might be kind of funny." She paused to adjust her strap, and then turned to see him better. Crossing a leg made her hips face him. She made no attempt to adjust her shorts that had ridden up slightly. "Not to change the subject, but did you read Pao Lee's novel?"

"I skimmed through it, but found myself more concerned with the plot than its details."

"Well, I read it all the way through after you told me he was an author. Had you done the same, you would have picked up on the British references."

Nodding his agreement, Watts said, "He did seem to use 'chap' a fair amount."

"That's one term, but my point is it validates that Lee spoke the King's English. Of course, it still doesn't explain why he sought publication in the US versus Hong Kong."

Watts nodded, admiring her. If he was a kid, he would fall into her lap and she would think it was cute. Somehow, he didn't think that trick would work as well now. "Daisy, would you mind if I ask you a personal question?" he said, gazing into her eyes.

In a flash, her body turned pink. Tucking her hair behind her ear, she said, "Not at all. What is it?"

It was the first time since he arrived that she seemed to notice him. Her eyes were softer now, her demeanor warmer. There was no turning back. "Do you have any policies against dating a police officer?"

Smiling sweetly, she said, "Maxx, if this your way of asking me out, I'd say yes."

Suddenly the weight that had been crushing his chest was gone. "That's so great, because I've wanted to ask that for a long time."

"Now may I ask a question?" she said. "Why do you spell your name with two X's."

"Because Mom said I was extra special." He immediately added, "As for a date, how about tomorrow at seven?"

"Seven it is."

Now feeling awkward, he stood up. "I need to go," he said. "Thank you for the information on Lee. I really appreciate it."

"You're welcome," she said, walking him to the door. "See you around campus, Maxx."

"Count on it."

TWENTY EIGHT

Watts slept until his alarm went off. Not used to sleeping soundly, he attributed it to Daisy. He could hardly wait for their date tonight. But with a full day ahead of him, he rolled out of bed, showered, shaved, grabbed a piece of toast, and ran out the door. Although he arrived early, Spartan was already at his desk, staring at the murder board. Judging from Spartan's partner's whistling, it seemed he had a good evening, too.

Then Ryder appeared like the Wicked Witch. "Whenever you clowns finish doing whatever it is you're doing, you can come fetch your paperwork."

Watts' ears perked up. "Paperwork as in subpoena?"

"That's right, Maxx. The judge happened to be with the DA when I called this morning, so it's your lucky day. Don't screw this up."

"Thanks for the vote of confidence, sir. Please give my best to the DA and the mayor."

Ryder stormed off without responding.

Watts grinned at his partner. "It is a glorious morning, Blaine. Let's grab that paper and take a drive—and no, I do *not* want you calling her."

"Fine with me."

Writ in hand, they were soon heading toward Kat Coulter's house. Given the early hour, Watts saw no reason why she wouldn't be there. Even though he was certain she had deleted some files, calling ahead would have her double-checking her misdeeds. As they approached her house, her garage door cracked open. Watts blocked the driveway and climbed out of his car.

She rolled down her window, casting an angry gaze. "I have a hair appointment in twenty minutes," she said. "Move your car."

"This won't take long," Watts said, handing her the legal notice. "We'll be gone as soon as we load everything up."

After reading the fine print, she killed her engine and said, "If I miss my hair appointment, you're paying for it."

"No, if you miss your appointment it's because you wasted your time."

The detectives followed her through the front entry and immediately headed for the office. As best Watts could tell, everything looked and smelled the same. The blinds were drawn, the temperature tolerable. He quickly went to work unplugging the computer's wires and cords.

Hovering over him, she said, "Is this really necessary?" When he failed to answer, she added, "I want everything back in the same condition it is now. Do you hear me? Not one single mark!"

"The lab will be careful," Spartan said. "It shouldn't take them long. I'm curious, though. If you can't access your husband's computer, what good is it to you?"

"As I've explained before, my attachment is purely emotional. It's all that's left of my husband, and I can't bear to let it go."

"All we need is the tower and external hard drive," Watts said to her, getting to his feet. "Did you ever find the filing cabinet's key?"

"Actually, I did," she said, removing it from the desk drawer. "I found it the other day."

Watts tilted his head, unsure if he heard right. He seemed to recall her saying she refused to go into the office, but he wasn't about to challenge her now. He grabbed the electronic components he needed and left Spartan behind to retrieve the paper files. They had already decided that if she opened the cabinet, they would keep the file drawers intact to save time.

Spartan had the file drawers on the floor before Watts was back. Two trips each, and everything was loaded in the Crown Vic. Huffing and sweaty, Watts thanked Kat and backed his car out of the way. Still angry, she zipped past them and sped off.

"Wow," Watts said, dragging an old Whataburger napkin across his brow. "I had no idea hair appointments were so important to widows."

Spartan gave him that, "you are so clueless look." "Widow or not, she's still a woman."

Watts figured his partner was right on both counts.

* * * * *

Back at 350, Watts signed Kat's computer components over to their best hacker, Electronics Specialist Aaron Collingsworth. A large man with thinning hair, a soft belly, and an oversized head, Collingsworth inspected the tower and backup hard drive while listening to Watts.

"Here's the authorization to break into the computer," Watts said, handing him a copy. "I'm looking for anything concerning The Guillotine Press, and in particular, its author's contracts. We're pretty certain they're in there, but they may also have been deleted."

"No problem, the specialist said. "It shouldn't take long."

"Great. Call me when you get the results."

But Watts' mind was stuck on Daisy more than the case. Over the past few days, they had spent a fair amount of time together, but dating was completely different. It had been a long time since he had been on a date, and he didn't want to blow it. She was smart, had a great figure, and understood a police officer's life. *She was perfect.* His right brain wanted to dance through the halls like Gene Kelly, but his left brain kept things in check. For tonight, dinner and conversation was all he wanted. Digging into the first of CC's file drawers brought him back.

Spartan had been sorting through his files ever since they got back. When he heard Watts at his desk, he slid his chair back to see him. "Well? What does Aaron think?"

"I expect some results soon. If possible, I'd like to return everything to her today."

"That won't happen unless you start sorting through those files."

"Yeah, yeah," Watts said, pulling his first file. "Did you find anything of interest yet?"

"Nope. So far it's been phone bills, utility bills, auto repair bills, insurance bills, and medical bills. Nothing says The Guillotine Press."

"Well, keep digging. Something must be in here or it wouldn't have been locked."

* * * * *

In less than an hour, they had located the GP files. Hiding in the back of the final cabinet drawer were receipts for publishing costs, business travel, car leases, and accounting for their home office, but no author contracts or royalty payment records. Neither detective was surprised at the outcome.

After returning everything to its proper place, Watts said, "Shall we see what Collingsworth has found?"

Spartan's look made Watts uneasy. It implied he wasn't organized. Rather than start an argument, Watts let it go and led the way, hoping to see Daisy again. Thinking of her made him feel sixteen again. She never appeared before Collingsworth waved him over.

Collingsworth adjusted his Harry Potter glasses, and then slid a thick manila folder across the counter like a bartender would a beer. "I believe this is what you're looking for," he proudly said.

Watts opened the folder and spread its contents so Spartan could see, too. They counted thirteen book contracts, which seemed peculiar since they only knew of ten GP authors. Closer inspection revealed that CC was included in the thirteen, but that still left two unaccounted for. The folder also included The Guillotine Press' financial records, an IRS audit, and proceedings from their tax fraud trial which happened to be represented by Iron Fist Attorney Hank Azar.

Watts smiled at Collingsworth. "This is a gold mine, Aaron. Thank you very much."

The specialist grinned back. "I knew you'd be pleased."

Spartan smiled, too. "By the way, how did you break the password?"

Collingsworth held his grin, folding his big arms across his belly. "I don't waste time on passwords, detective. We have much better ways to access hard drives. Everything I gave you was recently deleted, though. I guess people don't realize that the only way to completely erase data is to reformat or destroy the hard drive, and that wasn't done to either one. Thankfully, their ignorance keeps me employed."

"I'm sure," Watts said. "Should we impound the computer, or can we return it?"

"That's up to you. Everything's been documented, photographed, the files have been copied onto disks, everything's been printed in hard copy, and I've made certified hard copies for the courts, so as far as I'm concerned, take it back. Here, it will collect dust in the evidence locker, and that's never good for electronics."

Spartan covered his lips, casting a worried look. "But if we give the computer back, can't an attorney claim that we planted the evidence? In this case, the lawyer in question has a contract he doesn't want to share, and I'm sure he'll do all he can do discredit it."

Collingsworth removed his glasses and calmly leaned over the counter. "Detective, I go to great lengths to ensure everything stands up in court. Attorneys who have taken that route have always failed. If there's a question, all I do is go to the courthouse and testify. We've never lost a case over data authenticity."

"Then that makes our decision easy," said Watts. "We'll give it back."

Spartan had no choice but to go along with it.

This time Spartan called to make sure Kat was home. The air seemed cleaner, the fire smell less intense. Either the firefighters had made progress, or the wind had shifted. Either way, Watts was pleased with the result. Perhaps one day the sky would be blue again. Unsure whether Spartan was bored or upset with him, he said, "How many more times you think we'll make this drive, Blaine?"

"Hopefully, this is our last."

"I agree," he said, staring at the dry sagebrush and barren landscape. Even through wildfires and drought, tumbleweeds managed to survive. Whenever human civilization ends, they'll still be around with the crickets, roaches, and cicadas. These days, few cattle wandered the ranches. Most had been sold off because they had nothing to graze on. Everyone prayed for rain, even if it came from a squall line. Spartan broke his thought.

"Maxx, why couldn't you get someone to deliver this stuff? There are plenty of local couriers that need the business."

Watts glanced at him and then back at the road. "First off, who'd pay for it? Second, by delivering it personally, Kat might not think we found anything. Third, I'm curious to see if this makes its way back to Ryder before we tell him."

Spartan looked at him. "I assume you're referring to Hank Azar?"

"That's one name that comes to mind. Fourth, it's another excuse to see Kat Coulter. I keep hoping she'll slip up and say something she'll regret. Maybe something about Mayor Jordan, Courtney Dridelle, or the files will tie everything together. Or maybe she'll admit to deleting the files. That would allow us to nail her for withholding or destroying evidence. Anyway, we'll know more once we scrutinize Collingsworth's data. By the way, I'm not telling Ryder anything because I don't want the mayor feeding it back to Kat."

"Whatever you say, Maxx."

But Spartan's tone told Watts he wasn't okay with it. Spartan liked doing things by the book, especially since he was just back from rehab. Offering an explanation, Watts said, "I want you to know I accept full responsibility for this, so hang in there, okay?"

"Maxx, if I wanted to bail, I would've have done so a long time ago. I'm your partner, remember?"

"Glad to hear it."

When they arrived, Watts backed the car up to Kat's garage door. She met them at the front door with a new hairstyle that suited her pretty face. Highlights in an auburn color gave it depth, but treatments like that cost big bucks, and Kat claimed she could barely afford to cool her house. Of course, if she had received payment from CC's two million dollar life insurance policy, then it wouldn't be a problem.

"Your hair looks nice," he said, carrying her components through the entry. "Glad you made it to your appointment."

"Thanks," she said, dryly. "Set it up exactly like you found it, and make sure it works."

She was barking orders like a pirate captain, but Watts did everything without protest. It wasn't quite the *Protect and Serve* duty he signed up for, but it wasn't a problem, either.

Watching Spartan with her hands on her hips, she said, "Are you sure you put those cabinet drawers back in the right order?"

"Yes, ma'am," he said. "We marked them so we would know where they went."

When they finished with the first load, Watts and Spartan walked back to the Crown Vic, together. Leaning inside the trunk, and pretending to grab another load, Watts looked his partner and kept his voice low.

"Did you notice she's never inquired about what we found?" he said.

"Why would she? After all, she deleted everything, right?"

"Yeah. Let's let her keep thinking that."

When they finished their work, Kat Coulter inspected it, and then promptly escorted them outside. Glancing at his partner on their way back to the car, Spartan said, "I think we've worn out our welcome."

"Can't say that I blame her," Watts said. "But we did help her get over her grief."

"If you say so. I still find it odd that she never asked about what we found."

Watts closed the trunk and opened his door. "I keep telling you, Blaine, this case has conspiracy written all over it."

"I can't go that far. I'm just saying it's odd."

Up ahead in the middle of the street, Magpies picked at a road kill until some blowing trash scared them off. After passing the dead animal, Watts checked his rear-view mirror. In seconds, the scavengers were back at it. Spartan tapped his fingernails on the door panel like a ten year old. Finally, he stopped and looked at his partner.

"So, Maxx, you have anything going on tonight?"

"Actually, I have a date. I'll let you know how it goes."

"Crap!"

Watts' head spun at Spartan. "What's your problem? You're married, I'm single, and it's only one date."

"It's not that," he angrily said, looking at his lap. "Somehow I got a stain on my pants, and I'm guessing it's grease from one of those cabinet drawers."

"Sorry, man. I don't know what to say."

Spartan kept his head down until Watts slowed the car. With the engine still running and the air conditioner blowing, Watts stared blankly through the windshield. His concern mounting, Spartan said, "What's wrong, Maxx?"

Watts pointed. "You see that red and white pickup over there?"

Spartan spotted the rust-bucket in a parking lot. No one appeared to be inside. The front license plate was missing. "Yeah."

"It looks like the same F-150 from the Dairy Queen." Watts threw his door open and climbed out. "You can come with me or stay in the car, but I'm not going anywhere until I check the registration."

"I've got your back," Spartan said, climbing out.

Watts darted across the street and approached the vehicle with one hand covering his pistol grip. Seeing no one, he pulled out his notepad, wrote down the license plate, and ran back to the car. He handed his notebook to Spartan once they were both inside.

"Run the plate, but I'm sure it's not the same truck. Someone put a ton of money into the Skinheads' rust-bucket exhaust, and I can't imagine them replacing them with rusty pipes."

"Especially if they stole them off someone else's truck."

"The thought occurred to me, but my point is it's not the Skinheads' truck. Shall we grab lunch before heading back to the office?"

"I'll do anything except DQ."

"I hear ya."

*   *   *   *   *

Watts' sub sandwich filled his gut, but it was hardly satisfying. He would have been better off grabbing some fried rice and an egg roll from The Garden Dragon, or whatever that restaurant was named this month. Spartan kept pressing for details on Watts' evening date, but Watts wasn't giving any details. It was more fun keeping his partner guessing.

When they got back to 350, Watts unlocked his desk and retrieved the GP folder. He was convinced there was a link between the author contracts and CC Coulter's murder, and now he hoped to prove it. He handed six of them to Spartan and kept seven for himself. At first, they looked identical, other than the author's names and book titles. Mick Taggart hinted there was a financial commitment, but neither detective expected it was this substantial. Assuming they were reading correctly, it appeared that each author had to chip in thirty thousand dollars. In return, The Guillotine Press would publish, distribute, and promote two of their books. From Watts' perspective, that was the least that they could do for such an exorbitant sum. They also learned why the authors were so tight-lipped. There was a clause that stated that under no circumstances would they divulge their contracts to anyone.

Watts set his papers aside and looked at his partner. "Are you getting the same vibe as me?" he said.

"If you're referring to them getting scammed, then yes. Let's keep digging."

Watts got on the Internet to research what it cost to self-publish a book. The first person he spoke to sounded eager to publish the book he had never written. She said she loved books written by cops because of their authenticity. Since Watts couldn't provide any specifics on the number of pages, words, font, paper quality, book jacket, copyright, or ISBN, he said he would call her back and hung up. Before he could make another call, he would need help from his Barnes and Noble friend to decipher what was needed. Johnny wasn't in, so Denise Rashad stepped in to answer Watts' questions.

Rashad explained that publishers normally provide the ISBN number that tracks the book. She went on to say that while authors normally register their work with the Library of Congress, the publisher owns the copyright. Paper quality determines the printing cost, and there is a huge cost difference between publishing hardback versus paperback.

"Normally, libraries only buy hardbacks so publishing houses release hardbacks first. However, the high cost of these books is driving many libraries toward trade paperbacks—a soft cover version the same size as a hardback. While Barnes and Noble doesn't normally stock self-published books, they will order them on prepaid request," she said.

Watts set his pen down. "Ms. Rashad, the publisher I spoke with said something about an extra charge for returns. What's that all about?"

"Returns depend on the type of book it is," she said. "Mass market paperbacks are never returned, but hardback and trade paperbacks can be. At Barnes and Noble, if books haven't sold within a specified period, they are returned to the distributor for a full refund. Thus, some publishers pass the charge on to their authors, either taking it out of their royalties, or in some cases, charging them up front. And since distributors charge for storage and shipping, you can imagine how this cuts into profits. Of course, this practice varies between publishers so you need to check with them for their specifics."

Thinking this over, Watts questioned why anyone would publish with someone who passed on these expenses. To him, it seemed the creator of the work should benefit the most, but that clearly wasn't the case. "One last question," he said. "Do you carry any Guillotine Press books?"

"Any particular title?"

"How about *Hard Ride to Cimarron*?"

The phone was silent for a few moments, then Rashad came back on the line. "We don't carry it, and it doesn't appear to be self-published."

"That's okay. I'll look for it on line. I really appreciate your time. Say hi to Johnny."

"I will. Have a good one."

Watts ended the call more confused than he was before. He may have had a better understanding about what questions to ask, but if The Guillotine Press wasn't a self-publisher, he wasn't sure what to think. Sticking his head into Spartan's cubicle, he said, "I'm not qualified to make any judgments on The Guillotine Press, but how can a press that uses authors' money to print books not be considered self-published?"

"Beats me," Spartan said, swinging his chair around to face his partner. "And good luck getting an explanation from Kat."

"Yeah. Like everything else, she'll claim she doesn't know anything."

"I'm sure. So, did you determine how much it costs to publish a book?"

Watts leaned against the cubicle and it started to move. He quickly recovered and stood there with his arms crossed. "I'll have a better idea when I talk to the next publisher. Didn't the GP novels average around two hundred and fifty pages?"

Spartan quickly scanned through his stack of books, comparing them. "Yeah, two-fifty's about right, and the formatting seems to vary to keep 'em in that range."

"The publisher I spoke to said the retail price is determined by its production costs, plus a forty percent mark-up. That's the same mark-up we used when I worked retail in high school. Imagine how bitter you'd be if you were suckered out of thirty grand knowing you'd never see a profit. These days, in some towns thirty grand will buy a house."

"That, or a bad-ass pickup."

"Good one, Blaine, but my point is these authors signed their contracts knowing the cost." Leaving to go back to his desk, he said, "I need to make some calls."

The next publisher Watts spoke to broke down the costs for him. Besides printing costs, there was the publisher's take, distributors take, and the book store's take. Assuming no discounts, an author earned about a buck thirty for every trade paperback book sold, but no royalties were paid until the amount reached one hundred dollars. In spite of paying an extra fee for returns, returned books cancel sales one-to-one. Topping that off, the authors are responsible for their own promotion. Watts hung up, empathizing with anyone who had invested so much time in writing a novel only to face these punishing hurdles. No wonder why Jolene Lundgren and Luke Harper sounded so bitter. It also explained Hank Azar's apathy. Why anyone would subject themselves to this was beyond him.

Based on the publisher's account, Watts calculated the publishing cost for two thousand copies was fifteen thousand dollars, and that figure corresponded with The Guillotine Press' two-book contract. But since CC was the only one to have a second novel published, what happened to the rest of the money? Was this a Ponzi scheme where only those at the top profited? He slid his chair next to Spartan's so they could mull that over. They each had thoughts on how CC managed his business, but Kat probably wouldn't offer any answers. Still, they had to ask.

Kat promptly answered her phone, making it clear she that didn't like hearing from them by threatening them with harassment. Watts let her vent, then said, "Mrs. Coulter, we really need to talk. We can meet you somewhere, or you can come to the station. It's your choice."

The phone was silent, and for a moment, the detectives weren't sure if she was still there. Watts was preparing to hang up when she came back on.

"Meet me at Whataburger in fifteen minutes," she said, making sure they knew which one. The burger joint seemed an unlikely place for someone like her, but Watts agreed to it.

Spotting her BMW near the back, Watts pulled up next to it and rolled down his window. When she did the same, he realized she wanted to hold their conversation this way, but that wasn't going to happen. "Thanks for coming," he said. "As long as we're here, can I buy you a burger?"

"No thanks. I don't eat red meat."

"They also have chicken."

"I'm not hungry."

"Then how about this? Your car or mine?"

She quickly got out and slid into the back seat of their Crown Victoria. Watts wanted to tell her that from the way she was acting, anyone watching might think she was a prostitute turning a trick. All he had to do to complete the picture was join her in the back. Needless to say, he used better judgment and instead leaned his arm over the back seat to look at her.

"Okay, here's the deal," he said, getting right to the point. "First, you obstructed justice for lying to us about your having computer access. Second, we can prove that you deleted The Guillotine Press files from your husband's computer, so that's tampering with evidence. Third, you claimed you would never touch it out of respect for him, so that's another lie. Feel free to destroy the hard drives when you get home, but since everything has been recorded and logged, that would be a waste of your time and money. Fourth, you have not been forthcoming about your husband's book business when your actions prove you were involved. Finally, you lied about not knowing your company's financial affairs. You see, we know about your Guillotine Press' audit. Your IRS returns also list your occupation as business manager. Care to explain yourself?"

Her makeup couldn't mask the red blotches that suddenly appeared on her face and neck. She pulled out her mirror and fixed her hair and makeup, refusing to acknowledge them until she had applied fresh lipstick.

Finally, she looked up with bedroom eyes. "So, Columbo, is this the part where I'm supposed to confess?"

Ignoring her reference to Peter Faulk's bumbling detective TV character, he said, "It would save us a lot of time if you did."

"I see," she said, pressing her finger to her lips. "And if I refuse?"

"Then we take you downtown and book you. But look at the bright side, your mug shot will look really nice."

"Hmm. No, I think I'll call my lawyer first," she said, playing along. "Promise me you won't go anywhere. I'll be right back."

She flew out the door and ducked into her car like it was pouring rain outside. She rolled her window up for privacy, but Watts kept his down to make sure her car didn't start.

Spartan yawned, stretched out his arms, and then folded them across his chest. "Are you're really gonna bust her?" he said.

"Only if I have to."

"I figured as much."

Spartan's stomach rumbled. It did it again a few seconds later. Tapping Watts' shoulder, he said, "My body says it's time to eat."

"No, Blaine, it's the burger scent teasing it. You're not really hungry."

"Tell that to my stomach," he said, massaging his belly. After fidgeting for a few seconds, he looked at Watts again. "Who do you suppose she's talking to? Hank Azar?"

"That's my guess, and if he's wise, he's advising her to cooperate. He knows we don't have anything incriminating or we'd have busted her, so there's no harm in her talking to us."

Spartan nodded, still distracted by the smell of flame-broiled burgers. "Considering our fast-food diet, it's a wonder we're not obese like Porgy Mulberry."

"I know," Watts said, keeping his eyes on Kat's Beemer. "He wasn't like that as a kid. I'm amazed he got so large."

Kat finally got out of her car and returned to the Crown Vic. Watts presented her his tape recorder and prepared to press the record button. "So, are you ready to talk now?"

"I've been advised to cooperate, but don't confuse that with volunteering anything."

"I wouldn't dream of it," he said, turning on the recorder.

Watts spoke a couple of test words, and then played it back to make sure it worked. He already knew it did, but this way it was more dramatic, and made her realize he would take her downtown if necessary. He was preparing to ask his first question when a distinctive noise was heading his way. Convinced it was the Skinhead's pickup, he scanned the streets for it. When he couldn't spot it, he considered requesting an All-Points Bulletin until he realized it would only create mayhem. The sound faded soon enough, but Watts wasn't upset. If those Skinheads were stupid enough to hang around, sooner or later they would get caught.

Watts noticed Kat Coulter squirming in the back seat, wrinkling her nose. He and Spartan had grown used to the air conditioner's dirty sock smell, but Kat was turning green. He let her suffer while he studied his tape recorder, realizing that by a fluke, his window was open when the vehicle drove by. Upon verifying that the exhaust noise was indeed recorded, he marked the tape, and then prepared to ask his first question.

"What's the holdup?" Kat said. "I have better things to do than sit in your stinky car."

Catching her image in the mirror, Watts couldn't believe how different she looked from when they first met. Anger had replaced her innocence. Her looks no longer captivated him. He hit the record button and rested the tape recorder on the seatback. After introducing all three of them for the record, he made his opening statement.

"Mrs. Coulter, the initial examination of your husband's desktop computer showed no Guillotine Press records, and yet your joint IRS returns show that you deducted the computer as a business expense. Our lab recovered recently deleted files from his computer's hard drive that pertain specifically to your business. This recovered data includes the contracts for all existing GP authors, as well as two potential ones. Would you mind telling us how those files got deleted?"

Inspecting her manicured nails, she said, "No comment."

"That's fine, but to avoid jail time, you might want to reconsider your response."

Now, she looked up. "Okay, I admit it. I deleted them. It's my computer now, and I have no reason to keep my late husband's files."

"But earlier you told us you didn't know the password and wouldn't touch his computer."

"And at the time that was true, but I found the password on a sticky note in his sock drawer when I was going through his belongings. I didn't think to mention it when you confiscated my computer because I was rather upset at the time. My computer works fine, so there's no reason to keep anything on CC's."

"Are you saying that you transferred his files to your computer?"

"Yes. I transferred everything before I cleaned up CC's computer."

"I see. So, do you plan to continue running the business?"

"I haven't decided. The Guillotine Press was CC's baby, not mine."

"Then you're going to fold?"

"Detective, I just lost my husband, and not a moment goes by when I don't think about him. I haven't even had time to grieve. For now, the business will run itself. Once a book is published, it takes on a life of its own. Our printer keeps records of everything, as does our distributor. There isn't a whole lot for me to do at this point."

"Then why would an author choose The Guillotine Press over self-publishing?"

"Because CC was like an author's choreographer. He danced them through the publishing process and then sent them on their own with their name in print. All but two of our authors are currently published, and some of our books are selling fairly well, so nothing will change anytime soon. I will distribute royalty checks whenever it's warranted. I assure you, no author has been hurt by my deleting those files. It was merely electronic house cleaning."

Watts paused the recorder, debating on how to follow that up. Before conducting the interview, he and Spartan had agreed that Watts would ask the questions. But her composure stumped him, and her responses were messing with his mind. When a thought came to him, he pressed the record button again.

"I take it you've always been supportive of your husband's business," he said.

She eased herself forward, hands in her lap, close enough so he could whiff her perfume, and low enough where he could check out her cleavage. Spartan was invisible to her.

"When I married CC, I vowed to support him. We lived back east in a beautiful home with a swimming pool. The beach was an hour away. Life was good. But this is fine, too. Granted, moving here took some adjusting, but CC and I were happy."

Watts gave a skeptical look. "You're sure he didn't ruin for you it by moving to Texas?"

She gently shook her head, her full lips curling slightly at the corners. "No, detective, my life wasn't ruined by moving here, and if you want to hear my story, you won't interrupt again."

"I apologize. Please continue."

She took a moment to tuck in her blouse and smooth it. She then leaned back in the seat, placed her hands on her lap, and looked at Watts like they were chatting over tea. "Before moving here CC was a stock broker earning a triple-digit salary," she said. "He always said he loved his job until he started writing novels. At first, writing was a hobby, but then it consumed him like cocaine. He would spend all of his free time banging away on his keyboard, convinced he would become the next James Patterson. We hadn't been married long when his grandmother died and willed him this home. CC took that as an omen, so he quit his job and we moved to Fort Worth. I came willingly because I loved him dearly.

"His first manuscript was accepted by a New York publisher, but he refused their contract. After investing so much time and energy in writing this Wall Street thriller and only getting pennies for it, he decided to form his own publishing company—The Guillotine Press. The name came from his sense that the New York publisher chopped his head off.

"I helped him expand the business by finding new talent through my literary agency. Almost immediately, queries began pouring in. Some were pathetic, but some were quite captivating. CC contacted some of these authors to ask if they might like to join our press. After discussing the terms of a two-book contract, he let them think it over. You've obviously read their contracts. No one was coerced into signing. Basically, we agreed to publish two of their books at cost and receive a commission from every book sold. But rising expenses rapidly depleted our savings. We lived on a shoestring budget and still had to pay taxes, utilities, food, gas, clothes, and car leases. The book money wasn't coming in like we expected, so I took a part-time bank job. I'd be lying if I said we were living the dream as publishing tycoons. We sweat every summer night and froze our tails in the winter, hoping that CC or one of our other authors would break out of the pack, but that never happened. Then again, it's probably the same for ranchers who toil year-round only to lose their cattle to drought and wildfires.

"Some of our authors took exception to CC publishing his own books, implying he was stealing the money they invested to publish their work. From their perspective, I can see how it might appear questionable. After all, they had each invested thirty thousand dollars, and only had one book published. Admittedly, some have yet to see a royalty check, but that's because of their dismal book sales. In the meantime, our business was going broke. When the IRS accused us of tax fraud, we hired Attorney Hank Azar to bail us out. Since Hank was also an aspiring writer, we gave him a two-book deal in exchange for his services. Hank thought it was a good deal so he agreed to it. When CC died, Hank offered me free legal counsel until I could figure out what to do with the business and my life. I know I don't want to stay here, but my house isn't worth squat, so at this point I'm not sure what I'll do."

Watts waited until he was sure she was finished. While her testimony provided some interesting insight into the business, it revealed little more than her admitting she deleted the files, and since it was her computer now, she was certainly entitled to do that. If she hadn't downloaded them onto her personal computer, he would have thought she did it to erase The Guillotine Press from her life. He found it interesting that she never mentioned anything about CC's love affairs. If she had strayed on her own, she kept mum about it. All things considered, it seemed inconceivable that Kat Coulter didn't harbor any resentment toward her husband or his book business. Still, there was no evidence to suggest she killed CC, or had him killed. Then again, only a passionate person would stuff a paper wad down someone's throat.

Watts studied her while reminiscing over their numerous encounters. Over the course of a few days, he had seen her play the grieving widow, eager volunteer, and woman under interrogation, and while all of these personalities interested him, he wasn't sure he knew the real Kat Coulter.

She tried crossing her leg, but after twisting her ankle, slid it back where it was. Visibly frustrated now, she said, "How long do you plan to keep me here?"

"Not much longer," he said, scanning through his notebook.

"Look, you can ask whatever you want, but these theatrical pauses are wasting time."

Spartan glanced over his shoulder at her and she squinted angrily at him. Watts wanted to laugh, but didn't. After making sure Spartan was backing up the recorder with notes, the lead detective picked up the pace.

"Where did you live on the east coast?" he said.

"Long Island."

"And how long did you live there?"

"Thirteen years."

"How long have you lived in Fort Worth?"

"Seven years."

"Do you like it here?"

"Honestly, Texas is the most godforsaken place I've ever lived."

"Sorry to hear that. I guess it's is one of those places you either love or hate."

"Finally, we agree on something. But to be fair, Texans don't transplant well in New York City either."

"Noted," Watts said, grinning. "Do you think you'll return to Long Island?"

She bowed her head, rubbing her forehead. Her pain seemed genuine, so Watts gave her a moment. When she was ready, she looked up.

"I already said I have no idea what I'll do. I need a job before I can move back, and I can't get a job unless I'm already there. Make no mistake, detective, if CC he was alive and wanted to stay here, I'd stay with him. But now that he's gone, I have no reason to do that. I miss him dearly."

He gave her another moment to blow her nose and dry her eyes. She must realize that her makeup was a mess, but she never pulled out her mirror. "Mrs. Coulter, what used to hang on your husband's office wall?"

She looked up, seemingly confused. "Pardon me?"

"Connecting the holes in the wall leaves a poster-size rectangle, so I was wondering what used to hang there."

"Oh, CC had an old Broadway poster that he took down a long time ago. I have no idea why he never bothered to patch those holes."

Watts nodded, still wondering the same thing. "Did you know your husband had an affair?"

"If you're referring to Courtney Dridelle, yes, he told me all about it. He said they were at a book festival and had some drinks afterwards. They both got caught up in the moment and it went from there. It wasn't premeditated, and obviously didn't last. We got through it because I loved him more than his affair bothered me. Don't get me wrong. What he did hurt us both, but things happen—especially when you don't have kids to keep you grounded."

Watts raised a brow. "Did you ever wish you had kids?"

"Oh, god no. I'm not the nurturing type. We both knew that before we married, so it never bothered CC either. Whenever we'd joke about having kids, we would visit to the zoo and be cured." She laughed at Spartan's disapproving double-take. "What? I'm being honest."

"Moving on," Watts said, "Your husband's affair with Ms. Dridelle was a one-time fling, is that correct?"

She adamantly shook her head to the side. "It lasted three months before Courtney got bored with him, exactly like in her books. In my opinion, she's a cross between a black widow and a whore. I hate thinking about how many men she's slept with."

Watts calmly turned his recorder off. He had accomplished everything he set out to do. Nothing more could be gained from prolonged questioning. "Thank you for your time," he said. "We appreciate your candor. We'll get back to you if we have any more questions."

She nodded and leaped from the car like it was on fire. Seconds later, her BMW shot from the Whataburger lot like she just robbed the place. Too bad Porgy Mulberry wasn't around to sight her for reckless driving. Seems there's never a cop around when you want one.

TWENTY NINE

Watts and Spartan went into the Whataburger for a snack after Kat left. The place was practically deserted, so they took their time, discussing her latest interview. Soon after getting back to 350, it was quitting time, and Watts was shifting modes from detective to beau. He locked his tape recorder and the paperwork Collingsworth gave him in his desk and slid his chair under his desk. He wanted tonight's date with Daisy to be special and didn't want to think about work. In fact, he hoped to get through the entire evening without once mentioning it. All he wanted was to stare into her beautiful green eyes and listen to her angelic voice. If things went well, he might brush her hair aside, lean over, and gently kiss her lips. That would end it perfectly.

He still had concerns about fishing in the company pond, but since he had never met her until the double-murder and they seemed to be hitting it off, it was worth the risk. The big question was where to take her on their first date. Pappasito's Cantina was great for casual dining, but it could get pretty noisy. The Stockyards' H3 Ranch Steakhouse had great food and a unique atmosphere, but it was pricey. He didn't want barbeque or Italian because they could be messy, and things got stuck in your teeth. He pictured Daisy staring at him, hinting he needed a toothpick. Few things could be worse than having food stuck between your teeth on a first kiss.

He climbed into Leroy feeling more anxious than during his Senior Prom blind date. During the drive home, he recounted everything that had happened since meeting Daisy in Forest Park. Her *Magnum PI* reference had him wondering if she thought his flowery shirts were silly. Her smile looked inviting, but some people could smile even when they were annoyed. Daisy possessed a reserved sense of humor, but was also quite witty. His apprehension increased when his cell phone rang. *It's her.* "Hi, Daisy, I was just thinking about you."

"That's sweet. I was calling to make sure we were still on for tonight."

"Absolutely. I'm on my way home, and am looking forward to it. Any idea where you'd like to go?"

As soon as he said that, he wanted to take it back because it showed he had no plan. Dad said women hate that, so without thinking, Watts blurted the first thing that came to mind, "The H-3 Ranch has great steaks—assuming you like steak."

Laughing heartily, she said, "I'm Texas born and raised. How could I not like steak?"

"Good," he said, relieved to have made the decision, but fearful of the bill. "H-3 it is."

His heartbeat now returning to normal, he spotted a flower shop and pulled into the parking lot. His next big question, daisies or roses?

* * * * *

At two minutes before seven, Watts stood in front of her door smoothing his hair. His polo shirt displayed his athletic physique, while his loose slacks concealed the revolver he had strapped to his ankle. His only problem was he couldn't ring her doorbell, even though he was here last night. He did a couple of nervous paces fearing the Skinheads followed him here, and then cursed himself for thinking about the job. At the very moment he reached for the button, the door opened. He was blown away by her green summer dress.

Smiling, she extended her arms and pulled him in by the hand. "I was watching you pacing on the porch, and thought you were going to chicken out."

"Why would I do that?" he said, hiding his embarrassment. "You look amazing."

"Thanks, but most guys don't date fellow department employees. I believe the expression is fishing in the company pond? I'm sure you've heard more graphic ones. Anyway, where's your *Magnum* shirt?"

"They're all dirty, and for the record, I'm not concerned about dating a fellow employee because we don't answer to the same supervisors." Right then, he pulled the bouquet from behind his back and presented it to her. "I hope you like them."

She held them to her nose, relishing their fragrance. "Umm, they smell wonderful. Thank you. I love yellow roses. They're so—Texas."

He followed her into the kitchen and watched her place the flowers in a vase. The care she gave them proved she truly loved them.

"I can't tell you how many daisies I've gotten over the years because of my name," she said as she worked. "Guys think it's cute, but daisies are really for funerals."

After silently giving thanks to the florist who suggested roses, Watts said, "Daisy, I don't mean to rush you, but our reservation is in fifteen minutes."

She set the vase aside and smiled. "Then what are we waiting for?"

* * * * *

Dinner was outstanding, the Merlot putting them at ease. Their conversation flowed like they had known each other for years. It turned out Daisy drove Japan's answer to American's full-size pickup, a Toyota Tundra. Watts bragged that his Dodge could eat her Toyota for breakfast. She countered by saying her five-year-old truck did everything his could while getting another hundred miles per tank. Laughing, or perhaps crying over gas prices, they both agreed that it was easier paying the pump than buying a replacement vehicle. But the best part of their evening was neither spoke of their jobs. Before they knew it, the restaurant had emptied and they were being coaxed to leave with frequent offers for more coffee. Taking the hint, Watts paid the bill and escorted her out.

Steadying her arm while she climbed into the seat, her bare leg sent a wave of excitement through his body. Watts may not have said a word, but his hormones were screaming, "Babe!" He walked her to her door expecting to leave right away, but she invited him inside.

"*Castle* is on in a few minutes," she said. "You want to watch?"

"Sure. I love that show."

"Me, too. Especially Kate Beckett. She's smart, funny, and never gives Castle a break."

"I agree. You can't help but love her. She's quite the survivor."

Smiling, she escorted him to the love seat in front of the television and sat him down. She then moved behind him, turned on the TV, and began rubbing his shoulders. "Care for anything to drink?"

Watts' stomach was already sloshing from wine and coffee. Looking at her over his shoulder, he said, "Are you having anything?" hoping her answer would be no.

"I thought I'd have a tiny glass of wine. Anything more and I'd feel like I'm on a water bed."

"A water bed?"

She cast a sly grin and said, "My parents had one when I was young. I loved bouncing on it, but it always made my stomach gurgle. That's why I mentioned it." She then went to the kitchen to pour their wine.

"I know the feeling," he said, patting his full tummy. "I've never been on a water bed, but I know about gurgling stomachs. So, what happened to the bed?"

When she leaned over the sofa to hand him his glass, her perfume went

184

straight to his head. It was the same scent as before. He knew he wasn't imagining it.

Still draped over the sofa, she admired his blue eyes. "One day it sprang a leak and that was the end of it," she said, invitingly.

Sensing she had too much to drink, he said, "No wonder no one has them anymore."

He felt like a dork saying that, but it got her to sit next to him. As much as he loved the view, he was determined to be a gentleman. At the end of the show, he looked at his watch and got up. "Big day at work tomorrow, so I should be going. I really enjoyed tonight."

"Me, too," she said, wrapping her arms around his neck. After planting a kiss, she gazed into his eyes again. "By the way, your mom was right. You are extra special."

His hands found her waist, and their embrace lasted longer than expected. Their first kiss was magical, but sticking to his plan, he headed for the door before things got any hotter. He left, eager to see what would happen on their next date.

THIRTY

Maxx Watts arrived at the office wearing the same glow his partner had worn the last two mornings. For Watts, last night had been impeccable because of their mental connection. It was so easy being with her. Outside of the office, Daisy Woods became a different person, and one he wanted to know better.

Spartan gloated in his chair, chewing gum. "Well," he said. "How did things go with your new girlfriend?"

"One date hardly makes her my girlfriend, but it went very well."

"That's great. Care to spill any details? Like maybe her name?"

"No, thanks," he said, downplaying his excitement. "Moving on, I was thinking about Kat Coulter when I drove in this morning."

Spartan's jaw dropped. "Please don't tell me she's the one you're dating. I mean, I saw how she looked at you and how she treated me, but come on, you're investigating her for Christ's sake."

Chuckling, Watts said, "No, I'm not dating Kat, but I do feel sorry for her, having to live alone in a place she hates. By the way, how are things in your home?"

"Great. Couldn't be better."

"Uh oh. That word combination is never good, at least not when it comes from a guy."

"I'm serious, Maxx. Ever since Sandy and I started getting romantic, the kids aren't acting up anymore. My guess is they feel more secure, and the better they behave, the more loving Sandy becomes. I love it, and I love her."

"Well, I'm happy for you, Blaine, and I hope it keeps getting better. You both deserve to be happy."

"I reckon we do," he said before downing a big gulp of coffee. Setting his mug down, he added, "It's like we're falling in love all over again. It's a great feeling, isn't it, Maxx?"

Seeing where this was heading, Watts opened his desk drawer and pulled out his tape recorder. "Different subject," he said, wearing his detective hat now. "You remember that loud exhaust right before Kat's interview?"

"I do, and from the way you reacted, I thought you were gonna ditch her to go pickup hunting."

"As tempted as I was, we had to finish what we started. I got it on tape, though."

"Of course you did. You taped the whole interview."

"No, I mean the exhaust, and I'm ninety-nine percent certain it's the same truck."

Spartan nodded his understanding. If he begged to differ, he stopped himself when Watts' phone rang. It was Daisy, but he didn't smile.

"I hope I'm not interrupting," she said.

Watts excused himself and returned to his desk. Speaking softly, he said, "Not at all. Nice to hear from you. How are you doing? Where are you?"

"I'm glad, too, I'm here, and I'm fine," she said, answering all of his questions at once. "I was wondering if you'd like to have dinner at my place this evening. It's nothing fancy. Just my way of saying thanks."

"I'd love to. What can I bring?"

"Just your cute little self. And wear your Hawaiian shirt—with pants, of course."

His face reddened and grin widened. Nice to know she enjoyed their time together as much as he did. He moved as far away from Spartan as possible and cupped his hand over the phone. "Okay, pants with shirt. Glad you clarified that."

"It sounds like your partner is near. At least I hope it's your partner you're hiding from."

"You're very astute, and yes, he's at his desk. Can I call you later?"

"No need to. Be here at seven."

"Sounds great. Aloha"

When Watts closed his phone and spun his chair around, he saw Spartan leaning over his cubicle, smirking, Jimmy Dean style.

"It was her, wasn't it?" Spartan said. He grew impatient when Watts didn't respond. "You know, Maxx, I've patiently sat through your interviews and phone calls and never complained, but ignoring me is like a school teacher scraping her fingernails on the chalkboard. Can't you at least tell me her name?"

Watts smiled, shaking his head, thinking about the women he had dated. None of them came close to Daisy, and none asked him over for dinner on their second date. He tried to remember which Hawaiian shirt he wore the day they met at Forest Park. Black one with gold leaves or red one with silver? Either go well with gray slacks.

Spartan gave an annoyed look as he entered Watts' space. "I believe we were going to discuss Kat Coulter," he said. "That is, unless you're not finished daydreaming about your girlfriend."

"Ouch, that hurts. And for the record, Kat Coulter is still my top priority. The next step is to compare her statements to whatever evidence we have."

"Like the inconsistencies in her IRS returns?"

"That's a good start, but we need to find something that justifies our subpoena."

Spartan nodded, looking at his shoes. He raised his right pant leg and polished his left shoe on his black sock. Reversing the process made them both shine. "Ryder won't be happy if we come up empty."

"Don't remind me." Watts stood up and looked around. "There are too many people within earshot. Let's find a quiet room."

He grabbed the recorder and led the way to an empty interrogation room. After confirming the cameras and recorders were off and no one was behind the mirror, Watts set the recorder on the stainless steel table and hit Play. Although everything would be transcribed, he wanted to hear it audibly because hardcopy lacked emotion. Without her emotion, they are simply words. He also wanted Spartan to hear the truck exhaust.

As Watts listened to the interview, he recalled Kat's changing expressions. Spartan wasn't as tuned in because he had spent so much time facing forward and checking mirrors. For the most part, Kat sounded surprisingly candid, making no attempt to hide her computer deletions or her husband's love affair. She was equally open about her disdain for Fort Worth. Curiously, her New York accent didn't appear until after Watts brought up the Big Apple. He wondered why he didn't notice that before.

Watts found Kat's perspective on the book industry fascinating. He had no idea that bookstores catered to the major presses while casting small publishers aside. And book returns sounded a lot like expiration dates on food. Quick sales were crucial to a book's survival. Even the big name books headed to the value rack when their time was due. So, who carried The Guillotine Press books? Certainly, no one he knew of.

On many levels, Watts could understand Kat's dismay. Having a spouse that forfeits a successful career to write novels must have been dreadful. He figured they might have been better off letting Bernie Madoff handle their money. At least that way they could blame their losses on someone other than themselves. Considering their financial losses, Kat's resentment toward her husband must have been staggering, giving up her New York lifestyle for Brown Acres, as it were. So, did CC's extramarital affair push her over the top? This interview surely didn't reveal that. But in spite of her calm, Kat Coulter still had the best murder motive.

Another element that still intrigued Watts was how the Coulters lured potential author/investors. As a literary agent, what kind of research did Kat do to find authors desperate enough to spend thirty grand to publish their work? It seemed unimaginable, and yet twelve authors did it. Based on the numbers, the detectives agreed that The Guillotine Press' pot should be three hundred and sixty thousand dollars. Taking away one hundred fifty thousand to publish ten authors' books should leave a balance of two hundred and ten thousand dollars. Assuming CC used some of this money to publish his own books left one hundred and thirty thousand to publish fourteen more books. Any GP author knowing about this shortfall had good reason to be upset, but was it enough to commit murder?

Kat Coulters' checking account confirmed her dire debt situation. There was no indication that she had received her insurance settlement, and CC's account was equally bad. Nothing explained what happened to their savings, or how she paid her hair stylist. Most likely, she used her credit card, hoping her settlement would come through before her bill came due. But the bottom line was most Wall Street stockbrokers walk away with significant nest eggs, and it seemed unlikely the Coulters would have depleted all of their savings in seven years while living rent-free. So was CC's fortune hiding in a Swiss bank? Did Kat Coulter know this and kill her husband for the cash? Watts couldn't rule out the possibility.

Of the published Guillotine Press books, it readily became clear that some authors were more talented than others. In fact, CC's eclectic author mix made as much sense as his finances. And considering Kat's remarks about the timing of their Texas move, Watts still found it interesting that the move occurred within months of meeting Olyn Jordan. That move was more intriguing when considering the Medical Examiner never pin-pointed Mrs. Jordan's cause of death. Then there was Hank Azar neglecting to mention his legal counsel arrangement with the Coulters. Azar would probably say he didn't want to cheapen his novel or tarnish his "as seen on TV, acclaimed author" status, but who knows? At least Kat confirmed that Azar was still watching her back.

Kat spoke of her husband's affair as if Dridelle had instigated it, but considering CC's track record, Dridelle probably wasn't his first. Unless Kat accompanied CC on all of his travels, he had plenty of opportunity to roam, and being the smooth talker he was, probably had plenty of offers.

After playing the tape a third time, Watts looked at his partner. "I've heard enough," he said. "Any thoughts before we send it to get transcribed?"

Spartan nodded as he flipped his chair around. Straddling the chair so he could lean on its seatback, he said, "The Coulter's entire business model is bogus. The records show The Guillotine Press has had a negative cash flow ever since its inception, and in spite of Kat's income from her bank job, they haven't paid more than a thousand dollars in income taxes for the past five years because of their proclaimed business losses. I have yet to come across anything that shows CC Coulter has a nest egg, but we know that can't be true. To me, The Guillotine Press has been nothing but a tax shelter for the Coulters, and a bad investment for its authors."

Watts loosened his tie, which he not only found uncomfortable, but hazardous. More than once, he told Ryder that if a criminal grabbed his tie, he could lead him around like a horse. Ryder's response never changed. "Then keep the criminals from grabbing it", he would say, and then add, "That's why you wear a gun." Ryder's point never made a tie comfortable and Watts never found a clip-on he liked, so he dealt with it. But then as he leaned over, his stupid decorative bib dangled over the tax documents that Spartan had spread across his desk, blocking his view.

After tucking his tie in his shirt, Watts said, "We know that Hank Azar defended the Coulters against tax fraud charges. My question is how can you get in trouble with the IRS if you don't owe them money?"

"Oh, I forgot to tell you about that. Apparently, the Coulters weren't paying The Guillotine Press' corporate taxes. They either didn't know, or they fell behind because the book sales weren't adding up."

Watts nodded, checking off his notes. He wanted to hear Hank Azar's take, so he dialed his office and turned on the speaker. Azar's secretary refused to put his call through until he threatened legal action. Soon after, Azar was on the line.

"Good morning, detective," Azar said. "What can I do for you?"

"Sir, Detective Spartan and I would like to clear up a few things. As I'm sure you are aware, yesterday we met with Mrs. Coulter, and she told us about your bartering to represent them on their corporate tax evasion charges. I need to know how much The Guillotine Press owed the IRS, and if this matter has been resolved."

"We've been through this before, detectives. I cannot discuss matters involving lawyer/client privilege. If you need specifics, try calling the IRS. I understand they're good with numbers."

Spartan pointed to the facts and figures on the desk, giving a confused look. Watts signaled that he enjoyed playing cat-and-mouse with the attorney, and that he had no intention of telling Azar they already had the information.

"Mr. Azar," Watts said, "Let's put the IRS issue aside for now. Would you care to comment on your book contract, now that we have read it?"

"No, and since you already know its details, why are you wasting my time?"

"Because your contract doesn't specify how much legal advice you'll provide."

"Sure it does. I agreed to render services matching the value of the authors' investment."

"So, we're talking about thirty thousand dollars in legal services?"

"That's correct, and if you're looking for hidden clauses, you won't find any. Don't confuse reality with the fictional courts in *Forsaken Alibi*. By the way, did you read it?"

"I did, Watts said, noting a pleasant change in Azar's voice. "How are the sales going?"

"Honestly, I don't know or care. As you know, time is money, and I don't waste mine on trivial matters."

"But what about the time you invested in writing your book?"

"Detective, writing a book is a pleasure, but the book business is as painful as your interviews. Do you have any specific questions, or are you probing?"

Watts grinned at his partner. Azar's tone had shifted back to tense. He liked that. "Sir, I'm probing, just like you do in court."

"Well, at least you're man enough to admit it," he said, calmer now. "Ask away."

"Very well. How many royalty checks have you received since you were published?"

"Only one, and that came over a year ago. I remember it well because it was worth an hour of my time. Three hundred bucks."

"Did CC cut you this three hundred dollar royalty check while he owed the IRS money?"

"Oh, you're a sly one, detective. I'll give you that. As a trial lawyer, my court opponents are always trying to throw me off, but of course, I do the same to them. However, I assure you I will only answer questions that pertain directly to me. Anything else?"

"No, sir. I think we've covered all we can for now. Thanks for your time."

"No sweat. I'll send you my bill."

Watts cradled the phone and looked at his partner. "I hate to admit it, but Azar's right," he said. "The only benefit from that call is I realized our figures are wrong. We need to deduct thirty grand from the GP budget figures to reflect Azar's bartering."

"I agree," said Spartan. "Perhaps we should have Kat explain their tax situation."

Watts hesitated, wishing he had included that question in her interview. He didn't prepare his questions well enough, and now it would cost him.

"We'll review the transcript first, and then determine if we need to call her back."

"Sounds like a plan."

THIRTY ONE

The secretary delivered the transcript earlier than promised. Watts joked that she should put herself in for a pay raise for exceeding his expectations. She didn't even smile when she left. Her rejection cost him some confidence in the flirting department. Then again, not everyone shared his sense of humor. Hopefully, Daisy would.

He locked the original audiotape in the safe, then joined Spartan in his cubicle to read certain words out loud. Lowering the document, he glared at his partner. "According to Kat," he said, "we're supposed to believe her stockbroker husband gave up his triple digit salary because, as she put it, his writing consumed him like cocaine? What the hell does that mean?"

Spartan shrugged. "It's either a figure of speech or they snorted in Manhattan."

Watts could see a Wall Street executive dividing the favorite party drug of the rich and famous for his fellow Yuppie socialites. But cocaine addiction is hard to kick, and there was no evidence suggesting drugs were ever a part of the Coulter's lifestyle.

Not ready to choose sides on this one yet, he said, "Coke sniffer or not, CC must have created a significant financial portfolio for himself. So, did Kat take the bank job as a cover, or did Bernie make off with his money, too?"

Spartan shrugged again. "Surely CC was savvy enough to see the bear was poised to slaughter the bull, and sell before the market crashed."

"Since we haven't been able to find it, we may never know, but why risk losing your business and maybe do jail time over corporate taxes if you have the money to pay it?"

"Looking at it from another angle, let's say CC stashes his money before he gets married because he doesn't want Kat to know about it. He didn't want kids, so money was probably more important to him. Call hiding the money a sort of pre-nup. So if that's the case, Kat wouldn't know anything about it. We may never find his nest egg."

"Maybe, but don't stop looking."

After saying that, Watts stroked his whiskers, thinking. He lifted the transcript and read a few of his notes, then set them down. A long moment passed before he said, "If CC's money is gone for whatever the reason, then all Kat has left is his life insurance money."

"Two million is still a lot of money, Maxx. Especially if you're on a shoestring budget."

"I hear you," he said, tapping his finger on a page. "Check this out, and I'm paraphrasing here, 'Our expenses mounted and our savings dwindled. CC owned the house free and clear. The money wasn't coming in. Sweating every summer and freezing in the winter, praying for CC's big break that never happened.' Taken out of context, it reads like a woman scorned."

"Well, two million dollars might be a pittance compared to what his financial portfolio's worth, and I'm not giving up on finding it."

"That's good, but even if you find it, it's unlikely we can prove Kat knew about it."

Watts tilted his head back, staring at the ceiling. Stains streaked from every vent. Some of the ceiling tiles had yellow water marks. The office needed a make-over, but there was never any money for it. Wondering what kind of contaminated air was blowing from the vents, he slowly dropped his head to his partner's level.

"The other side of the coin is that Kat knew about CC's portfolio, and they chose a pauper's lifestyle to fool the IRS."

Spartan adamantly shook his head. "I would never let my wife suffer like that," he said.

"Well, Blaine, not everyone is as compassionate as you. Did you find anything on their capital gains? Monies previously unaccounted for? Royalties received or paid out?"

"If I'd known you wanted that, I would have studied accounting instead of criminology." Spartan waited as long as he could before slapping his partner's shoulder. "I'm kidding, for crying out loud. And to answer your question, the IRS says the Coulters earned a combined income of three hundred and twelve thousand dollars the year before they moved to Texas. About thirty six percent of that went to taxes because they leased an apartment instead of owning a home."

"Did they deduct their new BMW?"

"Actually, they deducted a leased car while in New York City, but they haven't done that since moving here. The IRS had no quarrel with them writing off their car. It was the four years of failing to pay corporate taxes that cost them their business license. That's when Azar got involved. After cutting his deal, he got their fine reduced to a fraction of what they owed, restored their license, and subsequently became an acclaimed author."

Watts scratched his nose, reading the murder board. His partner meant everything as a joke, and had it not had merit, it would have been funny. "I'm not buying into this dirt-poor business charade," he said. "If CC was anything like his wife, he was cunning enough not to blow his own money, so I'm with you. They must have money tucked away somewhere."

"I agree. Changing the subject, let's talk about Mayor Jordon's campaign fund. The Coulters' joint return shows they gave the maximum allowable contribution to OJ. Now, think about that for a moment. Why would New Yorkers care so much about a Fort Worth mayor's political campaign unless something was going on behind the scenes?"

"You got me, but while you're searching for that missing nest egg, keep looking for any financial connections with the mayor. For all we know, the Guillotine Press was laundering money for him. I'm not sure how much longer Ryder's gonna give us carte blanche authority, so we'd better dig while we have the chance."

"Agreed."

Letting Spartan focus on the Coulters' financial affairs, Watts looked into the GP's two unpublished authors. As of now, Hans Slater and Claudia McMaan were both out thirty grand and got nothing in return. Most people would be upset over that. The only problem was Watts didn't have any information on either author. Having no choice, he used a recorded line to call Kat Coulter back. She wasn't pleased to hear his voice.

"What now, *Colombo?*" she said, sounding agitated, like a cramping woman.

Making sure he was extra polite, Watts said, "I'm very sorry to bother you again, but I need some additional information. First off, why did you cut a royalty check for Hank Azar when you owed the IRS money?"

"Different accounts. Next?"

"Okay, let's talk about Hans Slater and Claudia McMaan, your two unpublished authors. Since you transferred all of The Guillotine Press files onto your computer, I was hoping you could tell me where they're from, what they're writing, and when their books are supposed to be published?"

"Hang on. I'm setting the phone down."

Watts heard background noises, like she was digging through files rather than looking on the computer. She came back on the line a few minutes later.

"Okay, if you're still there, my New Prospects file has that information. Hans Slater lives in San Marcos, Texas, and his book is titled *Killer Massage*. Claudia McMaan lives in Jacksonville, Florida, and her book is titled *Paradigm*. Both of these manuscripts were sent to the editor six months ago. That's all I know."

Watts jotted the information down. *Killer Massage* sounded interesting because it implied hands-on murder. "What's the editor's name and contact information?" he said.

"Perry Wellington. He lives in San Francisco. You ready to write this down?"

Watts jotted it in his notebook and read it back to make sure it was correct. He then thanked her, said he would be in touch, and hung up. He spent the next five minutes contemplating the possible roles these three could have played in CC's murder. As GP's editor-in-chief, Wellington didn't share any of the authors' financial risk, but he might be due back-pay. If Slater and McMaan's work had been with the editor all this time, they may be frustrated. Had they gone the self-publishing route, their books would be in print now, but like the other authors, they probably signed with The Guillotine Press for better credibility. Before calling anyone, Watts performed a Google search on all three names and came up empty. He also found it strange that there weren't any matching names on Facebook. The criminal data base came up equally empty, which meant none of them were wanted by the law, or they were writing under pseudonyms. Watts chose to speak with their editor first.

Perry Wellington sounded disappointed after Watts introduced himself, but had no problem in answering Watts' questions. His only request was that Watts be quick because he was expecting another call.

"I promise I'll be brief," Watts said. "As Editor-in-Chief for The Guillotine Press, do you work exclusively for them, or do you also do freelance?"

When Wellington stopped chuckling, he said, "My editing barely pays for my gas, detective. I do it because I love it. My day job is writing entertainment and restaurant reviews for the *San Francisco Chronicle*, which is another reason I need to be brief. If your questions pertain to Hans and Claudia, neither of them writes particularly well. I have been mentoring them as best I can, but it's not always easy. Don't get me wrong—they're both making progress, but it could be months, even years, before we'll be ready to publish their manuscripts."

"I'm confused. You're saying neither can write and yet they're picked up by The Guillotine Press. Why would any legitimate press teach someone how to write?"

"Sir, I've never been involved in those decisions, and frankly, I'm not real proud of some of the work we've published. Once an author signs the contract, CC passes their work on to me. My job is to mentor them into producing their best work. With CC's approval, it then went to the typesetter."

"Okay, let's discuss Hans Slater. I understand his novel concerns a brutal massage parlor killing. Is there anything in your dealings with him or his writing that suggests he could commit a violent crime?"

"It's been a while since I've read his manuscript, but if you're comparing his characters to CC's murder, Hans' victims were strangled, not gagged. Some questionable accidents occur at his fictional health center, too, but there's nothing in there that I would consider relevant to CC's death."

"What kind of accidents are you referring to?"

"Well, one guy does a face-plant when his towel jams the treadmill, another dies from a barbell crushing his trachea, and still another is found dead in the steam room—all at the same club where the killer massage takes place. I wouldn't want a membership there."

"Okay, I can see the treadmill, and maybe the weight machine, but a steam room accident? How can you die in a steam room? Does someone wrap a towel around his neck?"

"No, but you're on the right track. He slips on the floor and breaks his neck."

"Interesting," said Watts. "So, the only victim who dies from bare hands is the one receiving the massage?"

"That's correct. And in Claudia McMaan's *Paradigm*, her victim's body never turns up, which makes her story rather unique."

"How so?"

"Well, hers is a courtroom drama where the protagonist is convicted of murder on circumstantial evidence. The reader is constantly wondering if she did it, or if the killer is still at large. Its cliffhanger ending could easily turn this book into a series."

Doubting that, Watts said, "Although both stories sound fascinating, you imply that neither is well written. Why is that?"

"I never said their plots were bad. They're simply not ready for publication, which is why the authors are still refining them. Given time, I'm confident they'll both get there." He paused before adding, "If you talk to them, please remind them that I'm still waiting for their latest updates. Everything in this business is give and take, detective. Give and take."

"I see. Thanks for your time, Mr. Wellington. I hope you didn't miss your call."

"If I did, they'll call back. Have a nice day."

THIRTY TWO

Watts flipped a coin for the next call. It came up Heads, meaning Claudia McMaan won the toss. When you're out of ideas, sometimes flipping a coin helped. Then again, since she lived in Florida and it was an hour ahead, calling her first was the logical choice.

Following his introduction, he said, "I just got off the phone with your editor and he wants me to pass on that he's waiting for your latest changes."

"I know," she said, dolefully. "It's so hard to know what Perry wants. I write it one way, he says to write it another. I send it back, and he tells me to tweak the original version. It's very frustrating."

"I'm sure it is," he said, the sound of her voice suggesting she was in her mid-forties. "Is this your first book?"

"It is. Did Perry tell you it's bad? Be honest."

"Not at all. In fact, he said with a little refining, your manuscript has great potential." To avoid more follow-up questions from her, he quickly said, "How well did you know CC Coulter?"

"We spoke on the phone, exchanged a few e-mails, and that's about it."

"And did you send him the required money? Be advised that I've read your contract, know about the investment, and everything is perfectly legal."

"I'm not rich," she said, sounding like she was holding back tears. "I can't tell you how many times I hashed this over with my family and boyfriend. I mean, I could buy a really nice car for what I've spent on two books. CC's installment plan allowed me to pay him ten thousand upon signing, ten more when the first book is ready, and the remaining ten when it's published."

Even worse than I thought! "I would have guessed you would pay half when your first book came out, and the remainder when your second book is published."

"I actually proposed that, but he said it wouldn't work—whatever that means. Now that he's dead, I'm glad I only made the first payment. Do you think I'll get a refund?"

Seriously doubting that, he said, "You should discuss that with Mrs. Coulter."

"I was afraid you'd say that."

Sensing her hurt, he gave pause. He would probably feel the same, had he thrown that much time and money away, especially after Kat implied she would be leaving the publishing business.

To lighten the mood, he said, "Jacksonville's a nice city. I've only been there once, but my friend drove me in his boat to *The Landing*. I have to admit it was pretty cool docking right next to the restaurant."

"Jacksonville is very nice, especially if you own a boat."

"Have you ever been to the Dallas/Fort Worth area?"

"Once, when I was a kid—and no, I won't tell you how long ago that was."

He laughed harder than he should have, but why women worried about their age was beyond him. Nevertheless, her candid answer convinced him she was nowhere near Fort Worth the night CC died. "Do you have any alligator problems?" he said.

"Not personally, but they're definitely around. Like bees, if you leave them alone, they'll usually leave you alone. It's the snakes I worry about. They found a fifteen foot diamondback in a Jacksonville suburb."

"Fifteen feet?" Watts said. "That's gotta be a record."

"That's what they're saying. Sure makes me quiver."

"I'm sure." His watch reminded him the day was slipping by. "Anyway, thanks for your time. Good luck with your book. Like I said, your editor's waiting, so keep writing."

"I will. Bye now."

Watts immediately dialed Hans Slater's number. When no one answered, he left a voice message, then went back to his notes on Pao Lee. All he really knew about Pao was he commissioned the Writer's Block and was now left to the wind. Since Lee didn't die until after CC's murder, he could still be the killer. And if he was the killer, did someone silence him? Suddenly, Watts' brain ignited like fireflies in a Louisiana swamp. Lee, Jordan, Dridelle— Conspiracy! None of it made sense yet, but it kept him coming back to Mayor Jordan hiring Lee to kill CC so that OJ and Kat could be together. This love triangle theory still made more sense than any involving Courtney Dridelle. Maybe the hit financed Pao Lee's US book tour. And if Lee succeeded in his role as assassin, then Jordan would have to kill him to end the trail. Watts' phone rang.

His mind wrapped up in the case, he answered without checking the ID. "Detective Watts."

"Maxx, you really need to work on your phone etiquette."

"Daisy? Is that you?"

"Of course," she said, mocking him. "What other women are calling you about dinner?"

"None that I know of," he said, reveling in her sense of humor while that sultry voice of hers emptied his brain and released those pent up butterflies. "So, how are you?"

"I'm fine. I was wondering if you liked sushi."

Suddenly, the butterflies died from all the acid in Watts' stomach. There were plenty of reasons why he had an aversion to raw fish, and they were all good ones. Of course, he didn't want to share this with her right now, but how could they be soul mates if their food tastes were so dissimilar? Then again, maybe she didn't like to cook. Who does?

"Maxx?" she said, her tone implying concern. "Are you there?"

"Ah, yeah, but it's not the best connection. Did you say something about sushi?"

"Actually, I hate sushi, but since you're so chicken to answer, that's what we're having."

"Which one? Sushi or chicken?"

"Hmm. You're the detective and I said I hated sushi, so that means—"

"Great! I love chicken. You need any help? Can I bring something?"

"Tell you what. Show up at seven, and if I need any help I'll put you to work."

"Fair enough. See you soon."

Since Watts' mind was on Daisy and not the case, he took a quick bathroom break. Before sitting down at his desk, he stared at the copy of Lee's receipt for the Writer's Block that Lieutenant Ryder finally handed over. The answers as to why Lee commissioned the marble paperweight and why he used a Fort Worth trophy shop when he could have had it made in Hong Kong still eluded him. Was the block ready for Lee when he arrived? If so, did he order it from overseas? Since no one in the trophy shop had any recollection of Pao Lee, or the details concerning the Writer's Block, Kat Coulter seemed the only one who might unlock its mystery. Once again, Watts found himself dialing her number. He regretted it the moment she answered.

"I swear to God, Columbo, this had better be important."

"I'm sorry," he said to her, remembering how annoying Faulk's TV detective could be. Throughout the show, the bumbling Detective Columbo repeatedly returned for more answers. But Columbo was old and drove a beat-up Peugeot. In that regard, he and Columbo were nothing alike. The only weird thing about Watts was his squishy shoe.

Sighing heavily enough to be heard, she said, "What can I possibly tell you that we haven't already discussed?"

"I need to know more about Pao Lee," Watts calmly said. "Anything you can tell me would be great. I'll even take his height, weight, and shoe size if you have it."

"I hate to disappoint, but I only met him briefly on the night he gave CC the paperweight. Let me take a look at his file, though. I'm almost there," she said, shuffling papers. "Okay, here's what I have. Pao was born and raised in Hong Kong, he sent his query letter about four years ago, and CC and I agreed it would be beneficial having an international author, so we offered him the standard Guillotine Press contract. His book came out two years ago, and he has never submitted anything for his second book." She quickly added, "That's not unusual, though. Our contracts don't specify deadlines."

"You mean, your authors could go ten years between novels?"

"That would agree with the definition of no deadlines, Columbo."

Ignoring her sarcasm, Watts said, "Does the money for your authors' second books go into a savings account so it will be available whenever their books are ready?"

"Where are you going with this, detective?"

Watts leaned back in his chair, pleased she was listening. "I'm wondering if there's any money left to pay for their second books. A simple yes or no will suffice."

"In that case, the answer is no because we spent a lot of that money running the business. But like the tide, money is fluid. It comes in and goes out."

"I see. So, how much money is currently available for their second books?"

"Maybe sixteen thousand."

"Sixteen thousand is all? According to my research, that's barely enough for one book, assuming you're keeping to the same run. Do your authors know about this?"

"Of course not. But here's a little education on the book business. Big publishing houses may provide advances, but those authors don't see another dime until they've worked off their advance in book sales. Our authors may pay up front, but they get immediate royalties, so in the end it works out about the same. By the way, we've always paid our authors the royalties they've earned in case you're wondering why Hank Azar got a check."

Watts scratched his neck, unsure what to believe. "Getting back to Pao Lee, how did he find you?"

"Ever hear of the World Wide Web where everything imaginable is a click away?" After a brief pause, she said, "You really *are* Columbo."

Watts felt his muscles tense. Shifting in his seat and moving his feet helped, but an hour in the gym would be better. Like her, he couldn't wait to end the call.

"So you handled all of your correspondence with Lee over the web?" he said.

"Of course. By the way, they've also invented these wonderful devices called cell phones, scanners, iPads, e-readers, digital cameras . . ."

"Mrs. Coulter, there's no need to be so nasty. I'm only doing my job."

"You're right, and I'm sorry. It's been a rough week."

"I'm sure it has. Any idea how Pao funded his trip to Fort Worth?"

"Not a clue. Frankly, his ambitious book tour never made sense to me since he would probably have to sell fifty or sixty thousand books to break even. And while his novel is good, you need to be a celebrity to muster those figures."

Watts silently nodded. "Any idea what Lee did to have so much disposable income?"

"No, because we don't do background checks on our clients. If CC knew anything about Pao's personal life, he never divulged it to me."

Noting that, Watts said, "Do you have any contact information on Mr. Lee?"

"He was cremated, remember? He no longer has an address or cell phone."

Watts could just see her smirking over that one. On a physical scale, she might rate an Eight or even a Nine, but her personality deducted at least five points. Of course, you couldn't sink lower than grading women on a ten-point scale. Perhaps that was why he lost so many girlfriends. Hopefully, that wouldn't be the case with Daisy.

"You still there?" Kat said, as aggravated as ever.

"Sorry," he said, trying to catch up with where he left off. It took his brain a second to flash him back to Pao Lee's address. "Mrs. Coulter, you must have had some kind of physical address for him so your editor could reach him, or where you would send his royalty checks."

"Columbo, are you really this far behind the times? These days, everything's done on line. Most editors and authors correspond exclusively via e-mail, and royalties are always transferred electronically, even though we still call them checks. Pao Lee was a publisher's dream because he was responsive and pleasant to work with. There was no need to meet him in person, but when he wanted to stop by to say hello, we welcomed him. I can't believe he died in this godforsaken cow town."

"It's very sad, indeed." Watts let that hang for a second before asking for Lee's e-mail address and bank information."

"If I give it to you, will you promise to leave me alone?"

Watts squeezed his pen so tight it hurt. "How about if you promise to not call me Columbo, I'll leave you alone for the rest of the day?"

"But you *are* Columbo."

"No, ma'am, I'm not. I'm young, in great shape, and I drive a green 4X4 named Leroy."

"Leroy, huh? How utterly Texas. Anything else, Colom—*detective*?"

"Nope. That's it for now. I'll be in touch, but not before tomorrow. I always keep my promises."

"So do I, detective. Good day."

Watts hung up feeling like he had gone six rounds with Rocky Balboa. Kat Coulter was sharp all right. Maybe too sharp. So many things troubled him about this case. Lee's US tour for a book that came out two years prior, why he selected a Texas publisher and trophy shop, and why he visited the publisher he had never met just before he died. It was all very strange, and yet Watts believed Kat Coulter had some role in all of it. The hard part was finding the proof.

THIRTY THREE

350's air conditioner barely kept pace, but it was the lack of breakthroughs that was making Watts sweat. It was like cleaning out a latrine. The deeper he dug, the more it stank. Exhausted from talking to Kat, he slid his chair next to his partner.

"I feel like I'm standing in quicksand, Blaine. Please tell me you found something."

Spartan shook his head, and before he could say anything, the phone rang. It was Ryder, and he wanted them in his office, *now*.

After saying they were on the way, Watts stuck out his lower lip, thinking. Following a brief pause, he said to his partner, "Follow my lead, and trust me."

Spartan tossed his hands in the air, knowing they didn't have time to discuss it. Unannounced meetings like this rarely ended well. You could have banked a thousand Atta boys and one meeting like this could wipe them clean. As they marched The Green Mile to Ryder's office, the only noise in the corridor came from Watts' shoe.

Ryder waved them in wearing a smile as fake as the wood on his desk. His hands were resting on it like a king waiting to be fed. And like a king, Ryder had no idea what was on the menu. He only knew it had better be good.

"Gentlemen, I'm certain that after retrieving the data from Mrs. Coulter, you are ready to break this case."

Watts spotted a *Maxim* men's magazine on Ryder's desk. Even upside down, the scantily clad cover girl reminded him of Kat Coulter. Ryder saw him gawking and quickly tossed a folder over it. Watts held his grin, stalling for time.

"Lieutenant, I'll be blunt," he said, when the moment was right. "We have plenty of ideas, but still lack hard evidence. Mrs. Coulter has been forthcoming but remains a person of interest, and we still can't deny the possibility that the Forest Park murders are tied to our case."

"How can Kat Coulter still be a person of interest?" Ryder said, the veins in his neck ready to burst. "I get you your subpoena and you don't come

204

up with anything, and now you're telling me what—that you want to tear her house apart piece by piece? I guarantee the judge won't issue another warrant."

"That's okay, because Blaine and I are shifting our focus to Pao Lee."

If Spartan was closer, Watts would have nudged him so he knew he was ad-libbing. He didn't dare look at his partner because Ryder's eyes were locked on his.

"Sir, Lee had motive, opportunity, the Writer's Block, and left a hair sample in Coulter's office. We lost our focus when he died, but it all makes sense when you think about it."

Ryder rocked his chair, glaring back in apparent disbelief.

"I can't believe you two. You strike out with Mrs. Coulter so you go after a dead man. You're not detectives. You're insane. Forget Patrol, I should have you thrown off the force."

"With all due respect," Watts said, "You need to open your mind. You're the one refusing to believe our dead author may have murdered his publisher, in spite of evidence pointing in his direction. Unfortunately, the only ones who can confirm that are either dead or wanted by the police. Whenever Patrol finds our Skinheads, we'll know whether they killed Lee and Chow. If they're guilty, maybe they'll talk. If they're innocent, we have bigger issues."

Ryder blew his nose and tossed the tissue in the trash. Then his fingers found the back of his head and scratched vigorously. He stared at his detectives for a long time before reaching into his desk drawer for his stress ball. The veins in his arms pulsed as he squeezed.

Unable to stand the silence, Spartan jumped in. "Maxx is right, sir. Aren't you curious why a Chinese citizen would show up in Fort Worth for a belated book tour, and then a day after his publisher is murdered, he and his buddy are killed in Forest Park? And then one day after that, Lee and Chow are cremated? That may not bother you, but it sure as hell bothers us."

Ryder's hands levitated over the desk like they weren't sure whether to slam down or break something. "So your Skinheads are now part of this conspiracy?" he said. "Someone slap me so I know I'm not dreaming."

"Sir, had we known Lee was going to be cremated, we might have gathered more facts," Watts said, trying to draw the heat away from Spartan.

Ryder's eyes opened wide. "Oh, so now you're implying the ME screwed up?"

"Not at all, but I believe we should keep the communication flowing between all of these murders because Spartan and I are convinced they're related."

"Maxx, do you honestly believe that Pao Lee is your killer?"

"It's looking that way, sir."

"Then get out of here and do whatever you need to close this case"

The detectives left smiling. Ryder had no idea that a lot of what Watts said was spur-of-the-moment crap, and neither of them would ever admit to it. Keeping it secret was so important, they headed straight to the interrogation room, confirmed it was secure, and locked the door. Watts' smile was gone by the time he seated himself across from his partner.

"You know, Blaine, the more we discussed Lee in there, the more convincing it got. As far as I'm concerned, he *is* our number one suspect. Yes, Kat Coulter is still up there, but none of the other authors, including Courtney Dridelle and Ben Striker, are in the running anymore."

"Too bad Lee can't speak from the grave," Spartan sarcastically said.

Watts paused to ponder that. Something occurred to him during the meeting while Ryder was squeezing the ball. Needing Daisy's help, he said, "Keep looking for Coulter's nest egg, Blaine. I have something I need to check out. There's a slim chance that Lee can still speak from the grave."

"Yeah? Well, keep me posted."

THIRTY FOUR

Watts went to the lab to discuss his Lee premonitions with Daisy. He didn't want Spartan around because his partner was convinced they were dating, and didn't want to confuse the issue. Watts was brooding over how many times he could hear his partner say, "I told you so," when Daisy met him at the counter. She looked happy, but still addressed him as "detective".

Watts kept it professional, too. "I told Lieutenant Ryder that Pao Lee is our prime suspect in the Coulter murder," he said. "As before, he agreed to let us review everything on the Forest Park murders. Feel free to call to verify it."

"That's not necessary. What do you need?"

He was tempted to say, *Besides you*, but didn't. He saw no point in making this more awkward than it already was. Leaning over the counter and keeping his voice low, he said, "I need everything you have on Lee, and a place where we can talk freely."

"Sure. How about I meet you in the conference room?"

"That's fine. Oh, would you please bring CC Coulter's file, too?"

She nodded and went back to retrieve the files while he headed for the room. When she came in, she spread the files on the table and waited for him to speak. Watts looked around and touched the top of her hand.

"I have a hunch and I need your help."

"Of course. I'm here to help with whatever you need."

Watts smiled, knowing she meant that. "Okay, going back to the black hair found in CC's office, are you're certain it belongs to Pao Lee?"

"Absolutely. There are 3.1 billion bases of DNA, each bearing a generic code, and the hair from Mr. Coulter's home perfectly matches Pao Lee's DNA."

"Okay, but we know he visited the Coulter's house to give CC the Writer's Block, and according to Mrs. Coulter, never went into the office. Is there any way to know how long his hair had been there before it was found?"

"I see where you're going with this, but there's no definite way to tell that."

"That's what I thought," he said, removing his cell phone from his pocket.

He had turned it off for their meeting, but now needed to make a call. He pursed his lips while punching in the numbers. Daisy looked confused.

"What are you doing?" she said.

"Procrastinating. I really hate calling Kat Coulter, especially after I promised I wouldn't bother her again tonight. My connection with her is what you call strained."

"Then why call her?"

"Call it a fishing expedition," he said, without explaining himself.

Soon after, Kat's familiar voice answered. He set his phone to speaker so Daisy could hear.

"I thought we had a deal, Columbo. What do you want?"

"A simple answer, Mrs. Coulter. We're still trying to place Pao Lee at your house. Could he have gone to the restroom and perhaps ducked into the office for a second on his way back to the living room?"

"As I've said time and again, Pao Lee never left our living room, and he didn't stay long enough to use the restroom. He only wanted to give CC his paperweight. Why? Surely you don't think he's the killer?"

"I'm merely connecting dots, ma'am."

"Nice try, Columbo, but your tone suggests this is more about me than Pao Lee. You probably have someone listening in, or maybe I'm being taped, but that's okay. I have nothing to hide. I loved my husband, and my moving here proves that. You probably haven't learned this yet, but you don't have to realize every dream to have a full life. All that really matters is that you can share your life with someone who cares about you as much as you do them. CC and I had that, and I miss him dearly."

"We should all be so lucky," he said, eyeing Daisy. "Again, I'm sorry for your loss."

"Thanks—except you consider me a suspect, don't you."

"The proper term is person of interest, Mrs. Coulter, and that's only because we can't rule anyone out yet. It's nothing personal."

"Whatever. Any more promises you want to break?"

"Nope. I'll call if I need anything else. Thanks again for your cooperation."

He ended the call and looked at Daisy showing his palms at the phone.

"You heard her," he said. "What do you think?"

"She sounds nice enough. What matters is what you think."

"That's the problem. I don't know anymore. The last time we spoke, she growled at me. She started out that way again and suddenly she's Mary Poppins. She loves messing with me. Anyway, if she's telling the truth about Lee, the only way his hair could have gotten into the office is if he came back later. Based on the home's design, it seems unlikely a single hair could end up in the office even with the wind blowing through the house. That leaves the scenario where CC is sitting in his chair, he hears something, and then sees Pao Lee standing there. Recognizing Lee would be worse than seeing a stranger because he wouldn't be sure how to react. That gives Lee the advantage. A swift blow to the head, and CC's putty in his hands."

"Okay, let's say that Lee broke in. Why would he come all this way to kill his publisher?"

"We're still trying to sort that out," he said, unwilling to discuss their conspiracy theories right now. "Still no sign of Shing Chow's hair at the Coulters?"

"Nope. Only Lee's and the Coulters'."

"Well, at least we have something solid that steers us toward Lee and away from Kat Coulter. I'm sure Lieutenant Ryder will be happy about that."

She reached over and gently covered his hand with hers. "Maxx, whether we're in the office or out, I hope you'll say whatever's on your mind, personally or professionally. We're both rather intertwined in this case, so it's okay to talk shop over dinner or any other time. Got it?"

"Got it, and thank you."

Taking her hand back, she said, "By the way, what's with the Columbo reference? I've seen a few episodes on retro TV and I don't see any resemblance between you and Peter Faulk."

"She probably calls me that because I keep coming back for more even when she thinks she's given everything. But going back to Lee, he may have gone to CC because he hadn't received any royalties in two years. Maybe he used the Writer's Block as his Trojan Horse. I don't know if any of that is true, I'm just throwing it on the table."

"Keep talking."

"Okay, Lee's novel, *The Mariner's Club*, infers he was a seafarer. Most people can't write about sailing without having had prior experience, and I suspect few mariners have thirty grand to blow on a book deal, or have the time off for an international book tour."

Daisy crossed her arms, grinning. "You know, listening to you speak, you do kind of remind me of Columbo. It's not your voice, but you do have some similar mannerisms."

"Gee, thanks. Maybe I should grab some cigars and a trench coat on my way home. Any other insights?"

"Actually, yes. You are making value judgments on Lee that may not be warranted. Perhaps he was frugal, or maybe he was a ship's officer. If he was a mariner, he was probably at sea for weeks at a time, so he may have had weeks off between cruises. Merchant marines have little opportunity to spend their money at sea, so he could have saved a bundle over the years."

"Duly noted."

But Watts wasn't convinced. Something was still missing, but lacking ideas, he retrieved his papers and stood up. "Thanks for your time," he said, touching her arm. "If you discover anything new, please call me."

"I will, detective. And remember to call me."

"I promise."

Watts ran upstairs and filled Spartan in on his meeting with Daisy Woods. Detective Skip Parsons agreed to meet them in the interrogation room so they could all be on the same page. The wall clock ticked loudly to make whoever was inside uneasy. Since Parsons had yet to show, Watts grew anxious.

Spartan compared his watch to the wall clock. The wall clock was five minutes off, so he re-set it and went back to his chair. A moment later he got up again. "Since Skip's not here, I'm going to get some coffee. I'll be right back."

Watts barely looked up as his mind sorted thoughts between Daisy Woods, Pao Lee, and Kat Coulter. He was so involved that Spartan's words didn't register until he was out the door. Spartan must have run into Parsons because they both came back together.

Over the next thirty minutes, the three detectives compared notes on Pao Lee. It quickly became evident to Parsons that the two cases were more closely linked than he had previously thought. But Parsons still had reservations and the Skinheads were only one reason why. Another was the lack of knowledge on the part of the Chinese government. As far as they were concerned, Pao Lee and Shing Chow were ghosts.

Watts tugged at his eyebrows, staring at the evidence. "Skip, what did you use to positively identify your victims?"

"We've been over this, Maxx. Their passport photos matched their faces. I would have preferred to match fingerprints, but their passports didn't include any, and we didn't get any assistance from the Chinese. Even so, I'm confident that Lee and Chow are who they're supposed to be."

"Is there any way of knowing if the US did a background check on them before allowing them into this country?"

"Neither showed up on the No-Fly list, Maxx. That's one of the first things I checked."

Spartan kicked back in his chair, staring at them. "It's hard to imagine the bureaucracy in a country with over one point three *billion* people," he said. "I can't explain their lack of fingerprints either, but maybe we're reading more into their passports than what they really are. I mean, a passport merely identifies you as a citizen of a country, and it's up to the individual countries you visit to verify the information is correct. As far as I know, the US only runs visitors' fingerprints when there's an issue, and that only happens when passports have been coded to deny entry. For most people, passports are mementos that accompany travel photos from their one trip overseas."

"Point well taken," said Watts, "and I hate to sound racist, but considering Lee and Chow's ethnic background, I suspect there are a lot of Chinese men who bear an uncanny resemblance to either of them."

"So, what are you saying?" Parsons said. That Shing Chow and Pao Lee aren't really dead? That the Forest Park victims were posers?"

Spartan nodded. "That's an interesting possibility," he said.

Parsons shook his head in disgust. "Look, guys, I'm happy to share information, but I see little value in continuing this discussion. I need to get back to work. If you find anything significant, you know where to find me."

Watts waved a half-hearted good bye. In spite of Parsons' abrupt departure, he still felt the meeting was worthwhile. While he didn't partake in Spartan's body-swap theory, everything had to be considered.

Spartan kicked back in his chair, picking at his teeth. "I bet Skip thinks we're nuts."

"Maybe, but detectives should always think outside the box."

"I agree, but soon Pao Lee and Shing Chow will be nothing more than grim statistics for the City of Fort Worth. Unfortunate victims of violence. We should be grateful the Chinese government isn't using this as propaganda. Now that I think of it, the fact that they haven't capitalized on it gives credence to the possibility that Lee and Chow were actually Chinese agents, and to acknowledge them would be an admission that they existed. Had our media expressed any interest in their murders, our investigative reporters might have uncovered that."

"Okay, Blaine, now you're thinking way outside the box. People die every day in China without any mention on the news, so it's rather presumptuous to think the absence of a full report on Lee and Chow makes them spies."

"But don't you think the fact that they died in Fort Worth, Texas, sets them apart from the rest of China's population? I mean, we always hear about US citizen dying overseas."

Watts gave it some thought. He had never been to China, but he did keep up with the news. Spartan was right. It usually was a big deal when Americans died overseas. China might handle things differently, but it did seem peculiar that they wouldn't be screaming bloody murder over two of their citizens being carved up in a Fort Worth park.

"Blaine, as enlightening as this has been, I'm need to talk to someone in the lab about these murders."

"Yeah, right. Tell her I said hi."

"Keep guessing, partner. You're not even close."

THIRTY FIVE

On his way to see Daisy, Maxx Watts kept thinking about Kat Coulter. Even when she was sarcastic and rude, she had still spoken from the heart. She also seemed smart enough to know he could always demand a polygraph, so there would be no benefit in lying. He still found it amazing that with all the technology, no one could explain how Pao Lee's hair ended up in CC's office. That left everything to speculation, and speculation never resulted in a conviction. It seemed highly improbable that the wind blew a single hair in, and equally unlikely that only one hair would be ripped out during a fierce struggle. Watts still wondered what method Dr. Morton used to identify Lee's body, and what samples were taken before Lee and Chow were cremated.

Daisy immediately approached the counter when she saw him. "Detective Watts, I didn't expect to see you so soon. What can I do for you?"

"I don't know enough about body identification. Can we return to the conference room for a moment?"

"Sure. Let me tell my co-workers what's going on and I'll meet you there."

Watts nodded and moseyed toward the room. He took the same seat as before, twirling his thumbs while waiting. Soon, he heard footsteps and she came in, smiling.

"Sorry to keep you waiting," she said.

"Not a problem, and thanks for seeing me again."

"Detective, I already told you I'm available 24/7. All you need to do is ask."

"Thank you," he said, being cautious with his words. "Do you know how the ME determined the two mutilated bodies from the park were actually Pao Lee and Shing Chow?"

"I know the Chinese verified their passports and their photos matched the bodies. We also know that Lee and Chow arrived on the same Hong Kong flight two days before CC Coulter died. When their bodies were found in Forest Park, the ME took their fingerprints along with hair, skin, and blood samples, but the primary means of identification was their passports.

Personally, I prefer more, but I had no say in it. Lab techs lose credibility when they challenge detectives. I've been burned before, so I've learned to keep my thoughts to myself. You're the exception."

"Thanks. I'll take that as a compliment," he said, wondering what she might be holding back. "But here's what I'd like you to do. You obviously have some of the same doubts about Lee and Chow, so I'd like you to run their fingerprints through our national data base to see if anything comes up. If anyone asks, tell them I requested it."

"Sure. I can do that."

"Great. For now, let's keep this between us because I don't want you in the middle. As for Lee and Chow, most likely they are who they're supposed to be. We're only doing this as a precaution because we both know bodies have been swapped before."

"I understand."

"Well," he said, sliding his chair back, "I suppose I'd better get upstairs and brief everyone on what's going on."

She stood and collected her files, holding them against her chest. "Seven?"

"God willing and the creek don't rise," he said with a grin. "By the way, my partner says hi. I'll tell you more about him later. Thanks again for your help, Ms. Woods."

"You're welcome, detective."

When Watts returned to his desk, Spartan was sitting in his chair sipping coffee, sporting a Cheshire Cat grin. His chair squeaked when he leaned back. Then he eased it forward so it squeaked again. "So, how are things in the lab?" he said.

"Fine. I'm hoping to get some additional data to verify Chow and Lee's identities."

"You go downstairs to see your lady friend and that's all I get? My coffee gives me more excitement than that."

Watts lowered his head like a ram ready to butt. "First of all, she's not my lady friend, and second, I just said I went there to investigate their identities. Next time I'll drag you along, if you're so inclined. Finally, find some oil for that chair. It's annoying."

"Sorry. I'll see what I can find."

Watts puffed up his cheeks and then blew it out. He noticed a blob on his desk and rubbed it with his finger. When the mark didn't erase, he wiped his dirty finger on his sock. Looking at his finger reminded him that a single print could solve crimes as easily as a single hair. The ME had taken fingerprints from both Chinese victims, so some data base should turn up their identities.

It was such an obvious thing to do that Parsons must have checked them all. There were two reasons why Watts asked Daisy to double-check. First, she was technically savvy. Second, she was working both cases. He hoped this wouldn't cause any problems for her.

Daisy called ten minutes later saying she was on her way up with the data. By the time Watts passed the news on to his partner, she was standing at his desk. Spartan seemed surprised and also disappointed because she barely acknowledged either of them. Watts spoke first.

"So, did the data support what we discussed?" he said.

"Not exactly," she tentatively said.

The hair on Watts' arm stiffened with the news. He needed to tell Ryder about this, but also wanted Parsons to be in on it. Watts huddled the three of them together to discuss his plan. When they broke, he said, "We'll head down to Lieutenant Ryder's office as soon as I reach Detective Parsons. Everyone knows what they need to do, right?"

Once they nodded, Watts called Parsons and told him to meet them there. After he hung up, the three of them marched down the hall, line abreast, evidence in hand. Since Ryder's office only had two chairs, they all remained standing in front of his desk.

Ryder gave them a hard stare. "What's this? The Three Musketeers?"

"This is important," Watts said. "Skip Parsons should be here any second."

Parsons joined them seconds later, giving Ryder the "What am I missing" look. The look he fired at Watts wasn't as nice. Watts closed the door and then looked at Ryder. "Now that everyone's here," he said, "Ms. Woods has some interesting news for us."

"Thank you," she said, taking the opportunity to hand everyone copies of her report. "Sir, as you know, we already confirmed that the human hair found in Mr. Coulter's office belongs to the victim presumed to be Pao Lee. Detective Parsons worked with the Chinese government to confirm the identities of the Forest Park murder victims, which was appropriate considering Lee's and Chow's Chinese passports. However, running their fingerprints through the US database identified the park victim as Pao Lee's identical twin, Ming. We know this because Ming Lee is a naturalized US citizen, and lists an address near Forest Park. This means that if the real Pao Lee visited the Coulters' house, he is probably still alive."

Casting a desperate look, Parsons said, "How can DNA perfectly match two people?"

"The DNA from the hair found in Mr. Coulter's office matches the hair sample from the dead body in the morgue with a ninety-nine percent certainty.

In other words, identical twins will always share the exact DNA unless there has been a rare genetic mutation. However, in spite of this commonality among identical siblings, fingerprints are always unique."

"So you're telling me that Pao Lee stole his brother's identity?" Parsons said, accusingly.

"So it seems," Watts said, chiming in. "And murder is the best reason I can think of why Pao Lee is probably living at his brother's place right now."

Lieutenant Ryder kicked back in his chair, rubbing his chin. "Interesting theory, Maxx. The good news is we have his passport so he can't leave the country."

"He could if he uses his brother's passport," Spartan said, "and until we clear Pao Lee of murder, I suggest you talk to Homeland Security and see if Ming Lee has a current US passport. If so, then have them code it so he can't get through Customs."

"That's good," Ryder said." "Skip, how about taking care of that?"

Parsons looked miffed when Ryder assigned him the duty. On his way out, he gave disapproving gazes to all three musketeers.

Watts ignored him and took over. "Sir, based on this latest revelation, I recommend we arrest Pao Lee on murder charges."

Ryder's eyes tracked across Watts and Spartan before stopping at Daisy. "Allow me to play the Devil's Advocate," he said to her. "You say we have two people with identical DNA, but separate fingerprints. One is at large, and the other has been cremated. What makes you so sure the hair sample found in Mr. Coulter's office isn't Ming Lee's?"

Daisy looked him square in the eye. "Sir, while it's possible that Ming Lee could have posed as his brother when he gave Mr. Coulter the Writer's Block, it's unlikely he could discuss his brother's writing. Of course, this is just my opinion. I'm a forensics tech, not a detective."

Ryder nodded, shifting his gaze to his detectives. "Considering that you brought this evidence forward, you two can bring Pao in. Assuming Parsons did his job, then Ming's passport won't do him any good. I'd still like to know whether the Lee/Chow murders were hits or random acts."

"Maybe Pao Lee can offer some insight on that," Watts said.

"Or maybe Patrol will find Fazelli's kidnappers," Spartan added.

"Or maybe you should get going before the sun gets any lower," Ryder said. "If he's not home, we'll put out an APB." He then shifted his eyes back to Daisy. "Ms. Woods, if you come up with any more evidence, I want you to immediately bring it to my attention. Now get busy, all of you."

They wasted no time in leaving. Watts caught up with Daisy before she headed downstairs. "Please keep me in the loop, too," he said.

"I will, Columbo. Be careful bringing Lee in. Dinner can wait if need be."

"I'll call you when it's over."

THIRTY SIX

Watts and Spartan got on the computer as soon as they got back to their desks. Obtaining Ming Lee's address was easy. According to the Texas Department of Public Safety, it hadn't changed in years. Since it was already late in the day, they raced to their car, eager to wrap this up. The smothering smog had turned the sun red. Watts was glad red suns didn't blind.

Spartan watched for traffic while Watts steered onto Belknap. A Hispanic kid, eight years old tops, watched them drive off. Watts waved at him, and then watched him in the mirror. When they were a half block away, the kid flipped him off.

"I can't believe it," he said. "That little kid flipped us off for no reason."

"Maybe his dad got deported."

Watts nodded at the possibility, steering the big sedan through traffic. He had so many things going through his head he didn't want to converse. Finally, he looked at his partner and said, "I can't help thinking that if Parsons had been more thorough, Pao Lee might already be in custody. He's the only one who can piece together our puzzle and we really need him alive."

"I agree, but in Skip's defense, it did appear to be a match. I mean, who knew that Pao had a twin? Especially one that's living right here in Fort Worth."

Watts nodded, listening to him while scanning the streets. A scruffy dog sniffed a fire hydrant. Two blocks further, an angry bum was pushing his rusty Walmart cart at two kids that were making skateboard jumps. The scenes, typical of his beat cop days, reminded him why Porgy Mulberry blamed Watts for his not making detective. Watts wondered if Mulberry's weight gain had anything to do him not being promoted. If that was the case, then he felt sorry for Porgy, but not enough to forgive him for what he did to him. He let his thoughts shift back to Pao.

Looking at Spartan, he said, "Any idea how Pao's passport ended up in Ming's possession?"

"Not really."

"Me neither. Any ideas about Shing Chow?"

218

"Maybe he was Pao's accomplice. If Shing stayed in the getaway car, he wouldn't have left any DNA behind."

"True, except there weren't any tire tracks. At least none that could be traced."

Spartan nodded. "Either way, we should know soon."

Watts' brain was yarning possibilities all the way to Ming Lee's neighborhood. Located less than a mile from Forest Park, it explained why Ming might take Shing Chow out for a walk once the air cooled. Perhaps Pao stayed behind because of jet lag or didn't want to walk. If Pao had gone with them, he either would have saved his brother's life, or would have been killed with them. Once more, that was speculation.

Watts stopped the sedan in front of Ming's clapboard house and they both climbed out. Spartan headed around back while Watts started up the walkway. No one answered the door, no inside lights were on, and no one appeared to be home. Spartan soon joined Watts out front and unbuttoned his collar.

"Nothing out back," he said.

"Nothing out front either." Watts handed over the car keys. "How about keeping watch from inside the car while I talk to the neighbors. I don't want to alarm anyone, and both of us scouring the area could raise eyebrows."

"Is that why you didn't request a Patrol backup? I mean, Lee is a murder suspect."

"First, *you* are my backup. Second, Pao may not recognize our Crown Vic, but would certainly know a radio car that says Police. We don't want to scare him off."

Spartan accepted the keys. "You're the boss."

Ignoring him, Watts waited until Spartan was in the car before approaching the house to the right of Lee's. Soon after ringing the doorbell, an elderly Asian woman was squinting through her partially opened door. She didn't seem impressed with Watts' badge or introduction, so Watts didn't bother with chit-chat.

"Have you seen Mr. Lee?" he said.

The plump round-faced woman looked in the direction of Ming Lee's home and then back at Watts. Speaking with a thick accent, she said, "Mr. Lee not been himself lately. He come and go no particular time. He used to be very nice. Not so much now."

Her description convinced Watts that they had correctly identified Ming Lee's body in the morgue, and that Pao has assumed his brother's identity.

"Have you seen Mr. Lee come or go today?" he said.

"What I look like? Neighborhood watch? I no look out window all time."

"No, of course not. May I have your name for my report?"

Straightening her posture and sticking out her chest, she said, "My name Pak Sun Ye."

He nodded, recognizing her name as Korean. In Asian cultures, family names come first, but in America, many reverse it to conform to Anglo culture. Risking offending her, he addressed her as Mrs. Pak and thanked her for her time. Since she didn't correct him, he turned and walked away feeling her eyes stabbing his back. He joined Spartan in the car and fastened his seatbelt like he was going to drive off.

Spartan glanced at him, curious. "We're not going to watch Lee's house?"

Watts checked his mirrors and slowly pulled away from the curb. "We're watching, but also creating the illusion we're leaving. We have no way of knowing if the Korean next door is protecting Pao. Allowing her space should clear that up pretty quickly. Keep your eyes open for a place where we can see Lee's house, but she can't see us."

Spartan kept checking his mirror. "Since Ming's driver's license wasn't on his body, we should assume that Pao has it."

"I concur, and while we're at it, let's assume Ming's car is in the garage."

Spartan stared at Ming's house until Watts turned the corner. "What did the neighbor say about him?"

Watts put on his blinker and made two lefts until he was pointing down a shady street. The temperature dropped as soon as they hit the shadows. He waited until he had slowed to a crawl before saying, "Her name's Mrs. Pak, and she said Lee hasn't been himself lately. I thanked her and left." He took another left and stopped between two homes where he could see Ming's house, but Mrs. Pak couldn't see him. "This is perfect."

Spartan nodded, looking for curious neighbors and anything else that moved. Watching Watts fidget like a kid in Sunday School, he said, "You seem tense. What's going on?"

Watts stared out the windshield. "Narrow streets, dogs wandering all over the place, kids could pop out anywhere. If Pao's in there and decides to run, it could make for a tough pursuit, but if we park on his street, we may never know if he's in there."

"Or if he drives up, he might keep driving and we'd never know."

"Unless we recognize him, in which case we would go after him. Keep your head on a swivel and we should be fine."

Spartan slapped Watts' shoulder to get his attention. "There's movement in the house," he said. "Seconds later, the garage door was opening. "He's running, Maxx. Get moving!"

Watts threw it in gear and hit the gas. "Notify Dispatch. Tell them we're in pursuit."

Spartan flipped on the lights and siren, then called Dispatch. Their heavy sedan nearly swapped ends as they took the first left. By the time they turned onto Lee's street, Ming's silver Acura had a three block head start. Before they could get close enough to read the license plate, the Acura made an evasive left turn. The Acura cornered better than the Ford, but Watts managed to keep it in sight. Fearing this could end badly, Spartan requested assistance from the police helicopter so they could back off and still track Lee. Dispatch acknowledged his request, saying the chopper was on the way.

"Tell Dispatch Lee is heading for I-30, and I need radio cars in both directions."

No sooner had Watts said that, a kid on a bike rode into the street. Bracing against the wheel, Watts hit the brakes and skidded to a stop. Once the kid steered clear, Watts hit the gas, belching a trail of black smoke. Now being peak commuting time, the heavy traffic on Forest Park Boulevard forced Watts to back off. With the Acura no longer in sight and no way of knowing what direction it was traveling, he steered the Crown Vic to the side of the road and looked at the sky. "Where in the hell is that chopper?" he said.

"Still heading this way, I guess. Numerous patrol cars are converging on the area. The chopper can't be too far away. Lee isn't going anywhere."

"Yeah, right. Do you have any idea how many silver compact cars are on the road right now? All Lee has to do is blend in. It'll be a miracle if the helo can even find him. Call Parsons, ask him to run down Ming Lee's license plate, and request an APB on his Acura."

"Will do."

Watts sighed and pulled back into traffic. Still traveling north, he stopped at Rosedale to look for Lee's car. Since the traffic moved normally in every direction, he figured Lee's car must have slipped through. Crossing Rosedale, Forest Park turned into a divided road so Lee could have picked up speed, and that concerned Watts. "What do you think, Blaine? Is he gonna continue on Forest Park or take the freeway on-ramp?"

"If I didn't know the roads, I'd take the freeway."

Watts silently agreed as he listened to the radio cars closing in. Since 350 was only a few blocks away, there was an abundant supply of cops. Between the gawkers and nervous drivers, traffic quickly came to a halt and Watts couldn't move.

Sensing his partner's frustration, Spartan said, "If Lee stays on Forest Park, he'll run right into the Patrol cops."

"I was thinking the same thing, Blaine, but at this time of day, the downtown traffic's horrendous, and Lee is used to driving on the wrong side of the road. The worst thing that could happen is him plowing into someone head-on."

"All we can do is hope that the police chopper gets here soon to direct the intercept."

Watts scanned the sky again, but all he saw was brown. The air police would have a tough time spotting Lee's car in this haze.

"Let's hope Lee calls it quits before Forest Park turns into Weatherford Street. He could hurt a lot of people if he goes too fast around the bend."

Spartan nodded, tilting his head to the sky. "On any given day there's at least one news helicopter around, yet today the sky's empty. Amazing."

Watts took another glance out the windshield. "Money's tight, and those choppers drink gas. They're probably grounded today because their cameras can't see through the haze. Can't say that I blame 'em for not flying."

"I suppose."

Suddenly a radio report came in from an officer in pursuit. "Suspect Acura has crossed the median and hit an oncoming car," he said with a sense of urgency. "Request ambulance."

Watts pounded the wheel so hard his hand hurt. "Damn you, Pao!"

By the time they arrived on scene, five police cars had surrounded the Acura, rescue personnel were on the attack, and an ambulance a half block away still struggled to get through. Once the crash occurred, the police helicopter aborted to reduce the midair potential with the two news helicopters circling overhead. Watts got as close as he could get and then leaped from his car, flashing his badge at anyone who dared challenge him. Lee's Acura had hit at least two oncoming cars before rolling into a tree. Trapped inside the crumbled wreck, Lee's face was crushed, and several bones protruded from his chest and legs. Knowing he wasn't going to make it, Watts grabbed Lee's shoulder and squeezed hard.

"Mr. Lee, can you hear me?" he said, holding the pressure.

Tearing flowing from eyes squeezed shut, Lee nodded slightly, but didn't speak.

"Why did you run?"

"Kkkkk . . . killed my brother . . . and . . . Shing . . ."

"Pao, what happened to them? To CC Coulter?" No answer. "Stay with me, Pao! Did you kill CC Coulter?"

The EMT pressed his fingers against Lee's jugular vein and shook his head. "Sir, I'm afraid he's gone," he said. "He has no pulse."

Ignoring him, Watts repeated his questions, shaking Lee's body. Spartan grabbed Watts' shoulders and gently pulled him away. "He's gone, Maxx. There are cameras everywhere. You need to back off so the fire department can extract him. Patrol can write up the accident. We need to get back to the office to write our version of what happened."

Watts slumped. "You're right," he said. He withdrew, but not before slapping the Acura. His hand stung worse now, but it was worth it. As they walked away, someone fired up the Jaws of Life. Considering the car's condition, it would take quite an effort to extract Lee's body. Thinking about all that had transpired, Watts hoped the Lee brothers were together again in a more peaceful realm.

Watts parked the sedan at 350 and headed toward the door with his partner. Before they went through, Watts stopped and said, "Why don't you go home, Blaine? I'll take care of the paperwork. Sandy will have questions once she sees this on the news. I'm sure your version will differ from what they report. "

"Are you sure you don't want me to stick around? I don't mind."

Watts shook his head. "Family first, my friend. I'll call you if I need help."

"Okay. I'll see you in the morning."

Watts nodded and headed upstairs. If he hurried, he could still make it to Daisy's by seven, but right now he had to download his brain onto a Word document. He started with Pao Lee's final words, "Killed my brother and Shing." He paused, staring at the words, trying to ascertain who killed them, and why Pao ran. Watts found it interesting that Lee's dying words dealt with family and not CC Coulter. He thought about the Skinheads that witnesses saw leaving Forest Park and wondered if Pao ran because he thought they were after him, too. But how could that be when their badges were clearly visible? Sadly, they would never know.

When he finished his notes on the identity switch and how Pao died evading the police, he still wondered why Lee ran. Mistaking two suits in a Crown Vic with it lights on and siren blaring for two Skinheads in a pickup seemed highly improbable. And while experience told him that guilty people run, he wasn't so sure that was the case with this foreigner.

While writing his report, Watts learned that police had secured Lee's home, and Detective Parsons was on scene. Watts planned to return there tomorrow to dig up whatever Parsons may have missed. Maybe now that Pao was dead, Mrs. Pak would be more cooperative. Regardless of how things turned out, he probably wouldn't sleep tonight.

He saved the document and was e-mailing it to his partner for review. As soon as he sent it, his phone rang. *Daisy!*

"I saw it on the news," she said, sounding sad. "I'm so sorry, Maxx. I hope you're still coming over. It'll do you good."

"I'll definitely be there, but I need to shower first."

"No need. Just get your butt over here before dinner is ruined."

THIRTY SEVEN

Leroy flew out of the parking garage like a thoroughbred from a starting gate. Thankfully Watts' pickup knew the way because its driver was completely distracted. Watts steered around a pothole and some road trash, talking to his truck as if it understood.

"I'm telling you, Leroy, this job never gets easier," he said. "Having a woman in my life complicates things, but in a good way. Sorry I've been ignoring you. I can't remember the last time I detailed you."

The desperate eyes in Leroy's mirror told Watts to stop blabbing and turn on some music. The detective complied, sliding in John Fogerty's *Revival* CD, and then cranking up the volume. *Don't You Wish It Was True* was Watts' favorite song on that album because it spoke of a Utopian world where everyone loved and accepted everyone else. No war, only peace. Heaven on Earth. If Pao and Ming Lee, Shing Chow, and CC Coulter were lucky, they were already seeing that. Yes, Watts wished it was true. A world without war, only peace. Every day, society proved Utopia didn't exist, but having the right woman at his side made it seem possible.

His heart thumped when he reached Daisy's apartment complex. By the time he reached her door, it hammered in his chest. He heard footsteps, and then giggling from the other side of the door. The light changing in the peep hole confirmed she had been spying on him.

"What's the password?" she said through the closed door.

Smiling, Watts tucked his hands in his pockets and rocked on his heels. Feeling better already, he said, "Watts *is* the password."

Suddenly, the door opened and she stood there admiring him. The air conditioning exiting the apartment funneled through Watts open collar, giving immediate relief. Whatever she had baking in the oven smelled wonderful. She dragged him inside, sat him on the love seat, and handed him a Corona. Having never developed a taste for beer, he wanted to say he didn't drink it, but today it went down easy. She quickly sat next to him and tapped her bottle to his.

"To Pao Lee, Ming Lee, Shing Chow, and CC Coulter," she said. "May they rest in peace."

"Here, here," said Watts, taking a swig. "So, what did the news say about Pao Lee?"

"They showed images of the wreck, identified Pao as the driver, and identified the two injured victims as Juan Rodriquez and Michelle Jimenez. They didn't report many details other than that, but of course, I had a sense of what was going on. Much of the footage was devoted to firefighters trying to free Lee from the wreck."

Watts grimaced. "Let's forget about the job for a while. Thank you for having me over."

Grinning while swallowing her beer, she said, "Who says murder can't bring people together?" But Watts wasn't smiling with her, so she downed another gulp and draped her arm over his. "Maxx, I'm really sorry about the identity mess up with Ming and Pao. I know you'll say don't worry about it, but I do. I mean, it impacted two murder investigations."

"Skip Parsons should have caught it," he said, unable to shake it off. "Hopefully, that's why he's at Ming Lee's house now. But I'm really proud of you. Your revelation may have solved the Coulter case, so you should feel pretty darned good about it."

"How so?"

"I'll only tell you if you let me use your shower."

"Help yourself. All the towels are clean, and dinner's ready whenever you are."

"I'll be quick."

Ten minutes later he joined into her the living room feeling better. When he sat next to her, her legs pressed into his, and his energy was flowing again. They locked eyes, looking into each other's souls for what seemed an eternity before either of them spoke.

"I know we barely know each other," she said, "but it's so easy being with you, Maxx. I'm really glad you're here."

Sliding his arm over her shoulder, he said, "Thank you. I feel the same. You look so beautiful, I wish I had a portrait of you like this."

Her eyes widened and she backed away slightly. "Wow, what a great line! I've never heard that one before."

But Watts was serious. "It's not a line, it's a fact, and for the record, I have never said anything like that before—ever." His growling stomach broke the tension. Blushing, he said, "Sorry, I haven't eaten all day."

"I told you dinner's ready. Considering this afternoon's events and not knowing when you'd get here, I made chicken pot pie because it keeps well."

"Sounds great. I should have brought flowers, though."

"Why?" she said, with a look of surprise. "Your yellow roses are still fresh. Don't get me wrong, I love surprises, but you don't need to bring something every time we get together."

Watts gazed into her eyes, mesmerized. His heart fluttering, he craved to caress her. "I know this sounds hokey, but you are the most amazing woman I've ever met."

Smiling, she playfully poked his nose. "I'm flattered, Maxx, but it's time to eat, and be forewarned, I'm not the most amazing chef you'll ever met."

He smiled back. "My mom is the only other woman who ever cooked for me, so no matter what, it's special, and I appreciate it."

To avoid prolonging their conversation, she pulled him off the love seat and dragged him to the table. Once he sat down, she pulled the pot pie from the oven and served up healthy portions. Large chunks of chicken, carrots, green beans, onions, and potatoes floated on a light crust. "It has everything but the kitchen sink, and it's all fresh," she said, setting the plate in front of him.

Watts quietly inhaled the aroma. "It smells wonderful, Daisy."

She sat next to him and lifted her fork. "Stop smelling and dig in. I'm starving."

Sitting there, eating a delicious meal with soft music in the background, made small talk easy. Not once did either mention work while they ate. But when they finished and returned to the living room, the news was showing new footage of Pao Lee being extracted, the blood-soaked sheet covering his body a testament to his grizzly injuries. Watts was about to turn the volume down, but Daisy seemed intent on listening. Wondering what she found so fascinating, her answer came without a query.

"Maxx, look at Pao's shoes!"

Watts stared at Lee's flat-soled slippers. Right after he noticed them, the story changed to the wildfires in Texas and Arizona, the reporter saying there was no relief in sight.

"What about them?" he said to her, leaning back again.

"Remember how the ground at the Coulter's house was so hard and trampled that we couldn't find any footprints?" He nodded, picturing the scene. "Well, shoes like Lee's would be nearly impossible to detect." She faced him, gesturing with open hands. "Maxx, your shoes always give you away, but slippers like Lee's would make it easy to sneak up on CC Coulter."

Watts nodded. "Especially with gusty winds and screeching cicadas," he said, completing her sentence. "I'll call the ME to make sure he retains Lee's clothing. I'll also request he review Lee's skin and hair samples, and fingerprints."

"Maxx, I work with Dr. Morton a lot. Let me call him before it gets any later. He's getting kind of cranky these days, and he'll be less likely to yell at me than you."

"Thanks. I appreciate it."

She went into the kitchen to make the call, and plopped down next to Watts when she had finished. "Okay," she said, patting his thigh. "We're set to see him first thing in the morning. Anything else you want to discuss or shall we watch *Conan*?"

Slid his arm around her, he said, "*Conan* would be great."

As much as he wanted to stay, he left right after the show ended.

* * * * *

He didn't sleep well because his mind wouldn't shut down. Whenever he started dreaming about Daisy Woods, Pao Lee would interrupt like a chaperon at a high school dance. As a result, he spent a lot of time watching the digits change on his nightstand clock. When his alarm finally went off, it took more effort than it should have to roll out of bed. Last night's beer might have contributed, but more likely it was the unresolved issues. Either way, he would skip the beer next time.

As he ambled by the kitchen table, Coulter's manuscript pages caught his eye. Not the originals, but the copies of the ones they took from Coulter's throat. Scratching his head to wake up, he thought about his paper wad reenactment. Even soaked, it was still quite large, and would take considerable effort to force it down a man's throat, during which time any conscious victim would bite in self-defense. With that thought, he quickly downed a glass of orange juice and ran the shower. Following a quick shave and tooth brushing, he flew out the door.

Today he made no attempt to sneak past Lieutenant Ryder's office. Instead, he tapped on the door and barged in uninvited. "Mornin' lieutenant."

"Well, well, if it isn't my favorite detective. Come on in, Maxx. Have a seat so I can congratulate you on Pao Lee's arrest. It couldn't have gone worse if my newest rookie went to get him. So, now we have two innocent people in the hospital, had gridlock for hours, Lee is dead, but don't forget all that glorious breaking news coverage. Yes sir, you and your partner outdid yourselves on that one.

"Sir, as much as I appreciate your sarcasm, had you read my report, you would realize that we ended our pursuit before things got dangerous. We were two miles away when Lee crossed the median into those cars."

Ryder's face reddened. "I did read your report, and although parking around the corner may have given you cover, it also let the cat out of the bag. And then there's the backup issue. Granted, there was no official requirement to have a radio car there because Spartan was with you, but don't you think it might have been a good idea to have one anyway?"

"Hindsight is always twenty-twenty, lieutenant."

Ryder peered over his reading glasses. "I'll forget you said that because you obviously had a difficult night." He paused to look over a few things on his desk, then looked up again. "By the way, all that Skip Parsons found at Ming Lee's was confirmation that Shing Chow and Pao Lee were indeed staying there. Translate that to mean there's no need for you to go there."

Watts nodded, unprepared to debate the issue. "Lieutenant, how convinced are you that Pao Lee is our killer?"

Ryder removed his glasses and leaned back in his chair. "It's your case, Maxx. Do you have enough evidence to close it out?"

"Probably, but I still need some things from the ME and the lab. I want to be certain before we pin this on Lee."

"That's how the system works, so do whatever it takes to clear this up, but keep me in the loop—and don't start any more car chases."

Watts quietly nodded and retreated. He returned to his desk and reviewed the murder board, keeping his back to the entry so no one would interrupt. He spent the next several minutes re-reading the manuscript paper wad pages, and then raced to see Daisy. She met him at the counter and they returned to the conference room.

Practically out of breath, he said, "Before we see Dr. Morton, I'd like you to read these manuscript pages."

"Can I mark them up?" she said, glancing at them.

"Have at it." He offered a yellow marker.

Pen in hand, she proceeded to highlight the phrases, Tempers had been heating up between Anna and Gabriella . . . I can't see Anna and Gabriella ever getting along . . . Love triangles were never good . . . She still couldn't believe Pico was dead. He was an excellent actor, and to die on the set was horrific. The police seemed to be focusing on who traded Anna's prop gun for a real one rather than why? And why didn't the prop manager catch it . . . they weren't very close . . . off screen, they didn't get along at all . . . Detective, there are a lot of personalities in this business, and not everyone gets along. . . . Personally, I can't see Anna and Gabriella ever getting along . . . actors are deceivers, second only to politicians . . . I already told you they didn't get along, they both knew Pico on and off the set, and they were both fine actresses . . . Did either of them ever use firearms before? . . . Anna and I went to a shooting range as part of a self-protection class . . . Death comes to those deserving. She set her pen aside and she spent another five minutes re-reading everything she highlighted. When she finished, she looked at Watts.

"I'm not sure what I'm supposed to be looking for, but my take is there appears to be a love triangle where the person in the middle is murdered, and now the prime suspects are the two actresses. The phrase, 'Death comes to those deserving' seems to be a statement."

"That's very interesting. For me, the 'actors are deceivers' phrase was far more intriguing, particularly after I did a Web search on the Kat Bleuette Literary Agency. Don't misunderstand me, the agency itself appears legitimate, but since it had a recent photo of Kat Coulter, I did another search for Kat Bleuette, her maiden name, and it turns out she's a former Broadway actress Katherine Bleuette. Her Broadway photo is much earlier, but the pose almost perfectly matches Kat Coulter's literary agency photo. Now here's the kicker—when I asked Kat what used to hang in CC's office, she told me it was an old Broadway poster, so I searched through old playbill images on line. Unfortunately, I never found one featuring her, but considering that she was a stage actor and not a leading lady, that didn't surprise me. Anyway, considering this, does it have any impact on those manuscript passages?"

Daisy stuck out her lip. "If you combine the 'actors are deceivers' phrase with, 'there are a lot of personalities in this business, and not everyone gets along', it does raise flags."

Watts nodded. Leaning across the table brought a hint of her perfume. Reminding himself to ignore it, he said, "It sounds more incriminating when it's read aloud, doesn't it?"

She leaned into her chair back and made a face. "Now I'm totally confused," she said. "On the one hand, we have Pao Lee lying in the morgue with all the evidence pointing toward him, and now CC Coulter's own words suggest that his wife may have killed him. Are you saying that CC is the one speaking from the grave, not Lee? That Kat Coulter chose these pages to suffocate her husband because she couldn't take it anymore? How can Lieutenant Ryder approach the DA with this kind of uncertainty?"

"Which is precisely why I came to you." Having anticipated her uncertain expression, he said, "Daisy, I can easily pin Coulter's murder on Lee because he's dead, and has no apparent family outside of his dead brother. Pao lost money to Coulter, wore flat-soled shoes, his hair places him in the office, and he ran from the police, but it all seems too convenient. I mean, a single hair?"

"Okay, so where does that leave us?"

"I'm not sure, but remember, Kat Coulter was an actress, knew about her husband's affair, and the passages from her husband's manuscript mimic reality. No offense, but death by suffocation sounds like a woman scorned. The problem is we're comparing fiction to the real evidence pointing to Pao Lee."

"Which is why we need to get to the morgue. We're supposed to be there in thirty minutes."

"Okay, call Dr. Morton and let him know we're on the way. Remind him I want him to check Pao Lee's fingers for bite marks, or any cuts near his knuckles, healed or not."

"He's pretty good about noting those kinds of things."

Watts nodded, but needed to prove his point. "We still have a few minutes," he said. "I need to wash my hands."

He quickly returned, still drying his hands on the paper towel. He then put his hand in front of her mouth, folding his fingers so only the first two stuck out. "Okay, let's pretend you are CC Coulter sitting at his desk, he's been struck with the marble block, and is now secured to the chair. His attacker grabs his jaw, yanks it forward with one hand, and then stuffs the wad down his throat with the other. I want to see where my fingers would be relative to your teeth if I'm stuffing a paper wad so I'll know what to look for on Lee. I promise I won't hurt you."

"I'll tell you what. Since I'm closer in size to Mr. Lee and you're closer to CC, let's trade positions and I'll run my fingers down *your* throat?"

He chuckled. He wasn't thrilled, but it made sense.

"Fair enough, but wash your hands first."

"Gladly. I'll be right back."

Her hips swayed more than normal as she walked from the room. Watts hoped it was for his benefit. She returned moments later, her hands smelling like soap.

"There, all clean. Now relax, and gently bite down when they're all the way in." As he opened his mouth, she had a second thought and dropped her hand. "Nothing personal, but we should have someone with a camera witness this," she said. "Hang loose while I get someone."

"Good idea."

She soon returned with a large, unshaven man who wore a police ID around his neck. "This is Wilson," she said. "I've worked with him many times, and he's an excellent CSSU photographer."

Camera in one hand, tripod in the other, Wilson waved at Watts.

"Nice to meet you," Watts said. "How long before you're ready?"

Wilson wasted no time setting up his tripod. "About a minute." In no time, Wilson's camera was aimed at Watts, making make sure his camera was angled correctly. "Okay, Daisy, everything's good. Ready when you are."

"Great," she said. "Remember to shoot from multiple angles."

"Got it," Wilson said from behind the lens.

Daisy grinned as Watts' eyes opened with his mouth. "Don't worry, detective. I'll be gentle."

She used two fingers from her left hand to pull his jaw forward, and then inserted two from her right as far as she dared. When Watts bit down, his teeth left a minor impression slightly past her second knuckle. Once Wilson signaled he was done, she removed them and wiped them on her paper towel.

Packing his things, Wilson said, "I'll get these developed ASAP."

"Thanks," Watts said. "We appreciate it."

"Any time, detective."

Once Wilson left, Daisy smiled at Watts. "You okay, Columbo?"

Swishing his tongue to check for scrapes, he nodded. "I'm not sure you're ready to be a dentist, but we got what we needed. And stop calling me Columbo. By the way, what's there to develop? Isn't it digital?"

"Nope, it's 35 millimeter. Digital is too easily Photoshopped."

"Makes sense."

She checked the time. "We're running late. You ready to head to the morgue?"

"I need to call Spartan. He should be in on this."

THIRTY EIGHT

Spartan quickly joined them in the car. Watts brought him up to speed on the way to the morgue. Dr. Frank Morton met them at the door, not mentioning their tardiness. Morton immediately led them to Lee's badly damaged body, which lay naked on a steel gurney. Lee's right leg had been sliced through mid-calf, both arms had compound fractures, a rib protruded from his chest, and the left side of his face was smashed. Daisy had agreed to speak for them since she set up the appointment and was familiar with medical terminology.

"Dr. Morton, we'd like to see if there are any wounds above Mr. Lee's knuckles," she said. "We'd also like to see his shoes."

"You do realize that I haven't even started his autopsy, and that if I had, I would have noted these marks you're looking for?" he said.

Watts raised his hand like a school kid, but didn't wait to be called on. "Sir, we're not interested in the complete autopsy, just those two items. Seeing them will help determine if the deceased is also a murderer."

Morton shrugged like he could care less. "What do you want first? Cuts or shoes?"

"Cuts, please."

Morton nodded and started examining Lee's hands. "There is scaring on his front two fingers on both hands at the knuckles that could be a few days old," he said. "Some appear infected and haven't healed."

"Is there any way to identify where these cuts might have come from?" Watts said.

Morton hiked his shoulders. "Cuts happen. However, the infection suggests maybe from working in a garden, or on a car.

"How about from someone biting them?" Spartan said.

"Oh, I see where this is going." Morton said, backing off for a moment. "This concerns the paper wad murder, and you think Mr. Coulter bit his attacker. That's an interesting aspect, and one I wouldn't have considered had you not brought it up." He examined the fingers again and set them down. "Now that I know what I'm looking for, I'd have to say it's plausible that these marks came from human teeth. However, I'd have to do a lot more research to confirm that."

After snapping some close-ups of Lee's fingers with her personal camera, Daisy said, "By any chance, did you take any bite patterns from Mr. Coulter before you released his body?"

"Why would I when I just admitted this aspect is new to me," Morton said. "Perhaps his dentist can help you. As I recall, he had a new crown, and dentists need plates for that. Of course, there's no requirement for a dentist to keep them, but it's worth checking it out."

Watts remembered seeing a dentist appointment reminder on Coulter's desk and mentioned that to his partner. Spartan nodded, then left the room to find CC's dentist. Returning his attention to the ME, Watts said, "If we manage to find Mr. Coulter's dental plates, could you match his teeth to the marks on Mr. Lee's fingers?"

"Nothing has one hundred percent certainty, but I'd be willing to give it a shot."

"That's great. Now, can we take a look at Mr. Lee's shoes?"

"Sure. Follow me."

Dr. Morton led them into the storage area and pulled out a bin. Lee's bloody shoes were piled atop his tattered clothes. He made sure Watts and Daisy donned surgical gloves before they rummaged through them, but all they cared about were the shoes.

Watts carefully inspected the slipper-style shoes while Daisy snapped more shots. They were exactly what he expected. Chinese flat-soled slippers, typical for Hong Kong residents. He saw no reason to examine Lee's clothes. Handing them back, he said, "Thank you for your time, doctor. Please postpone Mr. Lee's autopsy until we can talk again. We'll be in touch soon."

Morton looked over the body and pulled a sheet over him. "I suppose Mr. Lee can wait."

* * * * *

Spartan called Kat Coulter from the car to get their dentist's name. He immediately contacted the dentist and learned that CC's crown was fitted three weeks before his murder. That date jibed with the appointment reminder they found on Coulter's desk. He then asked about CC's dental plates. Thankfully, they still had them. He immediately passed the information to Watts.

"Great work, Blaine." Watts looked in the mirror at Daisy who sat in back. "Ms. Woods, we'll drop you off at 350 and then head out to the dentist's office. If you could download your photos and keep working this angle, I'd really appreciate it."

"No problem."

It didn't take long to swing by the dentist's office to pick up CC's plates. On their way back to the morgue, Spartan studied Coulter's replica teeth. "Who says dead men tell no tales?"

"Certainly not lab techs or medical examiners," Watts said. He paused and then looked at his partner. "You realize that if CC's teeth match the marks on Lee's fingers, we'll have a wrap?"

"I do, and we should call it a deadly wrap."

"Good one, Blaine. And so the irony continues. By the way, I wasn't holding out on you. Something on the news inspired me, but I didn't want to say anything until I was more certain. I hope you understand."

"I know how you operate, Maxx. I've had some private thoughts of my own, but they didn't pan out. You and that lab tech did some great detective work coming up with this. You should both be commended."

"Thanks, but I hardly feel that way. The signs were always there, but I never saw them because I kept focusing on Kat Coulter. As for Lee's blundered arrest, you and Ryder were right. If I had asked for backup like you suggested, Lee would be alive, and there would be two less people in the hospital. I assume full responsibility."

"Don't be so hard on yourself, Maxx. Like you said, had we done it differently, Lee may never have shown himself, which means the result could have been the same, but on a different day. We do the best we can and that's all we can do. Besides, if Lee had gone to trial, think of the media circus it would have caused. His death saved the taxpayers a lot of money."

"Good point, Blaine. If the bite marks match, then Lee's death is probably a blessing."

"But what if they don't?"

"Then we'll scratch Lee off our list and take a different direction."

* * * * *

Dr. Morton had left Pao Lee's body on the exam table because the detectives were already on the way back. When Watts and Spartan came through the door, he flipped on the overhead lights, giving Lee's skin a gray reptilian effect. Morton took CC's dental plates from Spartan, examining them carefully. As Watts moved around the table, his squishing shoe made Morton look. Watts backed out of the way to stay clear of Morton's assistant who was taking photos. Morton took several minutes before facing the detectives.

"Realize that I'm limited in how I can stage these photos," he said. "Several of Mr. Lee's fingers were broken in the crash, and all have lost their flexibility."

Watts could see that. "Do whatever you can, Doc. I need answers."

The ME grabbed Lee's right hand and tried to straighten the index finger. A loud *pop* had Spartan running for the door. Watts chuckled at the photographer's smirk. Ignoring them, Morton carefully slid the dental plates over Lee's fingers and the photographer took his shots. When they finished, Morton handed the dental plates back to Watts.

"As I said before, I cannot say with certainty because of the damage to Mr. Lee's fingers, but it's still plausible that Mr. Lee's wounds were caused by Mr. Coulter biting them. I'd be happy to document that if it will help."

"That would be great, Doc. Also, could you please send copies of the photos?"

"You can expect them later today."

* * * * *

Watts couldn't believe what he saw when he got to the car. Spartan had been baking in it with the doors open for at least fifteen minutes. Spartan's coat was off, his tie loose, and his sweat stains made him look like a drunk. Watts climbed in, started the engine, and turned the a/c on full blast. "Had I known you were gonna bail on me, I would have tossed you the keys," he said.

"That's okay, Maxx. I need to shed a few pounds, and sweating is an easy way to lose weight. I'd go so far as to say it's healthier than any Hollywood diet."

"Glad you have a sense of humor, but you also stink."

"Thanks, Maxx. I never would've known. So, what's the verdict with Lee?"

"The ME believes Coulter bit Pao Lee's fingers and is willing to put that in writing, so it looks like Lee's our man. I'm sure Ryder and the mayor will be pleased to close this one out."

Casting an angry gaze, Spartan said, "Maxx, we've known each other a long time and you've never looked like this after closing a case. How about leveling with me?"

Watts chewed his lower lip, contemplating his answer. Spartan was right, but he didn't want to discuss it until he had explored some areas that troubled him. While watching Dr. Morton work, it occurred to him what had bothered him when Ryder pulled out that squeeze ball. It was a long shot, and he needed to talk to Daisy about it first. In the meantime, he had to run down another loose end. He set the car in gear, looked over his shoulder, and pulled out of his parking space.

Feeling better now, Watts said, "Since we have some free time, let's stop by Mrs. Pak's. I'm not sure she was being honest with me the first time. She might be more cooperative now that Lee's dead."

"Fine with me. You want me to talk to her while you stay in the car?"

"No, this time we'll go together. Who knows? Maybe that will help."

Light traffic made for a quick drive to Mrs. Pak's residence. Next door, Ming Lee's house looked as it had the day before. Its crime scene tape was gone. There were no patrol cars in the vicinity. Watts and Spartan readied their badges as they approached her door and rang the doorbell. When the door cracked open, they showed them to her.

"Hello, Mrs. Pak. I'm Detective Watts and this is—"

"I know you," she said, squinting into Watts' eyes. "What you want? I already tell you and that other detective everything."

"Yes, I'm sure. However, Detective Spartan and I still have a few questions. Can you please spare a few moments? I promise we won't take long."

"Ask away, but I make no promises."

"Okay, did you know that Ming's brother Pao and his friend Shing Chow were visiting from China?"

She hesitated. After peeking up and down the street, she opened the door and hurriedly waved them inside. "You come in now, but no stay long."

Watts followed Spartan inside, remembering that Arlene Buck had said the same thing, and they were out the door minutes later. Hopefully Mrs. Pak would outlast the author.

Spartan blocked the hallway, overwhelmed by the smell of Kimchi. Deciding to take the lead so they could quickly leave, he said, "Mrs. Pak, outside we were discussing Shing Chow and Pao Lee when you stopped talking and invited us in. Could you please tell us if you knew they were visiting from China?"

Her face wrinkled when she squinted. "I tell you this once only," she said, waving her finger at them. "I met Pao Lee and Shing Chow one time. Pao nice man. Shing, nice but quiet. Ming say his brother come from China for book tour, and I very impressed. Pao like playing with engines like his brother, so one day he help Ming at work and like it. Then Ming and Shing Chow never come home, and Pao sees on news they dead. After that, Pao never leave house because police stole his passport."

"What exactly did Pao say about his passport?"

"That Ming borrow his cargo pants that had his passport and never came home. After Ming die, Pao say he be accused of murdering brother so he became his brother." She stopped suddenly, her face wrinkling even more. "Why you not write this down? I say I only tell once!"

Watts and Spartan both whipped out their notepads, nodding at her once they caught up.

"So when you show up," Pak continued, "Pao certain you there to arrest him. Why you flush him like quail? He still be alive if you left him alone!"

Her abruptness caught them so off guard that neither had any follow-up questions. Without warning, anger filled her face and she rushed to the door. Holding it open, she said, "No more talk! You go now!"

They did so without protest. On their way to the car, Spartan glanced over his shoulder. She was still glaring, and hadn't moved an inch. "Well, Maxx, was it worth the trip?"

"Actually, it was. We learned that Pao Lee was staying there, believed he was being accused of murder, assumed his brother's identity, and remained in the most likely place we could find him. I'm not surprised she didn't say anything about Skinheads."

Spartan turned toward his partner. "Pao shouldn't have known about the Skinheads because they were never mentioned on the news."

"You're right, which makes his last words about killed my brother even more curious."

"But from what Mrs. Pak said, Pao believed the police were out to arrest him for murder. The only reason he would think that is if he killed CC, and then someone took his brother out thinking it was him."

Watts gave an affirmative nod, settled into his seat, and looked out the window. He was eager to get back to 350 to see what they really had.

* * * * *

By early afternoon, Watts had Dr. Morton's statement and photos in hand. After reading everything over, he went to see Daisy Woods about the toy ball in the evidence room. Watching Ryder squeezing his stress ball, Watts realized it could only compress so much. The super ball they found at the Coulters was smaller and harder, which meant it would compress less. Daisy agreed to do some research and Watts headed back upstairs.

After grabbing his murder file, he and Spartan marched to Ryder's office to present their case. Watts started with Dr. Morton's statement and photos, and concluded with Pao's actions and Mrs. Pak's words. Spartan added his thoughts on the bite marks on Lee's fingers, and then wrapped things up with his general agreement. When they finished, Lieutenant Ryder pushed himself away from the table, rested his hands on his lap, and smiled.

"Congratulations to you all," he said after a brief pause. "Frankly, I wasn't sure we would wrap this one up. You faced a lot of dead ends, but you got it done. I wish we were as lucky with Parson's double-murder case."

Watts snubbed his boss, more intent on spotting his *Maxim* magazine. If it was there, he had it buried. The room was quiet. His boss was staring at him.

"You have a problem?" Ryder said.

"Not really. But I prefer handling cases that leave no doubt."

"Well, from everything you've told me, there shouldn't be any. I'm sure the DA will agree that Pao Lee is your killer, case closed."

Spartan shuffled his feet, frowning, but not saying anything.

Rolling his eyes at him, Ryder said, "What's *your* problem, Blaine?"

"I keep wondering where Pao's buddy, Shing Chow, fits into the scheme of things? He came here with Pao, ended up dead, and then the Chinese government says his passport address is invalid and he had no family in Hong Kong. I can buy one of them not having a family, but two men seems unlikely in a culture that places so much emphasis on family ties."

Ryder's look deferred the question to Watts. As much as Watts wanted to add his opinion about Ming being a case of mistaken identity, he knew that would only confuse his boss. Instead, he looked at his partner and stated the facts. "I understand what you're saying, Blaine, but we never uncovered anything that even remotely suggests Shing Chow and Ming Lee were anything more than victims of random violence, and since we have no way of arguing with the Chinese government, we have to assume they are telling us the truth."

"And according to Skip Parsons, Ming Lee spent the last ten years working in an auto repair shop where his boss deemed him a model employee," Ryder added. "Ming became a naturalized citizen as soon as he was eligible. Correspondence obtained from Ming's computer showed that he idolized his twin brother, and spent a lot of time discussing Pao's frustrations with finding a suitable publisher. Pao wrote that he settled with The Guillotine Press because he didn't receive any interest with other publishers, but was angry he hadn't seen any royalties."

Spartan shuffled some more, looking a bit frustrated. "That may be true, but according to Kat Coulter, Pao was working on his next book, and looked forward to his US tour."

Ryder sighed and leaned back in his chair. He picked up a pencil, tapped it a few times, and then tossed it back on the desk. "Blaine, if you planned to kill your publisher at his house, would you say everything was great, or go on a traceable rant?" He paused, expecting a rebuttal, but Spartan remained silent. "My gut says Ming Lee had no knowledge of his brother's assassination plot, and there is no way to ever know why Pao Lee snapped. So here's the thing, guys, if we could predict people's behavior and be proactive, we would have fewer murders, but the only government programs that have succeeded with that are the ones that kill prospective murderers before the murderers can act. For some reason, most people in this country object to that approach, so instead they accept occasional murders as a way of life."

"I'd like to proactively take out some Skinheads," Watts said.

"Easy, Maxx," Ryder said. "The only Skinheads we're looking for are the ones that molested Tony Fazelli, and since we don't have their license plate, who knows if we'll ever find them?"

Taking that as a dig, Watts said, "I'm sorry, sir. The next time I meet menacing Skinheads at a Dairy Queen, I'll be sure to ask them for their license plate number *before* they want to fight."

"Okay, I've heard enough. You two get back to work. I'll approach the DA about closing the Coulter case. And thanks for your hard work."

"Yes, sir," Watts said, before doing an about-face. He went in having doubts, but left with even more after Ryder's reminder that Ming Lee worked as a mechanic. Mrs. Pak had said that Pao liked to work on engines with Ming. So, how certain could anyone be that the marks on Pao's fingers came from CC's teeth, especially when the ME also suggested the marks could have been scrapes? Was it coincidence that the dental plates lined up, or did Pao injure himself at Ming's workplace? Any attorney would be asking these questions and the case would be thrown out like dirty bath water. There was more to this case than an author becoming so discouraged over his book that he murdered his publisher. He checked in with Daisy on the phone, but she hadn't been able to investigate the toy ball yet due to higher priorities. When he made his request, he probably should have said he needed it, pronto.

Having another thought, he turned to his partner. "You ready for another drive?"

"I suppose," Spartan said, as if he had nothing better to do. "I need to hit the head first."

"Make it fast. I want Kat Coulter to hear the news from us, not Ryder or Jordan."

They headed for the door as soon as Spartan returned, but Watts stayed silent until they were underway. "I'm not trying to be secretive," he said. "I just didn't want anyone tipping Kat off that we're heading her way."

"You really think we have a mole in the office?"

"Let me put it this way, Blaine. Pao Lee's case is full of holes and we shouldn't have moved forward on it. So that leaves our actress, and I think she's been playing us the whole time. Her Columbo thing with me was a nice touch. But if we arrive at her place and find her bags packed, we'll know someone's protecting her."

Spartan looked at him, bewildered. "Forgive me for sounding stupid, but exactly when did you start having these second thoughts?"

"Probably at the morgue when the ME was fiddling with CC's dental plates. My initial thoughts took me back to Ryder squeezing his stress ball, and then I wondered if that tiny ball found in the Coulter's trash could have propped CC's mouth open. Before we went to see Ryder, I asked the lab to check on the toy ball. Then when Ryder mentioned Ming's auto mechanic experience, I started re-thinking the evidence against Pao. I'm sorry, man. I feel I set you up, but I promise you I'll take the blame if Lee's innocent. Hopefully, the lab will have some answers by the time we get back. For now, please trust me while we set some bait."

THIRTY NINE

The blinds were drawn at the Coulter's house. The wind blew and dogs barked, but not one cicada sang. The news said it never hit 100 today, but 98 was still too damned hot. Watts approached the front door the same as always except neither held up their badges. She knew them too well.

Kat Coulter, AKA, Katherine Bleuette, promptly answered, but rather than invite them in, she came outside and pulled her door shut. Wearing perfect makeup and a stunning gray pant suit, she looked ready for a business meeting, but her pearl necklace and matching earrings couldn't mask her disappointment.

"Detective Watts, Detective Spartan, what a surprise," she said. "What now?"

Watts stood there with his hands at his side, evaluating her tired posture and worn expression. Her eyes were red, perhaps from crying, but more likely from lack of sleep. He wondered if she had been arranging the funeral, but didn't ask. Watching her eyes, he said, "I suppose you heard about Pao Lee."

With no delay, she said, "If you're referring to him dying in the car crash, yes, I heard it on the news. What else?"

Spartan raised a brow. "Did you hear that Pao killed your husband?"

"Actually, I did. Mayor Jordan called shortly before you arrived. I can't believe Pao's the killer. I mean, I only met him once, but he was so kind and gentle I can't imagine him hurting anyone. Are you certain it's him?"

Watts saw something in his peripheral vision. He calmly loosened his tie as he scanned the area. When he spotted the Jack Russell, it took off running. Now the only moving objects were leaves, and the sweat running down his back. "Mrs. Coulter, it's mighty hot out here," he said. "We'd be happy to fill you in over a glass of fresh-squeezed lemonade."

She ran her fingers through her hair, staring at them. In spite of her melting face, she made no attempt to open the door. "My house is a mess and I'm fresh out of lemonade," she said. As she paused to rub her eyes, her chin started to quiver. "Have you ever noticed how quickly sympathy drops off after a memorial service? CC's was yesterday evening, but from the way everyone's acting, you'd think he's been dead for months." When she stopped again, a tear dribbled down her cheek. "I'm sorry," she said, wiping it dry. "It's just that no one's even called to check on me, not that it matters. We didn't have that many friends."

"We would have attended the service, had we known," Watts said.

"Thanks," she said, peering down the road as if she was expecting someone. She held her gaze for a moment, oblivious to everything else around her. Finally, she said, "It was a very small ceremony. Only our closest friends attended."

"Well, I'm sure you're relieved to have that behind you," Watts said, certain the mayor had attended. He kept hoping to be invited in, but she had made it clear that wouldn't happen. Still, he wanted to press the issue. "Mrs. Coulter, Detective Spartan and I don't mind if your house is untidy, but we would like to get out of the sun."

"I'm sorry, but this isn't the best time to chat. Had you called, I would have told you I was meeting someone for lunch," she said, making a point of checking her iPhone. "I can give you five more minutes, tops."

"That's all right. We only came to tell you Pao Lee did it, and I figured it would mean more coming directly from us. Anyway, should you ever want to hear the whole story, give us a call. Otherwise, have a good lunch."

"Thank you. Good day, gentlemen."

Watts walked away smiling. Neither he nor Spartan turned around to steal a glance. As they reached their car, Watts heard her front door shut. Suspecting she was watching, he spun the Crown Victoria around and headed down the road. He was so confident that she was watching, there was no need to check his mirror.

A mile down the road, Spartan broke the stillness. "You think she bought it?"

Watts rolled his head at him. "She's an intelligent Broadway actress, and the first rule in our line of work is to never underestimate your opponent. That's *especially* true for attractive women, and we both know the outcome of that."

"Yes, Maxx, I'm well aware. But I'm not as convinced she's up to something."

Watts' phone rang. "Hang on," he said, checking his phone. Seeing that it was Daisy, he answered. After filling him in on her findings, he said, "That's great. We just left Kat's place and I'm pretty sure she's running. Check the international flights first. We'll be back soon."

"Will do," she said. "See you soon."

Spartan's forehead dropped and eyes looked up, giving his partner the "have you gone insane" look. He waited until Watts stowed his phone, then said, "Now you're thinking Kat's gonna run?"

"I do, because in her mind she's a free woman. She also hates Texas and wants to start over. I'm sure glad we can track her passport. At least that will keep her stateside."

"If you say so."

When they arrived at 350, Watts took Spartan with him to confer with Daisy Woods. Not only had Daisy found new incriminating evidence against Kat Coulter, she had tracked down Kat's flight number. By the time their meeting was over, it was clear that leaving CC's dental plates with Daisy was the best decision Watts ever made. Every once in a while a hunch paid off, but this time he hit the Mother Lode.

For the second time in two hours, Watts and Spartan were briefing Lieutenant Ryder, but this time they had Daisy with them. As Ryder put it, The Three Musketeers ride again. At first, the lieutenant seemed upset with the idea of a toy ball being key evidence, but as more evidence was presented, he agreed to their proposed DFW airport sting.

Once everyone had been briefed, The Three Musketeers took off in the Crown Vic while Ryder and Skip Parsons followed in Parson's car. Also in on the plan was Officer Porgy Mulberry, whom the DFW Department of Public Safety Police would allow access to the flight line in his radio car.

Before they arrived, DPS police relayed that Katherine Bleuette had checked in for her American Airlines Flight 48 non-stop flight to Paris, cleared security, and was being monitored on Gate 23A's security camera. The Three Musketeers badged their way through the security checkpoint closest to D23A and spread out. Parsons and Ryder passed through the checkpoint near D-28 so they could bracket her. As requested, DPS police remained clear so as not to blow the operation. So far, all was proceeding according to plan.

When Kat spotted Watts, she immediately turned and headed south, but by doing so, she was heading toward Ryder and Parsons. She must have recognized Ryder from a photo because she immediately turned around and headed north. Trying to blend into the endless stream of concourse traffic, she managed to maintain her composure until she spotted Spartan and Daisy closing in. Seeing that she was trapped, Watts circled back to the gate and cued the agent to announce Flight 48 was ready to board. Kat immediately ran to the gate agent, showed her ticket, he scanned it, and then let her pass. Once she went through the door, the agent replaced the barrier strap to hold the other passengers back.

Twenty steps in, Porgy Mulberry blocked her path like an inflated raft. Before she could turn around, Watts came stomping down the jetway letting his shoe announce his arrival. Spartan and Daisy arrived in time to witness Kat's dark expression. Then Ryder and Parsons joined the gathering before a word was spoken.

Taking two squishes forward, Watts said. "So, how was your lunch?"

"Fine," said Kat, staring back. "What's this all about?"

Watts lost his grin and his eyes grew cold. When he was sure he had her attention, he reached into his pocket and pulled out the tiny ball. When her eyes looked at it, he said, "Yes, Mrs. Coulter, it's the same chewed-up ball we found in your trash the day your husband was murdered. Of course, at the time I had no idea it would identify you as the killer. You see, while it contains canine impressions like you said, it also contains bite marks that match your husband's teeth."

"I have no idea what you're talking about."

"Allow me to refresh your memory. During our first interview, you admitted that you seduced your husband the night of his murder, but you failed to provide a few details. So, this is how it came down. You were standing in the entry probably wearing a thin negligée with your hair draped over your shoulders. Smelling your perfume, your husband turned around to admire you. Smiling back, you slowly approached him, letting your hips sway so his eyes stayed locked on you. When you got to him, you playfully leaned over his shoulder, caressing him, kissing him, distracting him while you reached for the Writer's Block. Now, with the paperweight firmly in hand, you suddenly stood and swung your arm, striking his forehead. With CC now dazed and confused, you easily strapped him to the chair, pulled his head back, jammed this tiny ball between his molars to protect your fingers, and then stuffed the paper wad down his throat. Tell me, Kat, what was it like watching him die? Did you enjoy seeing his eyes and veins bulge, his chest heave, his arms strain against their straps?"

"Nice try, Columbo, but I still don't know what you're talking about."

"I figured you would say that, but did you know CC's eyes were still wide open when we found him? He had a look of astonishment, like how could the woman I love be doing this to me? Under the circumstances, I suppose any victim would feel that way, but I am curious—did you stay until he was dead? Did you watch his chest expand and his veins bulge while he struggled for air?"

Watts paused, not to let that sink in, but rather his anger was rising like a drowning kid's last air bubble. He glanced at Mulberry, but only for a second. *Porgy, you sonofabitch!* After pinching his eyes to shake off the memory, he fired a gaze at Kat Coulter. "So, tell me, *Kat*. How could you watch the man you loved strain against tie straps until he suffocated?"

"I told you before," she fired back, you know nothing about what it's like!"

Ryder tapped Watts's shoulder. "What's she talking about?" he said.

Kat fired back, "Marriage, you poker-playing bastard! For that matter, all men are bastards! I gave up everything for him. My acting career, my Long Island home, the beach, my life! And that son of a bitch goes and cheats on me with the biggest whore of them all! And then the bastard has the nerve to tell me all about it as if it made everything right! Death came to him all right. And he deserved it."

Watts thought about her well-spoken words, knowing none could be used against her since no one had read her rights. Still, it was the first time he felt she was telling the truth. Hank Azar would have no problem refuting her admission, but he couldn't deny the physical evidence. The best he could do was to discredit it, and that would prove far more difficult.

"I've heard enough," Watts said, "Lucky for you, where you're going, you won't have to deal with any bastards. Only women, who will certainly enjoy having you. But before I officially charge you with murder, I want to thank you for referring us to your husband's dentist. Without CC's plates, we wouldn't have much of a case against you. Oh, the toy ball in the trash helped, too. Just for future reference, it's usually best to get rid of the trash after you murder someone."

"Screw you, Columbo."

He smirked, finding it interesting how over the course of a few days, her once mesmerizing eyes now resembled a rattler's. No, strike that, because vipers never pose as something they're not. But the beautiful actress before him had spent her life perfecting her roles, making her lines believable. Too bad her role as a murderess wasn't an act.

"Oh, by the way," Watts continued, "it took a while, but we finally located your husband's Swiss bank account, and at today's prices, his nest egg is right at five million. Of course, you'll lose all that, plus your husband's two million dollar life insurance policy. For some reason, life insurance companies refuse to reward the people who murder their clients."

Kat's face got redder, but she refused to say anything else. During the silence, the gate agent came down the jetway, whispered something to Ryder, and then left.

Ryder nodded, waited a moment, and then said, "Folks, we need to clear the jetway so the real passengers can board. Detective Watts, please get on with it."

"Yes, sir." Watts took a moment to clear his throat and said, "Kat Coulter, or Katherine Bleuette as you prefer to be called, you are under arrest for the murder of Charlie CC Coulter. Officer Mulberry will read you your rights and take you into custody. Next time I see you, you'll be wearing prison garb. Get used to it."

While Mulberry recited his spiel, Kat Coulter stared blankly at the super ball in Watts' palm. In the course of Mulberry's condemning words, her look went from shock, to hurt, to resignation. She said nothing as Mulberry walked her down the jetway's exterior stairs to his radio car. Watts had planned it this way to minimize her humiliation because the mayor was her friend. By now, Ryder, Parsons, Daisy, and Spartan had already exited the jetway and the footsteps of boarding First Class passengers rapidly approached. Watts wouldn't leave the stairwell until he saw Mulberry drive off, though. He had to personally witness that to have closure. Once Mulberry's car was out of sight, Watts joined Daisy and Spartan at the gate. Daisy looked relieved, but Spartan looked glum, standing there with his hands in his pockets.

"Lieutenant Ryder and Detective Parsons already left," Spartan said as Watts approached. "Ryder looked surprisingly pleased, considering a few hours earlier we were blaming everything on Lee. He said he'd clear Pao's name and approach the DA about Kat as soon as he got back."

When Spartan finished, Daisy batted her eyes at Watts with no regard for his partner. "It was a good call," she said. "Without those dental plates the toy ball was useless, but under a microscope CC's tooth impressions became clear. I'm glad you went with your gut instead of the evidence we had on Pao Lee."

Watts managed to grin. "Even blind squirrels find nuts now and then," he said. But his grin faded as he squeezed the chewed up ball in his hand. "What kind of woman would do something like this?"

"No one I know," she said. "I can't imagine hurting someone you loved. I wish we could have drawn her blood at the crime scene. That would have told us her sleeping pill dosage."

"It's a moot point, Ms. Woods. Nothing can be gained from thinking about it."

After saying that, Watts scanned the line of waiting passengers. Those in business suits played with their smart phones, while those more casually dressed were all smiles, clinging to each other, eager to embark on their grand European adventure. Had they not tracked Katherine Bleuette through her passport, she would have easily blended into the crowd. Another lucky break, he mused as he checked the time.

Smiling at Daisy and Spartan, he said, "The freeways are probably gridlocked, and there's a Fuddruckers's a few gates from here. How about I buy you guys dinner?"

Spartan's eyes lit up. "If you're buying, I'm in."

"Me, too," said Daisy.

FORTY

Traffic was moving again by the time they had finished their burgers. Watts figured the time difference between delaying for their meal versus heading directly into the gridlock was nominal. Besides, he rarely ate at Fudd's, and he was happy to treat his crime fighting partners. The only problem was throughout the meal, Spartan kept trying to make a romantic connection between Daisy and Watts. They managed to elude him with smiles and shop talk, like all detectives do.

None of them expected Kat Bleuette Coulter to admit that she planted Lee's hair in the office and bent her own window screen, but Watts felt confident the new evidence would tell the story. The only reasonable explanation for CC's tooth impressions in the tiny super ball was it had to be forced into his mouth. Even the least educated juror should understand that. It would be difficult for any attorney to beat this case. Even cunning ones like Hank Azar.

When the trio arrived at 350, Watts went upstairs to write his report. A quick call confirmed that Mulberry was still busy booking Kat. Watts' issues with Porgy would never disappear, but it felt good including him in the D/FW airport operation. Even better, just like retro TV's Detective Columbo, Watts kept returning to the killer for more questions, and in the end, put her away.

As much as Watts would have loved spending more time with Daisy, he was exhausted by the time he finished with work. He gave her a quick call to congratulate her on her forensics work, but made no mention of any evening plans. She must have sensed how he felt because she didn't say anything either.

Leroy waited for him like a trusty steed. When Watts fired him up, exhaust pipes blasted the parking garage, its harmonics giving a sense of the raw power hidden under his hood. The sound reminded Watts of the one that interrupted his interview with Kat Coulter at the Whataburger. Replaying that moment, he subconsciously revved the engine as though challenging the Skinheads to a duel. Turning the heads of his curious peers, he quickly backed off and the tachometer dropped to nine hundred.

Leroy turned onto the street while Watts looked for that elusive Ford pickup. He didn't expect to find it, but doing so took his mind off Tony Fazelli, Pao and Ming Lee, Shing Chow, and the Coulters.

Since the Dairy Queen was less than two miles from the Whataburger where he interviewed Kat Coulter, he thought the Skinheads might live nearby. But driving the streets, baiting them with occasional accelerations, only produced curious looks. Some people raised thumbs, but most shot angry gazes.

The area between the Dairy Queen and Whataburger was as diverse as Dallas and Fort Worth. The Montgomery Street Dairy Queen located near Trinity Park and the Will Rogers Coliseum was surrounded by mixed housing, while the property near the Whataburger on 28th and North Main was primarily industrial. Both drive-ins were located on major arteries near commercial and residential areas. As such, both provided excellent escape routes. The Skinheads would have had no trouble dumping Tony Fazelli in Forest Park and then getting away. Maybe that's how Lee and Chow got there, too.

Watts headed toward the Whataburger neighborhood where rust bucket relics seemed to be viewed as collector's items. Slightly north on Main, rust buckets like that Ford F-150 would go unnoticed in the auto salvage yards, but in this area, Leroy would stand out like a raisin in oatmeal. If the Skinheads were anywhere near, they'd spot Leroy a mile away.

He cracked his window and kept his head on a swivel as he drove north on Main. At Long Avenue, he made a one-eighty and then hung a right on 28th. Squinting into the setting sun was giving him a headache, so a mile later he made another one-eighty and drove east to the Santa Fe railroad tracks. After thirty minutes of cruising with no sign of any Skinheads, cleaning the dust layer from his truck took priority. Some people saw their dirty vehicles as macho, but Watts preferred to keep Leroy shiny. And since his fuel gauge was dropping like the sun, he steered his truck into the gas station, filled the tank, and drove into the car wash lane. When he was next in line, and with three cars behind him, he heard a familiar sound. There was no mistaking that rust-bucket's exhaust. Trapped between the car wash and cars, he helplessly watched as it zoomed by. Even if he could follow, Watts figured that one car chase was enough for a while. If it truly was the same pickup, sooner or later the Skinheads would be caught. Watts hoped he would spot them first.

FORTY ONE

Watts got home at seven thirty-three, but it seemed much later. Even with the television on, his place felt empty. He stripped off his clothes and turned on the shower. While the suds slid off his skin, he thought about Daisy, wondering what she was doing right then. Like a mythical Siren in *The Odyssey*, she seduced his mind long after seeing her. After toweling himself dry, he slipped on his khaki pants, black and gold Hawaiian shirt, and sandals, and then dialed her number.

"Hope I'm not bothering you, but I can't get you out of my head," he said to her. "Did you have any plans for this evening?"

"Not really. You want to come over?"

"Love to. What time?"

"It's up to you."

"Okay, then I'll be there in twenty minutes. See you soon."

On the way, he stopped by the grocery store he knew was open. By sheer luck, they were busy unpacking fresh cut flowers. While he favored roses, the ones he saw didn't look so great. He chose a flower arrangement labeled "summer collection" because they looked fresh and smelled good. He recognized the carnations. Everything else he called "pretty".

When he arrived at her place, he held the flowers behind his back as he had done before, rang the doorbell, and stepped back. It took longer than expected before he heard footsteps. Finally, the door cracked open. She greeted him in a blue and white Hawaiian dress that tied around her neck and snugly fit around her waist, a flower in her hair. He could hardly believe she was the same person he saw at the station a few hours ago.

"Wow!" he said, his eyes wide, mouth open. "You look amazing." Handing her the flowers was almost an afterthought.

"Why, thank you, Maxx. They're beautiful. Come on in."

She led the way into the kitchen where she immediately put the flowers in the sink. Since her vase still held the yellow roses, she took the water pitcher from the shelf and cut the stems to size. When she finished, her arrangement looked as beautiful as she.

"I love them," she said, holding his hand. "Don't they smell wonderful?"

Watts drew in a breath. "Yes they do, but so do you. Do you always sit around the house in a Hawaiian dress after a long day at work?"

Smiling coyly, she said, "Of course not. I slipped it on after you called. I had a hunch you'd be wearing a flowered shirt, and thought we'd make a cute couple in case you wanted to go out somewhere."

"Well, it really is beautiful, and since we make such a great couple, where would you like to go?"

"I know a great wine and cheese bar, and don't worry, they have non-alcoholic drinks, too."

Watts smiled and squeezed her hand. Somewhere in their brief history together, she had already figured out that he didn't care much for alcohol, and loved how she said she was fine with it. As she wrapped her arms around his neck and leaned into him, he kissed her neck, savoring her fragrance. Neither was sure of where this was heading, but both seemed willing to explore it. He released his embrace so he could gaze into her pretty green eyes.

"The wine and cheese place sounds great," he said. "Let's go."

She grabbed her purse, locked her apartment, and pressed her hand over his heart. "Maxx, I know you don't like talking shop, but I want you to know you truly impressed me today. Had it not been for you, an innocent man would have been labeled a murderer, and Kat would have gone free."

"Thank you, but I couldn't have done it without you. We make a great team, you, me, and Spartan. Maybe we are The Three Musketeers. But for now, let's leave Spartan out of this while we chase the sunset to get some wine and cheese."

"As romantic as that sounds, the bistro is due east."

"Then we'll make due with a moonrise."

THE END

Mark W. Danielson is an active international airline pilot, retired fighter pilot, suspense novelist and long-time Texas resident. *Writer's Block* is the first in his Maxx Watts detective series.